# OCTOGEN

## Geoff Cook

Published by Rotercracker Copyrights, 2024
Copyright © Geoff Cook, 2024
Geoff Cook has asserted his right under the Copyright,
Designs and Patents Act 1988 to be identified
as the author of this work
This novel is a work of fiction. Names and characters
are the product of the author's imagination and any
resemblance to persons living or dead is entirely coincidental

This book is sold subject to the condition that it shall not,
by way of trade or otherwise, be lent, resold, hired out,
or otherwise circulated without the publisher's prior
consent in any form of binding or cover other than that
in which it is published and without a similar condition,
including this condition, being imposed on the
subsequent purchaser

First published in Great Britain in 2024 by Rotercracker Copyrights
Pacific Heights South, 16 Golden Gate Way, Eastbourne,
East Sussex, BN23 5PU

Paperback ISBN 9789893362693 Int. Edition

A CIP catalogue record for this book is available
from the British Library

For Steve and Charly
Simon and Justin
Dan and Cobi
Miguel, Sol e Gaspar
"Today a reader, tomorrow a leader."

# GENESIS

## BROADBENT – DERBYSHIRE - ENGLAND

### Forty years and one week ago – November 2025

'Hurry up. It's Doctor Who. We'll miss the last episode. She will never find out. Trust me.'

The younger of the two boys wriggled away from the hands gripping his shoulders, his face turned to avoid the pleading stare. 'Mum says we mustn't go this way. It's dangerous. She made a rule.'

With his eleventh birthday just two weeks away, Aashif Firman was the elder of the two by almost three years. Seniority determined his will would prevail. 'And what does Dad say?' He winked. 'Rules are for bending. What harm can it do? It will save us ten minutes. You want to see it too, don't you?'

Jamil knew it was pointless to argue with his brother. Mum would find out and they would get into trouble. It didn't matter if Aashif claimed total responsibility, Mum would tell Dad to cuff them both. Dad would shake his head sadly, as if to say none of us can defy her.

One last try. 'I'm frightened,' Jamil said. 'It's scary going that way.'

The quickest route from the mosque in Broadbent to their house was across the common, past Witches Oak, around the Roman Wells and along the track used by the mountain bikers until it re-joined the main road. The problem was it had been raining heavily; the ground was muddy and taking a shortcut would mean getting the bottom of their dishdashas wet and dirty. Their mother would be furious. She was proud of her sons' upbringing, insisting they wore the long, embroidered gowns to the weekly children's halaqah. Most of their friends wore jeans and would look at them with a smirk on their faces. Aashif had got into a fight after someone called them 'Mummy's boys'.

It was a week since the clocks went back an hour to GMT and dusk was fast approaching.

'Let's get a move on,' Aashif said forcefully. 'Remember, I'm your big brother.' There was an unconvincing quiver in his voice. 'You don't need to feel scared when I'm around.'

As Jamil feared, the walk across the deserted common saturated the porous material, which stuck to his chapped legs. Although Aashif ordered him to pull up the dishdasha around his knees, Jamil found it impossible to match his brother's stride and keep the gown above his ankles. He turned his head so his brother would not see the tears of shame flow down his cheeks. To make his sense of foreboding even worse, he could tell Aashif was regretting his decision.

As they passed Witches Oak and neared the old Roman Wells, Aashif stopped, his hand drawing Jamil to his side. They both heard the noises, giggling, shushing and then a forced laugh coming from within the thicket.

Aashif ran, pulling on Jamil to keep up, but the bikers were upon them before they cleared the trees. The two leading riders performed expert show-off wheelies, forcing the two brothers to stop as mud sprayed over the front of their dishdashas. The four remaining bikers, three more boys and a girl, formed a semi-circle behind them, blocking any means of escape. Aashif stood still, manoeuvring Jamil to stand shielded behind him.

Aashif recognised the gang members as second-year students from the comprehensive school he had recently joined. From classroom gossip, he knew the two ringleaders were from Middle-England Tower, the high-rise council block of flats he could see from his bedroom window. Both had been in trouble with the police on more than one occasion.

Heads turned as the last of the group made his way toward them. He was younger than the others, small and frail in stature. Aashif could not take his eyes off the metal calliper, which held in place a withered right leg, little wider than a stick of seaside rock. It was shorter than his left, causing the boy to lurch to one side as he approached.

The taller of the two ringleaders, the one with the unruly mop of blond hair, addressed the newcomer but looked at his captives as he did so. 'Arrived just in time for some fun, Stanley. Let me introduce you to the "Furkin Firmans". This one 'ere is "Arsehole Aashif" and the little wanker hiding behind him is his little bruvver, "Jam Rag Jamil". There were titters as the boy, emboldened by his sycophantic audience, held his palms together as if in prayer. 'They think they're better than us, 'cause they live in their posh houses and not on the Estate. As you can see, Mussies walk around in their nightdresses, always ready for a little sleep, so we won't disappoint them.'

Aashif moved to protect Jamil as the boy darted to one side and then feigned a move to the other.

'How would you like me to take Jam Rag . . .?' He sprang to the left; a move countered by Aashif.

'Austin. Help me.'

His sidekick, a shorter, stockier boy with tight ginger hair, pushed his bike to the ground in a violent gesture. He jumped to the right. Aashif countered by widening his stride and swaying from side to side to maintain cover for Jamil. The first boy lunged forward. Aasif reared backwards to counter the attack, digging his fingers hard into the arm as it reached to pull his brother to the ground. The blond-haired boy yelped in pain, loosening his grip and pitching forward to land unceremoniously on the muddy track.

It was their one chance to escape. Seeing the gap, Aashif yanked Jamil to his feet, screaming for him to run. They had taken only two strides when Jamil's shoe caught in the loosened hem of his gown, causing him to pitch forward into his brother. Aashif stumbled headfirst into the mud with Jamil on top of him.

In an instant, the group was upon them, hands frisking, fists pummelling, and kicks aimed wildly at their torsos.

The blond boy was back on his feet, jeans caked in mud, his expression displaying both fury and resentment at the damage to his street cred. He reached into the inside pocket of a frayed denim jacket and withdrew a small kitchen knife. Sitting astride Aashif's body, he wiggled the point under his eye. 'Your lot know all about knives, don't you, Mussie,' he said. 'It's your lot likes to slit white people's throats, you scummy bastards!' He pricked Aashif's cheek. A spot of blood welled into a trickle and fed into his mouth. 'Think you deserve a little memento of our meeting today, a little something to remember us by. And don't think you can rush home to mummy and tell her, 'cause if you do, little Jam Rag 'ere will wish he'd never been born.

It was late, pitch black. The only sounds were the branches rustling in the wind and the low-pitched moaning coming from alongside him. Aashif opened his eyes, unsure of his surroundings or of what had happened. He went to move, but someone had tied him to a tree. Then he remembered.

They had stripped the gowns from their bodies and bound him and Jamil with them. Reduced to their underwear, the bitter wind chafed their skin. Jamil was sobbing, the mucus from his nostrils coating his mouth and chin, his breathing shuddering as his eyes, wide open, followed his captors move in single file toward them.

'Close your eyes,' Aashif had said. 'Don't let them see your fear.'

One by one, with prompting from Austin and the blond leader, the four gang followers stopped in front of each brother, noisily collecting saliva in their mouths and closing to spit into their faces. Aashif looked at each one as they spat, a sneer on his lips as they turned away to avoid eye contact with him.

Austin lifted the disabled boy and whispered in his ear as he undid the fly on his short trousers. He held the boy out in front of him. 'Let them have it, Stanley,' he said. The boy held his tiny penis, directing a stream of urine into Jamil's face, who, still crying, could not help ingesting some of the steaming waste. Austin wheeled the boy around toward Aashif, but the flow petered out before reaching its target.

'Never mind,' the blond boy crowed. 'I have a special treat for Arsehole here.'

Aashif fainted as the knife scarred his back for the third time. How long had he been unconscious? He traced a finger against the streaks of congealed blood. His back stung, but to his relief, the blade had done little more than pierce the skin.

The realisation that Jamil needed help roused him from his stupor. He prised his arms free and stumbled toward the noise, fists clenched. The frail, half-naked body of his brother was slumped forward, restrained from collapsing by the robe binding him to the tree.

Jamil shivered in his brother's arms; the sound was barely audible as he pleaded for his mother. Aashif looked up toward the starless sky. 'By all that is holy, Allah will make you infidels pay for this.'

A week passed, and the brothers had long since suffered the consequences of their misadventure. With Jamil sworn to secrecy, Aashif took the heavy beating his mother commanded her husband to exact for the state in which they returned home. Whether their parents believed the fabrication of slipping in the mud and falling down an incline into bushes and brambles, Aashif knew they would not probe for a fuller explanation. However cowardly and unfair the stance, their parents would not be prepared to seek a confrontation with a community that harboured suspicion and was prepared to display its prejudices. With illegal immigration a major political issue, public sentiment was turning against certain minority ethnic groups, more so a mixed-race family insisting the children prioritise a mother's Muslim doctrine over the father's Christian background. The boys must learn a lesson; their mother insisted. They had to keep out of harm's way.

Today, the boys, clothed in jumpers and jeans, crouched, hidden by the bushes around Witches Oak. Aashif clasped the baseball bat a friend had loaned him. Their classmates would be halfway through the halaqah by now. Aasif told the Imam his brother was feeling unwell. He would have to take him home.

It wasn't really a lie. Looking down at Jamil, his body shaking, his head turned so as not to catch his brother's eye, he didn't look good. Was it the cold or fear? Both, Aashif guessed. He put his arm around those bony shoulders. 'Don't worry, my brother,' he said. 'My name means bold and brave and those things we shall be. You, too.'

Jamil looked unconvinced. 'There's a lot of them.'

'We are early, and they won't all come together. This time, they will expect us to go home along the main road past Fisher's warehouse. If they are waiting for us, it will be there. Eventually, one or two will drift back this way and we'll be ready.'

Aashif reacted to the sound of a steady tapping on the path by crouching lower and holding his finger to his mouth. He glanced around the bush at the approaching figure, reached for the bat, and sprang forward.

The sudden appearance of someone jumping out from the shadows took the little boy, Stanley, by surprise. Startled, he stopped in his tracks and lurched to one side, placing his weight on his good leg. 'You scared the life out of me!' he shouted. 'Where are the others?'

As Jamil appeared from behind his brother, the little boy realised he was not addressing another gang member. 'You!' he snarled, holding his ground.

'Yes, me!' Aashif held the boy under his arms, dragging him into the undergrowth.

There was no concern in Stanley's voice, just anger and contempt. 'Let me go.' He looked up at Aashif standing over him. 'Terry is my brother. Do you know who he is? He's a psycho. Touch me and I'll swear he'll kill both of you.'

'Maybe, but he's not here, is he, Stanley?' Aashif stuffed a handkerchief into the boy's mouth, dragging him to his feet and frogmarched him toward the smaller of the two Roman wells. The external fencing, designed to stop people from encroaching, had been partially trampled, providing easy access. Once inside, Aashif had no problem in prising the rusty wire netting cover away from the nails holding it in place. It provided a gap just big enough for what he had in mind.

Aashif turned to encourage Jamil forward, then back to Stanley. 'That explains why the bunch of cowards you hang around with were being so nice to you last week, doesn't it? Scared of your brother, are they?'

'Just like you'll be when I go home and tell him,' he mumbled through the handkerchief.

'We'll see about that. Come here, Jamil. Undo your fly.' Aashif grabbed the boy under his arms and lifted him. He was surprisingly light, even though he was of a slight build.

Ordering Jamil to join him, Aashif stood behind the boy on the parapet circling the well. It was wide enough for the three of them. Stanley shuffled to keep his balance, the calliper around his withered leg scraping against the masonry, dislodging small pieces of mortar which fell into the pitch black, lost in silence until the hollow plop echoed from the depths. The rustling of the rats, as they reacted to the disturbance, subsided as quickly as it began.

'Our Imam tells us you Christians believe in an eye for an eye, a tooth for a tooth. Is that right?'

For the first time, fear registered in Stanley's eyes. Aashif grasped him around the shoulders, pushing his body forward so that his head dangled over the void. 'Jamil, move around and hold on to me.'

Stanley cried out, his predicament apparent.

Gingerly, Jamil edged around to stand next to his brother, his hand grasping a handful of T-shirt. 'Now, piss all over him,' Aashif ordered.

Jamil's hand shook as he fiddled with the buttons on his trousers. His eyes darted nervously between his brother and the boy, whose head and half his torso extended over the ledge, his face peering into the void. His bravado dissipated with the thought of what was to come. Loud sobs now competed with the screams of desperation.

Jamil's tiny penis hung flaccid just outside his fly. 'I can't,' he said. 'No wee.' As he spoke, a rat sprang from the inside of the well, leaping over Aashif's shoulder. Jamil screamed. The momentum sent Aashif backwards, releasing his hold on Stanley's midriff. Desperately, he held onto the boy's good leg and arrested the forward movement, stopping the falling body as it tottered on the edge of the parapet.

'Hold on to his other leg, Jamil. I need to pull him back.'

Jamil wrapped his hands around the calliper, gripping as hard as he could, his head buried against the boy's thigh. He saw nothing through the tears clouding his eyes.

Aashif released the boy's leg, leaning forward to grasp him around the waist. What he did not expect was an arm thrusting wildly upward and a finger poking him in the eye. It stopped him in his tracks, the reflex to use his hand to rub and cover the eye to ease the pain.

Jamil reacted to the heavier burden by clinging even harder onto the calliper. But as he did so, his hands slipped against the shiny metal surface. His thumb jammed against the catch which held the calliper in place.

Neither brother would ever forget the events of the next ten seconds, nor the days ahead, which would change their young lives forever. As if a ship slowly launched from its moorings, Stanley slipped headfirst into the darkness, his withered leg the last thing to disappear. Jamil looked at his brother in disbelief, holding out the calliper in front of him. The scream echoed in his ears, faded and was gone. For Jamil, that scream would live on every night as he closed his eyes and prayed.

Aashif was the first to react, grabbing the calliper out of his brother's hand and tossing it into the well.

'He won't be able to find it to put it on,' Jamil said. 'We must call for help.'

Aashif pulled him from the parapet, his gaze fixed on his brother's eyes, willing him to obey. 'He's gone. Dead. Do you understand, Jamil? Nobody can help him. We must go. Now. We were never here. Do you understand? We were never here! This never happened. It was all just make-believe.'

Four days passed with no change to the normal routine of the neighbourhood. Aashif convinced himself the entire incident was some weird turn of his imagination or, on the occasions confronted by reality, how Stanley somehow climbed from the well and returned home unharmed.

It was only the silent, morose world into which Jamil had lapsed, uncommunicative and distant when spoken to, which prompted Aashif to focus on the stark reality of the chain of events he had instigated. Fortunately, their parents treated Jamil's mood swings as a function of his development, a phase in growing up about which they were knowledgeable, and he knew nothing.

Their mother worked as an auxiliary nurse at the local health centre. Aashif strained to listen behind the closed door later that night as she recounted to her husband the tragic revelation of the young boy who had fallen into one of the Roman wells. His elder brother reported him missing four days ago, but, as rumour had it, the child had only died during the last forty-eight hours. Can you imagine the horror of surviving for two days in such a place with no one to listen to your calls for help? May Allah comfort his soul.

The Council would have a lot to answer for, their father said. Allowing the safeguards around the place to fall into a state of disrepair was nothing short of criminal.

The next day, the news broke. The police suspected others were involved. They questioned eight students who attended a local comprehensive school. Two boys with a history of bullying were kept in the police station overnight.

It was the following Saturday. Aashif and Jamil, dressed in new dishdashas, returned home from the mosque to find their parents waiting for them in the lounge with three men in suits. Their mother had been crying. Their father told them to sit. 'We have welcomed these gentlemen into our home,' he said, his voice deeper than usual. 'They need to ask you both some questions. You will tell them everything you know.'

# EXODUS

## THREE RIVERS – TEXAS, USA

### Thirty-five years and one week ago -
### November 2030

Mary Jo Hammond drew long and hard on the cigarette wedged between her chapped lips.

As she looked out from the porch of their single-storey wood cabin, the tall leaves of the filler tobacco grown from Cuban seed swayed gently back and forth in the half-light as night approached. In happier days, before Bobby took ill, they had chosen the six-acre field for cultivation with just one aim in mind. When the plants were fully grown, they would hide the federal correction centre on Highway 72 from view. Out of sight, out of mind.

The signs on the entry roads into Three Rivers in Live Oak County described the township as the oil capital of Texas. It was an august boast. The guidebooks made only a passing reference to the penitentiary where many of the most dangerous redneck reactionaries, renegade murderers, and rapists in the Union were incarcerated.

On a still night, if she strained hard, Mary Jo could just make out the sound of the oil rigs humming some five miles away, alongside the refinery. She had been born and bred in Three Rivers and was mighty proud of her birthright.

The rasping, mucus-filled cough started up as she exhaled, forcing her to spit a ball of yellow phlegm onto the parched earth. It was ironic, she thought. That very plant, growing so high and strong just a stone's throw away, would consign her husband's body to the ground in a week or two and, most likely, see her lying in the soil next to him within the year. The thought caused her to laugh out loud, provoking another bout of coughing and spitting.

'You see this, Mother?' Bobby had called her 'Mother' ever since their only child was born some thirty-odd years ago. Millie survived until she was two when the consumption had taken her, but Bobby just went on calling Mary Jo 'Mother' until this very day.

'What is it, Bobby?'

Her husband was propped up on a make-do sofa bed in the lounge, his watery gaze fixed on the television. The sound was turned down because the noise hurt his ears. Nothing but skin and bones, cancer racked the body of this former fifteen-stone hard man and federal prison guard. Bones poked through the grey/blue skin of his skeletal frame. Pain and suffering were all he knew. Once, he inflicted these two ills: now, he had to endure them.

The image on the screen was like a scene from a science fiction movie. The sky above some desert location was full of drones, small, black-painted craft swarming incessantly like bees about a larger, torpedo-shaped drone with mechanical arms embracing a package the size of a small suitcase. From time to time, a smaller drone would explode into flames and fall to earth, causing the rest to realign to protect their queen.

An industrial complex came into view on the horizon. Within minutes, the drones were hovering over a series of circular metal towers, losing height and numbers as mid-air explosions sent many crashing to the ground. The larger unit came to a halt, the sound of its motor whirring as it hovered in position. The mechanical arms opened, and the package fell to the ground.

Spontaneously, a large red and orange mushroom cloud lit up the screen. As it expanded and dispersed, the camera trembled. The earth below creased in a ripple effect, as though some gigantic prehistoric monster was moving at breakneck speed just under the surface. Suddenly, the image froze and then disappeared before a visibly shaken announcer appeared in the studio, framed against a 'Breaking News' background.

'What's he saying?' Mary Jo asked.

Bobby half turned his head. 'I guess it's just another of those damn Arab killing Arab terrorist attacks, somewhere in the desert. I don't know why we don't drop a bomb on the whole fuckin' lot of 'em. He grimaced. The strain of talking sapped his energy. 'It's the third one they've shown.'

'More likely the same one the third time,' she retorted, losing interest and walking back onto the porch.

Thank God she lived in the good old US of A, the land of the free. She laughed to herself again as she reached into her housecoat pocket for another cigarette. Free, that is, if you're not on the other side of the six-acre field, banged up in a prison cell.

It was dusk. The only sounds to break the eerie silence were the flapping of the leaves of the tobacco plants, the occasional bark of a dog, and the swish of the rigs as they travelled the highway.

Today was Veterans' Day. She would pick up on the news after Bobby had taken his morphine and was asleep. She enjoyed the late shows.

From the distance came a low humming sound. The night sky lit up over Three Rivers as if dawn had broken. A pall of red and orange smoke, just like the one Bobby had pointed to on TV, rose in the sky, reaching out toward her, turning white as it moved. The sound came seconds later, an ear-shattering noise that pierced and burst her eardrums. She watched in horror as the earth vibrated beneath her feet, gradually at first and then violently as the tremors increased.

On the horizon, a curtain of water erupted from the ground. Her eyes stung. The federal correction centre, enveloped by the cloud a second ago was no longer there.

Mary Jo rushed into the cabin. Bobby dozed in the chair as she dug urgently at his arm. 'We're gonna die, baby. We're gonna see Millie.' She glanced down at the cigarette in her hand. Her last thought was how she had finally beaten the curse of tobacco.

The six-acre field vaporised a split second before she did.

# ONE

## SANDYS HALL -DEVON

## 14.30 – 11 November 2065

Could it be ten years since he stood in this same spot? It hardly seemed possible. So vivid were his memories of this place, it could have been yesterday. Then again, if he charted his achievements, a decade was no time at all to encompass his rapid rise through the political ranks. Jack Tirrand was a name to watch, destined for greater things if the talk bandied about in certain influential circles was to be believed. Not bad, he thought, for the boy from the humble origins of a foster home.

His nostrils flared as he breathed in the crisp autumn air and contemplated the reception he could expect beyond the sweeping driveway that led to the imposing manor house of Sandys Hall, the home of his wife's family.

The Fitzwilliams had witnessed the passage of time take its toll, much akin to the formidable wrought iron double gates marking the entrance to the estate. Ten years ago, these gates were freshly painted and closed, proudly defining the territorial integrity of the property. Now, they were open, pressed flat against the wall, the paint chipped and faded; the hinges rusted and broken. They were, he thought, a metaphor for the woman whose eightieth birthday he now came to celebrate: neither performed a useful function anymore.

At seventy, Verity had been the pragmatic and outspoken firebrand who ran her husband's family estate with an iron fist. In the intervening years, progressive dementia transformed her world into one of fantasy, the reversion to perpetual childhood as a pupil experiencing the emotions and responses of daily life in an all-girls boarding school.

He felt apprehensive about how he would react to Verity and to those around her who willingly took part in the charade that was now her life. Surely there would be periods of remission when she would remember she was Charles's wife. They had two children, a son, a man of the cloth – what a ridiculous term that was. It made him sound like a tailor – and a daughter, Rebecca, grandchildren and great-grandchildren. For Charles's sake, he hoped so. It had always been Verity's strength of character that gave Charles the backbone he lacked. Jack dreaded to think of him trying to cope without her support.

The impatient neigh of one of the two horses, as it exhaled a cloud of hot air into the chill autumn afternoon, brought him back to the moment. 'Sorry, cabby. This place stirs a wealth of memories.'

'I reckon it does,' the old man said, patting the flank of the Norman cob. 'Must be on my way. Bringing these two out of retirement to ferry clients is a far cry from turning the key in the ignition.'

'Out of fuel credits?' Jack asked.

The old man nodded. 'Used the last one yesterday. Have to wait until tomorrow to put the taxi on the road and these stalwarts back in the field until needs must.' He hesitated. 'Forgive me for asking, but you're Jack Tirrand, aren't you? I recognise you from the bulletins.'

Jack nodded. 'You can leave me here,' he said, eager to avoid being sidetracked into a political to-and-fro he sensed was imminent. 'I'll walk the rest of the way. What's your VI?'

The cabby recited the vehicle identification number, which Jack tapped into his mobile, selecting the menu option of a short journey credit. As the phone beeped its confirmation, Jack asked for the FTS reference. The tip was generous, and the old man voiced his appreciation. 'Free To Spend' credits were prized for the little luxuries they provided alongside the necessities to which all citizens were entitled.

The cob tapped his rear hoof on the tarmac as if impatient to be on its way. The old man nodded toward the horses and smiled. 'I'll thank you on their behalf. They'll be grateful you haven't made them take you up to the Hall. They desperately need new shoes and the gravel gets wedged in the gaps.'

Jack waved as the ancient carriage with its two-horsepower momentum came to life and trundled onwards to its next fare.

'Sandys Hall', the plaque affixed to the gate read. 'An Ancestral Estate Controlled by The Tangible Heritage Trust.' Jack laughed to himself. 'An Ancestral Estate'? That was rich. Undoubtedly, a description insisted upon by Rebecca to describe the crumbling ruin. His wife was always determined to display her social status, even though the new order frowned upon talk of class and breeding. His daughter, Alison, once voiced the opinion that her mother adopted a posher accent than normal whenever around her parents. Much to Alison's annoyance, he scoffed at the observation, but today's call confirmed just how perceptive his daughter had been.

Rebecca had put on her part pleading, part condescending tone as she reeled off a list of instructions that morning. It was her mother's special day, and he must not step out of line. He was to humour Verity by adopting whatever role she attributed to him, school inspector, janitor, or clandestine visitor from the adjacent, equally imaginary boys' school. On no account was he to recall actual instances from the past, become argumentative or short-tempered as was in his nature, or ignore her mother when she addressed him. The entire family was making enormous sacrifices to be with Verity over the weekend and the least he could do was spare a few hours away from his political masters to join the celebrations. He smiled to himself. As always, Rebecca's emotional blackmail was irresistible.

On the eleventh of November ten years ago, he recalled, it was raining, that fine drizzle that feels like nothing but ends up soaking you. Today, the sun was an hour from setting out of a watery blue sky. The air was still, the silence all around him broken only by the deafening sound of the gravel crunching under his shoes.

He felt a sense of peace, an illusion, he knew, as though nothing bad could ever happen. But it had. Thirty-five years ago, to this very day, the world changed forever. As if in sympathy with the sentiment, the sun faded, eclipsed by the canopy of foliage on the tall cedars in the copse, before reappearing to cast lengthening shadows on the driveway.

The scene was now of ploughed fields stretching as far as the brow, laying fallow, awaiting next year's crop of whatever the cooperative determined was desirable. Before eleven/eleven, one of the finest eighteen-hole golf courses in south-west England, designed by an American sporting legend of the time, occupied this rolling landscape. What an idle pastime, he mused, striking a little ball toward a distant hole set in a manicured lawn; so many simple pleasures sacrificed for the sake of survival. There must still be a few golf courses in existence around the world, links courses where the land was unsuitable for agriculture, but there were none he could recall. Golf was now a virtual game, played against a screen by a fast-declining band of followers, humorously branded in the media as eccentrics from another era.

As the main building of Sandys Hall came into view, he heard the strain of children giggling and shouting long before he could see them. His grandchildren. 'Twins ran in the family,' Rebecca had laughingly told him when she announced her pregnancy. 'The Fitzwilliams specialise in "double yokers"'. Two sets of twin girls in successive generations proved the point.

His stride quickened. Nothing could lighten his mood more than seeing the innocent reverie of two six-year-old girls who derived so much pleasure from each other's company. Enjoy the experience, girls, he said to himself. Regrettably, your trouble-free world will be short-lived.

They had seen him. Unsure of who was approaching, they stopped in their tracks like startled fawns. He sensed they were about to turn and run.

'Faith. Felicity!' he called out. 'It's me. Poppa Jack.'

They looked at each other, uncertain, seeking confirmation.

'It's Poppa Jack,' he repeated as he closed the distance between them.

Recognition came in an instant. 'It *is* Poppa Jack,' Felicity shouted as they ran toward him and launched themselves into his outstretched arms.

'How wonderful.' He hugged them each in turn. 'How are my most favourite little girls in the whole, wide world?'

Faith clung to him, her arms tight around his neck, her expression confused. 'Grandma said you were dead.' She hesitated as if pondering the obvious. 'But you're not.'

'Dead? Grandma said I was dead?'

'She did, didn't she, Felicity?'

Felicity wagged a finger at him. 'She did. We swear. She told Uncle Robert you would be late for your own funeral.'

'And he is a rector,' Faith added with a six-year-old's idea of gravitas.

He laughed. 'Grandma was only joking.' He took each one by the hand. 'Come on. Let's go show everyone Poppa Jack is still alive.'

The girls hopped and skipped alongside him as they made their way through the rose garden to the front of the building. Behind the majesty of the facade, the exactly proportioned and spaced window frames, the uniform stonework, and the sturdy Palladian columns which marked the entrance, there were signs of terminal decay, of a lack of attention and maintenance.

Sandys Hall had once been an impressive example of Georgian architecture. It was now just a slowly crumbling monument.

There was no forewarning. As little hands squeezed his, an image, so intense, so terrifying, flashed through his mind and was gone before his brain could process the memory. His entire body shuddered. And then came the debilitating pain, the acrid sensation of burning flesh at the back of his nose, channelling into his throat and down into his lungs.

His grip on those tender hands loosened. He struggled for breath, feeling the panic well inside him as he fought to get air into his lungs. Unsteady on his feet, he leaned back against the front door to support his weight, his eyes pinched closed, unsure of his surroundings.

'Are you all right, old man?'

As the first breath of air filtered past the bile scorching his parched throat, Jack opened his eyes. Robert was standing in front of him, a look of bewildered concern on his face. The twins ran off, reacting to their mother's call and eager to confirm Poppa Jack was still in the land of the living.

'I could do with a glass of water,' Jack said. 'God, it's cold in here.' His voice echoed around the great entrance gallery.

Robert thrust the bible he was clutching into Jack's outstretched hand. 'Here's some spiritual comfort while I'm gone,' he said with a laugh in his voice as he turned on his heels. 'Be right back.'

Jack sat down on a step of the sweeping staircase leading to the bedrooms in the east wing of the building. His breathing became more regular as the sense of dread subsided and he focussed on his surroundings. A dozen pairs of eyes stared down at him from the walls with that ubiquitous, pursuing gaze associated with the Mona Lisa. Charles would claim the ornately framed portraits hung strategically on either side of the staircase were of Fitzwilliam nobility dating back six centuries, of a dynasty commanding powerful sway in the West Country since Tudor times. It was all bullshit, a fabrication which did not stand the test of public record. Jack learned the truth early in his relationship with Rebecca, following a fierce row with her parents over her choice of suitor. One of Charles's great-greats won the estate at a game of cards in the early nineteenth century, stood accused of cheating and cemented his claim by emerging victorious from a duel to the death.

Most of the earlier portraits were of forebears of the unfortunate last Lord Sandys since re-dubbed by Charles to be a Fitzwilliam in all but name. There is a certain type of individual, Charles being one such, who, if they tell a lie long and often enough, comes to accept it as an immutable truth. Regrettably, Jack thought, Charles's tendency to dogma had rubbed off on his daughter, Alison.

Jack's gaze came to rest on the striking portrait of a dashing cavalier decked in a flowing white wig, brandished sword in hand as he sat astride a rearing black stallion. Replete with the King's standard, this Royalist was more than ready for the fray. Jack shook his head. The Sandys clan appeared to have been prone to making the wrong choices when life and death decisions were concerned.

'Why are you shaking your head? You look terrible. What's happened?' Rebecca glared at him.

'Nothing. Just some stress relief. I'm fine now.' He took the glass of water she held out toward him. 'Everybody around here thinks I'm dead or dying.'

Robert reappeared at his side. 'You gave me a shock, old man, and that's no word of a lie.' He reached for the bible Jack was still holding. 'Better give me that. If I leave it with you, you'll be tearing out the pages to light the fire.'

'And a damn sight more practical application than as a source for all those fairy stories you concoct every Sunday.' Jack started to feel better. The look on Robert's face told him the patronising smile and reprimanding tut-tut were simply stalling tactics as his brother-in-law searched for a witty retort.

When the eleven/eleven attacks came, Robert had just started university, set on a degree in humanities. Before the dust settled, he abandoned the course to seek a ministry in the Anglican church. Rebecca claimed the scale of the atrocities prompted him to embark on a stint of missionary work in the *favela* slums of Brazil. It cemented his attraction to the Country, especially Rio, and his love for the people. The experience both humbled him and strengthened his resolve to make a difference.

Of course, organised religion was now a declining influence in a changed world. Now there was a new order striving for survival by discarding the religious dogma and conflict of faiths that had plagued civilisation since man climbed up onto two legs and contemplated his mortality. Political power was centred on strategic regional strongholds. Dictates were swiftly enacted, designed to neutralise religious influence and convert dog-collar devotees like Robert into little more than social workers, sounding off with platitudes to the masses and preaching to an ever-diminishing number of the converted. The guiding forces had been clever not to confuse religion with faith, trust and aspiration; careful not to ban or drive worship underground. That would have been dangerous, creating a subversive force with objectives incompatible with the common good. Dissent could not be tolerated.

Against a background branding organised religion as an irrelevance, Jack could only admire his brother-in-law. Robert fought to uphold his convictions, not with the fervour of a revolutionary but with a pragmatic stubbornness which endeared him to the members of his local congregation. Jack suspected Robert would not give up on him, biding his time until he detected a crack in Jack's armoury. Until then, their exchanges on all things biblical were reduced to mild insults and banter.

'I'll have you know, old man, my fairy stories, as you call them, put a fire in people's bellies when there's no heat in the grate.' He chuckled, convinced he had put Jack in his place.

'Listen, old man,' Jack fired back. 'You have the infuriating habit of putting "old man" in every sentence you utter. Do you do it to everybody?'

Robert sniggered and gripped his arm. 'I only do it to you because I know how much you hate it.'

'I don't know if I believe you.'

'Stop it, you two!' Rebecca interrupted. 'You are like overgrown schoolboys with your silly point scoring.' She linked arms with her husband, leaving Robert to look on as they walked toward the study. 'I thought you were never coming. Father keeps asking after you. I'm sick of making excuses for an absentee husband making it obvious he is trying to avoid his in-laws.'

'Not guilty. The journey was horrendous. A collective, two trains, both late with no food, rounded off by a bone-shaking, twenty-minute ride in some strange stagecoach contraption the taxi driver is obliged to use when he has no fuel credits left.'

Rebecca ignored his attempt at an excuse, pulling his head closer to whisper. 'Alison is being prickly today. See if you can get her out of this mood. I don't want her upsetting mother.'

'Alison is always prickly, as you call it. So, what's new?'

Rebecca shook her head. 'The atmosphere at lunch was impossible. Such a shame you weren't here to distract her. My parents did not comment, but everybody else picked up on it. She kept attacking Harriet, criticising her domesticity, lack of ambition and deriding her for having no interest in any subject outside of family issues. You would not have tolerated her behaviour.' She paused to take a deep breath. 'I found several of her remarks spiteful and out of order. I took her to one side after lunch. She didn't take kindly to my rebuke and went off in a sulk.'

'Do you think your parents realised?'

They stopped outside the study door. There was no sound from inside. 'I think Daddy did, although he made no mention afterwards.' Jack strained to hear her conspiratorial whisper. 'Poor Mummy. She was still revelling in the euphoria of a school assembly. The local rector, alias Robert, was taking prayers and reading a scripture from the bible. She's having a bad day; doesn't recognise any of us; addresses Daddy as the headmaster and calls him "Sir" all the time.' She opened the door and pulled at his sleeve. 'Keep your eye on Alison.'

Jack sighed. Their daughters, officially Harriet One and Alison Two were twins. As with most of their character traits, they had little in common and were unrecognisable as sisters, let alone twins.

Harriet arrived in this world thirteen minutes earlier than her sister, entitling her to firstborn status and the obligatory suffix of 'One' following her first Christian name. Alison's birth certificate registered her as 'Two' and established the limit to which the birth quota legislation restricted the family size. Thereafter, many couples chose for one of them to be sterilised, a choice encouraged by the authorities with the award of additional family credits. Should Rebecca have fallen pregnant again, legislation required the baby be put up for adoption by a couple on the 'Infertiles Register'.

Throughout the world, the controlling union of INCOL, the acronym for the International Coalition Legislative to Preserve the Human Race, was attempting to ensure population levels gradually declined to achieve the delicate balance between the availability of resources and the requirements necessary to feed and clothe every citizen. The goal was still a long way off.

The study was crowded and decidedly chilly, a couple of degrees less cold than the rest of the building, but still unpleasant. Charles and Verity, wrapped in blankets, occupied the two winged leather armchairs facing each other. Charles appeared relieved to note Jack's arrival.

'How gracious of you to come, Deputy,' he said. 'You missed a wonderful lunch, all credit to the ladies present.'

Jack acknowledged the comment with a smile. Protocol was served. Addressing his son-in-law by his political rank was deliberate, intended to illicit a courtesy in return. Jack had no desire to disappoint his host. 'Glad I could make it, your Grace. Only sorry I couldn't get here earlier.'

Charles's chest expanded, head erect, at the sound of the reference to his hereditary title. The satisfaction he once derived from being known as Lord Fitzwilliam when he took his seat in the House of Lords was short-lived. In the interlude between assuming the title upon his father's death and the enactment of the INCOL Articles of Existence, which abolished both the upper and lower houses of Parliament, there had been precious little time to enjoy his status.

Although he paid lip service to the provisions of the new legislation which forbade any recognition of or allegiance to class distinction, Charles insisted, within the confines of Sandys Hall, that family and retainers dutifully respected his hereditary title. The fact his son-in-law, an up-and-coming member of the UK Assembly, deferred to him was a recognition of the esteem in which Charles was held. He would have been least impressed had he known Jack's concession to him was only intended to humour the old man's caprice.

Robert entered the study, closing the door firmly and rubbed his hands together aggressively as he acknowledged the assembled group.

'Sorry we cannot offer you the comfort of a little warmth,' Charles said. He glanced over at the open fireplace where once a dozen logs would have been blazing away, now given over to a lonely-looking gas fire which was turned off. 'We used the last of today's heating credits to keep the fire going over lunch.' His arm waved in the air, his finger pointed at the high, wood-panelled ceiling and the large single-glazed panel window overlooking the rose garden and the grounds beyond. 'Like a sieve this place. Impossible to heat. Needs three times the allowance your lot gives us just to be bearable.'

Jack avoided Rebecca's censorious glare. 'I thought the THT was supposed to look after the place since you conceded the property rights? Haven't you asked them for a concessionary heating grant?'

Charles's cheeks flushed. 'Don't talk to me about your precious Tangible Heritage Trust. They do bugger all except use their informers to spy on me and make sure I don't cut down any trees. And what do you mean by "ceded"?' His voice became shriller. 'It was hardly a voluntary act. They ex-appropriated the estate citing a historical and cultural preservation enactment coming from Berlin, of all places. I ask you, what do the bloody Krauts know about the culture of English stately homes?'

Rebecca placed a restraining hand on her father's shoulder, at the same time as giving her husband a withering look which said seek appeasement.

Charles was a dumpy, but well-built man with those same piercing blue eyes Rebecca had inherited. His pronounced chin sported a snow-white goatee beard. Jack recognised the Charles of old as his cheeks took on the red glow of passion, his chin lifted from his chest and his eyes, vital and charged, ready for the challenge.

Jack went to speak, change the subject, but Charles, brooking no interruption, frustrated the opportunity. 'Did you see the grounds on the way in?' He did not wait for an answer. 'I ask you, call themselves landscape gardeners. They are an affront to the job description; taken at random off the available to work register. Skills – zero; intelligence – zero; willingness and application – non-existent. Look over at the rose garden. It's more like the Amazon jungle! Your people in charge of INCOL have no idea what is happening in the outside world.'

The twins playing quietly in the corner now reacted to the charged atmosphere by clambering onto the sofa next to their mother, tugging at her knitted skirt and jumper and pleading to be allowed back out to play. Jack smiled inwardly at what must be a well-rehearsed scenario, a persistent coercion which tender Harriet could not resist. The searching look toward her husband must have only convinced her that further resistance was pointless. With his knees tucked up under his chin, Mac was lost to the world, absorbed in one of Charles's leather-bound compendia of forty-year-old motorsport magazines.

'Go on then,' she conceded. 'But stay in view. It will be dark soon and we will have to light the candles together. You like that.'

As the twins scurried out of the study, Jack moved to lighten the mood with his father-in-law. 'Listen, Charles. I understand these frustrations, especially for somebody who has lived over half his life in the world of plenty before eleven/eleven, but you must accept the conditions in which we exist have changed, perhaps forever.'

'For the worse.'

'Of course, for the worse. The experts say it will be at least another thirty years before the contaminated oilfields start to come back on stream. And that's assuming the new breed of climate do-gooders don't get their way. Until then, it's the responsibility of us all to do everything in our power to preserve humanity from a path of self-destruction.'

Charles shook his head. 'I've heard all this claptrap a million times.' He wheeled in his armchair to face Jack, ignoring the blanket slipping from his knees onto the floor. 'It strikes me, whilst ninety-nine per cent of the population are living in squalor to make the sacrifice possible, there are elitist cliques in Berlin, New York, Moscow and God knows where else living the good life under INCOL's protective umbrella.'

'I agree.' The rejoinder came from the slender, boyish figure sitting in an armchair three sizes too large for her. Jack had waved to Alison as he entered the study, but they had not spoken. 'It's a disgrace. And it pains me to see my father as part of it.'

In retrospect, Jack knew the mature reaction would have been to use his political skills to sideline the topic and not meet their criticism head-on. His need to rebuff the allegation was both a response to the anger surging inside him and the constant fear someone was monitoring careless talk and foolhardy assertions to undermine his position.

The election of deputies in the London Assembly division of the Senate was always hotly contested and peppered with invasive, personal attacks and wild innuendos intended to defame the candidate. As a relative newcomer to the political classes with a non-white strain in his heritage,

Jack's opponents aggressively contested his nomination and election with distasteful racial undertones.

The public conception was of elected deputies enjoying a favoured lifestyle and a status enviously sought by the politically motivated. It was far from the truth, perpetuated on hearsay and rumour, but nobody would lament his passing if a chink in the family armour could bring about his downfall.

'Can't you see the two of you are condemning the system there to protect you? It may have its failings. It's run by humans, after all.'

'I can certainly see it's there to protect *you*,' Charles retorted, plainly buoyed by the support of Alison.

Rebecca tut-tutted. 'Now, come on, Daddy. Be fair. Jack never takes advantage of his position. He was well within his rights to use his deputy's six-monthly travel concession and requisition a pool car and driver to bring him to join us. But no. He chose a collective and public transport to show he wants no favours from his position.'

Jack groaned inside. By speaking out in his defence, Rebecca simply amplified the objection raised by her father—time for Jack to play hardball.

'That's where you're wrong, Charles. You harbour a belief the world you live in today must embrace the outdated twentieth-century concept of a democratic society where free speech, human rights and expressing dissent are all solid building blocks to some open-minded utopia.'

'It's an aspiration; certainly not a reality.' His cheeks flushed. 'You find my view amusing?'

'I'm sorry.' The condescending smile and sardonic twist of the mouth were reflexes Jack consciously sought to suppress. It was an unfortunate habit he found he adopted when an argument irritated him. 'No, of course not. Though I must say, I find your naivety disturbing. The values you crave are those which spawned an army of disillusioned, fanatical individuals who thought they had the one-time solution to realign the direction in which civilization was travelling. And they were allowed, some would say encouraged, by a largely passive response from a political class resigned to fighting talk rather than direct action, to take up arms to maim and destroy in the name of some ill-matched, warped environmental and religious doctrines. *That* is the reason we are shivering in the cold today.'

The room fell silent. Jack fully expected his brother-in-law to react at the mention of religion, but Robert was having an intense, whispered conversation with his sister.

Charles's face almost glowed incandescent in the half-light. 'Are you suggesting I . . . my generation somehow encouraged or provoked the terrorists and degenerates responsible for eleven/eleven into doing so? If this is your belief, you are plainly deranged, Deputy.'

Again, Jack knew he should close the exchange with some placatory remark, but he could not. It was not to Charles he needed to press home his argument, but to the younger audience present, who looked on with hostility borne out of confusion. It would be the responsibility of this new generation to steer the world out of its mess and into an era of opportunity and recovery. No easy task, he thought to himself.

Whatever provoked the hostilities three decades ago was a lesson for historians to analyse. In the following months, the world tottered on the brink of self-destruction. Overnight, feast turned to famine and famine to death.

At the eleventh hour, calculating, wise heads, the founding fathers of their day, established order. Collective sanity prevailed, out of which INCOL was born. In a move of worldwide solidarity, every sovereign nation coalesced and empowered the organisation to save the planet. Its charter demanded powers to steer humanity through the rigours of realigning private gain to the common interest. Where there had been greed and consumption, there were now shortages, hardship and suffering. The challenge was to convert mentalities from personal gratification toward striving for society as a whole. Such a seismic shift of attitude would never come about by popular consensus.

The rules had to change. The rights of the individual were curtailed. Tough enactments on birth control, religious freedoms, crimes against society and rationing were introduced and gradually assimilated into the public psyche. Above all, personal liberties and privacy, once cherished as basic rights, were severely curtailed. Initially, the resentment was fierce, laws flouted, and social upheaval widespread. It took hardship, brutal enforcement and the imposition of a virtual dictatorship based on necessity, but INCOL survived and thrived. Today, a new generation knows of no other world, its hopes and ambitions fuelled by the prospect of a brighter future. It was only the cynics of Charles's era, and the hot-headed revolutionaries to succeed it, who practised dissent. These citizens, who would never accept the status quo, must be dealt with.'

'Of course, I'm not accusing you,' Jack said. 'Listen. INCOL is not some demonic force. It comprises representatives from every corner of the globe, ordinary people like us . . . like me. It's as benign as it can be under the circumstances but still a minority criticise and are determined to flout the rules.'

'Benign! I don't know how you have the nerve to use the word. We live in a police state akin to any other in history where those prepared to express an alternative opinion are censored and often removed, lost without a trace.'

Jack could see Alison nodding her head out of the corner of his eye, but the hand pressing on her shoulder appeared to restrain her from interrupting.

Again, Jack realised they needed to move on. It was futile trying to appeal to Charles, whose viewpoint was ingrained and, without fear of retribution, available to all who were prepared to listen. The trouble was that elements within the security service could well learn of Charles's reckless remarks and put the rest of the family, including Jack, under suspicion.

As much as he knew Rebecca's constant stare was willing him to change the subject, he needed to avoid any future accusation that he did not react to Charles's defamatory statement. 'The security services are empowered to ensure compliance with the law, no more, no less. Collectively, we are all obliged to obey the rules. We cannot afford the luxury of dissent. Look at the facts and stop seeing the injustice in rumour and speculation.' He shook his head to preface an admonishment. 'We have established regulations for your own good yet, in this room, you ignore one of the most important security enactments.'

Charles raised his eyebrows as he searched for an explanation. It was Alison who picked up on her father's comment. 'He's talking about the television, grandpa,' she said wryly. 'We haven't got the bloody thing switched on.'

Jack turned to face his daughter. 'Quite right. The requirement was introduced to protect you. The television must be always online when individuals are in residence.' He was quoting verbatim from memory. 'How do you expect to keep up to date with breaking news, the release of civil edicts if, as you call it, the bloody thing is switched off? Compliance means TV indoors, mobile on outside. Does that simple requirement warrant dissent?'

'For Christ's sake, somebody put me out to graze.' Charles leaned over to squeeze Verity's hand as the bile rose in his throat. 'If life has been reduced to a mandatory blank screen or watching endless sports programmes, fifty-year-old situation comedies or a court scene as they condemn some poor wretch to the cells . . . I'd rather slit my throat.'

Alison stood up, a finger waving at her father. 'Don't worry, Grandpa. His lot will do it for you.'

The exchange charged the atmosphere. Jack feared they were heading for a full-blooded confrontation with neither able nor willing to back off.

'You've changed, Jack, you know that?' Charles adopted a softer tone. 'You used to have opinions and respect other people's points of view. Now, you spout the party line.'

Jack gritted his teeth, his fists clenched. He was ready to explode. God Almighty! Charles was one of the breed who selfishly took advantage of the spoils, ostracised and disenfranchised all who got in their way and, unthinkingly, left succeeding generations to clear up the mess. It was no wonder an unholy alliance between religious extremists and environmentalists obsessed with revolutionary change sought a solution through violence. To excuse Charles now, on the grounds of age, would be to patronise him, and Jack was not prepared to accept that compromise.

A hand pinched at the sleeve of his jacket. It was down to Rebecca to avert the train crash. She knew her father and husband too well to let a full-blown argument develop. 'Let's not forget why we're here,' she whispered in Jack's ear before leaning forward to tap Verity on the knee. 'Mummy, look who has come just to wish you a happy birthday. We thought he would never get here, didn't we? But he's finally arrived. Look. It's Jack.'

If Rebecca hoped for a lucid reaction to the announcement, she was to be disappointed. Verity raised unseeing eyes to stare in front of her before returning her gaze downward to study whatever she believed was couched in her lap.

Rebecca repeated his name.

'Jack, be nimble; Jack, be quick; Jack, jump over the candlestick.' The nursery rhyme erupted in an emotionless monotone. Verity laughed to herself, a smirk which was transformed into a stern glance as she focussed on the new arrival. 'This Jack is neither nimble nor quick,' she said. Her eyes fixed on his. 'I will have him know I am the milk monitor this month and I distinctly remember ordering a third of a pint for every girl, plus three pints for the staff room and whatever the kitchen ladies require. He's late again, as usual.' She gave a cursory wave of her hand. 'Now, put the crates down there and be off with you.'

Jack took a step back, at a loss for words.

'What are you waiting for? Don't stand there gawping!' The look she gave him put him in the food chain somewhere between rodent and viper. He recognised the look of unspoken rebuke passed on from mother to daughter. 'Are you deaf or something?'

'If I may butt in,' Charles whispered.

Verity reacted by sitting bolt upright, her hands pressed flat against her thighs, palms turned inwards. 'Yes, Sir,' she shouted at the top of her voice.

The collection of compendia on Mac's lap slid to the floor. 'Jesus wept,' he said in a soft Scottish brogue.

Charles stretched forward to pat Verity on the hand. 'It's today we have to pay the milk bill,' he said tenderly. 'I've asked the secretary to draw a cheque, so he will have to wait until it's ready.'

'Yes, Sir!' in an even more strident tone.

Rebecca linked arms with her husband, a nonchalant smile on her face as if the last passage of conversation was nothing out of the usual. She led him across the room. 'Alison has invited a chum from Uni to stay for the weekend. Say hello to Rolf.' She acknowledged the tall, athletic young man with the crop of untidy, ultra-black hair, standing behind the winged armchair in which Alison was sitting. 'This is my husband, the Deputy, you've been so longing to talk to.'

Jack reacted to the cue and extended his arm for a firm, uncompromising handshake. Rolf remained planted behind the chair in a pose reminiscent of a formal, studied Victorian photo portrait. A restraining hand remained on Alison's shoulder, suggesting the young man was aware of the fiery temper his girlfriend possessed. The fact she responded to the gesture suggested a degree of intimacy and respect, which took them well beyond the mere 'chums' level.

'Pleased to meet you, Sir,' Rolf said, a broad deferential smile on his face. 'I have heard a great deal about you.'

'None of it complimentary, I guess, if it came from Alison. Where's the accent from, Germany?'

'Blackpool, actually,' he replied, much to Alison's amusement.

Jack smiled. Seeing Alison look so radiant and happy was a rare and comforting experience. 'When did they start talking like that in Blackpool?'

'Apologies. It sounded facetious. It is German. My father is retired and lives near Stuttgart, but I am on the Dweller's Register at my mother's address in Lytham Saint Anne.' He hesitated. 'She is English – separated from my father.'

Jack curbed the urge to enquire further. At worst, it would seem like an interrogation; at best, an assessment of his suitability as his daughter's suitor. 'What are you studying?'

Rolf exchanged a complicit smile with Alison. 'I'm glad you asked, Sir. I have just enrolled in the mature student programme, a degree course in social mobility for all non-CR actives.'

'Very worthwhile,'

'To be honest, Sir, when Alison invited me to join the family for the weekend, I jumped at the opportunity. I was hoping . . . ' He glanced at Alison, seeking support.

'Spit it out, Rolf,' Alison prompted. 'He doesn't bite unless he's wearing someone else's teeth and do stop calling him "Sir". It's a title reserved for seniority.'

Jack ignored the barb, prompting the young man to continue.

'Well, as you are an Assembly deputy with special responsibility for the care of the elderly and those excused from the Cooperative Register, an appreciation of your insight would be invaluable for my coursework. I was hoping you might give me a moment to discuss the challenges.'

Rebecca gave a knowing shake of the head. 'You don't know what you're asking for, Rolf,' she cautioned light-heartedly. 'Once you get him started, the floodgates will open, and he will not stop banging on about work. I've suffered years of it.'

'I'll second that,' Alison said.

'Sorry to interrupt everybody.' The sense of alarm in the demure voice stilled the various conversations taking place. Harriet sat on her own next to the picture window, a thick blanket decked around her shoulders.

'The girls were playing on the lawn a minute ago. I turned around for a second and when I looked back, they'd disappeared.'

# TWO

## SANDYS HALL -DEVON

## 16.00 – 11 November 2065

Robert shuffled across to the window and looked out. 'I'll go and check,' he said.

'No!' In one word, she managed to convey both anger and panic. 'Mac, I can't see the girls outside. They are not playing on the lawn. Can you find them and bring them in, please? The light is failing.'

'They'll be fine. Where can they go?' Mac's casual response suggested a seasoned familiarity with his wife's concerns. The compendia of motor magazines remained firmly raised as a barrier between them.

'Find them, please!' She spoke through gritted teeth, aware that others were witnessing this marital disharmony.

In Jack's head, an alarm sounded – not for the well-being of the twins – but for a father's concern for his daughter's relationship with her husband. Something told him this was not an isolated incident. Since infancy, Harriet had a sensitivity and fragile personality so easily damaged, yet she was as single-minded and persistent as her sister when those she loved were challenged. Jack would speak to her on his own as soon as the opportunity arose. Right now, there was another priority.

'Why don't we all take a stroll before the light finally goes?' he proposed. 'The men can go first to round up the twins and leave you ladies to accompany Charles and Verity to the portico.' He saw Alison's raised eyebrows as akin to calling him a sexist bastard, but he needed to get Mac away from the study and out of his lethargy.

He pulled Mac to his feet and told him to swap his slippers for his shoes. Jack followed Rolf and Robert into the courtyard. There was no sign of the twins or any response when Robert's booming voice called out their names.

Rolf turned to Jack. 'We've got about fifteen minutes before we need torches,' he said. 'Let's split up.' He suggested sweeping a wide arc to cover the immediate acreage. 'Are there any natural hazards?' he asked.

The answer came in a shrill scream piercing the still air, followed by a crack like a twig snapping as the sound reverberated against the building.

'Out of the way,' Robert shouted as a chunk of weathered masonry fell, narrowly missing them. 'The place is falling to bits.'

Felicity emerged from the long grass leading down to the lily pond. She stumbled forward, bedraggled and struggling for air. Mac appeared, and they ran towards her.

'Where's Faith?' Mac asked, clutching his daughter to him.

In between desperate breaths, she spoke. 'The man. Scared me. Jumped up. Faith fell in the water.'

Jack had run three full marathons over the last year and considered himself in decent shape, but Rolf reached the pond a good ten seconds before him. Faith's slender figure, dishevelled and trembling from the soaking she had received, sat on the muddy ground at the water's edge. Petrified, she sobbed as Jack picked her up and held her close to him.

'I'm sorry, Poppa Jack.' She looked up at him, pleading with those entrancing brown eyes full of tears. 'Will Mummy be angry with me?' she asked through chattering teeth.

'Of course not, darling. How did you come to fall into the water?' He looked at the mass of vegetation under the surface and thought, more to the point, how, on earth, did you get out?

'The man scared me,' she said. Her breathing was becoming more regular.

'What man?' Jack asked.

She waved toward the long, untended grassland. 'The man pulled me out. He told me to hold his hand.' In stilted, disjointed phrases, Faith told how the man suddenly appeared in front of her, rising from the ground like a ghost. Felicity stood rooted to the spot, but Faith, stunned by the stranger's appearance, took two steps backwards and fell into the pond. She moved her arms, just as Mummy had taught her, but something pulled at her legs, forcing her down.

She told of hearing Felicity scream in the distance and then a loud bang. Suddenly, the man reappeared, reached under the water and pulled her onto the bank. He ran off at the sound of voices.

Mac arrived, Felicity in his arms. Harriet's cry of relief came from not far behind.

'Did you know the man?' Rolf asked.

She shook her head. 'He wasn't like us,' she said.

'What do you mean, sweetheart?' Jack gripped her hands and looked into those innocent eyes, still full of fear and confusion.

'Brown. Like muddy. His hands and face.' She held out her tiny palms.

Rolf took the lead as they careered through the long prairie grass. His arm shot out to block Jack's passage forward. It was unyielding as it collided with Jack's chest, forcing the breath from his body. Head bowed, hands on thighs, Jack sucked in air.

'Sorry,' Rolf said, pointing to the area in front of them. 'Best not to trample all over it.' The grass was flattened as though someone had been lying down. They were only thirty metres beyond the pond, but the topography had changed. From where the two men stood, there was an uninterrupted view of the front of the main building.

Rolf settled on his haunches, hands palm down, tracing the contours of the compacted area, adjusting his position as he moved forward toward the small pile of rocks arranged at the end.

'You seem to know what you're doing, Rolf,' Jack said, more intrigued by his companion than the scene they were surveying. 'Is crime scene analysis another one of your talents?'

'My father worked for ISE. He used to talk about the techniques of investigation. I am an avid listener.'

'He was an operative with the security service?' There was both admiration and suspicion in his tone. ISE, the acronym for INCOL Security and Enforcement, was feared or admired, hated or respected, dependent upon your status, be it suspect or enforcer. The overriding mantra of the policing authority, which had few limitations, was the protection of society from any threat to INCOL's governing mandate.

Rolf stood and turned to meet Jack's questioning look. 'In his younger days,' he replied, matter of fact. 'Now, he's desk-bound, shuffling papers from one tray to another: his words, not mine. Shall we go back?'

Jack could hear Rebecca's voice nearby, rising above the others, calling for him. He returned the call, his attention still directed at the young man. 'So, what would ISE make of this? A vagrant or would-be thief attempting to hide when he heard the commotion?'

Rolf shrugged. 'Possibly. Whatever the motive, he has long since gone and, excluding the possibility of one or two disturbing nightmares over the next few days, the girls have not suffered.'

By the time they made their way back to the Hall, night had closed in, and a chill wind was blowing in from the north. The promise of a warming soup and cold snacks found them in the study, huddled together, wrapped in blankets.

Harriet stayed close to the twins, who were now tucked up in bed, sound asleep and, surprisingly, unphased by their ordeal. Verity dozed off in her wheelchair alongside Charles, and Mac was again immersed in the collection of ancient motoring magazines. For the rest, a bout of conjecture and speculation around the stranger in the grass evolved into a general and spirited exchange of views on crime and the criminal classes. Finally, Robert's decision to attempt a thoroughly forgettable rendition of 'Onward, Christian Soldiers' on an ancient harpsichord badly in need of tuning sent everybody to seek solace out of earshot in their bedrooms.

For Jack, sleep would not come. Rebecca wound herself around him like a boa constrictor, more for warmth than intimacy he regretted. Any thought of caressing her into wakefulness quickly dissipated at the sound of her gentle snoring in his ear.

As the rays of sunlight filtered in between the join in the curtains, he felt as if he had lain awake all night. Lack of sleep doused his customary early morning cheer, replaced by a sense of foreboding he could not dispel. He determined to confront his demons with a strong cup of tea and return to bed, where he would couch into Rebecca's back and doze for a couple of hours.

Barefoot, the floorboards were ice cold to the touch as he dashed toward the kitchen wrapped in Rebecca's fluffy woollen, pink dressing gown. He paused at the study. He could hear a steady tapping on the exterior brickwork, a sound which grew louder as he neared the window but came from a point which was just outside his line of vision.

Although unprepared for any physical challenge, curiosity got the better of him.

As the hinges on the front door creaked, a stealthy approach was not an option. He winced as he stepped onto the gravel and took in the scene before him. Balanced on a chair at the point where the masonry had fallen the previous afternoon, Rolf stood, dressed in a tracksuit with a hammer raised to strike in one hand and a chisel in the other. The look of surprise relaxed into a wide smile as he recognised the apparition in front of him.

'An explanation wouldn't go amiss,' Jack said sternly, to hide his embarrassment.

Rolf failed to wipe the smile from his face. 'I didn't want to alarm anybody until I was certain,' he said. The chair wobbled on the uneven gravel. Jack moved forward to steady it, cursing as the stones dug into his feet.

'Certain about what?' Jack said, becoming more irritable with every passing second. 'Let's carry on this conversation inside.'

Sitting back in a rocking chair in the scullery, his feet entwined in a blanket from the dog's basket, and with a mug of tea clasped between his hands, Jack's sense of well-being returned. 'So, what's all this early morning demolition about?'

Rolf remained standing. He placed a matching mug on a gnarled oak chopping board, twisting it so that the handle was lined up parallel to the edge of the board. A minute adjustment was necessary to satisfy him before he looked up to answer and reached with his free hand into a pocket.

He held out a bullet casing between his thumb and index finger. 'It's from a *Sturmgewher*, a military assault rifle. I recognised it from my training as a reservist. I found it on the ground yesterday, close to where the intruder was lying.'

'Why didn't you say anything?'

'I needed to be sure, and now I am.' He gave a rueful smile. 'The bullet is lodged in the brickwork. My guess is your granddaughter's scream saved one of our lives.'

Jack ignored the droplets from his mug spilling onto the dressing gown. 'You're suggesting someone was lying in wait to commit murder? Everybody was outside.'

'No. It was just the three of us: Robert, you and me. Mac was walking toward us but some distance away. We were talking about how to organise the search when the girl appeared.'

'*You* were working it out, as I recall.' Jack was wide-eyed.

Rolf ignored the comment. 'I assume the shooter was waiting for his target to emerge from the house, no doubt prepared to hold up for as long as it took. From where he lay, there was a clear shot. He was no amateur. The little mound of rocks acted as a support for the barrel.'

'The twins disturbed him.'

'That's my conclusion. He must have reacted when they neared him, so startling the girls and provoking the accident. There was just time for one shot, but the diversion must have distracted his aim. He had to make his escape in a hurry.'

Jack nodded his agreement. 'But he still took the risk of being caught by stopping to pull Faith from the water?'

'What can I tell you?' He shrugged his shoulders. 'A would-be assassin with a conscience.'

'The authorities will have to be advised.'

They moved back into the study. Jack shivered as he noticed the frost on the inside of the picture window. There was still no movement from anyone else in the house. He couldn't blame them: better to snuggle down in bed than face the chill of a freezing winter morning.

Neither man spoke, Jack pensive, Rolf hesitating over his choice of words.

'I don't want to appear too pushy, Sir . . .' He was nervous, waiting for a positive sign to carry on.

'But?' Jack prompted. The young man was hard to fathom, forceful yet reverential at the same time. Was he putting on an act for his benefit?

'I would like to suggest you hold fire on that decision until we have some more facts to hand. You know the methods ISE will employ.' He hesitated. 'I was thinking more of Charles and, I have to admit, Alison as well.'

He was right, of course, Jack thought, although loath to admit it. ISE would be all over the estate. No one would escape interrogation or be allowed to leave the premises. Charles was bound to let loose one of his critical outbursts, almost certainly supported by Alison, who would vociferously take her grandfather's side. One problem would morph into several and put the family – above all, Assembly Deputy, Jack Tirrand – under the microscope.

In the circumstances, as uncomfortable as he felt, Jack would leave the disturbing occurrence in temporary abeyance until a few discreet enquiries could be made. Regretfully, he agreed to play his part in a conspiracy of silence.

'I suppose the question is which one of us was he after?' Rolf asked, raising his eyebrows. 'Do you have any enemies?' The reverential tone was now gone.

'Seen and unseen,' Jack said. 'I'd need to borrow most of your fingers to count, but I doubt I've upset anybody enough to want to kill me.'

'There are just three options. One, a local rector; another, a poor student; and the third, a senior politician ambitious for promotion. I know which one I'd bet on.'

Jack gave the comment some thought. 'You may well be right, but the local rector has his demons to contend with and the poor university student, as you describe him, appears to have several strings to his bow and family connections leading right back to ISE headquarters in Berlin. Maybe all is not as it seems. Somebody who blacks himself up to commit murder, if such was the intention, has to have a military background.'

Rolf's brow creased. 'You've got that wrong, I'm afraid. I spoke with Mac before he went to bed. The man who scared the girls and rescued Faith was not camouflaged. He was a black man, as in Caribbean or African descent.'

Jack clasped his head with both hands. The ringing in his ears; the throbbing forehead; the sensation of seared flesh in his nostrils; vivid abstract images evaporating into a haze. The pain was excruciating, but somehow enticing. Where have the memories gone? His eyes closed as his breathing faltered.

# THREE

## ALEXANDRA PALACE – LONDON

## 10.00 – 13 November 2065

Arnold Roach hoisted his not-inconsiderable posterior onto the corner of Jack's desk with an ease that belied his size. He shuffled into a comfortable position, his feet no longer touching the floor. Glancing around the large room crammed with desks and filing cabinets, he acknowledged the greetings from several of the London Chapter members with a slight bow of his balding head. As senior coordinator, Roach enjoyed a position of status and a direct reporting role to the UK Assembly leader and INCOL Senate representative.

'Thought so, Jack,' he boomed, aware he now had an audience. 'The Chinese have finally admitted what we all suspected and asked for help. What do you think about that?' He didn't wait for an answer. 'Serves them right for being so damn secretive. Now we know one has finally managed to escape.'

Jack gave a peremptory nod. His weekly report had to be ready in thirty minutes, and Roach's appearance was a distraction he could do without. What's more, since he arrived back in London, the last thing he wanted to do was turn up the volume on the TV. He had paid no attention to the news.

Several heads turned in Roach's direction, prompting him to ignore Jack's apparent disinterest. 'Since China occupied Australasia, no Australian or New Zealander has escaped and lived to tell the tale. Now, it looks as though this lone sailor in a catamaran has made it out of Tasmania whilst nobody was paying attention.'

He waited for a reaction which did not come. 'After several weeks of rumour and denial, INCOL Asia has now asked ships and aircraft in the southern oceans to be on the lookout. Mind you, if the military and their drones can't find him, what is the chance of some tramp steamer spotting him in that mass of water?' He reflected on his rhetorical question. 'Probably dead by now. If he's not and they find him, he'll wish he was. The Chinese hate to be embarrassed. What do you reckon, Jack?'

'Can we leave it for later, AR?' Jack did not take his eyes off the screen in front of him. 'You know Monday's a bitch, and I need to work through these site reports for the Chapter briefing. Alright with you?'

AR, as Roach liked to be known, appeared unmoved by the plea. He plucked at the retro braces with the inverted V-shaped leather fasteners, which hiked his pinstripe trousers over the girth of his thighs to fold loosely around his waist. His shirt sleeves were rolled up tight to meet the sweat marks under his armpits, a red bow tie set below a long, scrawny neck with a pronounced Adam's apple. Well into his fifties with veined red cheeks and a dietary reputation said to exclude anything coloured green, he was a prime candidate for a coronary within the next ten years. Not that many of the inmates in the glass-domed Assembly building would shed a tear if he did. Amongst the Deputies and support staff, he was known as 'pigeon', given his capacity to shit on anybody below him. Nobody was immune from a pigeon smear or major muck spread if he felt he could impress his superiors.

In the time before INCOL, when there was a sovereign government operating in the Houses of Parliament in Westminster, AR would have been described as a chief whip, responsible for herding his flock around the inner sanctum as the order paper dictated.

As a young, aspirant civil servant, Jack vividly recalled the TV images of that last highly charged sitting of a packed House. The prime minister stood at the Despatch Box, tension and emotion in his voice, as he outlined the democratic role the United Kingdom would play in a new worldwide order created to maintain peace and security for all nations. The Houses of Parliament, he explained, would cease to be the seat of government until sovereign rule was returned to these shores. In the intervening period, Britain would be represented at the highest level in the INCOL Europe Senate in Berlin, and the Westminster Estate converted into a museum, open to the public, a fitting tribute and reminder of the UK's democratic heritage.

'Good weekend, Jack? You got back early? I thought you might have taken the extra day. Didn't take a staff car, I note.'

Jack gave a cursory nod. AR was on a fishing expedition. Best to feed him a sprat, at least. 'I needed to be back for this Chapter meeting. The memo said we have important guests.'

'You were lucky with your lifts? It's a damn long way from Devon.'

'Two hitches; one from Barnstaple to Guildford, and the next dropped me off at Muswell Hill. If you mention your Assembly status to the driver, it's as good as a taxi service.'

'Never done it myself,' Roach said. 'I know by law motorists must stop for hitchhikers if they have a spare seat, but I always tell my drivers to ignore the requirement on the grounds of political expediency. If they're reported and subject to a fine or loss of fuel credits, I request a dispensation notice. Works every time.'

Jack turned to catch the eye of fellow Deputy, Les Hawkins and raised his eyebrows.

'Rebecca and the family stay down at Sandys Hall?' Roach asked, ignoring Jack's impatient sigh.

'For a day or so. I expect they'll travel back together midweek. I need to . . .'

'Verity's eightieth, wasn't it?' A wintry smile bared a set of immaculate dentures – a rarity these days, Jack thought – 'Significant age, eighty, don't you think?'

Jack's puzzled glance was more of concern as to the source of Roach's information than to acknowledge the comment. The Deputies' Movement Log showed a two-day visit to Devon. He had not discussed the reason with any colleagues.

'I don't expect too many of your clients worry about the future when they reach the old four-score, do you?'

'My clients?' Jack queried. 'If you mean the residents of the care and nursing homes under my watch, the average life expectancy is now eighty-two. As to worrying about the future at that age, I expect their chief aim is to get to eighty-three. You must let me know how you feel when you reach their age.'

'Just making polite conversation, Jack. No need to get tetchy and defensive.'

'I have to get some work done.'

For a man his size, Roach slid off the desk with surprising grace. 'By the way, Jack,' he said. 'The big man wants to see you after the meeting. Go straight to his office.'

Jack acknowledged the order. You push it, AR, he thought. Had Jack referred to their leader, Simeon Hill, in such a derogatory manner, his name was likely to end up on a delegate performance report as an accusation of seniority disrespect, submitted anonymously, of course.

'Any idea what for?' Jack asked. 'I can come prepared.'

'No idea.'

'You're lying,' Jack said to himself. Roach was privy to virtually everything that went on at the Palace. His nose got everywhere, including into some dark and smelly places.

'Jack Tirrand is the man of the moment,' Roach said loud enough for those around to hear. 'You know we all think highly of you. It must be important. His Monday routine doesn't include one-to-one meetings with deputies.' He hesitated for effect. 'Disciplinary issues apart, of course.'

For a second, the mysterious events of the weekend came to mind, but Jack dismissed the notion. Not even AR could have unearthed that one so rapidly.

Heads turned as Roach threaded between the rows of desks and open-plan partitions. 'Mind you,' he announced with a crackle of amusement in his voice. 'If this Aussie evades detection and makes it as far as South America and the Open Territory, we are going to get some first-hand evidence of exactly what is going on behind the Bamboo Curtain. I guarantee it won't be pretty.'

# FOUR

## ALEXANDRA PALACE – LONDON

## 10.30 – 13 November 2065

There were under thirty minutes left for Jack to complete his weekly report and join the other forty deputies who made up the London and Southern Chapter of the UK Assembly. The meeting would be held in the Chamber, a cavernous room converted from a bar many years earlier when Alexandra Palace was a tourist attraction. Whether it was auto-suggestion or some chemical reaction between the hops, nicotine and the woodwork, it was widely agreed the auditorium bore a feint trace of beer and cigarettes.

The deputies shuffled to their allotted places, monitors before them showing the agenda for the day and, as the meeting progressed, a draft of the minutes in real time prepared by the stenographer. Any changes could be suggested by commenting alongside the relevant text.

Monday morning's gathering was primarily for the submission of weekly updates by the senior deputies, of which Jack was one, detailing the performance of their departments over the previous seven days and their aspirations for the following week. It was routine business and rarely attended by the upper echelons of the Chapter or a representative from the UK Assembly headquarters in Preston.

Today would be different, Jack sensed. For what reason, he had no idea. His curiosity heightened. As individuals filled the seats at the top table, Assembly member and Senate representative, Simeon Hill, took the chair. The two officials who normally controlled the agenda sat next to an elderly woman whom Jack knew as a branch coordinator from Preston. Toward the end of the table sat the internal auditor, Roach, and the HR executive. Alongside, two men Jack did not recognise moved into position, their chairs slightly set back from the main body of dignitaries. From their muscular build and the uncomfortable manner, the taller and more substantial of the two constantly poked his finger between his neck and the starched white shirt collar, Jack guessed wearing a formal suit and tie was not their standard dress code. The woman who took the seat behind them bent forward to speak to the taller of the two, who nodded curtly in reply.

'Germans,' whispered a gruff male voice from alongside Jack. 'By the look of them, ISE security and enforcement. They don't look like they're from intelligence.' Jack flashed a smile of agreement at his colleague, Les Hawkins, who raised his bushy eyebrows questioningly.

Simeon Hall called the meeting to order.

The major topics of local finance, crime and security, education and health, were each covered within the ten-minute segments allotted, stimulating no significant reaction from the top table. Jack was preparing to follow Hawkins, an amiable deputy in his mid-thirties, who was rounding up his presentation on SocioLine, the only official social media outlet allowed following the purge of those responsible for eleven/eleven. INCOL had taken offline Facebook, WhatsApp, X, Instagram, and dozens of other clones. Held under draconian anti-terrorist enactments, thousands of senior and middle management executives were convicted of complicity in a conspiracy to aid and abet a coordinated nuclear attack on fossil fuel sites around the globe. The penalties were severe. Many were summarily tried and executed. The fate of hundreds more was unknown.

Hawkins was about to sit down just as Simeon Hill's microphone buzzed. The room fell silent as he rose to speak.

At one metre-ninety-three, Simeon was an imposing man who had preserved the svelte figure of the outstanding athlete he had been a quarter of a century earlier. He came to prominence in the first INCOL Olympics established seven years after the catastrophe. His haul of seven golds and four silvers in disciplines ranging from track and field to basketball, cycling and rowing only once ever came close to being surpassed, by Simeon himself, at the following Olympics, two years later. With so many non-productive leisure and learning hours to fill, sport was considered an integral component of every citizen's life. The period between each Olympic Games and soccer World Cup was shortened from four to two years, so that one or other was taking place annually.

Sadly, the atmosphere at the selected venues, many and varied as they were, could never match the atmosphere of anticipation and excitement witnessed in the olden days. Onerous travel and displacement enactments restricted the number of spectators present at any one venue to residents and guests with special clearance authority. With billions of television viewers throughout the world glued to their sets, new sporting heroes were born and revered every year. As the first and most prominent of these titans, Simeon Hill enjoyed a godlike status amongst the public, notably within the orbit of INCOL Europe.

Simeon began by asking Hawkins to elaborate on certain data from the latest set of statistics posted on SocioLine the previous week. Jack's brow creased. Why was Hawkins trying to answer questions concerning the health deputy's report? Surely, this information was the responsibility of Samantha Kahn, the health deputy appointed by Simeon eighteen months earlier? She had already given her presentation, which was received without comment. This was a deliberate snub to Kahn and an embarrassment to witness Hawkins's faltering attempt to provide answers about statistics he had simply compiled.

Simeon persisted with his questioning. What were the age ranges of patients occupying hospital beds? How many were terminally ill? What percentage transferred to receive palliative care? The interrogation was about to border on territory for which Jack was responsible. He glanced over at the two guests. They were listening carefully to the interpreter as they made notes.

By the time Jack stood to make his presentation, the atmosphere in the room was nervous and unsettled. Hawkins had finished stumbling through a series of answers, most outside his remit. Occasionally, he deferred to the health deputy as better placed to answer, but as Kahn rose to follow on, Simeon motioned for her to remain seated. Curious eyes glanced across to see how Kahn was reacting to the belittling tactics used to undermine her. There was a tight smile on her lips which, to Jack, suggested defiance.

The two Germans stopped taking notes and were studying Jack as he reported on the various homes and institutions for which he was responsible. A wave of the hand silenced the interpreter.

As Jack began his concluding statement, his casual glance caught AR leaving his seat and making his way to the side of the auditorium, where he began a conversation with the intern recently appointed as Jack's researcher. The young woman was still at the stage of fetching and carrying along with relaying messages when Jack was absent from the Assembly building. If AR has planted her as an informant, Jack would need to be circumspect with the personal information he entrusted to her. He would not rush to judgment, but if AR was monitoring Jack's whereabouts, he needed to know why.

Simeon was on his feet again, one hand caressing his chin as he framed the next question. The persistent probing into the number and categorisation of care and nursing home residents in the region niggled at Jack. Simeon was uncomfortable in the role of inquisitor, his questions random and with no logical sequence. Above all, he showed no interest in the answers. It appeared he was testing Jack's patience and competence rather than having a genuine interest in the subject.

The charade was annoying Jack. As the question-and-answer session progressed, he sensed Simeon was baiting him, waiting for a challenge. He was not to be disappointed.

Simeon claimed he was concerned with the apparent increase in numbers of the generation he described as 'in God's waiting room'; the over eighties, a group he allied with those suffering from incapacities who also occupied places in the homes.

'Look, the statistics simply do not provide an accurate picture or tell the complete story,' Jack retorted.

'Why is that?' Simeon looked relieved to have provoked a challenging reaction.

Jack discarded the report from which he was quoting and lifted his eyes to address Simeon 'The Third Age Enactment is a fine piece of legislation, but it has one serious flaw. It lumps together men and women from sixty-five through to over a hundred. That's a thirty-five-year plus span with which to band together individuals with different upbringings, cultural,' – he almost said, "and religious," but thought better of it – 'and with a wide variety of physical and mental conditions and needs.'

Simeon sat back, his posture more relaxed. 'Do explain.'

'Throughout this community,' Jack said. 'There are varying and contrasting levels of physical and mental capability, incapacity, and illness. Last week I visited a centre where I met a seventy-year-old who could scale a mountain but recognised neither of his sons. He was living in the next room to a ninety-plus lady who could recite, at will, from any Shakespeare play, but was chair-bound and required lifting around the place. In between these two extremes, you have a million variants. Trying to generalise with statistics is impossible.'

The broader of the two Germans spoke to the interpreter, who stood, brushing down her pleated skirt as she did so, her face expressionless. 'How would you choose to classify the statistics?' she asked and received a curt nod from the man.

'What I already do, as best I can. The priority is to identify those residents, irrespective of age, at risk or with the onset or existence of degenerative diseases expanding at a faster rate than our ability to cope adequately. I am talking about dementia, principally Alzheimer's, acute depression and Parkinson's.'

He felt the room's undivided attention. In a world with insufficient work for everyone, he explained, there were not enough alternative stimuli to keep minds healthy and vital. Lump this factor together with nature's random selection of victims – he had Verity in mind – and the means existed to delve beyond the figures to discover solutions to curtail the rampant expansion of these debilitating illnesses.

'In a world of limited resources and output, it would pay us to deal with the causes rather than treat the symptoms. Before eleven/eleven, generations invested fortunes in assisting people to live longer in a positive environment. The average life span now stretches well into the eighties, but this bland statistic disguises the fact most see no purpose in a world where there is no quality of life.'

'Better off dead.' The German spoke in heavily accented English.

'Can we ever say that?' Jack frowned as he looked at the man.

There was a ripple of applause as Jack sat. Simeon stilled the delegates by bringing the meeting to a close.

'Point of order.' The voice came from behind Jack.

Simeon looked around to identify the speaker. 'This is irregular, Miss Kahn.' Roach appeared at his side, bending to speak out of range of the microphone. 'Are you certain you wish to proceed?' Simeon asked.

'I am,' Kahn replied, crossing her arms.

Jack knew of Deputy Khan as the delegate for Eastern Suburbs and a keen defender of minority interests, not a fashionable or sympathetic cause since the social repatriation enactments of twenty years ago, which saw the widespread resettlement of citizens back to their ancestral homelands. Kahn was younger than most of the delegates, mid-thirties, he guessed, an attractive woman of Pakistani extraction, second-generation immigrant status. She had a reputation for speaking her mind on constituency issues. Was her desire to raise a point of order the reason she was snubbed earlier in the session? He was about to discover why.

Kahn rose and drew breath. 'My intervention concerns compliance with Section 14 of the INCOL Europe Establishment Treaty.'

Simeon's brow creased. Jack looked around to spot Roach, who was standing talking to a member of the security staff. AR knew exactly what she intended to say.

'As you will recall, Mr Chairman, the section I refer to decrees that, irrespective of the language in which a draft or final document is prepared, the official INCOL release will be in English. For months, we have been receiving a variety of official communications only in German. These all originate from Berlin. The relaxation of Section 14 specifically contravenes the Treaty and I appeal to the Chair to make the appropriate representations.'

Roach handed Simeon a note, which he acknowledged with a nod. 'The Assembly will recognise the technological advances within all our administrative systems have superseded the aim of this requirement. We all now have the facility of instantaneous translation.'

Kahn came straight back with a reply. She smiled and raised her gaze to look at the two guests. 'Over the years, the Treaty has been amended by various codicils to recognise changing circumstances. No attempt or proposal has been made to alter this section.'

There was a nervous buzz in the room. Everyone knew the Americans would never tolerate a change to the norm, giving English preferential status.

'In addition,' Kahn said, a hint of self-righteousness in her voice. 'I submit, with respect, that the translation software is inadequate to reflect the nuances present in any language.'

The more commanding of the two Germans glared at Simeon and drew a finger across his throat.

'Your point of order is noted, Deputy,' Simeon said icily.

# FIVE

## ALEXANDRA PALACE – LONDON

## Midday – 13 November 2065

As Jack made his way to the second floor, he was still trying to process the strange train of events of what should have been a routine meeting.

The only other person waiting in reception was a woman in a severe dark-blue tailored suit, who acknowledged him with a clipped smile. There was something vaguely familiar about her, the unfashionably short, grey hair, either a rinse or natural and premature for somebody in her early forties. She wore no make-up to soften the heavy features and dark pouches under reddened eyes, which signalled too many hours in front of a screen. He couldn't place her and was about to strike up a conversation when an anxious voice from the adjacent corridor leading to the service elevator distracted him.

Kahn insisted she needed to tell her mother she would be delayed and home later than promised. Roach mumbled something in reply as he and a security guard escorted her past the open door of reception toward Simeon's suite of offices. Jack and the woman exchanged a questioning glance as the closed-circuit cameras whirred above their heads and repositioned after reacting to the noise, but neither spoke.

'Do you two not know each other?' Simeon appeared at the doorway a few minutes later. 'Do come through,' he said with a disarming smile as he stood aside to lead them into the boardroom.

Introductions were made. Jack recognised the name of Ramona Usher from a security briefing. 'Ramona's a section head in Homeland Affairs.' Simeon said. 'And our Jack Tirrand is the deputy responsible for care and the elderly in the Chapter.'

Pleasantries exchanged, the two visitors sat alongside each other at a polished mahogany boardroom table sufficient for twenty people. Simeon took a seat facing them. 'While we wait for our two guests from Berlin to join us, let me give you a heads-up on why I've asked you to this meeting.' He studied them both. 'You look pensive, Jack. Something wrong?'

Pensive was the wrong word. Preoccupied would be more appropriate. Why hadn't Kahn passed them on her way out? Maybe there was another exit. The place was a rabbit warren. She must be all right, surely, but raising the subject would be inappropriate and provocative. He made an excuse about the start of a cold.

Simeon nodded and relaxed into a narrative Jack had heard before. Usher adopted an expression of reverent concentration.

'When INCOL International sub-divided into the six INCOL regional zones we know today, the founding charters decreed that all would trade and cooperate on a transparent and constructive basis with mutual respect. In sport, we have always promoted these noble aspirations.' He paused and nodded with eyes closed. 'However, in the commercial world, this laudable aim has proved difficult, if not impossible, to achieve.'

Roach's voice, full of bonhomie, echoed in the corridor as he greeted someone. Jack's head turned as he strained to listen for evidence of Kahn's presence.

'Something on your mind, Jack?' Simeon was studying him.

'I was hoping to have a word with Samantha Kahn before she left.' He saw the irritated expression on Simeon's face. 'It's not important.'

'I appreciate your sympathies and allegiance to Kahn,' Simeon said, adopting the tone of a benign father. 'I was watching you as she spoke at the meeting. But, believe me, now is not the time to be distracted from a far more important issue. Now is the time to worry about furthering your career. Do you take my point?'

Jack nodded. 'I apologise. Please continue.'

Simeon tugged gently at his beard. 'In the Senate's opinion, INCOL Europe is now more isolated from the world than ever before. Before eleven/eleven, we talked magnanimously about globalisation and a world dominated by social media.' He shook his head. 'What a haven for hatred and evil was nurtured in the name of free speech.' He stopped at the sound of people approaching the room.

Although espousing Berlin's policy line, Jack accepted the facts that bore out Simeon's condemnation. Long since banned and dismantled, the worldwide web, emailing and all social media platforms, coupled with the astute application of malicious AI, had provided the means for the eleven/eleven terrorists to plan and coordinate their attacks.

He recalled how it all started. What seemed, at first, an unfortunate IT glitch corrupted the data in the Europe-wide lottery system. A machine virus code-named 'Greed' began sending bogus results to ten thousand online punters selected from the neediest, vulnerable and volatile profiles hacked from the data files of Facebook, Instagram, WhatsApp and a clutch of smaller niche sites. Every one of the ten thousand was fed a lottery result corresponding to a winning line on their ticket, leading them to believe for that night and the following day they had won a hundred million Euros. Media outlets reporting the correct results found their communication channels blocked or corrupted.

The celebrations and excesses of those initial hours turned into pandemonium and despair as the reality came to light. In the days that followed, there were forty suicides, six murders and the assassination of two of the principal executives in the corporation running the lottery.

A new breed of malicious actor was manipulating artificial intelligence to stir unrest. Over the following months, it would get infinitely worse, and the Establishment just didn't see it coming.

There was a tap on the boardroom door. 'May we?' Roach entered briefly and held the door open for the Germans to enter.

Simeon's extended hand was ignored as the stockier of the two, with the clean-shaven head set on a bull neck, gave a curt nod to those present. His eyes, inset and without eyebrows gave him an oriental look as he appraised both Usher and Jack at length. Simeon introduced him as Willi Schmidt, undoubtedly the more senior of the two men.

His companion, Tomas Muller, was of a similar age, late thirties, taller and less bulky than Schmidt. The aggressive and purposeful expression on his face looked to Jack as practised as if he trained himself to convey a tough and ruthless persona. Schmidt didn't need to pretend. His menacing and intimidating air was natural, not the sort of individual Jack would ever wish to cross. Their suits were carefully tailored to disguise muscular frames, doubtless the result of a dedicated regime of gym workouts.

Jack listened with scepticism as Simeon described their roles as liaison officers with the INCOL Human Resources Division in Berlin. The word 'bullshit' came to mind. These were no stooges from personnel. Both men had ISE enforcers written all over them.

Simeon deferred to the new arrivals. 'I was just explaining to Ramona and Jack how INCOL Europe is now more isolated from the rest of the world than ever before. Consider the facts. Russian-controlled INCOL Northern Territories straddles the globe from what was Finland in the west to Kazakhstan and Mongolia in the east. Russia and its satellites are now more secretive and wary than in the Cold War many decades ago.

'Since the bombardment of North Korea in retaliation for supplying the terrorists with salted nuclear devices so effective in destroying and contaminating large parts of the world's fossil fuel extraction and refining resources, sizeable areas of the globe have become uninhabitable. The impact on the Korean peninsula, Japan, and north-eastern China produced an unholy Sino-Japanese alliance and a response to move south. With the forced occupation of the Malay Archipelago and Australasia, the bamboo curtain descended on INCOL Asia. You can understand why our senate is so concerned about global protectionism.'

Usher stole a glance at Jack, which said where is this preamble going and why are we here? Neither ventured to comment.

'Of course, I know I make it sound bleaker than it is,' Simeon said. 'There is still free trade between zones, but it is slowly declining. Every INCOL area wants barter. What can you do with IMEX credits if there is an acute shortage of raw materials and little to buy and sell? The experts tell us it will be between thirty and fifty years before we can work in the contaminated areas. While we wait, half of INCOL Indo Africa and the central and equatorial chapters of INCOL America remain basket cases with insufficient means to feed their populations. I am excluding Tomorrow World. That zone is isolated from any shitstorm.'

Usher looked up as the monologue stalled. 'There is still a surplus of productive capacity in North America,' she said. 'They are net exporters.'

Simeon gave a wry smile and shook his head. 'The Americans espouse the virtues of transparency and fairness, but the truth is the most powerful zone on earth is preoccupied with parochial considerations and self-serving interests. INCOL Americas has faced an ongoing humanitarian crisis in Venezuela and neighbouring countries in Central and South America ever since the oilfields were attacked. There are still major repercussions from the chaos and mass flight from the contaminated areas to resettle in poor countries with no capacity to absorb large numbers of starving refugees. Couple this cauldron with a large influx of desperate people into North America and Canada, together with the need to keep the Russians and Chinese under control in Tomorrow World, and you see the issue from the American perspective.' He stopped to reach for a glass of water. 'No, the sad truth obliges INCOL Europe to survive in an isolationist world.'

'Are you saying we should also become inward-looking?' Jack's question harboured both alarm and disbelief. He glanced at the two Germans, who appeared disinterested in the exchanges. 'It sounds dangerous and provocative.'

'It's only logic. We must calculate the total resources available to provide for all our citizens and plan as necessary. We cannot rely on other INCOL regions to underwrite our consumption.' He extended his arms to encompass both Jack and Usher. 'That is why you are both here.'

Usher's brow creased underneath a mousey-brown fringe. 'I don't see the connection. Our roles are in different spheres.'

'All will be made clear in good time.' Simeon gave a condescending smile. 'You, Ramona, have been responsible for looking after criminal welfare and rehabilitation for many years at Homeland Stability.' He turned to face Jack. 'You are here with an unquestioned expertise in dealing with the needs of the elderly and long-term infirm.'

Listening to Usher's job description triggered Jack's memory. Three years earlier, she was one of the guest speakers at a highbrow, time-wasting seminar he had to attend dealing with social integration in a changing world. He had a vague recollection of her contribution as standing out amidst a deluge of stale cliched offerings.

Simeon leaned forward as if to impart a secret. 'A Senate sub-committee has been debating the creation of a new task force to implement a draft programme, which is still under wraps. I don't need to remind you of your oath of allegiance to INCOL and its principles binding you to total secrecy regarding what I am about to say.'

Usher's eyes widened. 'Sounds very cloak and dagger?'

'Hardly,' he said. 'Whilst still in a formative stage, the Committee of Resources Executive, CORE to you and me, has voted to avoid public speculation until it has trialled measures to regulate consumption. Once approved, CORE will submit the findings to the Senate. We must avoid leaks, which may give rise to public disquiet and hoarding.'

'You're saying people won't like what they are going to hear?' Jack asked.

'I didn't say that.' The response was curt. 'Rumour and distortion of the facts are disruptive. CORE needs to avoid malicious leaks until the enactment becomes law.' His voice tailed off. 'I have said enough for now. Let me pass you over to Herr Schmidt, who will explain your participation.'

So, they spoke English, Jack mused. Why the interpreter? His thoughts returned to Kahn's point of order. Where was she? Where were they keeping her?

Schmidt's English was as good as fluent, spoken with the mere trace of an Eastern European accent. His role was to present a travel schedule with non-negotiable fixed dates. Jack and Usher would leave for Germany by train the following Monday. Roach would organise the official travel vouchers necessary to move between jurisdictions. On arrival, they would be met by Muller and his team. They should pack for a week. Further details will be provided.

'Where in Berlin will we be staying?' Four years earlier, Jack had been housed in a *Kiez* near a vacant industrial site dating back to Cold War days. He was not fussy, but a third-rate fleapit in a road of bars full of drunken youths, prostitutes and vagrants alongside abandoned streets of crumbling buildings was not Jack's idea of hospitality.

Folds of flesh rippled around Schmidt's neck as he shook his head. 'You're not going to Berlin. Your requisitions will be submitted for transit to Lorrach. It's near Freiburg in the Black Forest. Very beautiful.' He said something in German to Muller, which brought a smile to their faces. 'They used to make chocolate there,' he explained.

The meeting was over. Jack and Usher were escorted from the office with a parting glance, which said what the hell is going on. On Monday, they would find out.

Right now, Jack had something far more pressing on his mind.

# SIX

## OUTSIDE ALEXANDRA PALACE – LONDON

## 13.00 – 13 November 2065

How long before they released the bloody minutes? The Assembly press office was late. Normally, by this time, Seth Morgan would be back in the newsroom of *The Capital Review*, working alongside the ranks of the unwashed as he churned out another boring rendition of today's Chapter meeting, which he knew few would be bothered to read.

Unlike most of his fellow journalists, Seth had a thing about personal hygiene. He used the water allowance in his apartment sparingly but to great effect. He had the foresight to have installed a forty-gallon water butt which occupied the best part of the small outside terrace. It fed a simple system which filtered and recycled rainwater into the system whenever he exhausted the rationed mains supply. He hated the stench of body odour; all those course heterosexual humpers, as he called them, with sweaty armpits and smelly bums. At least Damien was on his wavelength. Dear Damien. What a catch for an old queen! Seth could never have believed his luck. Pinch himself. It was true.

What was holding things up? The minutes should appear just before lunch. Seth would write up his piece for tomorrow's edition by five, back home by six, and be well advanced with preparing an evening meal before Damien arrived. Just thinking of Damien and he massaged his crotch. With tonight's culinary masterpiece in the oven, he would spoil Damien with a contraband gin and tonic, accompanied by a stress-relieving blowjob before they settled down for the evening. His turn would come later. Jesus! Where in God's name were those fucking minutes?

Disgruntled, he sank back into the driving seat of the two-seater van parked in the restricted area where all the hacks congregated. His gaze was fixed on the doorway from where his junior assistant would appear with the official release. Any second now, he willed.

Why wait for the minutes? He had been in the public gallery. Tomorrow's piece almost wrote itself. Putting all the normal, boring routine stuff to one side, he would do a cameo on the two visitors and highlight

Kahn's controversial point-of-order with an editorial on the encroachment of the German language as a spearhead designed to undermine INCOL Europe's Anglo-Saxon influence.

What a pipe dream! He could never write a piece like that and get it published. Free press? Come on! The Senate might talk about a liberal attitude, but it was a mirage. The Treaty prohibited any reporting which was deemed to provoke civil disobedience or contravene the objects of the coalition, an all-encompassing restriction which strangled anything controversial at birth. If that isn't censorship, what is? Journalists and commentators were as eunuchs in a brothel. Chaos might break out on the streets, but his job was to make any crisis sound like a children's birthday party.

Seth shrugged. So, what if he couldn't be the investigative journalist by-lining the exclusive scoops which would make his name? He still had a life. On the credit side, he was in a stable, full-on relationship, the best he could recall in his fifty-five years. Thanks to Damien's greedy nature and innocent little scams, they had plenty of credits available for all their needs and the occasional luxury.

Sure, he could remember a time when you could say and write almost anything about anybody. No holds barred. The stupidity of leaving the journalists to regulate themselves. Put a 'maybe' or 'alleged' in the right place and you could get away with murder. Political correctness. What was that? Seth and his cohorts were upholding the banner of free speech.

How it all changed when those religious extremists found common ground with the activists from a generation of disillusioned young people. For years resentment festered as successive generations witnessed an ever-increasing, ageing population enjoying a perceived entitlement to the fruits of their labours at the expense of the working population. A century of excess consumption created a crisis within society and brought the planet to the verge of an environmental catastrophe. Yet the Establishment paid little more than lip service, promising change that never came, creating an imbalance impossible to correct. Something had to give. It was just the way they went about it.

Seth exhaled, misting up the windscreen in front of him. He would be long dead before any semblance of the old normality returned. Maybe it never would, and the press would always be subject to government oversight.

These days, the only worthwhile scoop was to discredit some celebrity in the public gaze: sportsman, actor, perhaps a politician. Sexual indiscretions were part of the human makeup, but still fair game for the tabloids. He could do with a good kiss-and-tell story to enhance his standing in the newsroom and restore his waning reputation. Just ten more years and the censoring editor could stick his biro firmly placed right where the sun doesn't shine. Seth would put his feet up and count his retirement credits.

He fidgeted in his seat. Where was the boy with the damn minutes? Ogling at some cleaning girl, most likely. At least Arthur knew his limitations. He could count his lucky stars he was still around, lucky to escape the last round of repatriations.

He caught sight of the black face as the boy emerged from the doorway and edged through the crowded concourse with a sheaf of papers held above his head. A woman with a scarf pulled tight around her head struggled as she crossed his path. Her head turned as if she was looking straight at Seth. There was no mistake. He was watching Samantha Kahn. The man who was walking up to her, waving to attract her attention, had been waiting by the exit door for ages. Seth noticed him because he was not wearing an overcoat in the biting icy wind. They talked – no; she was shaking her head – he held her arm and was talking and gesticulating with his free hand. Hold up! The man was Deputy Tirrand. What was this, a lovers' tryst? Whatever he said must have convinced her. They walked off together.

This was more than mere coincidence. Ninety-nine per cent of anonymous tip-offs naming a rising political star such as Tirrand were baseless. Just last week, Seth followed up a call claiming the deputy was seen in the company of a well-known call girl. Petra Quilter was one of the high-class hookers known in the newsroom as the SS girls, a synonym for the Society Slags. He was sceptical from the start, and a meeting in a nightclub proved a waste of time and, more to the point, the sacrifice of a chunk of some FTS credits on a bottle of disgusting, sparkling wine. The woman was after money for an exclusive story, but after he chipped away at her narrative with a few pointed questions, it became apparent that if she had met Tirrand, it was at a social event and never went beyond a brief handshake. But that was then and, by the look of it, there was now something worth following up.

'You see that couple? Recognise them?'

Arthur appeared at the window of the van, one hand massaging the pitted skin of his cheek. 'She just passed me. It's the Paki woman who was giving it all that.' He made a gesture with his fingers to imitate somebody talking.

'Give me those!' Seth grabbed the sheets of paper. 'Follow them. Send me a text when they reach wherever they're going. I'll come and get you. Remember to keep watching and make a note of the time and place. Wait for me to arrive. The censors will have to check your text message before they release it to me. Keep following until they settle somewhere or part. Now get moving and don't let them see you. *Capiche?*'

Seth watched the boy jog away. He felt he was on to something. The headline wrote itself. 'Rising Political Star Cheats With Chapter Firebrand', along with a teaser, 'Rumours of a clandestine liaison with high-class call girl yet to be disclosed'.

This was big, big enough to put the name of Seth Morgan in lights.

# SEVEN

## MUSWELL HILL – LONDON

## 15.00 – 13 November 2065

If it hadn't been for the warmth from holding two steaming hot cups of something wet that passed as coffee from the vending machine in the foyer, Jack would have curtailed his vigil and gone home. The early morning sunshine had flattered to deceive, and he had left his topcoat at the apartment. Waiting outside the Assembly Hall, the weather closed in with a blustery northerly wind, and he was freezing.

Surely, he couldn't have missed her. She was bound to take the metro home to Eastern Suburbs and to do so, she had to pass him. Have they kept her inside?

She was about to walk past him. With a hijab wrapped tight around her head, chin on chest and striding out, Jack grabbed her arm as she passed.

She wheeled around, taking a step back as she did so, her hijab slipping to reveal a face flushed from crying. 'You, too!' The accusation was full of venom, her head shaking.

'What's that supposed to mean, Samantha?'

'You're just like the rest of them, Jack. Wait until the right moment to take advantage.' She recoiled from the hand he held out as if it held a deadly weapon.

'What the hell happened in there? When I didn't see you leave, I was concerned. I heard what you said in Chapter and guessed you would get into difficulties with Simeon.'

A look of confusion crossed her face. 'This isn't some trick, is it, Jack, getting that disgusting man to try to shut me up?' She held her fists against her chest. 'I will do something about it. I'll not be threatened like that.'

Jack raised his hands as if in surrender. 'I have no idea what is going on or who you are talking about. I'm here only because I was worried about you.'

There was a moment's indecision as she decided. Her chin quivered as she moved toward him, placing her hands on his shoulders, her face resting against the front of his jacket. She tried to dry the tears running down her cheeks. He detected the scent of perfumed soap. 'Sorry to doubt you, Jack. I'm so wound up, I could explode. That sexist bastard, Roach, and his sneering sidekick of a bodyguard. I feel hate and contempt in my heart.'

He suggested she explain what had happened over a coffee. There was a social lounge on the ground floor of the building in which he lived. They could walk and talk on the way.

Twenty minutes later, he was opening the front door of his apartment. The lounge had just closed, prompting an invitation to join him for a drink upstairs.

Kahn hesitated, plainly influenced by her experience earlier that afternoon. 'I don't think I've got the time,' she said. 'There is a meal to organise for my mother and father. They are elderly.' She felt the excuse was insufficient. 'I'm the youngest of the family, an afterthought, you might say. They rely on me, and I've used up all my spare travel area credits for a communal taxi. It means taking buses or hitching.'

Jack smiled with what he hoped was a fatherly expression on his face. Stripped of her Deputy gravitas, Kahn was younger than she tried to appear, her striking feature large, oval-shaped, olive-green eyes accentuated by the classic red *bindi* painted in the centre of her forehead.

'Don't worry,' he said. 'I'll make us a cup of lemon balm tea. It's good for anxiety and stress and you look as though you could do with it. When you're ready, you can use some of my credits. I try to walk most of the time. The collective won't take too long to get you home.' From the look on her face, he felt he almost convinced her. 'I think it's important I know what's going on, don't you?'

As much as he sensed she wanted to confide in him, he could see she felt uncomfortable at being alone with him in the apartment.

'I may have to interrupt you. I hope you don't mind.' He pretended to check his watch. 'I've got a video call booked with Rebecca. You've met my wife, haven't you? At the Olympic games' reception,' he prompted.

She nodded.

'You can say "Hello".'

The deception was complete. It may have been a white lie, but there was no sinister motive, just a compulsion to better understand the disquiet he felt about the meeting with Simeon and the Germans.

She smiled an acknowledgement, returning his smile for the first time. Perched on an antique leather armchair with the television flickering but muted in the background, a mug of tea clasped between her hands, the words came tumbling out.

As she was about to leave the Chapter meeting, Roach, together with one of his sergeant-at-arms - a euphemism for a heavyweight security guard – pulled her to one side and escorted her into one of the ground floor holding rooms. At this initial stage, Roach put on his all-embracing, buffoon-like geniality. Her point of order had caused unnecessary embarrassment to important overseas guests from INCOL headquarters. Would she accept her intervention be deleted from the minutes? All it would take was a simple signed statement, acknowledging it was inappropriate. The stenographer would then delete it from the record. Five minutes and they could all be on their way.

No. Kahn was adamant. She had done nothing wrong in trying to bring a procedural lapse to the attention of her superiors. Why should she retract?

The atmosphere changed. After one more failed attempt by Roach to coerce her, she was led upstairs, frog-marched, as she described it, to an interview room behind Simeon Hill's office. She noticed Jack waiting in reception and assumed he was part of the cabal summoned to apply pressure on her.

As Hill tried to reason with her, almost pleading at one point, Roach sat opposite, purposely thumbing slowly through her personnel file and looking from the page dealing with family history up at her with a questioning expression.

'Had it not been for that bastard's threatening attitude,' she went on. 'I was prepared to be convinced by Hill to concede on the day. There are plenty of ways to skin a cat. I could always come back to the point in open forum.'

But she had not, and in the face of her unequivocal refusal, Hill glanced at Roach and left the room without saying another word. As she went to stand, the guard yanked her arms behind her and cuffed her wrists.

Jack straightened at the comment. Unbelievable. An exaggeration? She sounded so convincing.

'Roach breathed his stale breath into my face. I was being treated as a hostile suspect, contrary to some clause he referred to in the Enforcement Act.' The breath shuddered in her mouth.

'Go on.'

'He returned to my personnel file and questioned my family's residence qualifications. It appeared, he said, that an omission had occurred. My grandmother and two elderly aunts should have been deported to Pakistan under the social repatriation enactments. Their status would have to be reviewed.'

Jack's brow creased. 'Surely, you must have misunderstood him?'

She shook her head. 'I told him. They are first-generation British citizens. I am a deputy. My family is excluded from the enactment.'

'You're telling me he threatened your family?'

She nodded. 'He said he has the authority to make it happen. He gave me twenty minutes to think it over, sign the waiver, and the subject would never be mentioned again. He left me in the room with his security guard.'

Jack sat back in his armchair. 'That must be when he joined the meeting in which I was involved. He was with the two visitors.'

'They came back into the room with him, one sitting on either side. Again, he emphasised my family would suffer the consequences. His self-satisfied, smug look charged me with a false sense of bravado. I flatly refused to sign the paper and demanded I be allowed to leave, threatening recriminations if he continued to hold me against my will.'

'And the response?'

'The Germans simply smiled at each other. It appeared to empower Roach. He said something to the guard.' She hesitated, shaking her head. Her eyes were wet, her chin quivering as she relived the memory.

'I can't help you if I don't know all the facts.' His voice was soft, as if encouraging a recalcitrant child.

She took a handkerchief from her pocket, blew her nose and composed herself. 'You must never repeat this to anyone,' she insisted.

He promised and waited for her to continue.

Roach and his guests pushed back their chairs to stand, forming an audience around the so-called sergeant-at-arms as he stretched a pair of thin white latex gloves over his fingers. Her protests were ignored, her wriggling to no avail as he loosened her jumper, picking at the buttons on her blouse, his hands roaming around the contours of her brassiere, forcing down the material to expose one of her breasts.

She looked down at the floor. 'I felt humiliated, vulnerable. I tried to stand, still with my hands cuffed behind me. I screamed and shouted for him to stop. The Germans looked on with apparent disinterest, talking to each other as if I was invisible. But Roach, that disgusting man: he was transfixed, like a rabbit caught in the headlights. He just stared at my breast.'

Her eyes flickered as if reliving the moment, her mouth open as if about to speak. She betrayed no emotion, her voice now a methodical monotone. 'The intention was obvious. They were prepared to defile me.'

Jack's mind was racing. Could this be true, or could she be concocting an elaborate fabrication to discredit the establishment for which they worked? If so, it made no sense. She must realise if a formal complaint was made, she would be branded as a deranged liar, her accusation nothing more than the aberration of a member of a hostile ethnic minority, set on disrupting the workings of the Chapter. 'Is that where it ended?' he asked.

She shook her head. 'The guard with the gloves tugged at my sari. I realised I had no option but to accede to their will. I could never live with the shame.'

'You envisaged he would assault you?'

'I am certain. Thank God for the sari. I had draped it in Andhra style. Look, like this.' She stood to show how the material was pulled between her legs, tucked in at the waist and knotted. 'He was trying to find a way into the material, but it is not straightforward.'

If his fleeting smile at the absurdity of the scene was unintentional, it provoked an immediate and angry response. She rounded on him, eyes blazing, demanding to know what he found so amusing. He raised his hands in supplication.

'I am sorry if I appeared callous,' he said. 'For one second, I had the absurd image of some heavy wearing latex gloves thrashing around at your clothing. I don't mean to minimise the gravity of your predicament.'

Her expression softened. The brief squeeze of the hand told him she understood. 'I know. One day, perhaps, the red mist in front of my eyes will disperse and the experience of feeling afraid will leave me. I was convinced

Roach's frustration, his pathetically embarrassing figure in front of the Germans who were treating the assault on me as some regular daily occurrence – I sensed it would lead to violence.'

Jack waited for her to continue.

'His eyes were full of hate. I took one look at him, the vile figure of a man consumed by a voyeur's lust. I gave in. I signed his dirty little piece of paper.'

'You did the right thing. Bide your time. The opportunity will come again. There was no more threatening behaviour?'

She shook her head. 'It was almost surreal, as though nothing had happened. The gloves disappeared as quickly as the bindings around my wrists. The entire atmosphere changed, as if we were exchanging pleasantries about the weather. I was halfway down the stairs when my legs gave way and I began to shake. I stopped in the washroom to compose myself.'

'Do you think Simeon was aware of what was likely to happen when he left the room?'

'I can only assume so. I never saw him again, but I was a captive in his suite of offices. I imagine he didn't want to be seen to be implicated.'

'It in no way excuses him, does it?' He spoke as if announcing the death of a close friend.

Long after they exchanged goodbyes with his parting promise not to let the matter rest, he lay in bed, restless, unable to sleep. He agreed with Kahn that reporting the incident to the authorities would be counterproductive. They would both be branded as minority troublemakers. It would be her word against the bastions of the establishment, the self-styled guardians of democracy. What chance? He would insist on a private word with Hill.

Whether it was frustration or over-tiredness, he could not dispel the sense of dread. There was just something about next week's trip to Germany, which did not sit well with him. What the hell was happening?

# EIGHT

## MUSWELL HILL – LONDON

## 19.00 – 13 November 2065

The queue for the soup kitchen at the homeless station stretched back as far as he could see. Seth put the average age in their early twenties, an equal mix of the sexes. Given the chill in the air, they appeared remarkably good-humoured, stamping their feet, exhaling clouds of breath as they exchanged banter, the prelude to one more night of a depressing reality with no outlet for their dreams and aspirations.

Good God, he thought. If that were me, I would strive to change my lot, and join a revolution. Even suicide would be preferable to just surviving. Man evolved to live, to stimulate and be stimulated, not to exist in some controlled bubble with no expectation beyond the certainty of death. No wonder there was an undercurrent of protest, causing the ISE to retaliate in an ever-harsher fashion. The scent of revolution might be in the wind, but the conquest was one thing; nobody offered a better solution for the aftermath. Could the people be trusted to determine their destiny? It was that fallacy which had reduced the world to its present dire state.

He shuddered, prompting a move to reach for the fan control to turn up the heat in the van. Come on, Arthur! Where are you? Damien would be getting anxious. If there was one thing Seth found difficult to handle in his relationship, it was his partner's highly strung and volatile nature. Still, nobody but Seth was perfect, he joked to himself.

For the nth time, he flicked through the pages of the minutes, finally tossing them onto the passenger seat. Tomorrow's piece almost wrote itself, the same old boring rehash of the briefing reports. Somebody must have got to Kahn and convinced her to withdraw the point of order. There was no mention of the two Germans. So what? His hands were tied should he contemplate acting outside *The Capital Review's* mandate.

A further temper-fraying ten minutes passed before Arthur made an appearance, shivering with the cold, eager to enter the van. Seth delayed, pretending the passenger door was stuck. 'You took your time'.

A cloud of hot air erupted from the boy's mouth. 'I thought you'd be pleased with me.' His tone was deflated. 'I hung around in the freezin' cold until she came out.' He was both anxious to please and scared of Seth. His Adam's apple coursed nervously up and down in the drainpipe of a neck.

'She was in his apartment?' Seth's voice moved up an octave.

'Stayed about an hour. He came down to see her off in a collective. Put his hands on her shoulders and kissed her on both cheeks, didn't he? Very chummy if you ask me.'

''Did you . . .?' Seth was too excited to finish the question.

'Course I did. Who do you think I am? Got a still of them both together as he's kissing her.'

Seth's mouth parted into an amiable smile, revealing an uneven row of yellowing teeth. 'The dirty old man. She must be a good twenty years younger than Tirrand.'

Arthur rolled his eyes upwards in a theatrical gesture.

'All right, Arthur, don't be a prick. Damien might be twenty years younger than me, but that's different. Besides, I'm not the one married to the human tigress. Wait until Rebecca finds out about this. She will go ballistic.'

'You gonna tell her? We've got no real proof. It was more like a father and daughter kiss.'

Seth tapped the side of his nose. 'Innuendo is my middle name. If we decide to publish, I'll give Rebecca the heads-up, and get a quote. I guarantee our society doyen will not miss the Film Festival this Friday. I'll have a quiet word.'

Arthur wrestled the minutes out from under his bottom. 'What shall I do with these?' he asked.

The gears ground as the van lurched forward into the stream of traffic. Seth smiled. 'You can write them up, Arthur. I've got bigger fish to fry..'

# NINE

## BARRA DA TIJUCA – RIO DE JANEIRO – TOMORROW WORLD (formerly part of Brazil)

## 19.00 local time – 13 November 2065

Lance Cody Jr. pushed the glass with the crushed lime remains of a caipirinha toward the centre of the rustic table and made to get up. Sweat caused the inside of his bare haunches to stick to the wooden slats of the chair and, as he rose, the effect was a loud slurping noise that amused the fellow clients of the beach bar.

From the corner of his eye, he recognised the appraising once-over he was getting from the two bikini-clad, mixed-race girls waiting on the sidewalk. He flashed a smile and received a wave of the hand in return. Picking up women was never a problem for Lance. His lean, tanned body, schoolboy good looks and an unruly mop of blond hair were his passport into many a new adventure, although recently he had tired of the chase and conquest.

In his mid-thirties, Lance was single with no steady partner on the horizon. Physical attraction apart, developing a lasting relationship was a problem. Amongst his workmates at the BC Complex in the satellite city of Campo Grande, he kept a distance which he knew people interpreted in him as being vain, egotistical, and self-centred. That was harsh. Lance considered he was none of those things. He recognised the old twentieth-century terminology of a nerd, someone immersed in the high-tech world to which his TW contract was bound. It proved to be an effective cover.

Outside work, nobody recognised Lance as a fully functioning member of society. One of his more stalwart girlfriends who stayed the course for a whole month departed with the weary comment he would only find relationships more meaningful if they were encrypted. She had a point, he conceded, but under the veneer, Lance Junior was a real maverick, just like his father.

He was just five when the family was forced to move from their home in the Santa Clara Valley, an area to the south of San Francisco Bay. His father, Lance Senior, otherwise known as Camel because of the cigarette wedged permanently between his lips, had been rounded up in the purge of Silicon Valley, euphemistically known as the HT (High Tec) Realignment Programme.

As the social media corporations were shut down, their owners and top executives incarcerated for aiding and abetting terrorist and non-compliant activities, the entire innovative technology industry collapsed in on itself, setting back the world of communication and IT by fifty years.

From the new thinking shaping INCOL's policy of control and reform came the acknowledgement that once a hundred years passed and radiation levels were manageable, oil would flow again. The renaissance of fossil fuels would be short-lived. Nobody was blind to the fact that in the thirty-five years since eleven/eleven, climatic conditions had improved, extremes of weather less prevalent, and average temperatures more constant. A significant increase in industrial activity would require major advances in green technology to maintain a clean environment and yet allow the global economy to grow and flourish.

Sure, parts of the globe would never recover. Retaliation against the North Koreans for sourcing the dirty bombs had been swift and total. The strikes on drone-making facilities in Turkey and Iran were carried out with laser precision. Northern China and the Korean Peninsula would be no-go areas for up to a hundred years, but the surviving populations now had new territories to populate. Elsewhere, a strategy to implement groundbreaking policies would be obligatory, no longer a worldwide sop to the idea of a green environment whilst the once powerful polluted land and sea.

The concept of TW, Tomorrow World, was the brainchild of INCOL Americas. Whilst the rest of the world readjusted and came to terms with the harsh realities of insufficient resources and personal restrictions, a proposal to ensure technological progress did not falter was presented and reluctantly accepted by every INCOL region. An area of central and southern Brazil was effectively cut off from the rest of the world and renamed.

Chosen both because it offered a neutral option acceptable to the major powers and was self-sufficient in all basic foodstuffs and consumer goods, the area had suffered minimal damage during the eleven/eleven onslaught. Under the auspices of INCOL Americas and the watchful eyes of the members of a security council made up of Europe, Russia and Asia, a form of democratic government was set up. A paper currency, the Inco, circulated and a more liberal social framework, designed to stimulate creative minds, was permitted.

Communities were structured to provide research and development in the fields of AI; engineering, both heavy and specialised; shipbuilding and the aero industries; innovation in the drug and health sectors, and above all, emphasis on advances in clean energy to fuel the new global economy destined to emerge from the shadows of a century of darkness.

'Camel' Cody and his family were amongst the lucky ones. Of the tens of thousands of skilled workers displaced by the Realignment Programme around the world, twenty thousand were assigned to TW. Adding family members, specialists and support staff in other critical industries, the total resettled swelled to two hundred thousand individuals embracing some thirty nationalities. A master plan envisaged the creation of scientific and industrial parks in satellite cities within easy reach of the major conurbations in Rio, São Paulo and further south around Curitiba and Porto Alegre.

The project took six years to come to fruition. Imposing secure borders and rigid immigration controls ensured the five million Brazilians, deemed lower caste or socially inadequate, could be uprooted from their homelands and relocated in areas to the north and east of the protected zone in hastily established resettlement camps. Civil unrest was ruthlessly quelled by imposing martial law under the iron hand of the ISE security forces. A rumour circulated citing the use of a revolutionary hallucinogenic substance to ensure social compliance as part of a classified programme known as *Operação Candida*. No official comment disavowing the rumour was ever issued, and no hacker managed to breach the protocol.

For many of the hundreds of thousands of skilled, technical, commercial and financial workers around the world who were excluded from TW, the future was bleak. Men and women who were once recognised and rewarded for their technical and business skills were now considered pariahs. Be it innocently or otherwise, they had failed to expose money laundering and allowed innovations in communications and AI to be hijacked by the terrorists. Many were reassigned to assist in the redevelopment of coal mines and shale reserves, previously abandoned as too uneconomic to exploit. Now, these reserves were priceless. Under extreme working conditions, many a soft hand which once glided across a keyboard became gnarled and ingrained with dirt and dust in the name of retribution.

As Camel Cody, with his wife and two sons, set about building a new life in the fenced-off township built around the BC Complex in Campo Grande, some fifty kilometres from downtown Rio, he found himself driven by two opposing forces. Foremost, he was a supporter of the new society, a technical genius, and ranked as among the leading exponents in the field of Blockchain development and cryptocurrencies. Yet, he was an out-and-out maverick revolutionary who despised authority and a set of rules, which he described as the product of little minds. His fellow man needed help, and he was prepared to do something about it.

Before eleven/eleven, Camel was a wealthy man. Amongst the early developers of Bitcoin, the leading digital currency, he took strategic positions over the years, turning his modest investments into millions. He could boast of a friendship with Laszlo Hanyecz in May 2010 when the first real trade in Bitcoins took place. Laszlo offered ten thousand Bitcoins for a pizza delivery. Ten years later, had the astute guy who took the deal held on to his ten thousand ticks, this one pizza deal would have been worth over eight point two million dollars.

Camel speculated on the growth of digital currencies, playing the market in Ethereum, Litecoin, Ripple and a dozen others amongst the over seven hundred available at the peak. His paper fortune rose to over one hundred million dollars, only to be wiped away in a single day as the drones landed on their targets.

His sons were too young to understand what was happening as their father tried to cope with the new reality. He had nothing with which to barter. Nobody wanted digital currencies, gold or a shoebox full of useless dollar bills. People needed to survive amongst the fear and panic. Somehow, he managed to feed his family.

As world order was established under INCOL, Camel's talents were once again recognised, and family life returned to a semblance of normality. The move to Campo Grande was a breath of fresh air, and the two boys were schooled and developed in an atmosphere of calm and purpose.

Unlike Elmer, his elder brother, Lance wanted nothing more in life than to be a carbon copy of his father. His skills in computer technology, communications and AI came on a pace in his early teens. His laid-back attitude, faith in his competence and dedicated approach to problem-solving were straight out of his father's life handbook. By the time he was twenty, the two men almost talked and acted as one.

Maybe Lance and his parents should not have been surprised when Elmer chose a different path. Sensitive and highly strung, Elmer showed a bias for music and the arts, isolating himself from the rest of the family. He immersed himself in his one ambition, to become an accomplished classical pianist, applying the one trait he gained from his father, that of single-minded application.

An approach to the TW Arts Council in Rio resulted in an opportunity to join the Opera House orchestra and the chance Elmer craved to move out of the family home to a downtown apartment which he would share with Ricardo, a trombonist with the resident orchestra. Early on, Lance guessed the two were a couple but said nothing to his parents, who he surmised must have arrived at the same conclusion. Surprisingly, for a family with such a modernistic outlook on life, it was a taboo subject none chose to confront.

The rift finally came when cancer struck. In the spate of a few weeks, Camel Cody succumbed to the disease and died. At twenty-five years of age, Lance knew loss at an intensity he could never have imagined. It was as if his guiding star had vanished from the sky. Elmer used a concert tour to North America to excuse him from attending the funeral, a decision which Lance saw as contemptible, and a snub intended to dishonour the memory of their father. They neither saw nor spoke to each other for ten years, distressing for their mother and made more so by the stubbornness on both their parts in refusing to make the first move to ease her pain.

Lance ignored the row of 'Ride and Leave' trotinettes, choosing to walk the three blocks back from the beach and checking regularly to ensure he was not being tailed. He made three detours, the last one in through the front door of a department store and out via the staff exit before ending up at the lock-up storage facility. He was confident he had not been followed.

Closing the roller-shutter door behind him, Lance moved between the various metal storage containers, pulling two away from the central concave floor area to expose the metal water drainage grid, which he prised with a screwdriver from its housing. He reached into the black void, his fingers grasping the canvas strapping holding the waterproof bag in place. He opened the rigid plastic case with the moulded foam insets, revealing the Iridium satellite phone, antenna, and charger. A thirty-minute charge would suffice. He expected the call to be brief. Releasing the marine antenna, he unwound the eight-metre cable and stood on one of the metal containers, reaching up to clip the antenna to the attachment fitted to the ceiling light.

Lance was early. Taking deep breaths, he slid onto crossed knees, body bowed forward, stretching out and down until his forehead touched the floor, arms held in front of him. The child's pose was one of his favourite yoga positions. He cleared his mind, a sensation of peace and tranquillity overtaking him.

All he needed to do now was relax, run through his schedule of exercises, and wait for the call.

# TEN

## SANDYS HALL – DEVON

## 23.30 – 13 November 2065

'Shit!' It was a low, painful hiss. Losing her bearings in a cemetery in the pitch black of night was a nerve-chilling experience, made worse by having just stubbed her toe on the protruding remains of an ancient headstone. Alison kicked off her canvas sneaker and frenetically massaged her foot. Regretting her decision to come, she felt annoyed at herself and cursed under her breath.

Robert had led the way, moving ahead until his silhouette was lost in the darkness. It was all right for him. As the local vicar, he would know his way through the cemetery. The chapel and its grounds had served the gentry and estate workers of Sandys Hall for centuries.

A strand of torchlight suddenly flickered into life, illuminating a pathway to the vestry door. 'This way.' Robert's disembodied voice urged her on. 'Mind your footing.'

'Too late for that,' Alison said. 'You should have told me to wear wellies. My feet are soaking, and I've cut my toe.'

He played the beam of light across the ground until she was safely inside, then closed the heavy oak door behind them. 'Welcome to the House of God.' The torchlight highlighted an inset grey stone wall at the far end of the nave. 'You all right?' he asked, taking her curt nod as a cue to continue. He parted two heavy curtains. 'See the Sedilia. Second row of bricks from the left; push hard on the fifth one up from the floor.'

Her discomfort forgotten, intrigued, she moved to the priest's seat and followed his instructions. The brickwork was set into a recessed doorframe which swung inwards with lubricated ease, suggesting regular use. A dozen stone steps led down into a black void. Robert moved past her, swinging the torch from side to side as he guided her, step by step. The air was even colder than outside, still and musty. 'You're now in the undercroft,' he said.

They stopped in front of a large steel door with a modern appearance. 'In all the times I've visited this chapel,' she said. 'I never knew it had a cellar or under . . . whatever you called it.' Her voice echoed in the stillness.

Keys rattled as he took them from his pocket, the torch playing on the double lock securing the door. 'Until early in the twentieth century, they used to keep the corpses down here before burial.' The sound of the second lock opening reverberated around the confined space. 'It served as a morgue cum undertaker's establishment. The temperature helped to preserve the corpses.'

She shivered and moved closer to the sound of his voice.

A fluorescent light flickered into life, illuminating a sizeable room with metal filing cabinets around two walls, a square central table, and four dining chairs stacked alongside. A large dehumidifier placed between the wall and an oil-filled portable radiator emitted a low whirring sound. 'I put this on a few hours ago,' Robert said apologetically. 'It takes the damp chill off of the room.'

'I'll take your word for it.' She stamped her feet. 'I'm bloody freezing.' Her gaze fixed on the series of maps pinned to cork boards and covering a third of the available wall space. 'What is this place?'

She moved closer. Three of the plasticised maps were reliefs of various areas of South America, each to a different scale, each with various coloured pins placed at intervals along the coastal strips. The lower bank of three maps displayed historical shipping routes around the globe. Her curiosity aroused, eyes fanning around the room with a new intensity, she fixed on a series of wires stretching up from behind one of the filing cabinets through a gap in the cross-vaulted ceiling.

'What are you up to, Uncle?' There was a trace of apprehensive humour in her voice. 'Why did you bring me here? This is something illicit, isn't it?'

Robert set two chairs around the table and beckoned her to sit.

'My apologies for the cloak and dagger invitation. I was waiting for your boyfriend to leave so we could speak in private. I'm taking a risk in confiding in you.' He hesitated. 'To put it bluntly, I need someone who believes in individual freedom; someone I can trust. My options are closing in on me. I pray you are the person I can let into my confidence.' He waved his arm at the three walls. 'If the authorities were to see all this, they would send me to the scaffold.'

Her brow creased. 'Hold up. Before you tell me exactly what is going on here and compromise your niece, am I to understand the bumbling, harmless persona of my religiously committed uncle is a front for somebody far more sinister?'

'I wouldn't have put it quite like that.'

'How would you put it?' She mimicked his arm-waving gesture. 'Whatever it is, it involves working against INCOL and the Establishment. Yes?'

He shrugged his agreement.

'You must be desperate. We see each other rarely. I may be close to you, but you don't know me from Adam. Yet, you're prepared to let me see all this. Why?'

Robert waved his index finger. 'I see you make a biblical reference. It's the time-honoured conundrum. Which Alison am I about to clasp to my bosom, Simon Peter or Judas Iscariot? Will you blossom in my shadow or kiss me before selling me to the Sanhedrin for thirty pieces of silver?' He laughed to himself. 'Intuition, I suppose, is the answer to your question. I believe we have the same proactive attitude to right and wrong. Of course, I'm taking a gamble – a calculated gamble. Sorry if I sound like I'm preaching.' He stood up. 'Fancy tea or coffee? Something a little stronger?'

She shook her head, eager for him to continue.

'Hang on a jiffy while I pour myself a shot. At my age, you feel the cold in your bones.'

A half-full tumbler in hand, he eased himself into a chair. 'Thirty minutes before I have to make a call. Let me tell you what's going on.'

It was tragic, he explained, for the peoples around the world who suffered such appalling atrocities as had followed eleven/eleven. A perverse alliance between religious and environmental extremists to develop and execute such a complex and wide-ranging attack said more about the culture of divisiveness in communities and the power of social media at the time than the ideologies the activists claimed to promote.

It came as no surprise that in the immediate aftermath, many found comfort by turning to their faith in whatever Almighty they believed. During those first months, coming to terms with what had happened involved seeking the guidance of practitioners of religion to restore some order or sanity in a climate of such dreadful chaos.

By the time INCOL had evolved into a functioning, authoritarian force, curbing the influence of the clergy became essential if total control was to be achieved.

He raised the glass to his lips and played a healthy swig around inside his mouth before he swallowed. 'Throughout history, there have been countless occasions where the State comes into conflict with the Church.' He sighed. 'The power struggle has never ceased. Somewhere in the world, it is ever-present. As you took your first breath, Alison, another purge was about to start.'

As soon as Christian, Jewish and Muslim voices united to oppose some of the more drastic, anti-social programmes introduced by INCOL, a campaign of disinformation started to question and discredit the motives and attitudes of the clergy. With the insidious impact of fake news and vociferous criticism from influential sources, public opinion turned, priests and religious practitioners were hounded, many denounced and detained, and culminating in the mob lynching of a lay-preacher and his wife who defied the law by harbouring an outspoken evangelist preacher.

'At the time, I was a humble vicar serving a parish, embracing the dock area of Plymouth. My parishioners comprised a transient collection of penniless, repentant merchant seamen and the ladies of ill repute who, nightly, reduced them to this state. The other resident community of churchgoers would struggle to fill the front two rows of pews.' He set down the empty glass on the table. 'One day, a visitor came to my quiet backwater. Names are irrelevant, save to say he was a senior member of the Anglican church on a visit to Winchester.'

There was a quizzical expression on her face.

'Intrigued? I know I was when he explained how the authorities tightened controls on movements in and out of the ports of Southampton and Portsmouth and he decided to examine the possibilities of ports in Devon and Cornwall.'

'To what end?'

He pinched his nostrils together and spent some seconds holding her gaze before committing himself to speak. 'He sought my help in facilitating the aims of an underground movement known as AF.'

'AF? Never heard of it.'

He smiled. "Soon to be seasonably topical. We have a Christmas Carol entitled 'O Come, All You Faithful'. It is a call to all Christians to unite, to find strength and solidarity in the Lord.' His teeth parted in a broad grin as he picked up the glass and attempted to drain the last drop. 'It translates from the Latin, *Adeste Fideles*. As preachers, we love Latin. It sets us apart from mere mortals.'

For the first time since they arrived, Alison returned his smile. 'And what does your band of Latin admirers get up to?'

'We help selected individuals persecuted by the authorities start a new life elsewhere.' He hesitated. 'I was loath to join AF. It seemed too risky for somebody like me.'

'What changed your mind?'

'A month after the initial meeting, my visitor turns up again. This time, he is desperate. ISE is on his tail. He needs to get out of the country. I seek a good friend in the merchant service who is willing to help. A day later, the fugitive is on a refrigerated cargo ship heading for South America.' He eases himself slowly from the chair and walks over to the filing cabinet. The charging light on the cell phone is green as he disengages it from the mains. 'Eight weeks later, my seafaring friend returns with a box of Brazilian sausages for me. Inside, I find this equipment and a letter from the man I helped.' He dialled the calling sequence. 'It's a satellite telephone,' he said. 'All will be revealed.'

He put the cell phone to his ear. 'This is Wet Feet calling,' he said. 'How is Roy?'

# ELEVEN

## BARRA DA TIJUCA – RIO DE JANEIRO –

## TOMORROW WORLD

## 20.00 local time – 13 November 2065

Lance always found the caller's English accent comical, as if mimicking an ancient American movie technique intended to represent the impression of high-society inbreeding.

The recognition code was always drawn from the world of twentieth-century entertainment. Currently, it was singer/composer, Roy Orbison.

Lance acknowledged the greeting with the corresponding reply. 'Only the lonely know how I feel tonight.' Quite apposite, he thought, given his current state of mind.

'The three parcels will be ready for despatch on Friday.' Lance recognised a hint of concern in the Englishman's voice. It had the same cultured ring, but there was an edge to it. He often wondered about Robert Fitzwilliam, a village pastor embroiled in a scheme to help dissidents flee from persecution to TW. He must realise he was risking his life to help people he did not know escape into the arms of an American he has never met – just a voice at the end of a satellite phone.

Lance had initial misgivings about accepting the suggestion from the ageing clergyman Robert helped smuggle across the Atlantic. The old man praised Fitzwilliam's actions. He would be a reliable contact for Lance and his group to use. Yes, the clergyman would write a letter to Robert, encouraging him to work with Lance. The same ship's captain who agreed to transport the old man and put him ashore disguised as a crew member, delivered the letter and satellite phone to Robert. The response was positive. Over the years, Robert acted as one of the five collaborators around the world, assisting some thirty dissident individuals from all over Europe to reach comparative safety on the other side of the Atlantic.

Lance listened as Robert quoted the colour code to identify the vessel on which the fugitives would be travelling.

'Your voice sounds strained,' Lance said. 'Is there a problem?'

There was a pause on the line. 'The answer is, I don't know. Maybe. I believe someone may have tried to kill me. I may have to seek refuge.'

'Explain.'

'I was at a family gathering on Saturday. A hidden assailant fired a shot which missed whoever he was aiming at.'

'You believe it was intended for you?'

'Not one hundred per cent. There were three of us standing together, but I was the likeliest target. As far as I know, neither of the other two merit a summary execution.'

'And the shooter?'

'Who knows? They would never let me get to a public trial. It would be an embarrassment. Summary judgement by assassination would be their preferred course.'

There was an audible sigh and obvious disappointment in Lance's voice. 'You should make contingency plans.'

'I am doing so. As much as one day I look forward to meeting the Almighty, I prefer to delay the privilege for as long as possible.'

'Was the occurrence reported to ISE?' Lance asked. If the answer was 'yes', they would have to move quickly.

'No. It did not suit another member of our group to formalise the incident. It will be kept between us.'

'And the third person?'

'He will say nothing.'

Given what he was hearing, Lance's next request would take Robert out of his comfort zone. 'For the time being, let's monitor the situation. Regrettably, it's come when I could do with your expertise and cooperation.'

'Unsolicited compliments from you suggest I'm not going to like what I'm about to hear.'

Lance ignored the comment. 'We have an urgent shipment to handle, originating in Continental Europe, an approach on behalf of a former intelligence operative who could prove extremely valuable. We need confirmation this is not an attempt to infiltrate INCOL into the network. Somebody is working on it, but I would rather rely on your judgement once you have met him. I trust your intuition.'

'You want us to do that?' Robert's voice was shrill.

'Us?'

There was a momentary silence. 'I thought it best to seek the assistance of a collaborator, a replacement should I not be around.'

'He's with you now?' Lance felt the perspiration on his forehead. 'Remember what we agreed? You don't bring anybody into our confidence without first checking with me. You are putting everything at risk.'

'The He is a She and she is my niece.'

'*Your what*?'

'You heard.' Lance sensed the mix of hurt and anger in the Englishman's voice. 'I'm at this end, taking the risk, not tucked up on some sunny beach giving orders. If I have to leave in a hurry, I don't want to see wasted everything I've set up. I made what you Yanks term a judgement call. My colleague is honest, discreet and reliable.'

Lance heard a young woman's voice in the background. 'Thanks for the eulogy, Uncle,' she said. 'Put it on my headstone.'

'She's got a point,' Lance said. 'If the game is up for you, it could be a death sentence for her.'

'Don't take me for a fool. I won't let any harm come to her.'

'Is she in agreement? She sounds young.'

'Since when have youth and beauty been an impediment? I'm simply giving her some background information at this stage.'

'Can we talk about this later? I need to give you the details to contact the subject of the shipment.' Lance recited a series of lower and uppercase letters, digits and punctuation marks. 'You now have the name of the individual concerned, his address and the contact of a trusted associate of ours who lives in the same region and will assume responsibility for moving the person to the drop-off point you establish once they have been vetted and cleared by you. I can't emphasise the need to be one hundred per cent sure.'

'Anything else?'

'Yes. What is your news channel saying about Ted Hubbard?'

'Who? The name rings no bells.'

'He's the guy who made it away from Australia on a yacht? Has there been any reaction?'

'Oh, him. The only official reaction is from the Chinese authorities, who have put out an all-areas alert for a small unidentified vessel using its AIS database identification.'

'No suggestion he's been located?' Lance's voice was shaded with a hint of elation.

'None. As far as we know, he is still out there somewhere. Can I ask why you're interested?'

'Just curious.'

'That sounds evasive.'

Lance chuckled. 'If you must know, we helped him with the software to hack the Blockchain maritime servers. It's quite an achievement to breach a Blockchain protocol and get away with it.'

There was a muffled exchange of conversation at the other end of the line. Finally, Robert spoke. 'I'm afraid neither of us has a clue what you are talking about.'

'It's complicated and technical.'

'Humour us.'

'In simple terms, once a day, every vessel on the high seas is tracked by a process akin to the old GPS, where the location is fed into a series of Blockchain servers. These servers use an authentication package to verify and approve the data by seeking registration by the actor so that the next step or block in the chain can be processed.'

There was a throaty laugh at the end of the line. 'Actor? Is this theatre?'

'In this context, it means the partner in the project who wishes to record the data. Ted Hubbard employed a variant of the 51 per cent attack to gain partial control of the chain, enabling him to corrupt the tracking reports so that vessels appeared to be all over the place. One day, a cargo ship could be identified in the Mediterranean: the next day, rounding the Cape — clearly impossible. So, the system is recalibrated. The next reading shows the same vessel in Macau. Crazy, isn't it?' The excitement was apparent in his voice, any attempt to simplify the explanation forgotten. 'Authentication could not occur whilst data remains unverified and not recorded. Delays ensue momentarily until the system is recalibrated. Ted's little gem of malware encourages the server to accept the location with a bogus consensus algorithm, move the block on, and produce logistical and financial chaos. Imagine, a motor part for a dealer in Calcutta appears as a chest of tea in Marseille. And whilst chaos reigns, Ted sails on undetected to his destination.'

'Which is?'

'That would be telling. Truth is, even I don't know. Happy with the explanation?'

'Clear as mud.'

'Good. I'll await news of our impending shipment.' Lance hesitated. Fitzwilliam sounded offhand, offended by his earlier reprimand. He would end on a lighter note. 'While I'm waiting for confirmation on this week's packages, I'll clean the sand off my feet and work on my tan.'

'You do that. If I wasn't a man of the cloth, I'd reply appropriately.' The off button was pressed before Lance could react.

Damn the Brit and this latest problem. Fitzwilliam was a valuable asset, the most important of his collaborators, somebody they could not afford to lose.

# TWELVE

## SANDYS HALL – DEVON

## 00.30 - 14 November 2065

'You're scary. Do you know that, Uncle? Or should I call you Robert?'

They were back in the study of the main house. Alison was couched into an armchair, a blanket pulled tight around her, leaving her head poking out as the only part of her body exposed to the chill in the room. The building was in silence.

'Robert is scary,' she said. 'Uncle is that harmless buffoon he makes himself out to be in front of everybody, like a character out of those Bertie Wooster novels on the permitted reading list. It's all an act, isn't it?'

Robert sat in the other reserved armchair; a large brandy glass nestled between his hands. He raised the glass in a toast. 'Here's to one more friendly merchant seaman,' he said. 'Contraband Dreher from Brazil. I've become quite partial to it, now I'm on the last bottle.'

She raised an imaginary glass. 'Here's to Alky Robert, revolutionary fixer and part-time vicar. Who would have believed it?' Her expression lost its smile. 'You realise they must be monitoring that satellite phone? The satellites they didn't destroy were all taken under INCOL control. It can only be a matter of time.'

'I made that observation, but Roy said not.'

'Don't you know his real name?'

He shook his head. 'This week it's Roy; next week, who knows? As they used to say in the spy films before your time, James Bond and all that.' He tapped the side of his nose. 'It's on a need-to-know basis.'

She laughed. 'Who is James Bond?'

'Don't let's get into that. There was so much junk in space, the powers-that-be could not control it all, and a few obscure, non-categorised transponder units evaded capture or registration. Roy's lot found one. It was put into space at the behest of the Kazakhstan Agricultural Cooperative to monitor, of all things, the movement of cattle.' He shook his head in mock amazement. 'You would never believe it, but Kazakhstan is so big, the size of Europe, and so sparsely populated, herds of cattle would go on walkabout.

The satellite allowed them to track the beasts and communicate with the bovine control central, or whatever it was called.'

'Even so, it could be traced.'

'Always a risk, I suppose. I'm no technical expert, but Roy tells me the solar panels continue to operate, and it transmits using some weird microwave frequency which nobody else uses. It could only be picked up by INCOL Russia and it's a little too far south for their lot to worry about. I don't know how, but if it were to be breached, Roy's group would know.'

'And do what?'

'I imagine they would find another satellite.'

As they talked, Robert balanced a notebook on his thigh, a pencil in his hand. With methodical precision, he referred to a chart to translate the list of letters, numbers, and symbols Lance had given him.

'You want me to help you ship dissidents to safety?' Alison asked.

'That's the general idea. Or take over from me if I'm not around.'

'Does my father know any of this?'

Robert jerked upright in his chair, the notebook slipping to the floor. 'Good Lord, no. Jack is a principled man, even if he is a politician. That means, ultimately, he works for INCOL. Whatever his moral compass, any inkling of my activities would put him in an impossible position. He would have to denounce me or live with the burden of knowing. I could not do that to my sister. You must promise never to say a word.'

'I haven't said I'll help you yet.'

'You now know everything. In fact, you have already unknowingly helped me.'

Alison's brow creased. 'I have?'

He nodded, bending to retrieve the notebook and evading her questioning gaze.

Their silence was born of concentration; his, working to decipher the names and addresses; hers, trying to fathom what he meant.

'You lied,' she said, suddenly. 'It had nothing to do with the article you were writing about influential people, was it?'

'I regret the deception, but I was in a bind.'

'You pleaded with me. The research I did in the university library on that female physicist and the civil servant from the Treasury. You were verifying their credentials. They are dissidents.' She got up, dragging the blanket along the floor and confronted him. 'You used me, Robert.'

His first reaction was to deny the allegation, but he thought better of it. 'I am sorry. It was underhand, but I was unsure about confiding in you. Your boyfriend had just arrived on the scene. I needed information, and fast. I prayed for forgiveness. Sometimes, the truth is such a difficult beast to harness.'

'And now, because you believe you were shot at, you have decided you can trust me; suddenly convinced I want to be involved.'

His hands were clasped together as if praying, the tips of his fingers grazing the underside of his chin. 'Had those two individuals remained, one would have already been hanged, the other interrogated and left to rot in some hell hole. Thanks in part to you, they are both safe and contributing to a better world.' He closed the notebook and studied her. 'We are witnessing the progression toward fascism, spawned from the well-intentioned attempt to maintain law and order which INCOL set in motion. Racial discrimination, deciding those members of society who will survive, those to be left by the wayside; controlling personal choices and brainwashing the populace with false information; providing incentives for one man to denounce his neighbour. The world has seen it all before in another age. The impact is likely to reach its zenith before society has the freedom to allow democracy to temper this downward spiral. Our small contribution gives the free-minded folk in TW the chance to make sure the transition is as painless as possible.'

Alison reached for his hand and gripped it. 'I don't know whether Robert is a realist or a dreamer, or, for that matter, whether I am. All I see is my parents being sucked into the system, good people yet obliged to conform to a regime I find abhorrent. Of course, I will help you.'

He nodded and opened the notebook to face down over his knee. 'I mentioned two things I wanted to talk with you about. I'm curious to know exactly what your relationship is with Rolf. How much do you know about him?'

'With Rolf? Why?'

'This secondary existence you are about to embrace countenances no pillow talk, no conscience-pricked confessionals when asked why you are in such a strange mood, why you won't confide in the person who loves you. If this other you exists outside your head, you could be signing a death warrant for you and others.'

'What do you want to know?' She yawned, her bottom jaw shuddering.

He took the cue. 'Plenty has happened tonight. Let's leave it and get some sleep. We can catch up in the morning before you leave for London.' He flipped over the notebook, glanced at the page, and covered it with his hand.

He rose from his chair. 'Just one thing for my records,' he said. 'Rolf's family name – Eigard, if I heard him correctly?'

Another puzzled look crossed her face. 'Yes. He told me it was an unusual name. Archaic.'

'We had a brief chat.' Robert smiled. 'He mentioned his family.' He wanted this to sound conversational rather than conduct an interrogation, but he sensed his pulse rate was increasing. 'Stuttgart, he said they came from. I've forgotten his father's Christian name.'

She looked confused. 'Is this going somewhere?'

'No, no,' he stuttered. 'I'm just going to make some diary notes before I settle down. Background stuff.' He gave her a warm smile. 'It can wait.'

'For the sake of your notes, Rolf is from a town near Stuttgart and, as far as I recall, his father's name is Dieter.'

Five minutes later, Robert locked his bedroom door. 'Shit!' he said out loud. 'Shit! Shit! Shit!'

Her involvement was now complicated beyond belief. He reread his note, decoding the name of the individual he was to assess for transportation. Surely, it couldn't be. He did not believe in coincidence, not even in the biblical sense. The name in the notebook was that of a Dieter Eigard from a place named Rottenburg, just to the south of Stuttgart.

# THIRTEEN

## MUSWELL HILL – LONDON

## 08.00 – 14 November 2065

The pool car arrived a few minutes after the scheduled pickup time.

Irritable through lack of sleep, Jack reprimanded the driver, an amiably annoying, elderly Welshman with a sing-song voice who, from his nonchalantly dismissive reaction, had ample experience of listening to deputies complaining.

The previous night, and with Kahn's story still vivid in his mind, he sat late into the night, troubled by her description of events. Did she have a reason to lie? Eventually, he gave up trying to find a logical explanation, let his mind wander and fell into a disturbed sleep, punctuated with grotesque images and the ricochet of a gunshot.

Jack was grateful for the apartment to himself. His fondness for falling asleep in an armchair had recently irked Rebecca. She considered it a personal affront and his habit of sitting in total darkness little more than a sign of a mean streak in his nature. It was true he recognised the need to conserve resources, but it had nothing to do with the comforting sensation he got from dimming the lights. And he wasn't mean-minded, damn it. He regularly donated a couple of credits to the national food bank system. Starvation was becoming a real problem and his family's relative affluence was a blessing, not the hereditary right to privilege which tainted Rebecca's outlook on life.

The message arrived on his mobile just after midnight. Simeon needed a meeting with Jack at his home at nine the next morning. A driver would pick him up.

They were right on time as the car pulled into the majestic tree-lined driveway, arriving at a large, modern detached house set into the hillside within the sprawling complex of St. George's Hill in Weybridge. As the electric gate whirred shut behind them, the imposing figure of Simeon Hill came to the top of the short flight of steps leading up to a pair of oak double doors.

A casual, collarless shirt and beige linen trousers were partially hidden by a flowing Kimono-style silk dressing gown, decorated with a series of highly coloured dragons breathing fire. He held on to one end of the matching belt, the other trailing on the ground behind him. Heavy wooden-soled sandals clunked on the steps as he advanced to welcome his guest.

Jack was taken aback by the effusive greeting, 'So good of you to come,' accompanied by the hug, over-the-top, he thought, for somebody who displayed a polite reserve in public. He detected a hint of alcohol on the other man's breath, not the stale odour of the previous night's consumption but the cool, fresh tang of juniper over ice and gin.

Simeon led him around the side of the house to a service door and into the kitchen, a spacious open-plan area with a breakfast buffet spread over an island counter built to seat six. If it crossed Jack's mind why he had been invited in through the kitchen and not through the front door, it now became apparent. Simeon was about to say something when he was interrupted by the sound of a fierce exchange between a man and a woman. Expelling the air from his cheeks, Simeon walked over to close the internal door, but it was a pointless gesture. Not even earplugs could have blotted out the no-holds-barred argument taking place.

Jack fully expected his host to react as he would have done in a working environment, to take immediate charge and quickly bring the situation under control. But Simeon made no move, other than to flash an embarrassed smile and a shrug of the shoulders before gesturing for Jack to take a seat.

The door Simeon had just closed was flung open, ricocheting against the tiled wall. Jack's recollection of the Senator's wife, Francesca, was a fleeting handshake from a well-groomed hostess at a couple of official functions. The striking woman who now stood framed in the doorway reminded him of a feral cat fleeing from a fight. Flushed with anger, eyes ablaze yet full of tears, long strands of thick, auburn hair matted to her cheeks, she made no move to enter the room. With her gaze transfixed on her husband, Jack doubted she even registered his presence. And that was fine by him.

In a gesture of defiance, elbows extended, she slowly placed her hands on her bare waist. The loose, beige blouse which silhouetted the unchecked movement of her breasts was tied in a knot some ten centimetres above the belt of the white harem pants. The folds of the flared material billowed around her hips and legs, tapering into elasticised grips around her ankles. Her bone structure, too heavy-set to grace a catwalk, appealed to a basic instinct in Jack, which took him by surprise. He failed to rationalise the sensation that made his spine tingle, grateful neither of the protagonists was paying him any attention.

'Simeon, this is the last time I will talk to you about this.' She spoke in a voice capable of freezing molten lava. 'You take your son in hand once and for all or, I swear by all that's holy, one of us will have to leave this house. Do you understand me?' She swivelled sideways, pulling down the collar of her blouse. 'You see what he did to me?' There was a red welt running across her neck. 'No man hits me and gets away with it.'

'I didn't hit her.' A gruff voice came from the passageway into the kitchen. 'I threw a punch in her direction. She walked into it. I didn't mean to hit her.' Then words were spoken with a pleading note of self-righteousness.

'A punch?' Simeon said in amazement, staring at his clenched fist.

'Not like that, you idiot. A hole punch. The little metal thing that puts holes in paper. I just brushed it off my desk. She was invading my space.' As he moved into the room, his bloodshot eyes flickered nervously between the two men. 'I'm sorry. I didn't realise you had company.'

He was in his early twenties, Jack calculated, one or two years younger than the twins. Everything about him said he was a troubled soul. The dishevelled, untended head of jet-black hair; the limp creases impressed into clothes by continuous wear; the incense of stale tobacco and alcohol around chapped lips. But his eyes gave the game away. Beyond the lack of sleep, how many times had Jack seen the hollow, helpless look in the eyes of a hundred beggars holding out their hands? In the old and forgotten, it was the look of despair and hopelessness. In the young, it was the barren landscape they saw in front of them when the effect of the drugs wore off and reality offered no respite.

Jack nodded a greeting. The woman looked over but made no gesture to acknowledge him. She turned to face her husband. 'Did you hear what I said?'

With outstretched arms, Simeon herded his two family members toward the door, but the woman stood firm. The look of raw anger changed. Her head shook as she adopted an expression of despair. 'I'm never in the right, am I?'

'Can we do this somewhere else?' Simeon pleaded.

He shepherded them through the door and closed it behind them before the conversation resumed. It made little difference. The passageway was like an echo chamber. Jack could hear every word.

'You always side with this little prick of a son of yours,' she said. 'I only asked him to look after your mother for the morning while I go out. It's the nurse's day off.' Her voice became louder. 'All your son has to do is get off his fat bottom once in a while to make sure she takes her medication. Asking too much, is it? Your mother won't leave her room.'

Simeon mumbled something which Jack did not catch.

'That's the trouble,' the young man said. 'Francesca never asks, she orders and, I've told her before, I don't take orders from her. She is not my mother. She is nothing to me.'

'Tell him, will you!' she demanded. 'If I can't get through his thick skull, maybe you can.'

There was some more mumbling.

'Upset, is she?' There was the sound of the victor in the young man's voice. 'You know something, Dad? That's the problem when you trade in those comfortable old slippers for the latest Italian fashion. You tell yourself the new shoes fit but, eventually, the toes pinch, and you take them off. Lo-and-behold, some other bugger has picked them up and runs off with them. You look around for the old slippers, but they're nowhere in sight. Suddenly, you're lying in the morgue in bare feet with a label around your toe that says *died with no shoes*.'

There was the sound of a slap and then footsteps receding into the interior of the house.

Simeon reappeared in the kitchen with his arm around his son's shoulders, his demeanour relaxed, as if nothing out of the ordinary had taken place. Maybe it hadn't, Jack thought. Maybe this was an everyday occurrence in the Hill household.

'My son, Christopher.' The young man offered a limp hand, clammy with sweat. Jack surreptitiously wiped his hand on his trouser leg.

'This is Deputy Jack Tirrand.'

Christopher's gaze was fixed on a point six inches to the left of Jack's face. 'Sorry about Francesca,' he said. 'My father's wife has a fiery Latin temperament. She–'

'Chris, you will be interested to learn Jack's daughter is a post-graduate.' Simeon gave his son a playful punch on the shoulder. 'Chris is an undergrad at Uni in Manchester, taking a degree in political philosophy and diplomacy.'

He's not grasped the basics yet, Jack thought. He smiled, his attention elsewhere. Under normal circumstances, Simeon would not have a clue about Jack's family background. Something had changed that.

Christopher stared at Jack, his jaw dropping. 'You're not Alison Tirrand's father, are you?'

Jack nodded.

'God, she's a stunner. There's Latin or Indian blood in your family?'

'Indonesian on the female side of the family.'

Christopher's expression was one of unbridled admiration. 'This is a real pleasure.' His entire demeanour adopted a new and positive dynamic. 'Alison is magnificent in every way.'

As hard as he tried, Jack could never have imagined an adjective less appropriate to describe his slender, soft-featured offspring with her hair cut short and dressed in unflattering clothes designed to make her look more butch than feminine. He felt a mix of pride and curiosity.

'She's two years ahead of my set, but what a firebrand of a woman. We all pile into the debating society to listen to her condemnation of the Establishment and the virtues of a freer, more inclusive, and open society. She's such a wonderful speaker. And brave. Been hauled up twice before the CP, but it doesn't stop her.'

'CP?' Jack queried.

'Censorship Panel. A bunch of crawlers. The sort of ingratiators who hang around dad all the time.' He tapped Jack's shoulder with his fist. 'Sorry, I thought that's what you were. Apologies.'

Simeon shook his head. 'Careful, Chris. These people have a role to play. Don't criticise what you don't fully understand.'

Christopher reeled around to face his father. 'Don't patronise . . .'

'You were talking about Alison?' Jack said, anxious they did not go off on a tangent. He needed to know more about a world in which his daughter circulated, and which he knew nothing about.

The boy turned back with a smile. 'As I said, it's the way she speaks, as if it's just you she's talking to. It's seductive. There must be a dozen guys who have wet dreams about Alison every night.'

'Chris!' Simeon cut in. 'Exercise some decorum, please.'

This conversation was about somebody Jack just did not recognise. His daughter, a symbol of sexual gratification? Conceivably, Harriet before she got married and had the twins, but Alison? Sure, she had a string of casual boyfriends. The ones he'd met all seemed quite keen, but he could never imagine her in the way she was being portrayed. Perhaps the power of oratory was an aphrodisiac, after all. Certainly not a quality he possessed.

'You should ask her out,' Simeon suggested. 'Be a pleasure to see you associate with someone who doesn't look as though they've just crawled out from under a stone.'

The boy ignored the barb. 'She's going out with a German guy. Tough cookie and super-protective. He's already floored one over-sexed, would-be interloper. I wouldn't fancy getting into his bad books.'

'This is Rolf you're talking about?' Again, Jack thought back to the weekend. The comment sounded out of character, but, on second thoughts, he didn't know Rolf sufficiently well enough to make a judgement.

'Never bothered to find out his name. Smack you first and ask questions afterwards: that would be his credo. I like my nose just the way it is, thank you.' He took the sound of his father's forced cough as a prompt. 'Better get back to the flat screen,' he said. 'Still working on the algorithm. Need to crack it.'

'Do as Francesca asks, will you?'

Christopher stopped in his tracks. 'Seriously?' he asked.

'Seriously,' Simeon replied.

The boy shook his head in a gesture of despair as he left the kitchen.

Jack accepted the offer of a cup of black coffee from his host. 'I could do with this.' There was silence as both men concentrated on their drinks, their thoughts elsewhere.

'Why did Chris go for a degree course in politics if he's so into computers?' Jack asked. 'I would have thought the IT route suited him better?'

'It's not challenging enough for somebody of Chris's standard. Since the end of all the social networking, internet development and the tech free-for-all, it's now predictable. As you know, restrictive licences are granted to special industrial and service sectors. The rest of the population has access to the INCOL social server and communication data lines. Technology has taken a step back – a breather if you like – and there is little to stimulate innovation outside the work going on in TW.'

'He sounds quite clued-up.'

Simeon nodded and smiled. 'He is. Rank offers some privileges. I use what influence I can to further his bent. One must be careful not to overstep the mark. The IT world is full of whistle-blowers and denouncers.' He took a deep breath. 'Shall we get down to business?'

Jack had just seen his host as a weak and ineffectual head of the family. The man who now spoke reverted to type as a competent politician. He came straight to the point. Why did Jack meet up with Kahn outside the Assembly?

Jack was not about to hide his concern. 'I invited her for a coffee. She was distressed at the turn of events, and I was concerned for her.'

'Concerned. Distressed. Do you have a relationship with her beyond your collegial association? She's not from the same minority racial group as the one you mentioned to my son?'

'There are no racial overtones and when I extended her my friendship, it's not in the way you infer.'

Simeon retrieved a pair of thick-rimmed glasses from the pocket of his kimono, along with a sheet of paper. He read the single paragraph, finally looking over his glasses at Jack. 'So, expand on what you meant by "concerned"?'

The reaction to the point Kahn raised at the Chapter meeting took Jack by surprise. It was a valid observation, mentioned in private by several deputies. 'The next thing, she is being treated like an errant school child, ushered into your office for a dressing-down. She fails to reappear for some considerable time. I was worried about her. I didn't understand the process.'

'The process? What does that mean?' His neck and cheeks were flushed.

Jack clenched his fists tight, burying them between his thighs. 'Can you tell me why you asked me here? Is this some form of vetting?'

'Vetting? Heavens, no. I simply need to resolve the situation before it gets out of hand.' His tone softened. 'Tell me, if you would, what is supposed to have happened?'

'I waited around for her, simply to offer my support. When she finally reappeared, she was in a bad way. She complained of harassment and sexual assault.'

'Who is supposed to have carried out this alleged assault?'

'Roach, together with one of the security guards and in the presence of your two German colleagues.'

Simeon rose, shook his head, and made a sound halfway between a cough and a coarse laugh. 'I trust you are prepared to accept my assurance this is a total fabrication. I must tell you, Kahn is a troublemaker. Nobody harassed or assaulted her.'

'She showed me the marks on her arms where she had been restrained. No fabrication there.'

'That's the word. Restraint. She lost her temper and attacked Roach; leaving a mark on his face. Of course, she was restrained for her own good. Security bound her hands until she calmed down.'

Simeon returned to his seat. As far as he was concerned, Kahn raised the point of order with the singular intention of embarrassing his guests. It was mischievous and showed bad faith. There were far less provocative ways, established channels, for making her point. Whilst Simeon was the last person to challenge her right to do so, the manner she chose was insulting and she had to be disciplined.

'She was asked to withdraw the point of order from the minutes. She refused point blank and became both angry and hostile. They managed to calm her and talk her around. She came to her senses.'

'Why insist?' Jack persisted. 'It's no big deal. We are all confused whenever these dictums turn up in German even if we do have translation software. Someone needed to raise the issue. Why is it suddenly so sensitive?'

The studied glance at Jack suggested an irritability. Simeon weighed his words. 'There is a growing concern amongst some of our friends in Continental Europe – how do I phrase it? - an acute sensitivity to the growing criticism and dissent from certain minority immigrant communities, if you get my drift?'

Jack did. This was blatantly racist. He could not let it pass. 'Kahn's as British as I am.'

Simeon's smile was tepid. 'Quite so.' His voice was a whisper. 'Let me say, however inappropriate the intervention, had it come from another quarter, I could have batted it away with a quip and offended nobody. Whatever I said to sidetrack Kahn would have appeared, on one hand, as having racial overtones yet, from the German perspective, a weakness on my part.'

'So, they're so thin-skinned we have to keep our mouths shut or they'll throw their toys out of the pram?'

Simeon glared. 'Calm down, Jack. You are becoming tedious. Get real. Like it or not, the Germans are the powerhouse of INCOL Europe. Their industries represent over fifty per cent of all finished goods produced in the zone. Together with the French and Italians, they account for seventy per cent of all agricultural needs. We must respect their position and recognise our dependence.'

'Tread carefully on the racial aspect or we'll go hungry. Is that it?'

Simeon exhaled slowly and studied his fingernails. After several seconds, he looked up. 'I put you down as an astute politician about to embark on an important project requiring not only tact and diplomacy but insight as well. The simple truth is we British have always been good at selling houses to each other, moving and shaking other people's money by providing quality banking and financial services and consuming lots of imported goods. These are sectors of the economy which no longer have any driving force. Our manufacturing base is tiny by comparison and scarce raw materials are now allocated to more efficient organisations. Most of these industries are in Continental Europe, principally Germany.'

The conversation had gone off at a dangerous tangent, questioning Jack's competence and loyalties. The issue troubling him had been discarded.

He hadn't asked for this meeting, but he needed answers. 'Was Kahn molested?'

'No.'

'With respect, how can you be certain? You weren't in the room, were you?'

'I looked in from time to time.' He shook his head. 'I recognise Roach, when provoked, has brutish tendencies.' The raised palm of his hand told Jack not to interrupt. 'That's verbally, of course, and we need someone like that. He assured me he never laid a hand on her. She persisted in refusing to cooperate–'

'To capitulate?'

'Call it what you like. Kahn has an agenda. Surely, you can see that?'

Recognising the threat from the exasperation in Simeon's voice, Jack chose not to react. He knew he was testing the man's patience.

'She represents the bias of a disgruntled section of society,' Simeon said. 'Look, I accept the immigration repatriation legislation was crude and imprecise. It was a knee-jerk reaction to eleven/eleven, necessary to cope with a potential mass backlash against minorities at a time of acute food shortage. Families were separated arbitrarily, many repatriated, others allowed to remain.' He clenched his fists. 'But it worked. Activists calmed down. Unnecessary bloodshed was avoided.'

At what cost? Jack thought. He nodded. There was truth in what had been said. In the urgency to stem the uprising from the so-called True British movement, the indiscriminate division of minorities had decimated tribal groupings and created a toxic mix of anger, resentment and fear of the additional measures ISE might choose to impose.

'Nowhere is this nationalist view more strongly held than in Germany. They believe a return to fascism can be avoided by ensuring minorities are fairly treated but kept in their place.'

'So, threatening reprisals against Kahn's family was Roach's interpretation of keeping her in her place?'

'Clearly not. He overreacted after she attacked him.'

'Just before she . . . capitulated?' Jack could not resist charging the remark with sarcasm.

Simeon did not react. 'I consider the matter was resolved to everyone's satisfaction.' He waved his fingers as if ticking the item off on an agenda. 'That's all on that one. Tell me, had you met Ramona Usher before yesterday's meeting?' His mood instantly lightened.

It was five minutes of general conversation before Jack could return to the Kahn issue. Simeon's lips tightened as he suggested they meet together to clear up any misunderstandings.

'Speak to my secretary when you're back from Germany,' Simeon said. 'She'll put a note in my diary to remind me in a month or two.'

Simeon held the kitchen door open as Jack stepped outside. 'I'll give you some gratuitous advice, Jack,' he said. 'There are advantages when you can live and work in the shadows, away from the public gaze. Fame is a difficult cloak to wear, doubly so when it's derived from a background as wholesome as sport. You have an enormous sway over a large section of the population. People look up to you as a figurehead, for some, a role model.'

Where was he going with this? Jack was intrigued.

'You might find it hard to believe, but popularity is not a prize. It's a responsibility, a burden which brings with it disadvantages. Many will gravitate toward you, some well-meaning, others, not so scrupulous, who will try to convince you to use your influence to support a particular cause or some end. It's a constant battle because I am just a regular guy with family pressures and all the positives and shortcomings of the rest of the population.'

Jack wondered. Was this some roundabout way of excusing the reaction to his family issues, an attempt to humanise him, perhaps?

Simeon reached to shake his hand. 'My advice to you is if you find yourself the focal point of public attention, think long and hard before leaving the shadows. It could be your downfall.'

The pool car was parked on a grass verge, the driver leaning against the bonnet, arms crossed, watching as Jack made his way down the drive. 'You don't see many of them around this part of the world,' he said, idly looking past Jack back toward the house.

Jack turned. Francesca was framed in a picture window on the first floor, motionless, staring straight at him. She slowly raised her arm and pressed her palm flat against the glass. What was it supposed to mean? Was she telling him to stay away or seeking some sort of bond?

Jack reacted to the sound of the car door opening. 'Sorry,' he said. 'What did you say?'

The driver pointed along the road to a figure astride a bicycle some fifty metres away. 'He's been standing casing the house you've been in for the last fifteen minutes. Moved off the moment he saw you come out.'

'It's an impressive house.'

The driver laughed. 'You're telling me. Way out of the league of a black man like him. Must have come to see how the other half lives.'

Jack attempted a smile, but his expression tightened as he sensed the acrid stench of burning flesh in his nostrils.

# FOURTEEN

## SANDYS HALL – DEVON

## Midday – 14 November 2065

Robert let out a loud sigh and stretched across the Aga to retrieve a mug of lukewarm tea. It had been a long morning, but he was finally alone. The sound of Harriet's voice came from the driveway as she tried manfully in one sentence to both coax the twins into the back of the taxi and harass Mac into assisting. Robert sympathised with the challenge she faced. As loving a father as Mac was, he was the human equivalent of a sloth.

Perhaps it was the stress she was under which provoked that morning's heated argument with Alison. It followed a pause in the conversation at the breakfast table, just after Rebecca excused herself to take an important phone call. At Harriet's insistence, Mac was sent upstairs with the twins to finish packing. Robert was on the point of inviting Alison into the study to take up from where they had left off the previous night when Harriet exploded.

'You've never worried about anything I've wanted, have you?' Her eyes glazed over as she stared at a point halfway between her sister and uncle.

'Sorry?' Robert said, the surprise in his voice apparent.

'I'm not talking to you. I'm talking to that selfish bitch.'

Alison brushed the crumbs from her hands. 'Don't start all that again. It won't make any difference.'

'Of course, it won't! Whatever Alison wants, Alison gets. What did he call you? *Daddy's little shining star?* And what was I whilst you were Dad's favourite? Harriet do this. Harriet fetch that. I cared about you, making sure everything was right. And what do I get in return? When I ask you to help me with the only thing that's really important to me, it's No! No! NO!'

'We've been through all this.' Alison adopted a wearisome tone as she gave Robert a half smile. 'What does she expect me to do?' She turned back to her sister. 'If you acted more responsibly, you wouldn't be in this position.'

'Don't you lecture me, you fucking cow!' She rose to her feet, leaning forward, her knuckles white as she gripped the table. 'You're nothing but a total egotist, only interested in yourself and incapable of lifting your little finger to help anybody.' Tears ran down her cheeks. 'I hate you and hope you get some terrible illness and die in pain.'

Rebecca rushed into the room, oblivious to the atmosphere, her hand grasping a mobile to her chest. 'Quick, somebody! Give me a pen and paper.' She returned the mobile to her ear. 'Hold on a minute, Seth, will you?' She shook her hand at Alison to hurry. Robert checked his notepad. He had already removed last night's annotations. Alison took the blank page he proffered and held it ready with a pen.

'Go on, Seth.' Rebecca indicated for Alison to take the details. She repeated a telephone number, time and location, which Alison wrote at the bottom of the page.

'Now Seth, tell me what sort of topics we're . . .' Her voice tailed off into the distance as she quit the kitchen.

Harriet stood; her face turned toward Robert. 'We're leaving, uncle. The stench of self-righteousness in here makes me want to vomit. I'll pop in to say goodbye to Charles and Verity before we leave.' She gave him a weak smile. 'Don't waste any time trying to teach the Devil's disciple anything about compassion. She has a heart of stone.'

As much as he longed to pry, Robert could tell from Alison's attitude that she didn't want to offer any explanation and, now Harriet had left, they were alone and there were more important things to discuss.

'Time for a chat?' he asked.

'Alison!' Rebecca's voice rang from the hall. 'If you want a lift back to London, you had better be quick.' Her head appeared around the door. 'You'll never believe it,' she said, her voice full of excitement. 'They're going to do a full page on my work for charity. It's so exciting. Seth is such a sweetie. I've got a lot to organise.'

Alison folded the sheet of paper, tearing off the strip with the information she had jotted down. 'There you are,' she said.

'Can you give us five minutes?' Robert asked.

'Provided it is only five minutes and not one of your bloody - did I really go on for two hours? - sermons.' Rebecca snatched the scrap of paper and was gone.

Robert swigged the last of the tea and put down the mug. Okay, the conversation did not last five minutes, more like fifteen, but even fifteen minutes was not enough to dispel all his misgivings.

He had been too hasty in entrusting Alison with the details of his involvement with Lance. Stupid. The incident on Saturday had unnerved him. The more he thought about it, the more convinced he was the bullet was meant for him. If ISE was behind it, they would try again.

In the cold light of day, analysing Alison's unequivocal agreement to join him told him to be wary. Her innocent enthusiasm was no substitute for experience, and the necessity to acquire a skill set would need weeks of patient instruction. It was time he did not have. Logic told him to back off. Inexperience apart, her relationship with Rolf would risk complicating the mission.

Listening to Alison talk, cheeks still flushed from the reaction to her sister's tirade, reminded him of those old cinema images of the young people who dashed to enlist in the forces at the start of the Great War, full of romantic ideals and never once imagining the horrors which would confront them.

It came as a relief when Rebecca's interruption ended their conversation. Five minutes for Alison to pack and be outside, or Rebecca was leaving without her.

Robert unfolded the pages torn from the notebook and flattened them on the kitchen work surface. There was no doubt in his mind as to the identity of Dieter Eigard. Confirmation had come via the INCOL, People and Places search engine. A good citizen's blog recorded the award of a special long-service commendation to ISE official, Dieter Eigard of Rottenburg in Oberbayern, Bavaria, following his sterling work for CORE and his retirement from operational duties. He would now assume a part-time consultative role, working from home to finalise the report specially commissioned by Berlin. His profile showed his wife as deceased, and one son, Rolf Andreas.

The contact who channelled the extraction request to Lance's organisation was Mila Kullenberg, with a Stuttgart address. From research on the *Bürgerregister*, Robert discovered she worked for the synod of the EKG, the evangelical church in Germany, which, in the current anti-religious climate, acted as a charitable organisation for the homeless.

Lance had already set the process in motion through a network member in Frankfurt, whom he knew under the codename of FreierMann. Both Eigard and Kullenberg had been subject to 24/7 surveillance for several weeks, with their movements monitored and relayed to Lance via the satellite phone arrangement.

Robert needed to speak to FreierMann before approving any initial contact. Why was Eigard not being extracted through a German port? Arranging for the man to enter the UK on some pretext and then disappear added a layer of risk and danger to an already precarious scenario. The quicker a plan was hatched, the better.

Even if everything went to plan, it would be a month, at least, before Robert could affect his escape. A month of dodging the authorities or avoiding another bullet would be challenging, but the only way forward was to suffer the anxiety and press on. In the meantime, he would put in place his exit plan.

# FIFTEEN

## CHELSEA HARBOUR – LONDON

## 02.00 - 15 November 2065

He opened the front door of the seventh-floor apartment with exaggerated care, losing his balance as he pulled off his shoes. 'Shush,' he said, as he steadied himself against the doorframe. By moving his head back, he could focus on the shoes as he shunted them gently to one side. 'Doesn't make any sense.'

'What doesn't?' The voice was heavy with sleep.

'Sorry. Did I wake you?'

'I said what doesn't make any sense?' Damien sounded edgy.

Seth wheeled around, leaning back against the wall to keep his balance. 'I was just thinking, it doesn't make any sense. Your shoes come off easily with the laces tied, but it would take a lifetime of failures to put them back on without undoing them.' He opened his eyes wide as he tried to focus on the living room. 'Must have a deeper meaning, that, don't you think?'

'You're drunk.'

'Master of the obvious,' he said, slumping into an ergonomic recliner.

Damien was lying on the sofa, dressed in black silk pyjamas, pillows puffed under his head and a Mexican-design throw-over across his legs. The television, with sound muted, was showing a fifty-year-old situation comedy.

'Does it notice?' Seth faced his partner. 'So what?' he said defiantly, but instantly regretted the challenge. Fair's fair, he thought. Courtesy of Damien's job at Homeland Security, they amassed enough housing credits to secure a status two-bed apartment in the centre of London, with a view of the Thames. It was listed in Seth's name to avoid anyone asking awkward questions. Most of the credits were thanks to Damien's little scams, with enough left over to pay for the furnishings. Sparsely equipped, perhaps, but the clean-cut Scandinavian-style units were both timeless and expensive. They were a sign of good taste, Damien insisted. Maybe, was Seth's unspoken reply, but the chairs were fucking uncomfortable. Instead of voicing his criticism, he just smiled.

Seth's contribution to the household budget was to provide enough credits for their day-to-day living needs with something left over for those little luxuries. That reminded him. He fished in his raincoat pocket. 'I bought these for you.'

He leaned forward, holding between his thumb and first finger a crumpled white, reusable paper bag, which Damien accepted reluctantly. He glanced inside the bag, letting it fall onto the shag pile carpet.

'Sorry,' Seth said. 'I know you like Turkish Delight. I bought them a few hours ago. The sugar has congealed. They've stuck together but they taste alright.' True enough. He'd tried one in the taxi. Bits were still stuck to his teeth.

Seth intended to come home around midnight, but the Chinese barman in the pub got talking to him. He hadn't quite worked out whether the young man was just chatty or gay or, with any luck, chatty and gay. It was an encounter to develop another time when he hadn't drunk so much.

Damien studied the television. 'Too bad if you're hungry. Your dinner is in the dog.'

Seth tried to focus. His brow creased. 'We don't have a dog.'

'It's what you say, isn't it? You're expecting "in the oven" and I make a joke of it. What stone have you been hiding under for the last thirty years?'

'Very droll, I'm sure.'

'Forget it. What kept you so late? We need to talk.' Damien's expression turned serious; his thin lips downturned at the corners.

Seth's eyes flickered as he tried to clear his head. He just wanted to go to bed. That would piss off Damien. He'd try to persevere. Five minutes, max.

'Sorry, I'm late.' An image of the Chinese boy flashed across his mind. 'I was just finishing the groundwork for a meeting with Rebecca Tirrand at the Film Festival on Friday. The snotty bitch thinks I want an interview about her charity work. I'm actually after some insight into the relationship with her hubby. Give me a sniff of an indiscretion and I can go to town on our upstanding politician, Jack Tirrand.'

'She'll never forgive you,' Damien said with a smile. 'You'll be off her Christmas card list.'

'What a relief that would be. I hope you're right. She never stops talking; totally up herself.'

Damien swung onto his feet, discarding the throw-over and fishing in his pyjama pocket for a Post-it note, which he tossed in Seth's general direction. He grabbed at his pyjama trousers as they slipped from his waist, glancing at Seth's expression as he did so. 'Forget it,' he said, readjusting his pyjamas. 'I'm not in the mood to have you gawping at me. The last thing I want tonight is sex with an old drunk with BO.'

Seth played with the headrest and adjusted the recliner to raise the level of his feet. 'Factually correct at all levels; I cannot argue.' He tried to read the Post-it but gave up. 'Perhaps I'd not call it BO, more a manly scent provoked by a high testosterone level.' He ignored the raised eyebrows. 'I was just marvelling at how somebody so well-endowed as you could have such a slight, bird-like body, the face of an angel and the tongue of a hardened bitch. It's a devilishly compelling mix.' He waved the note at Damien. 'Need my glasses. What does it say?'

'You forgot your gofer . . . What's his name?'

'Arthur.'

'Arthur, that's it. You forgot Arthur booked a call to you at eleven?'

'Oh, shit!'

'Lucky I was in. I pretended to be you and took the call. You had him tailing somebody, Tirrand, I'm assuming. According to Arthur, Tirrand met up with some woman outside his building late tonight – not the Kahn woman – he greeted her, and they both went up to his apartment. A scarf was wrapped around her head. Presumably to hide her identity. Arthur's opinion from the cut of her clothes and fancy shoes leads him to the conclusion she was a hooker, though I doubt from the sound of his adolescent, squeaky voice he has any first-hand experience.'

'Did he . . .?' The effect of the alcohol was fast wearing off.

'Relax. He took some snaps. No names were mentioned, just in case the censor was live to his conversation.'

'Good boy. He's learning fast.'

Damien finished adjusting his pyjamas and perched on the sofa. 'Are you in any condition to talk? I have a problem, but I'd rather leave it until the morning if you're not able to contribute.'

'Go on. Arthur's information has given me an adrenalin rush. Is this problem work-related?'

Damien nodded. 'Piece of terrible luck, coupled with an unfortunate coincidence. Just think. How many hundreds of thousands of hard copy files do you imagine I'm responsible for at Homeland?'

'Can't imagine. They were digitalising all the old stuff at the time of 11/11: must go back a hundred years or more: enough to fill a warehouse.'

'Exactly. The eight thousand metre unit at Nine Elms is stacked with High Court and County Court cases until 2028. From then on, everything was digitalised.'

'So, where's this going?'

'What do you think is the possibility of two enquiries for the same file within two days of each other?'

'I suppose, if it was topical.'

'Topical? No way. We're talking about the case of two mixed-race brothers sentenced as juveniles for a murder committed in 2025. The file's not been requisitioned by anybody over the last twenty-five years.'

'I don't understand. Why your strife?'

Damien sat back, crossing his legs and folding them under his body, yoga style.

As the SEO for the closed-case historic records, Damien's primary role was to oversee the movement of hard copy within and beyond the storage facility. A computerised register showed the summary detail and location of every file listed. Whenever a Homeland department needed to consult the details of some criminal case before 2028, the requisition would pass over Damien's desk for authorisation to allow his second-in-command at Nine Elms to register and release the documentation.

'It's Janet's responsibility to make sure the damn file comes back when it should,' he said. 'That's what she's paid for.' He shook his head.

Two years ago, Phil Silverman, a lawyer-cum-private investigator who specialised in looking into cold cases, side-lined Damien at a cocktail party. He had a problem. Occasionally, his investigation would hit a brick wall when certain information could not be sourced because the file he needed was classified exclusively for Homeland use and needed special clearance. It would be much appreciated if he could come to some arrangement with

Damien, allowing him an unofficial look at a confidential record from time to time. Over the intervening period, spasmodically at first, but with increasing regularity, currently, on two or three occasions per month, Damien would 'lose' a file from the system overnight for a transfer of fifty FTS credits to his account.

'I give ten credits a pop to Janet for running the scam. She controls the storage facility and, until now, everything has gone smoothly.' He puffed air into his cheeks.

'Where do you store the credits?'

Damien's eyes widened. 'What's that got to do with anything? Afraid I might hide them from you?' He put on a wounded voice. 'How could you think that of me?'

'Don't give me the hurt little boy act. You've told me all about the scam before. Just humour me.'

'The credits go into my account. Where else could they go?'

Seth shook his head. 'You know you're taking a risk? If they decide to audit you, how do you explain the dodgy credits? Why didn't you buy a mobile on the black market with an embedded proxy account? I've got the contacts.'

Damien massaged eyelids resembling crumpled tissue paper and picked at his eyelashes, causing dried white flakes of the excretion from his limpid blue eyes to settle on his pyjama collar. 'Relax,' he said. 'It's not an issue. Nobody's going to be looking into the financial records of a Homeland official. After all, we're the ones responsible for requisitioning the audits. So, chill out. My problem is Phil's got a file which has been requested by somebody in Homeland.'

'With all that paperwork, you're not going to tell me files never go adrift and suddenly reappear. Get it back from this Phil character and pass it on to whoever wants it.'

'I wish it were that simple. It's Ramona Usher, a bigwig in the department who has signed the requisition. She wants it before Monday.'

Seth looked bemused. 'So, over the next couple of days, it turns up.'

Damien shook his head. 'She's on the warpath. Won't accept it's gone missing. She's sending a team of ten people from her section tomorrow to comb through the records. It's put the wind-up Janet. She's on the point of confessing all. I told her to stay strong, and that I'd sort it out. But I'm up against it. This Usher is a tough cookie.'

Seth said nothing. A weak smile cloaked his thoughts. Damien was under suspicion. Seth could guarantee the issue extended well beyond one missing file. Janet was a fragile link. She would succumb under interrogation. The only panacea he could offer was to sleep on it and work out a solution in the morning.

'If that's the best you can offer, it will have to do.' Damien sounded irritable.

He looked a sorry sight, Seth thought. If things did go south, getting out of the relationship before he could be implicated was a priority. It would be a pity . . . His line of thought suddenly changed. If the file was so important, what was in it to warrant all this manpower set to find the damn thing? Seth needed to read it. If he could come up with another scoop for the paper with his by-line, he wouldn't need Damien's financial support. Maybe he could kill the proverbial two birds.

He rose and reached out to pull Damien up by his clammy hand. 'Come on,' he said. 'Let's go to bed. I'll work something out. I always do, don't I?'

# SIXTEEN

## MUSWELL HILL – LONDON

## 03.00 – 15 November 2065

Around the same time as Seth Llewellyn Morgan lay in bed, listening to his partner's even breathing, his mind racing on how he could capitalise on Damien's predicament, thirteen miles away, Jack sat alone in darkness, waiting for his wife to return home.

The journey from Devon should have seen her home by eleven the previous evening, but he wasn't unduly worried. The TV news was reporting civil disturbances by unpatriotic factions, and protests following the alleged suicide of a leading member of the disgraced and long-since disbanded Meta Facebook empire. Sentenced to a full life term of imprisonment for treason and sedition, the woman was an outspoken and vociferous dissenting voice when criticising alleged INCOL human rights abuses. Despite a conviction for failing to monitor and report plans coordinated through social media to perpetrate the 11/11 atrocities, thousands responded to her call for a demonstration of public disobedience. Jack suspected the rise of the underground 'Facebook Forever' movement was as much a troubling manifestation of public weariness of four decades of austerity as it was support for the deceased figurehead.

As rumours of her death circulated, large groups took to the streets. Roadblocks were set up on all the major roads to forestall a major convergence of the rioters. The reporter confirmed the ringleaders had been identified and were being apprehended whilst steps were well underway to disband the misguided protestors and send them home.

Rebecca was likely to have been caught up in the confusion. There was no cause for concern. Besides, he had something far more pressing on his mind.

He had been returning to the apartment building from the community bakery when she approached him; so cleverly disguised, he failed to recognise her. The last person he could have imagined was standing in front of him, her expression as she removed the scarf more of discomfort than embarrassment.

Francesca Hill had stayed for three hours. The two pizzas Jack brought from the bakery remained untouched, now cold and congealed in their boxes on the kitchen table.

She had made the journey on the off chance he would be at home. 'Simeon told me you were expecting your family to return later tonight. I hoped I might catch you on your own.'

'You intrigue me. Please explain.'

'That terrible argument; you were present. The way you looked. It was as if you understood what I was going through.'

'It was none of my business.'

'Even so, I knew you could sense the undercurrent. I desperately need someone understanding to talk to.' She looked into his eyes. 'I know I am taking a risk. Can I rely on your discretion?'

He listened as she talked. Occasionally, he would pose a question, encourage her to explain something or make a helpful comment. After two hours, the conversation widened to embrace more general topics and she relaxed, at one point even chancing to laugh at an off-the-cuff aside he made.

Jack checked his watch. His wife would arrive shortly. At this prompt, Francesca was on her feet, apologising for taking up so much of his time, surprised at how late it was and how it would soon be difficult to find a collective heading in her direction. He didn't need to say it would be inappropriate for them to be chanced upon by Rebecca. Not that she was likely to be suspicious, but given their conversation, it was better to avoid unnecessary explanations. The consensus was unspoken.

He was lost in thought as he watched Francesca leave the apartment and walk into the road under the hazy glow of the street lights. Thank God, Rebecca was due back. During those last ten minutes, the atmosphere between them had been charged with a primaeval urge he knew they had both felt. Had it been allowed to develop, the night could have been so different. His breathing faltered as an image of them entwined together entered his head and hardened his crotch. The dreamlike state ended abruptly when the sound from the hallway of the elevator told him Rebecca had finally arrived.

She entered the apartment like a tsunami reaching the shore. In machine gun fire sentences, she talked of six vehicle checks between Aldershot and London that left her ready to explode. Unable to sit down in the same place for more than a few seconds, she played with a glass of brandy, which she would constantly sniff but not drink.

'Thank God your daughter kept her mouth shut,' she said. 'When one of the more objectionable road marshals made his presence felt, I expected Alison would berate him with her customary outburst on democratic rights. She said nothing, just gave him her pathetic little man smile.'

'Maybe she's in love.'

Rebecca scoffed. 'Love? You must be joking. I doubt she's experienced the emotion: far too self-centred.'

'I wonder which one of us she takes after?'

'Glanced in the mirror recently?' She playfully shook her head. 'Joking apart, I was busy gearing up for this interview with Seth on Friday. You look confused. Did I forget to tell you? Sorry, thought I did. I'll fill you in later.' The excitement went out of her voice to be replaced by concern. 'Robert told me the twins ended up having the most terrible argument this morning. They almost came to blows. Harriet was in a state. Neither would say what it was about. Alison was brooding on it in the car, quiet and distant. I tried to make conversation but gave up.'

'You didn't ask her? God knows you were stuck in the car with her for hours.'

'I have a lot on my mind. I don't approve of your censorial attitude. If you must know, this interview will publicise my charity work. It's a golden opportunity.' She raised her eyebrows as if waiting to be challenged. 'As for Alison, I dropped her off at a girlfriend's in Islington. She's coming round tomorrow morning. You can interrogate her then.' She strained to read the clock flashing hypnotically in the corner of the television screen. 'God, is that the time? I need to go to bed. I'm shattered.'

The following morning, found Jack working in his office when a voice on the intercom told him his daughter was on the way up. A little earlier, breakfast with Rebecca consisted of watching her stand alongside the kitchen counter as she downed two double espressos and a slice of dried toast, all in quick order, followed by a command charging him to resolve whatever was troubling Alison. Rebecca was too busy and, in her own words, 'not in the right place to exercise the patience needed to deal with Alison's minor emotional disturbance.' Would he be a darling and handle it? She was already late for an appointment with the seamstress about altering possible dress wear for Friday. She would catch up with him later. With that, she was gone.

Jack opened the door, and to his surprise, found Harriet standing there. A weak smile and a mumbled apology for turning up unannounced spelt trouble.

Her chubby cheeks with that warm red glow were now pale and drawn. Her tired, hollow eyes, normally so bright and positive, told him she had been crying. She hugged him tight, longer than normal, her face turned away from his.

He broke the clinch to offer coffee and one of those exclusive Belgian chocolate biscuits for which Rebecca would spend a couple of luxury credits just in case somebody important dropped by.

'Your mother will kill me if she finds out I'm wasting her precious biscuits on the likes of you,' he said.

Harriet gave him a knowing smile and leaned forward. 'Just for that, I'll take another one.' Her mood quickly darkened again. 'I need your help.'

Jack watched her nibble at the biscuit. Harriet was the quieter of the two girls, more thoughtful before reacting and far less spontaneous than her livewire sister. Dads shouldn't have favourites. He didn't, but there had always been something more vulnerable and wounded about Harriet, which made him more protective of her. Mind you, she could be single-minded if the situation demanded, with a callous streak Jack attributed to her mother's Fitzwilliam lineage. Jack knew, when provoked, she could be ruthless in her response.

There was no point in making small talk. 'Spit it out,' he said. 'Tell me all about it.'

'I'm desperate. I've got nobody else to turn to.'

'What are we talking about? Financial? Matrimonial?'

She gave a dismissive shake of the head. 'I'm pregnant, three months. Mac doesn't know yet. It's a boy, I'm sure. You always wanted a grandson, didn't you?'

An image of Mac came into his mind, a man with a lethargic disinterest in anything physically demanding. 'Why haven't you told Mac? It is his, I presume?'

'It's a *he,* Dad, not an *it,* and don't be crass. Of course, he's Mac's. I'm not like Alison, opening and closing her legs so often, it creates a draught.' She gave an oblique smile.

Jack ignored the slight. 'What do you intend to do?'

She looked at her father with an expression of stark amazement. 'What do you mean, *what* do I intend to do? What do you think? I intend to give birth to a normal healthy baby boy and keep him within our family.'

Jack smiled, stood and walked toward her, arms outstretched. Grown-up, maybe she was, but still vulnerable. He understood the dilemma she faced, keeping the secret to herself, the terrifying mix of joy and fear. She hugged him as the tears flowed.

'You asked Alison to help?' Jack continued to hold her, but she pulled back.

Her cheeks were blotched, but her eyes were dry with a cold and hostile glint. 'Bitch! She knows I'm not allowed to keep a third child. As the law says I must put him up for adoption, she could step in if she wanted to support me. She knows she wouldn't have to take care of him. I will be his actual mother. It would just be her name on the adoption papers.'

'And she refused?'

'She told you?' The question was accusatory.

'No, I haven't spoken to Alison. I expect to see her later today.'

'I'm never speaking to the bitch again. She's ruined my life. The only part missing was a son. I craved for a boy ever since we were married. I adore the twins, but how I wish it were one of each sex. Forgive me for saying that.' She slumped back in the chair. 'What shall I do?'

'You keep saying *I* and *Me.* Surely, Mac has some say on the subject? You can't avoid telling him.'

'I haven't. I see it as somewhat of an irrelevance. He's so wrapped up in his little world that I doubt he'll have anything meaningful to say other than to obey the law. It's not what I want to hear from a man who pays lip service to being a father.'

Jack swallowed hard. 'You are contemplating bringing a child into a relationship which, by your admission, appears to have stalled. Do you love your husband?'

She pulled a face. 'What's love got to do with it?' She tossed her head back and looked away. 'Of course I do. Mac's the father of my twins. You know, for better or worse; I took the vow. I'm sure a boy would bring us closer.'

'I've never subscribed to the belief that having a child to keep a relationship together is well-founded.'

She tut-tutted and shook her head. 'What are you talking about, Dad? You're wandering off the point. My relationship with Mac is not at the heart of this. We're married and we're staying married. I'm desperate to keep my baby boy and I'm here to ask for your help, not to listen to some amateur marriage guidance counselling.'

'And getting angry with me is going to help you achieve this? Have you spoken with your mother?'

The mention of Rebecca softened her. 'I'm sorry. I didn't mean to offend you. Yes, it was Mum who suggested I talk with you. I hesitated. You're always so busy.' Her face flushed. 'Please, Dad, can you help me? I've never wanted anything so much in my life. There must be a way.' She hesitated. 'I could try a surrogate deal with somebody.'

Jack knew there were women prepared to take the risk, addicts and social outcasts, all notoriously unreliable and volatile. Most were found out when they tried to register the child as their own before handing it back to the biological mother. Even if successful, the future was bleak. After spending months trying to hide the pregnancy, the parents were then faced with the unstainable pressures of trying to bring up a family of three children away from prying eyes. It only took a suspicious neighbour, or a spurned blackmailer, prepared to denounce the parents for the prize of extra credits. The punishment was brutal. Both parents would be sterilised and, together with the surrogate, sent to a penal land farm where they would spend a lengthy sentence. All three children would be placed into care and onto the adoption register, never again to see their natural parents.

There were exceptions. The Family Equity Enactment made an allowance where the mother died in childbirth, was disabled, or suffered a debilitating or fatal accident. In these instances, the immediate family could opt to assume responsibility for the child, irrespective of the size of the household.

Jack sighed. He treated the outburst as a sign of desperation. Harriet would never put the twins at risk. He handed her a handkerchief. She rubbed her eyes and blew her nose fiercely.

'Can't you do something?' she pleaded. 'You're a lawmaker. Can't you change the rules?' There was a half-hearted laugh. Even she could see how ridiculous the question was.

'You know I can't ask for the legislation to be amended to suit my requirements, but I can ask our constitutional expert at the Assembly to see if there is any angle which can be exploited.'

Harriet looked up at the ceiling.

'I agree,' Jack said. 'It probably won't achieve anything, but I can try. Your best bet is to persist with your line of approach through Alison, though you must respect her position if she intends to have her own family.'

'She doesn't. She was adamant. No permanent attachments, men or kids. She prefers a life of selfish freedom. It's a joke. As twins, we're supposed to experience special bonding, shared emotions and a heightened sense of responsibility for each other. What a load of bullshit! Aside from the argument, we must have exchanged half a dozen words all weekend. She's self-centred; spent all weekend conspiring with Uncle Robert.'

Jack held back from asking exactly about what they were conspiring. They were in danger of moving away from the important issue. 'Let me guess,' he said. 'The way it went is that Alison gave you a spontaneous and unconsidered reaction to a badly phrased ultimatum from you, to which you reacted by immediately flying off the handle. Is that about right?'

Her little snigger answered the question.

'Thought so,' he acknowledged. 'I promise to sit down with Alison and try to appeal to her on your behalf. No guarantees. Perhaps, if she thinks it through, she won't see it as a bad idea if what you say about her is true.'

Harriet shrugged. 'You can try, but I'm not holding out any hopes.'

The intercom interrupted the silence as they exchanged understanding smiles.

Jack told the caretaker to send up the visitor. 'What the hell does he want, turning up unannounced?' he asked himself out loud.

# SEVENTEEN

## MUSWELL HILL – LONDON

## 10.00 – 15 November 2065

'I'd better go, Dad.' Harriet made to get up.

'Please hang on.' Jack was insistent. 'It's only a colleague. I'm sure it won't take long.' He was determined not to let their conversation end without impressing on her the need to confide in her husband. Her matter-of-fact, fatalistic approach to the marriage saddened him. It might not be the case of a burden shared, a burden halved, but Mac needed to be a part of the discussion, if not the solution.

There was a tap on the door. Jack blew his daughter a kiss as he walked across the room.

'Hope I'm not intruding.' A perspiring and breathless Arnold Roach peered over Jack's shoulder into the lounge. 'Heard talking. Thought you might be busy.'

He was, so he said nothing, ushering the man into the room and gathering the raincoat thrust at him.

'And this would be . . .?' He grinned at Harriet as he took a handkerchief from his pocket to wipe his forehead.

'You remember my daughter, Harriet, don't you, AR?' Jack said.

They spent five minutes trolling through historic pleasantries. My, my, how she had blossomed since the last time they met. When was that? When she was at university? That long ago? Her degree course? Domestic science? That's cooking, isn't it? She laughed off the put-down. She had a family? He couldn't believe it. Twins? My goodness, how time flies!

In Jack's eyes, AR possessed the unfortunate ability to impress his superiority complex on those with whom he deigned to talk. He could sense Harriet was in awe of the man's pompous manner, deferring to the status of someone she saw as several rungs above her father on the political ladder.

'Where are you bringing up this delightful family?' Roach asked.

'We've got an SCH semi-detached in Ware . . . Hertfordshire,' she added when Roach looked at her askew as if she was unsure as to the location of her home.

'Oh, yes,' he said in a tone which suggested, oh well, somebody's got to live there, I suppose.

'It's with the Clearers at the moment. We'd like a move to Devon. My husband is a civil servant working on energy conservation. There's an opening for him in Exeter.'

They talked for a while about the property market. With the shortage of construction materials, private home ownership had gradually eroded since eleven/eleven. New housing construction was minimal, as available resources were directed toward existing properties in need of renovation. The Social Community Housing scheme, SCH for short, would requisition the property and permit an approved contractor with a licence to order materials to complete the renovation and refurbishment work.

An individual's or family's equity in their home was recognised by the Department of Habitation through a division known colloquially as the Clearers, which attributed a value in habitation credits to every residential unit based on size and location. The formulae and appeals procedures were complicated and established amidst a constant barrage of accusations of favouritism, inconsistency, and corruption.

Would-be buyers and sellers could consult the Open Transaction Register maintained by the Clearers for a suitable swap. Under the rules, a buyer could add a maximum of ten per cent of their existing property value in accumulated credits from a savings account to buy a more expensive residence. Mortgage habitational credits were available to good citizens, and first-time buyers whenever starter units came onto the market.

'Are there many people in your chain?' Roach asked.

Jack's brow furrowed. Whenever AR became intrusive and asked searching questions, there was an ulterior motive. He decided to hear him out before interrupting and redirecting the conversation.

'Six,' Harriet said. 'It's complicated because somebody in the chain has a criminal conviction.'

'Property reallocation?' Roach queried, referring to the rule of invoking an automatic accommodation downgrade if someone in the household was convicted of a minor social crime. With a serious offence involving attempts to undermine INCOL's authority, eviction of the entire family and confiscation of the property was a legal option.

Harriet nodded. 'There's an appeal. We're told it could drag on for ages.'

'Give your father the details and I'll look into it. I expect I can get things moving. There's often a way around these bureaucratic hold-ups.' He gave her a patronising smile. 'After all, if we can't help our flesh and blood, what is the point of holding a position of responsibility? Don't you agree, Jack?'

So, that's your ploy, is it? Jack thought. Undermine my status by asserting your own, and you have an ally in the Tirrand camp. And it was working. Harriet's idolatry gaze at him with eyes wide open said this is my saviour. No words were needed for Jack to understand his daughter's thought process. As far as seeking Roach's influence was concerned, moving house was the last thing on her mind.

'I know you'll do everything in your power to take full advantage of the system, AR.'

Roach wriggled in the armchair, leaning from side to side. 'I've gone numb in the bum,' he joked, to which Harriet gave a false laugh. He sat forward. 'Now, where was I?' He had her complete attention. 'Your father knows I am always willing to help an old and trusted friend.' He closed his eyes as he nodded. 'You realise,' he said, 'the provisions for dealing with individuals who work against the philosophy of INCOL are draconian, but they have to be. We must maintain a united front to support authority, or we put at risk all the good work we've achieved over the last thirty years and anarchy will prevail.'

'I'm sure it's nothing as serious as that,' Harriet said, unaware of the actual target of Roach's remarks. 'I think he was trying to use somebody else's credits.'

'Quite so.' Roach was dismissive. 'Do not lose sight of the fact; anybody guilty of undermining *our* authority will suffer the consequences. Not only will they be deprived of a place to live, but of all their treasured possessions and, more significantly, the loss of status and the respect of family and friends. The system is designed to deny any serial offender his rights, and it is my responsibility to make the suspect aware of the pitfalls.' His triple chin shuddered with the gravity of his warning. 'In your case, Harriet, perhaps we can convince the offender to withdraw his appeal. That would do the trick, wouldn't it?'

Harriet beamed. Jack could see she believed AR was a kindred spirit who not only understood her plight but had the power and influence to resolve the problem. Jack had to get her alone to explain Roach's motives before she made a weapon for him of her vulnerabilities.

'Are you travelling back to Hertfordshire now?' Roach was sliding his talons into a willing victim and was not about to release his prey.

It was too late. Despite Jack's protestations that they needed to talk, Harriet jumped at the offer of a lift in Roach's pool car.

While she went to the bathroom, Jack stood over his visitor as the man struggled to raise himself from the chair. 'You didn't call round on the off chance you could play the Good Samaritan for my daughter. You had something to say to me?'

Roach's arms shuddered as he heaved himself up. Their faces were inches apart. Roach avoided eye contact. 'It can wait,' he said, breathless. 'It was only an impromptu, spur-of-the-moment thing, old man. Give me a hand, will you?'

Jack backed off, allowing Roach to get to his feet.

'All I wanted was to see if you were at home,' Roach said. 'I need you to attend a meeting at the Palace tomorrow. There are several pressing matters to resolve. Can we say mid-afternoon, just after lunch?' He did not wait for a response. 'Tell Harriet to come down as soon as she is ready. I'll find out where the driver has parked.' With that, he was out of the door.

Harriet's cursory nod of the head as she ran toward the elevator left Jack with a heavy heart. He grabbed her arm as she mouthed a hurried goodbye, determined not to miss her lift. She tried to pull away. 'Dad. Let me go.'

They needed to talk again tomorrow when Rebecca was around, and he had spoken with Alison. Surely, Mac could babysit the twins.

Again, he restrained her from leaving. 'Listen,' he said, his tone serious. 'Be discreet with AR. Keep our conversation private and do not mention the pregnancy. Believe me, he is not the solution nor a confidant.'

From the window, he watched the car pull away. Roach was an opportunist who would try to use Harriet to expose any vulnerability in Jack to his advantage. And he would do it without a second thought for Harriet's wellbeing.

# EIGHTEEN

## NINE ELMS – LONDON

## MIDDAY – 15 November 2065

Climbing the dozen steps to the entrance of the storage facility left Seth immobile and straining to pretend he wasn't gasping for breath. He stooped, leaning forward, hands on his thighs as he took large gulps of air, counting the beats of his racing heart, avoiding eye contact with the trickle of people moving around him.

He turned his head to follow the line of the building back to where the perimeter fence separated it from what was once New Covent Garden, a thriving fruit and vegetable market in the days of plenty and now, a windswept container park. As his breathing stabilised, his gaze centred on the side wall of the building and the grimy shadow of where the plastic lettering of the emblematic trademark 'Amazon' once figured proud. Seth laughed out loud. Once upon a time, you hardly had time to tap a key on your laptop before a delivery man was knocking at your door with whatever you ordered from an endless list of possibilities. Long gone were those days.

Seth was doing this favour for Damien. That is what he told himself. He was taking a risk, a risk he would take to cement their relationship. Come off it! Who was he fucking kidding? Okay, point taken. He was past fifty and a little portly around the stomach – an area he would gently pat and call his savings account – and the simple truth was Damien would soon tire of him. There were already telltale signs he was looking elsewhere for action. So what? A hard-on for a skilled investigative journalist like Seth was the scent of a real story. Experience and instinct told him the file hidden in the van could well be the scoop he craved for all his working life. If the fallout from his investigation meant hanging Damien out to dry, then sobeit. It's called collateral damage.

Seth's first visit that morning was at Phil Silverman's office in Shoreditch. Damien had telephoned ahead to okay handing over the missing file to Seth.

The solicitor, who introduced himself as Phil the Brief – 'it's what my clients call me, and the name has stuck' - was in his late thirties and slight in stature. There was nothing remarkable about him other than a lingering scent of cooking oil. It was only as the man sidled past him that Seth detected the aroma of animal fat in the man's brilliantined and groomed jet-black hair. What price vanity, Seth thought, when Brylcreem is no more?

'While you're looking for the file,' Seth said, his voice heavy with sarcasm. 'Make another copy for me, will you?'

The illegal photocopier would be hidden in the basement. Registered users had to license all photocopiers and printers. A scanner was installed in every unit to photograph and record each document copied. A small, unique symbol printed in the page's corner identified the source machine, should the origin of a copy be questioned. Periodic online machine audits were carried out by Homeland personnel, commonly known as "sheet turners".

For those individuals operating on the margins, a black-market copier could be arranged at a premium price from an underground dealer, one of a number who thrived from providing and servicing these machines.

'There you are,' Phil the Brief said, slapping the original and a copy on the desk. 'Are you and Damien . . .?' He hesitated. 'Intimate, like?'

'We have our moments.'

'I bet you do,' he said with a throaty chuckle then, suddenly turned serious. 'Don't leave around or show these copies to anyone. It's a year's black and white if they catch me.'

Seth nodded. The reference was to the striped armband those convicted of crimes against society were forced to wear throughout the term of community service imposed by the court. The population was encouraged to ostracise these lawbreakers, whose access to credits was severely restricted.

Seth pushed open the large double door fronting the building and followed the sign showing 'Homeland Security – Closed Case Storage – Reception (Search Requisitions)'. This was his first-time visit to the facility. Accredited journalists were allowed six discretionary searches per year. He handed two requisitions to the counter clerk, both for high-profile cases where his only selection criterion was the large number of files he expected would be generated by the request. The more the paperwork surrounding him, the more straightforward his assignment.

The clerk countersigned the requisitions, passed them to an employee clad in a luminous yellow hi-vis vest, and waved a languid hand at Seth toward the security guard.

Feigning attention to his mobile, Seth waited until a woman on her way out was held whilst her briefcase was examined. He put his case on the scanning machine, his demeanour one of mild impatience as he waited for the guard to finish attending to the woman.

The man walked over to him. Seth's smile at the blank expression on the guard's face hid the acute anxiety he felt. He prayed the contents of the case would not be checked and the missing file, hidden between the pages of today's newspaper, would evade detection.

In the event, the inspection was cursory, and Seth was waved through. Stands to reason, he thought, as he regained his composure: security would be much more concerned with the control over files being removed than the possibility of somebody trying to smuggle documents into the facility.

The visitors' examination area comprised a group of a dozen tables, neatly arranged in rows of three, separated by wire fencing from what appeared endless corridors of metal storage racks, all crammed with shelves of manila, blue and rose-coloured covers, most bound in tape, some in thin plastic strapping.

Two pickers, one of whom Seth saw take his requisitions from the counter clerk, pushed trolleys along the corridors, matching location references to those fixed to the shelving. Files were removed or replaced as the pickers moved back and forth in total silence, other than the squeak of unoiled trolley wheels as they passed over the concrete floor.

Seth looked around to check the location of the surveillance cameras, choosing a table where he could sit with his back partially obscuring a view of whatever file he was examining. Over to the right on a mezzanine floor was a glass-partitioned office giving both visual access to the visitors' area and, through a bank of screens with alternating images, coverage throughout the entire building. A young woman in the office glanced down in Seth's direction. He nodded and smiled, causing her to avert her gaze and move back into the room. There are eyes everywhere, he thought. I am going to have to do this with real precision.

Seth waited, arms folded, a studied look of boredom on his face. Occasionally, he glanced at the occupants of the other two tables, noting how they worked. An electronic alarm buzzed as the restricted access barrier clicked open, preceding the picker and a trolley packed with files. One by one, eleven buff-coloured folders of varying thickness were placed on Seth's table, a pained expression on the face of the picker, as if the burden of his efforts would continue to go unappreciated.

Seth mumbled his thanks and set about thumbing through the pages, pretending to study the contents and making copious notes. An hour passed. It was lunchtime. Personnel were changing, the woman in the office in intense conversation with a younger man who did little more than nod as he took her seat. It was now or never.

Seth ambled over to the large, inverted umbrella-style container for returned files and deposited three bulky folders. As he went to walk away, he shook his head, appeared to chastise himself, and turned back to retrieve one of the files. A skin-coloured latex glove covered his right hand as he manoeuvred his body to stand back on to the surveillance camera. He picked a folder somebody had discarded earlier that morning and laid it open on the table in front of him.

The lunch hour was over. Most of the tables were filling up with earnest-looking individuals Seth guessed were civil servants. The pickers were busy, and nobody was interested in what he was doing. Even the woman in the office who was back from her break paid little attention to the screens as she attended to her duties.

He removed the newspaper from his briefcase, slowly opening it and allowing the file he retrieved from Phil the Brief to slip onto his lap. After appearing to read the newspaper for a few minutes, he folded it and, as he did, dislodged a pile of files onto the floor along with the missing file. He rearranged them carefully, making sure the missing file nestled within the pages of the folder he had not requisitioned.

Seth looked at the clock. This pantomime had been going on for the best part of four hours. He would give it another fifteen minutes before emitting a loud sigh, collecting his notes and returning everything, making sure the folder containing the missing file was placed in the container well away from the others he had requisitioned.

A chill wind was blowing off the Thames as he stood on the pavement outside the building. He deserved a few stiff drinks and a suitable penance from Damien when he got home later that evening.

Out of curiosity, he would take a closer look at the paperwork Phil the Brief copied for him. Why were people so interested in a schoolboy prank forty years ago that went tragically wrong? A young boy suffering from polio was found dead at the bottom of a dry well, the victim of two young brothers who wanted to scare him and exact revenge. Why was it coming to light now after all these years? Instinct told him he needed to investigate further.

Toward the end of the afternoon, back at Nine Elms, Janet Hamilton, the woman Seth spotted in the mezzanine office, was expecting a visit from Ramona Usher. It was thirty minutes after her regular leaving time, and she had missed her normal collective back to the family home in Hanwell. Her parents would worry if there was no message. She played nervously with the tassels on the fake Burberry scarf her mother had given her as a birthday present. Usher was insistent. There was to be no contact with anybody until they talked.

The commotion began toward the end of the afternoon as the returns container was emptied and the files and folders were replaced on the racks. A picker came across a file on the "Requisitioned but Missing" critical register. It fell from a folder returned by a visitor as the picker was about to replace the document. Usher ordered that nothing be touched until two of her forensic investigators arrived to carry out an inspection.

Usher was shorter than Janet had imagined as she stood behind a table in the examination area. Wearing a tailored, figure-enhancing two-piece suit, which partially disguised a tendency to overweight, Usher was small in stature. With clipped grey hair and heavy features with no make-up, she was not conventionally attractive, but Janet saw something in her demeanour that she found appealing, yet both unsettling and hostile. It was those wide, cold and emotionless, brown eyes staring at her, appraising her, searching for unspoken answers. Janet averted her gaze and studied the floor.

Janet's boss, Damien, had been insistent. If questioned, she must not lose her nerve. He assured her the latest missing file was on its way back. It was best she didn't know how, by whom, and when. Just play it cool and everything would be fine. She could rely on Damien, she told herself.

'Is it correct for you to be interviewing me without my boss being present?' Janet said, filling her chest with air and standing upright to emphasise her height advantage.

'Sit down and shut up!' Usher shuffled a pack of A5-sized screenshots from the surveillance cameras and laid them out on the table. Mouth open, Janet did as she was told.

'Do you know any of these people?' Usher asked.

'What do you mean, *know*?'

'Do you have a problem with English?'

Janet felt the surge of blood in her cheeks. 'I don't know what all this is about, but the answer is no. If you're asking me whether I recognise any of them, I do. They are all visitors to the search area today, people I identified on the monitors.'

Usher pointed to a grainy image of one man. 'What about him?'

Janet fired the same question back at Usher. The icy stare unnerved her. 'Yes, he was here,' she said.

'His name is Peterson from Finance,' Usher said. 'He requisitioned the document in which the missing file was discovered. His concern was to check one set of figures and he could not swear if there was a separate file in his folder. He doesn't think so. He only needed it for a few minutes. Tie in with your recollection?'

'I told you. I don't understand what all the fuss is about.' Janet blinked, this time determined to hold Usher's stare. 'Files go missing from time to time, but they always turn up, eventually. What's so special about this one?'

Usher ignored the question. 'What about him?' She pushed forward another screenshot.

'Again, same answer,'

'His name is Seth Llewellyn Morgan, a journalist. It's his first time here.'

'Yeah, I remember the requisition. The picker complained about the number of folders involved. The guy wanted information on two paedophile cases tried in 2000. Must be writing an article or something.'

'Have you ever seen him before?'

'How many times do you want me to answer the same question?'

'Watch the playback. He drops several files into the completed bin and then returns to retrieve one. His back is to the camera, obscuring the view, but the file is put back on his table. Later, some files slip from the table whilst he's reading a newspaper. Looks a little contrived, don't you think?'

'Happens nearly every day. Somebody goes back to retrieve a file they thought they'd finished with. I've told Damien we should have a non-accessible system once the file has been discarded. If it's needed again, there should be a supplementary requisition. Like most things here, you can try to make a difference, but nothing ever changes.'

Usher nodded. 'Now you mention Damien Spencer . . .' She took a sheaf of papers from her case. 'Perhaps you could give me an insight into what your manager is like and how he works? In confidence, of course.'

# NINETEEN

## MUSWELL HILL – LONDON

### Late afternoon – 15 November 2065

Rebecca burst in through the front door, dragging three 'for life' plastic bags. 'That's the last time I shop at Harrods.' It sounded like a declaration of war. She released the bags onto the floor with a groan of relief. 'You used to count on their integrity and straight dealing. Not anymore.'

Jack glanced up from the sheaf of papers he was annotating at the dining table. 'Oh, why's that?' He carried on writing in the margin, hesitated and shuffled the page back into its place.

Rebecca reacted to the gesture. 'Not interrupting anything important, am I?'

He smiled, prompting her to continue. What could be more important than shopping? Certainly not making a judgement on a disciplinary hearing concerning the alleged mistreatment of a resident with advanced Parkinson's disease. That could take a supporting role, he mused. Sarcasm apart, it was not a straightforward case and needed careful analysis and concentration. Better left for later. 'You were saying?' he said.

'I was in the Just Worn Once department. They have some beautiful dresses there. Timeless. Not like the shoddy rubbish they turn out today.' She waved a hand toward the drinks cabinet. 'I found this off-the-shoulder creation, just perfect for the Film Festival on Friday.' She took the drink from his outstretched hand. 'God, I deserve this.'

'I thought you were getting a dress altered?'

She held out the glass for a refill. 'Trouble is, you might tinker with the appearance, but the fact remains, everybody has seen it before.' She took a large swig from the replenished glass.

'Is that so bad?'

Her face took on an expression somewhere between amazed and offended. 'For a private soirée, it wouldn't matter, but this is a major social event, and I am being interviewed, almost certainly photographed, for an exclusive article. Come on. I'm the wife of the hot-shot deputy. I have to do you proud.'

'Considerate of you.'

'Let me get to the point, will you?' She ran her fingers through shoulder-length, blond hair, ruffling her head as if allowing the curls to settle like waves rolling onto the shore. Her hand dropped to play with a necklace made up of oversized, white plastic pearls, slowly fingering each one as if on a rosary. 'I am guessing this amazing creation was designed by a once-famous fashion house for a world-renowned actress, worn once for an award ceremony, never again to see the light of day.' She breathed in through distended nostrils. 'Until now,' she added. 'What could be more fitting?'

'Sounds expensive.'

'That's the point I'm trying to make.' She gave a close-lipped grimace. 'It was on the peg for seventy-five regular credits.'

It was Jack's turn to take in air, sucked in through pursed lips. 'Why so much?'

Rebecca ignored the question. 'I told the young man to convert the seventy-five regular into luxury credits. At the current swap rate, I calculated it converted to fifty luxury credits. Do you know what he said?' She shook her head, eyes staring at her husband. 'You won't believe it. And Harrods of all the places. He had the brazen effrontery to tell me Harrods had introduced a new rate of one-for-one.'

She waited for a reaction. 'Well, haven't you got anything to say?'

'I'm afraid he's right.' He gave her shocked expression a conciliatory smile. 'Even if Harrods are precipitous.'

'You're joking.'

'It's political rather than financial,' he said. 'The powers-that-be sense a groundswell of discontent amongst the population, resentment toward those "haves", like us, if you like, who enjoy benefits the majority do not. Luxury credits are a manifestation of the widening gap.'

'I get all that,' Rebecca said, clipping her words. 'But they exist and yesterday they were worth more than they are today?'

'I can explain?'

'Quickly, and in words of one syllable. None of your financial mumbo-jumbo.' She held out the dress in front of her and sighed with satisfaction. 'I want to show you how it looks on me.'

Jack nodded approvingly. 'The various credits we use as currency were known as cryptocurrencies, like the dealer's note for the once famous Bitcoin your father has framed in his study.'

'One syllable, remember,' she cautioned.

'The credits have a relative value to each other, based on what they can buy and how many have been mined.'

'Mined? Do you dig them up?'

'Mined is the term used: issued if you like.'

Her eyes were casting around the room. She was losing interest.

'To put it simply, the Finance Secretariat has done away with luxury credits as being divisive in the current climate.'

She shrugged. 'If you say so. I still maintain Harrods should give special consideration to those it calls its valued customers.' She draped the dress over her arm with exaggerated care and headed for the bedroom.

Jack returned to his paperwork, briefly punctuated by admiring a few twirls when his wife reappeared to show off her acquisition. He made some positive noises as he watched the impromptu catwalk performance, judging it better to keep quiet than to comment on his calculation that every square ten centimetres of material cost one credit. He must broach the state of their finances with her, and the sooner, the better.

The intercom buzzed.

'That will be Alison,' Rebecca said. 'I suggested she call around about now. We can all go out for dinner.'

'I thought we were eating in.'

Rebecca gave a final twirl and a mock curtsey. 'Too busy, don't you know. That's unless you've rustled up something?'

His daughter was unrecognisable. Gone was the equality dressing code in favour of a one-piece, tailored, knitted dress with a roll collar. Nylon stockings and fashionable mid-heel shoes replaced the calf-length socks and black lace-up boots she preferred. To his amazement, she was wearing make-up.

'This is a surprise on two levels,' Jack said, taking the coat she held folded over her arm and laying it over a chair. 'One, it a surprise you have deigned to visit us and, two, you have, for once, appealed to your feminine side. I approve.'

'A bog-standard male interpretation, but I suppose I should say thanks if there was a compliment somewhere in that remark.' She took in the lounge with a panoramic sweep of the head. 'I'd forgotten what a delightful apartment this is. Jack Tirrand with bourgeois tastes. One thing is missing.'

'What's that?'

'I can't detect the waft of your culinary pièce de résistance, spaghetti Bolognese, so I guess we are dining out.'

'Provided it's on your credits.'

'You're on,' she said as Rebecca walked into the room.

'What have I missed?' Rebecca raised an eyebrow at her daughter.

'Dad suggested I pay for dinner, and I agreed.'

'Don't be silly.' Rebecca said dismissively, looking sternly at Jack. 'Students have no income. Everybody knows that. Your father was kidding.'

'I wasn't.' Jack shuffled some papers into a pile, aligning the corners with care. What was the point? Sending subliminal messages to Rebecca implying restraint, when faced with the largesse of a film festival charity event, was about as effective as trying to turn a screw with a hammer. They would have to have a serious conversation. Even then . . . ? Rebecca's reality treated a life of privilege as an unfailing constant.

'Of course you were,' she said. 'You are escorting a celebrity . . . and her daughter,' she added as an afterthought.

Perhaps the Ying and Yang Oriental Style Eatery would not aspire to Rebecca's idea of a celebrity venue, but the two British chefs who assumed responsibility when their Chinese employers were forced to return to Macau, carried on the tradition with gusto, even down to using make-up and strips of adhesive tape to pull their eyes into oriental slants. The food was a passable imitation of the description on the menu, inexpensive at seven credits for a set meal for three and the atmosphere with most of the tables occupied broaching on the festive.

Jack used the relaxed atmosphere to raise the subject. 'You should know Harriet came to see us yesterday. You know why, so I won't go into it.' He looked over at a distracted Rebecca for solidarity. 'We just hate to see one of our children distressed and disorientated. We all need to play a part in helping her.'

'By all, you mean me?' Alison's tone was measured, in no way argumentative.

'No. I include us all. Her disappointment and resentment are directed at you, but it's unfair. I explained your attitude toward family could well change in the future. You might decide to be with somebody who wants children and, if you went along with her plan, put your happiness at risk.' He took the dessert menu from the waiter and cradled it in his lap. 'Give us a minute, would you?'

Rebecca reached for the menu. 'It all sounds so fattening. I have to fit into my new dress. Do you think tinned pineapple slices in tempura has many calories?'

'Oodles,' Alison said. 'Everything on offer is a dietary hazard. Makes you wonder. All the images I've seen present the Chinese as thin, bordering on emaciated. Suggests our interpretation of what they eat is a far cry from their actual dietary habits.'

Rebecca picked up her wine glass and deliberately placed the menu back on Jack's lap. 'I'll chance it,' she said. 'But just a small scoop of ice cream to go with it.' She smiled at the couple on the neighbouring table, lowering her head as she did so.

'Can we please focus on what I was talking to you both about?' Jack looked from one to the other.

'Okay.' Alison dragged out the word. 'Let's talk about my sister if we must.'

'Let's try not to get heated and exasperated. You've already fallen out with your sister. We must come together as a family and understand each other's position. Harriet faces a crisis and is desperate. Desperate people do crazy things.'

Rebecca shook her head. 'I think she got pregnant on purpose.'

'You do?' Jack's brow creased. 'Do you know that for a fact?'

'Feminine intuition. Her conversation is dominated by talk of children and sadness one of the twins wasn't a boy. Planned it, I shouldn't wonder.' She gave Alison a fleeting smile. 'After all, how many times has she heard you say you have no maternal instincts or desires? Must be dozens.'

The waiter was hovering. 'Give us a few more minutes. We'll let . . '

Rebecca interrupted. 'I'll have the pineapple in tempura batter with a scoop of ice cream and whatever synthetic gunk you use to substitute Chantilly. Anybody else?'

The waiter hesitated.

Jack was about to speak, but Alison beat him to it. 'Bring an extra spoon, will you? I'll steal some of my mother's.' She cast a glance in Jack's direction. 'Dad will pass, I'm sure. Just a small espresso.' She looked at Jack for confirmation. 'That's all, thanks.'

Jack reached under the table to squeeze her hand. 'I see the first step as helping Harriet to treat her predicament without all the heightened emotion, which makes her feel she is alone and we either don't care . .' He stopped and waited while the waiter placed the cutlery on the table. 'Or we are unsympathetic to her aim.'

'What a ridiculous thing to suggest.' Rebecca said. 'Harriet knows we will do everything we can to help her.'

'She certainly feels I'm against her,' Alison acknowledged. 'And, in a way, it's my fault. You're right, I've made such an empiric argument against motherhood so many times in her presence that she came to believe my agreement was a slam dunk.'

'A what?' Rebecca looked askance.

'A fait accompli, if you like.'

'Why do you bang on so much about it?' Jack asked.

A nervous-looking slip of a girl placed the dessert, pineapple rings, in a crisp, brown batter coated with melting ice cream, in the middle of the table. Rebecca pushed it toward Alison, who held up her hand. 'You first, I'll dig in a minute.' She watched her mother clean around the melting ice cream with a spoon. 'If it lasts that long.'

Alison turned to face Jack. 'I've been giving this whole mess some thought. I suppose the answer to your question is I was disappointed in her lifestyle choices, yet, at the same time, jealous of the happiness she appears to find in those choices. It was always my hope we would be two rebels, bucking convention and avoiding the dreaded nine-to-five. We would shun the cosy family option and make our mark on the world together.' She shook her head. 'For me, she took the easy way out, a boring but faithful husband, two children delivered on cue and getting more satisfaction from a soufflé than a soundbite.' Rebecca offered her the dessert plate. 'No thanks, you finish it.'

'You were explaining,' Jack prompted.

'So, I taunted her for letting me down and being so bloody smug and self-satisfied.'

'Hardly her fault.' Jack sipped his coffee. 'She rebelled at your condemnation of motherhood. What do you want out of life?'

'I wish I knew. I can't see myself with kids. The twins are lovely, but they do nothing for me.'

Rebecca put down her spoon. 'I've had better,' she said.

Jack glanced at the empty plate. 'Bit late to complain now.'

Rebecca ignored the jibe. 'And what if Mr Right comes along and sweeps you off your feet and longs for a family? Do you tell him you hate kids?'

'I don't hate kids, Mother. I never said that.'

'Alright, don't bite my head off.'

'I've just never felt maternal. Is that so wrong?'

Jack signalled to the waiter for the AS touchpad. 'Do I take it, as far as Harriet's proposal is concerned, you want to keep your option open? If so, we should both sit down with her and try to end up as friends, whatever the outcome.'

'I would prefer to give it some more thought before we include Harriet. I can't forget she was always there for me whenever I was a needy teenager; got me out of plenty of scrapes. I guess she feels my agreeing to help her would put the account straight. There's no side to her. In her mind, it's a simple case of I did all this for you, now it's your turn.'

Rebecca excused herself and made her way slowly between the tables toward the restrooms.

'Whatever decision you come to, we need to speak with Harriet as soon as possible.' The image of AR escorting her to his car came to mind. 'She is unstable and acting irrationally, clinging to any solution suggested to her. I don't want her doing anything to put her at risk.'

'Is that likely?'

'Possibly. I worried about her after she left last evening.'

Alison gripped his hand with both of hers. 'Here's the thing. I need a few days to think everything through, preferably away from everybody who feels they can influence the outcome. I'll make a deal with you.'

Jack opened his eyes wide. 'Provided it doesn't cost me. Finances are a little tight right now.'

'It won't. Rebecca told me you are off to Germany next week on business. How about I join you? Lectures are finished now for the semester. I'm sure you can arrange a travel pass and I promise I won't get in your hair. Going for some long walks in the country will help to clear my head and put everything into perspective. It's not only Harriet. I need to consider where and if I'm going anywhere with Rolf. Say yes, please.'

Jack said nothing, his eyes closed.

'Well? What about it?'

'Let me think. It's complicated.'

She shook her head. 'I don't want to know all the ins and outs of why and where you're going. Organise a pass for me and drop me off at any big city on the way through. I'll handle the rest. I've got plenty of credits to use for a cheap in-transit hostel, and I'll be back at the train station to meet you for the return journey. Job done.'

His first reaction was to refuse outright; mixing work and family was always a line he didn't cross. But this time, it was different. A refusal would weigh heavily in 'the one-for me, one-for-you' competitive credo his girls had developed over the years. Rebecca's influence, he thought wryly. Alison could blame Harriet for the trait, but she was just as judgemental. And what harm could it possibly do? He asked for a few favours from his position as a deputy. What would be wrong in asking for an additional travel pass? The journey would be long and tedious, and Usher didn't seem like the worldly conversationalist with whom the time would fly by. Having Alison around would, at least, break up the monotony.

'Subject to authorisation and my travelling companion's agreement, I'll go along with it,' he said. 'You'd best clear it with your mother.'

'What's her mother got to clear?' Rebecca asked as she retook her seat. 'Have you settled the bill? I have a thousand things to do.'

'Alison intends to travel through Germany with me, a week away to think over everything.'

'Great,' Rebecca said offhandedly as she smiled back at a diner across the room. 'Shall we go? People are staring at us.'

Alison was tucked up under a duvet in the spare bedroom when Jack knocked and entered.

'I expect I'll say "yes" in the end,' she said. 'Otherwise, I'd almost feel obliged to have two children of my own just to show I wasn't being churlish.'

'You shouldn't look at it that way. The decision is yours and the consequences of that decision must not distort the way you react. What's more, yours is the only voice you should listen to.'

'You're talking about mother?' she said.

'She prefers harmony, which is often the easier option. It's only one piece of the jigsaw. You've got a few days to weigh up the pros and cons.' He tucked her in.

'You do know I'm not a child anymore?'

He laughed. 'Old habits and all that.' They both laughed. 'It's not why I popped in to say goodnight.' He squatted on the end of the bed. 'I was going to mention I was introduced to Chris Hill today. He knows you from Uni and is a definite admirer.' He smiled inwardly as he recalled the young man's adulation.

'Really? I've seen him around. He's been to a few debates. Contributes nothing. I only know of him because he makes sure everyone knows he's a senator's son with privileges when it concerns access to computer equipment and networks which are rarely available to the masses in this so-called equitable society you represent.' A flash of anger came into her eyes.

'Please.' He held his hands together. 'Let's not politicise this conversation.'

'Sorry. His study mates call him "mono" because he's forever going on about his digital skills.'

'Mono?'

'I assume it stands for monotonous. Is there something I should know about him?'

'No, not about him.' Jack weighed up whether he should say what was troubling him. 'He talked about Rolf, implying he is jealous as far as you are concerned. Rolf has warned certain fellow students to stay clear of you. Is he the possessive type?'

'No. It doesn't sound like Rolf.' She hesitated. 'Perhaps, occasionally. He does like to influence what we do as a couple or where we go. It's intermittent, and I put it down to his Teutonic background. He's not demanding. I don't think you call that possessive, do you?'

'Maybe not, but the tendency to control needs watching. It's not healthy in a long-term relationship and often causes serious problems. I've witnessed the consequences first-hand at work, so be careful.'

'One more thing to weigh up while I'm on this retreat next week.'

As she watched the bedroom door close behind him, Alison reached under her pillow for the remains of the sheet of paper Robert had given her to write the telephone number for her mother. A light pencil brushed over the indentation left by Robert's imprint had confirmed the name and address of Dieter Eigard as the subject of the extraction. The trouble was, if she ruled out coincidence, it cast a whole new slant on her relationship with Eigard's son, her boyfriend, Rolf. She could not wait to discover the truth.

# TWENTY

## CAMPO GRANDE – RIO DE JANEIRO STATE

## TOMORROW WORLD

### Late Afternoon – 15 November 2065

There was no breeze to relieve the unseasonable heat. It was spring, but the temperatures were in line with what would be expected in high summer. Ironic, Lance thought. The previous generations spent decades talking of their concerns about environmental conditions, and global warming, but doing little. Look what happened. The actions of determined minorities changed everything in one day. Carbon and methane emissions were severely reduced; the output of petroleum products slowed to a trickle; recycling became holier than religion – yet, what has changed? The world still suffers violent temperature distortions, hurricanes, floods and forest fires. The ice caps are still melting, and Venice is still predicted to vanish like Atlantis within the next fifty years. Looks like the course correction came too late.

Lance watched a group of kids doing dive bombs into the communal pool. Water splattered onto the legs of a woman lying on a lounger. The woman reacted with shock and went to say something to the lad preparing to jump, but smiled instead. Good on you, Lance thought. There wasn't much to enjoy in life for these kids. They were just having some innocent fun.

He picked up a magazine entitled *Hyperledger Chaincodes* and turned to the centrefold where he had hidden the transcript of the satellite phone conversation the previous evening with his German contact, codename FreierMann, regarding the surveillance of Dieter Eigard and the go-between, Mila Kullenberg.

As FreierMann explained his tactics, Lance sensed the led weight of discomfort in the pit of his stomach. It was all so amateurish, like listening to the Boy Scouts of America taking part in a CIA covert mission.

According to FreierMann, his subject kept a low profile, rarely leaving his house in the middle-class suburb of Rottenburg. He relied mainly on the support of social services and the visits of a local woman who came to clean once a week. FreierMann had engaged the woman in casual conversation whilst they waited for a bus. She rarely saw her employer, who stayed in his office, which was out of bounds to her. He left her money in a jar in the kitchen. It suited her that way. He was a 'bit of an oddball', she had confided.

As FreierMann was working on his own, 24/7 surveillance relied on an old-style, battery-operated motion detection camera, hidden in the branches of a tree and trained on the front door with any activity recorded on a micro disk. It didn't exclude the possibility of Eigard leaving the property via the rear garden gate, which led straight into the adjoining park, but FreierMann was certain it was not an exit he used.

Maintaining a watch on Mila Kullenberg had resulted in a different and far less successful outcome. The woman was in her fifties with an active professional and social life, always on the move and spending little time in her one-bedroom condominium apartment in a Stuttgart suburb. FreierMann entrusted surveillance responsibilities to a friend whose commitment and reliability could not be questioned. Like FreierMann, his friend depended on Lance's promise to help change and secure his future.

Regretfully, FreierMann had to admit his friend screwed up. The woman noticed him tailing her and confronted him. She accused him of stalking her with sexual intent, a crime punishable by death, and threatened to report him.

FreierMann was forced to confront the woman as she returned to her parked vehicle late one evening. Hostile and suspicious at first, he explained she was under surveillance because she was seeking safe passage for a colleague. If she went to the authorities, she would put the opportunity to help Eigard in jeopardy.

Her composure restored, she said she never intended to carry out the threat. She even invited the man to attend a group therapy session with her at the Evangelical Centre for the Homeless.

Kullenberg was a first-generation Brazilian, born of German parents who emigrated after the Berlin Wall fell. At age seventeen and two years before eleven/eleven and the chaos that followed, she left Brazil for Germany to finish her education in Heidelberg. Following the inception of INCOL, and the appropriation of land in Brazil to establish Tomorrow World, her parents were relocated to the regional city of Salvador, where her father spent his remaining days in a nursing home. Formerly a pastor in the Lutheran church, he still maintained contact with like-minded friends and acquaintances, some of whom were citizens of Tomorrow World. The family background was influential in her joining the EKD as a practising evangelical and where, over time, she gained the trust of the synod and the Bishop of Baden.

Official contact with her father was restricted to one censored telephone conversation per month. A more private channel was established via a clandestine system of letter exchanges facilitated by a churchgoer who traded regularly in machine parts with merchants in what was the rest of old Brazil, now denominated as a region of INCOL Americas (South).

She and Professor Eigard, as she called him, became friends through the church. He was a devoted Protestant and, although she was aware of his former involvement with ISE, their friendship blossomed. He confided in her. His last assignment before retiring was for CORE, the Committee for Resources Executive, a top-secret project with a report he was working on at the final draft stage. Her assistance as a proofreader and sounding board was invaluable to him. He knew he could trust her.

Suddenly, from one day to the next, he cut her off. Her calls went unanswered; he no longer attended church gatherings; it was so out of character.

Confused at what she could have done to turn him against her, she almost gave up hope of ever seeing him again when he turned up unannounced at her apartment. He was troubled and gave no reason for his absence and failure to communicate, other than it was to safeguard her. He needed help. She once told him she had family in Brazil. Could she reach out to them? He needed a contact to flee the country and seek haven in Tomorrow World. The letter to her father was answered during their monthly telephone call. He told her to be strong and rely on the preachings of the Lord in Ephesians 3:20. She could tell Eigard his plea had been answered. Somebody would be in touch. This contact tonight with FreierMann was the first sign of progress; though she feared it might be too late.

Two weeks ago, she was taken to ISE headquarters in Stuttgart and questioned about her relationship with the Professor. She admitted to helping him with his report and attending the same church. Beyond that, she knew nothing of Eigard or his whereabouts. Nobody mentioned his plan to flee, so, possibly, he either avoided disclosing his intention or kept her name out of a confession. She had not spoken to Eigard since and did not intend to do so.

When Lance quizzed him, FreierMann said he believed her story and her promise not to warn Eigard he was under surveillance. She understood why it had to be.

Lance shuffled the pages back into the centrefold of the magazine. He would shred and burn them later. Doubts lingered. He would like to feel as convinced as FreierMann. The involvement of ISE complicated any extraction. Perhaps the English padre would provide additional information. Lance trusted his agent's judgement. The stakes were high. If Eigard was genuine, he would be an important source of information about this secret CORE project and the workings of the security service. Kullenberg's letter suggested he was a high-level official with access to a great deal of ISE classified data. It was a big gamble. Alternatively, if Eigard was a plant, Lance and the *Adeste Fidelis* operation were finished. ISE hitmen would see to that.

Lance missed having someone like-minded with whom to exchange ideas. True, he had a brother, but Elmer would not have been much help. He regretted the rift that developed between them following their father's death. Would it ever be resolved? Lance hoped so, but his brother remained a stranger, even at their mother's funeral. Lance took the initiative, but Elmer did not respond in kind, replying in one or two syllables, and leaving the wake without warning.

Parallel with the decision on whether to proceed with Eigard's request was the delicate issue of how to resolve the problem posed by Robert Fitzwilliam. The arbitrary introduction of his niece as a prospective replacement was out of character and signalled desperation. They should have discussed the possibility in private, not presented it as a *fait accompli*. The *AF* operation depended upon a small band of helpers around the globe, individuals with religious beliefs, well intentioned but with limited practical experience who were prepared to accept and not question the motives of the candidate seeking asylum. Lance introduced elements of control, scepticism and interrogation into the vetting procedure and, until now, their luck was holding. He sensed things were about to change.

Lance wrestled with the dilemma for the rest of the afternoon, and it was still on his mind in the early evening as he rode his motorcycle into the city. He returned to the lock-up to check for new messages. There was nothing new, so he spent an hour clearing out surplus paperwork, which he shredded and then burned in a portable barbecue.

Bolting and double locking the external door, he turned to stroll along the narrow street toward the sound of laughter and the flashing, intermittent light of the neon signs, advertising the bars and nightclubs in the area known as the *Boca do Lixo*, literally the mouth of garbage. The noise increased, shouting and cheering from the packed bars.

It had slipped his mind. Tonight was the local soccer derby between Flamengo and Botafogo, the two Rio teams vying for leadership of the league. Emotions were running high and everybody's attention was directed at the barrage of oversized screens in a dozen gaudy bars where sex workers mixed with potential clients. Lance decided a drink and ten minutes of soaking up the atmosphere would improve his mood.

He strolled into the shadows of a tarpaulin-clad building under renovation. From out of the darkness, a hand grabbed his arm, forcing him to turn and pressing his face and torso into the plastic curtain. A section parted as he was bundled into an area smelling of wet cement. His legs were kicked apart as the grip on his arm tightened, forcing it upward against his back. The hand on his wrist was large and weathered.

'Jesus, that hurts,' Lance half-spoke, half-cried in Portuguese. 'If it's money you want, try my back pocket.'

Lance was panicking. 'Tell me what you want, for fuck's sake!'

'Speak in English.' The order was spoken in a deep voice with an accent Lance could not place.

'What is this? Who are you?'

'Your name!'

'It's on my identity card. You've got my wallet, only I don't keep my money in it. I told you. It's in my back pocket.'

'I *said*, your name?'

'Lance Franklin Cody,' he said with a resigned sigh. 'Who's asking?'

'Your father's name?' A knee pushed into his thigh.

'What do you want, the family tree?'

'Forget the bravado, just answer the question.'

'He was also Lance, but everybody knew him as Camel.'

The man's mouth was close to Lance's ear. 'Lance Cody Senior published a famous paper following a lecture he gave to the US Marine Corps. What was the subject of that paper?'

Lance forced a laugh. 'Do I win a prize if I tell you?' he quipped.

The knee pressed harder into his thigh. 'The subject?'

'There was a Presidential commendation framed in the living room at home. Dad was proud of that. His paper dealt with Red Teaming against cyberattacks.'

The man turned him and pushed him back out into the street. Lance spun around to face his assailant. The man was a head taller than Lance, easily ten years older, with bleached blond hair and an impressive tan. He held out the muscular arm that had secured Lance minutes earlier, his hand extended. His blue eyes registered no emotion.

'Pleased to have finally made your acquaintance,' he said. 'I've come all the way from Australia to meet you. My name is Ted Hubbard.'

# TWENTY-ONE

## SOUTHBANK SOCIAL CENTRE – IEFI – LONDON

## CHARITY FILM FESTIVAL

### 19.00 - 17 November 2065

Seth was having trouble with his cummerbund. By leaving undone the top two buttons of his dress suit trousers and using a knotted length of string around the button and through the buttonhole, he could secure the trousers around his waist. The cummerbund was necessary to hide the repair, but the damn thing kept moving around, exposing a fold of white flesh between the tail of his shirt and elasticated briefs. To add to his discomfort, Damien was finding the whole exercise amusing.

'If you won't help, piss off,' Seth snarled as he tried to safety pin the cummerbund into place.

'How long is it since you wore a monkey suit? It looks as ancient as the films you're going to watch tonight.'

'It's been a good few years. I didn't think I'd put on so much weight.'

Damien ran a polished fingernail down the satin lapel, flicking away a strand of cotton with his slender index finger. 'This is tailoring from an era long ago,' Damien said with false gravity in his voice. 'The dim and distant past when you could look straight down and see your cock.' He burst out laughing.

Seth gripped his partner's wrist, squeezing hard.

'Ouch, you bully. That hurts.'

It was meant to. Seth was seething inside. Right at that moment, he could forget the wretched Film Festival. He wanted to hurt Damien, make him feel genuine pain before he stripped off and fucked him hard, so hard it hurt. He could feel the erection straining inside his briefs. It was tight against Damien's leg. He tightened his grip on the wrist.

'Stop it, will you?' Damien yanked his hand away, flicking the fringe back off his forehead as he fought to regain his composure. 'Look what you've done!' He displayed a red welt. 'You've become a monster. You don't respect me. Look at the state you're in.' He looked at Seth's crotch and laughed to himself as the thought came into his head. 'If you can keep the hard-on going, which from recent experience is unlikely, it will hold up your trousers.' He gave a derisory laugh and stomped out of the room.

Seth dismissed the urge to chase after him. He was running late. There were more important issues in prospect. He would teach Damien just who was calling the shots when he got back. 'I'll be late,' he called out. 'Don't wait up. I've remembered my key'.

There was no response.

The foyer of the venue on the south bank of the Thames was crowded with guests, the men, most in identical dress suits, many as ill-fitting as Seth's, and their partners, in lavish, attention-seeking, one-night-only creations. As they milled together, the greetings loud and insincere, the conversations exaggerated, the laughter forced and effusive, all but a few strived to catch the eye of the press corps, hoping for a photo or comment in the society pages of tomorrow's editions.

There was a heavy scent of contraband cologne mixed with camphor in the air, Seth detected, wrinkling his nose as he passed a group concentrating on the canapes. As he made a minor adjustment to re-centre his cummerbund, he felt exonerated. It wasn't only his dinner suit hidden away in a wardrobe for years. How many men within a ten-metre radius, he mused, also relied on a piece of string to stop their trousers from collapsing around their ankles? Quite a few, he wagered.

He caught sight of Rebecca standing with a group of charity trustees welcoming newcomers as the cameras clicked around them. She was positioned alongside a small, portly man who was hanging on her every word. Brilliant, Seth thought. Choose a victim to engage in conversation who will not upstage you. As if in response, Rebecca peeled away from the man as a photographer beckoned her to pose on the red carpet. Almost elbowing the smaller man as she swung around, she adopted a stance Seth associated with a statue of Aphrodite, one arm raised with her hand caressing the nape of her neck, the other, holding the stem of a wine glass with her arm modestly shielding her ample breast. 'Like this?' she moaned, as if in pain.

Seth caught her eye as the photographer moved on. 'Rebecca,' he said. 'So glad to see you.'

She looked askew at him. 'Don't tell me.' She hesitated. 'It's Seth, isn't it?' She waved a finger across his outstretched hand and pointed at his dinner suit. 'I thought all journalists walked around in dirty raincoats with the collars turned up.'

'I've got several of them I can wear if it makes you feel more comfortable.'

She twitched a smile. 'Now, I remember,' she said. 'You wanted to do an interview, wasn't it? It slipped my mind, what with all the charity work for this event.'

'If you haven't got the time, we can . . .'

He did not finish. 'Of course not,' she said. 'A deal is a deal, and I am a woman of my word.' She felt for a watch on his arm, pushing up the starched cuff and reading the dial. 'There's forty minutes before the programme starts. Better get on with it. There's a meeting room on the first floor we can use. Where's your photographer?'

'I have an arrangement with the official photographer here tonight,' he lied. 'I just saw him take your picture.'

Ten minutes of question and answer on the aspirations of the charity were what neither wanted, but the charade was played out with all the sound bites needed to fill a few column inches of newsprint.

Plied with a series of understated compliments, a technique Seth used with frequent success, Rebecca relaxed as he took control of the interview. This is going to be a walk in the park, he thought to himself.

Deftly changing the subject, he asked questions about her upbringing, family, childhood friendships, and adolescent relationships. At first, she answered by leaning forward, her eyes taking in the small black recorder he placed on the table between them. As her self-assurance and inbred arrogance came to the fore, she sat back in her chair, a coquettish smile on her face, half-turned toward him. Journalistic instinct told him when he had gained sufficient trust to broach the storyline he intended to feature.

He called a brief halt to leave the room to arrange a fresh chalice of gin tonic, which she willingly took, sipped from, and nestled between the palms of her hands.

'Our readers will be interested in the relationship you have with your husband. How does a deputy's wife manage both a family and a professional life? No simple task, I would imagine?'

She beamed at the implied compliment. 'Absolutely, Seth. Family chores aside, we try to entertain as much as possible. I am always there to support Jack. You know what they say, behind every successful man etcetera.'

'How did you two come to meet?'

'Gosh, all those years ago. We were both at Warwick University. I was one of the first INCOL intake student groups. Jack was already there, approaching his final year.'

'Love at first sight?'

'Hardly. We came from vastly different family backgrounds. Jack is mixed race. Don't print this, but I thought him uncouth at first.'

'Really?'

'True, but then, I heard him give a talk at a debating society meeting on social justice within a controlled society. He was a powerful speaker; quite swept me off my feet.'

'You talk about his family background. I can't find out much about him before university. What are his roots?'

'It's not something he relishes talking about. As far as I know, his father worked overseas for the Foreign Office. There was an accident on a German autobahn. Jack was travelling in the back of the car and was lucky to survive. Both his parents died. There were no relatives in the UK, so he ended up in a foster home. Beyond that, you will need to speak with him.' She took a draught from the chalice. 'I thought this interview was about me. All we've talked about so far is the charity and Jack.' She gave him an uncomfortable smile.

'Just background info.' He would have to back off for a while or risk losing her cooperation.

After ten minutes of idle conversation about her youth and development, likes and dislikes and social tittle-tattle, he forced himself to stifle a yawn. He was losing patience.

'Do you consider you have a good marriage, based on trust?' he asked.

'What a ridiculous question,' she retorted with a half-laugh. 'We have a wonderful marriage and two lovely girls, twins, who are making their mark on the world.'

'Of course, goes without saying. No, I simply mean, well, let's face it, you are two high-powered individuals in the public eye. Do you ever get the opposite sex interested in you, trying to chat you up? You know what I mean: a mature woman, who knows the ropes, attractive to the younger man. You *are* not going to tell me no one has ever tried it on?'

She studied her shoes, cheeks flushed. 'I won't say there hasn't been the odd suggestion or a little flirting. Some mature men find me attractive.' She paused. 'But it's all harmless fun. I make sure of that.'

'What about Jack? Does he get propositioned? He's not unattractive.'

She looked at Seth as if he had just stepped off an alien spacecraft and laughed. 'Good Lord! The only competition I face for his attention is his infatuation with his work.'

'Does he ever bring his work home?' He widened his eyes as he asked the question.

'What is that supposed to mean?' Her brow creased. 'Aren't you wandering off script with all this?'

*Coup de grâce*, he thought. Time to strike. 'The readers like a little titillation. It enhances the allure of your appeal in their eyes, a woman of the world who has seen it all.'

She appeared to accept the explanation. 'He brings homework occasionally,' she advanced, cautiously.

'No, I mean in the flesh; like the Kahn woman who instigated that set-to at the Monday meeting. She was in your apartment afterwards for a couple of hours.'

He put on his innocent smile. Give her credit. The old cow was making a good fist of pretending she knew.

'Jack has regular meetings with fellow deputies all the time. This meeting you refer to was nothing out of the ordinary.'

'You must have thought it was tactless, inviting a single woman into the apartment when you were not there?'

She pushed the empty chalice across the table. 'I don't see the relevance of this line of questioning.' She pulled his arm toward her. 'It's time for the programme to start. I suggest we call it a day.'

Her cheeks were crimson, lips pressed tightly together. She steadied herself as she rose, sending the chalice spinning across the table. He reached for the recorder. 'Where do you get all this random information?' she countered. 'Anybody would think we are under surveillance. There are people in and out of the apartment all the time. We are a busy household. You must have noticed that?'

'Just one more thing.' He held her gaze. 'Just between the two of us, what would you do if you discovered your husband was unfaithful?'

She staggered as she stood. 'Getting up too quickly mixed with that gin you made me drink; I feel quite lightheaded.' There were beads of perspiration on her neck.

'I'm not suggesting he has been,' Seth prompted.

She pressed the back of her hand against her cheek. 'I'd chop off his balls and feed them to the dogs.'

# TWENTY-TWO

## SOUTHBANK SOCIAL CENTRE –IEFI-LONDON

## CHARITY FILM FESTIVAL

### 20.30 - 17 November 2065

Guests were making their way to the auditorium where a line-up of the great and good was assembled to welcome the visitors. Already regretting her final indiscretion, Rebecca parted company with Seth, insisting her phraseology was for his consumption only and, on no account, could be on the record.

Her attention was now directed to joining the welcoming committee of charity trustees. At the front of the group were two political appointees who rarely appeared other than at social events. She picked on the next in line, the Society treasurer, whispered a question about today's receipts in his ear, and squeezed in front of him.

Although he had no intention of spending three precious hours watching a Hitchcock classic made over a century ago, Seth moved down the line, touching hands and muttering as he progressed. He made a mental note of those names he could drop into a cameo piece he was thinking of doing as a follow-up to his forthcoming exclusive on Jack Tirrand. It might be valuable to get a few quotes – *I could never have believed it of him – His poor wife. She does so much for the charity*. His flight into fancy came to an abrupt halt when he saw he was about to shake the hand of Simeon Hill. His senses came alive. It wasn't Hill's practised smile, the gentle nod of the head or the assured way he thanked the guest for coming; it was the fact that on the wrist of the person next in line was an item of jewellery he immediately recognised.

'Good evening, Mrs Hill,' he said. 'So rewarding to have met you at last. Seth Llewellyn Morgan, with the *Capital Review*. Would you have a quote for us?'

Her hand was clad in a tight-fitting, white silk, wrist-length glove, fingers together pointing downward. She was someone who didn't like the common touch, he calculated, unsure of whether she expected him to shake her hand or bow and kiss it.

She stared through him, ignoring the question.

Seth recognised the distant look in her eyes, the fixed smile, her attention to the present no more than somebody going through the motions. From long ago, he recalled people with that same disassociation from the here and now, refugees reliving the atrocities they had witnessed, faces recalling the remains of a home in ruins or witnessing the still body of a loved one. It wasn't fear or sadness, but the look of someone when desperation has turned to resignation.

He held her fingers, pulling her hand gently toward him to study the gold band securing the glove around her wrist. The piece was studied with large squares of a dark blue stone he guessed were sapphires set into the bracelet and secured by a delicate filigree of silver. It was a one-off and figured in the photograph assembled for the Jack Tirrand exclusive. The shot of the farewell hug they exchanged outside his apartment building illustrated the bracelet. The enlarged inset enhanced the detail. There could be no mistake.

He released her hand, returned the waxen smile and moved on, looking for the opportunity to turn around and find an exit.

'Guest or Press?' the usher asked.

'Press.'

'Follow me.' The man led Seth toward the front of the auditorium. 'Row two, on the left,' he pointed.

Seth was too wrapped up in his good fortune to object. He might as well stay for the first half of the programme. No point in getting home too early and ending up in another bitching contest with Damien. He sat back in his seat. What a night! Not only had Rebecca provided a quote to headline the article, but he could also now identify – hint at, might be safer legally – the mystery woman who visited Jack, the ladies' man.

To his surprise, Seth enjoyed the film: a good plot, fine acting and a remastered version of commendable quality. Earlier events left him in a positive mood. He would stay past the interval and catch the second half of the film. There was a buffet reception to follow and a charity auction of a variety of timeless cinema keepsakes. It could be fun.

Holding up a complimentary glass of what passed as bubbly, Seth toasted a fellow journalist sitting at the end of the interval bar. The ostentatious gesture was too much for the string holding up his trousers to withstand. As if in slow motion, the string separated from the waistband, the cummerbund loosened, and exposed at first, his briefs with the printed red hearts and then, as the trousers bunched around his knees, an expanse of pale white flesh. In desperation, he opened his legs wide to secure the trousers before they ended up around his ankles.

The bar was filling. The more tactful pretended not to notice; others surreptitiously pointed and giggled; some laughed openly. His glass fell to the floor, shattering and attracting even more attention. Seth fished desperately to grasp the two ends of the waistband, yanking them together and forcing the trousers up in a movement that pushed the cummerbund toward his chest like an external brassiere. His antics now became the focal point of the bar, an interval spectacle performed by an embarrassed and impromptu participant.

With both hands grasping the ends of the waistband and using his chin to push the cummerbund down to its rightful position, he stumbled toward the exit, the crowd parting before him as he advanced. 'Looks like a dinosaur on the charge,' he heard someone say as he shouldered his way forward.

Straining for breath and perspiring, his face cardiac-arrest red, he made it to the sanctity of the gents, locking the stool door behind him. Struggling with the cummerbund, he used it as a makeshift belt to tighten around the waistband. It was the best he could do, but far from perfect. The second part of the film was just starting as he made his way through the deserted foyer to the exit, hands in trouser pockets as an extra precaution against another unscripted accident. The plethora of emotions he experienced in the last thirty minutes condensed into a terrible rage inside him, a rage directed at his partner. Had Damien the sensitivity to help him get ready and not stand there poking fun at him, Seth would not have experienced the discomfort and embarrassment to which he had been subjected. It was all Damien's fault and Seth would damn well make him pay, the unfeeling and inconsiderate bastard.

The collective dropped him at the entrance to Chelsea Harbour, the remaining three passengers smiling politely as he struggled to leave the vehicle. He shuffled along the pavement in short steps, his hands still wedged into the trouser pockets. The apartment was in darkness. He fumbled for his keys. No point in sounding the entry buzzer. He expected Damien to be out, flirting in some underground club with his grubby friends.

Once inside, he breathed out with a grunt, pulled off the cummerbund, and kicked off his shoes and trousers. Clad in a dinner jacket over a perspiration-stained shirt, briefs and woollen socks, he made for the kitchen to pour himself a stiff drink. He frowned at the sight of the two half-full gin tonic glasses on the work surface.

The noise stopped him in his tracks. It was unmistakable. Seth crept along the corridor to the master bedroom. The volume increased. Damien was moaning, moaning the way he once moaned with Seth, the sound of sexual fulfilment. He stood outside the closed door and listened. An icy calm came over him; a decision taken out of his hands. His hand nestled on the door handle.

'Come on, you bitch! Harder!' The sound of hands clapping on bare flesh. 'Again. Harder!' Damien was hissing instructions. 'I love it. I love what you do to me!'

Seth inched open the door. Damien was lying face down on the bed. Damn it! On their bed, the bed they shared, the bed on which they pledged their commitment, one to the other. The other man was kneeling astride him, supported by both outstretched hands on the mattress, his pale white, pimpled back tinged with perspiration. Seth crept nearer, neither man registering his presence.

With one stride, Seth was at the foot of the bed. He lunged forward, grabbing a tuft of curly blond hair and yanking the kneeling man backwards off the bed. The sound of the man's penis exiting Damien's body was like a plunger unblocking a sink. It caused Seth to smile amidst the anger. The man fell, spread-eagled on the floor, his face a mask of fear.

'What the fuck are you doing?' Damien was still face down, unaware of Seth's presence.

Seth reached for the nearest thing he could use as a weapon, a braided cord lying on the bed, used for securing one arm to the slatted rungs of the bedhead. He flayed the cord several times across Damien's back. A jagged red welt stood out against his porcelain white skin. Damien yelped, as much in surprise as in pain, and wheeled over, whimpering and bellowing as he did so.

The blond-haired man scrambled to his feet, rummaging for the clothes lying scattered across the floor. Seth recognised him as the neighbourhood security guard who patrolled the complex at night. How long had these sexual liaisons been going on? Seth could only imagine.

'Look what you've done to me, you bitch. I'll bleed to death.' Damien was attempting to study his back in the full-length mirror. 'I'll sue you.'

'No, you won't and there's no blood. Not yet.' Seth wheeled around to confront the security guard who, half-dressed, was making for the bedroom door.

'I know who you are,' Seth said. 'I'll have a word with your employer. Don't worry, you shouldn't find it too difficult getting another job.'

The man stopped in his tracks. 'Please, Guvnor, don't say nothing. I've got a family to support. It's him. He won't leave me alone. He found me asleep one night during a shift. Told me unless I did what he asked, he'd shop me. He's sex mad. Wish I'd told him to do his damnedest. He's all yours.' The words tumbled out in a torrent.

Seth appraised the man cowering by the door. He was in his mid-thirties, around Damien's age, with slack cheeks, downcast eyes, and a weak face. He was going to fat. His blond hair was wispy, thinning on the crown. Damien wasn't as fussy as he once was. He must be desperate and losing his charisma if he was settling for someone as common as this pathetic individual.

The man's eyes were pleading. 'Piss off and don't show your face here again.' Seth slammed the door behind him.

Damien sat back in bed, knees bent, a top sheet pulled up over his naked body. His expression said he had recovered the cocksure composure, the fragile arrogance necessary to mask his apprehension. 'What are you doing back?' A crooked smile split his face. 'Embarrass yourself looking like that in front of everybody, did you?'

Seth took a step toward the bed, his arm raised. Damien pulled back, his knees now under his chin.

'You little prick! I should have told you to bugger off months ago. That's it. Pack your things and get out.' Seth hovered over the bed, his fists clenched so tight his knuckles turned white.

'Ooh, listen to him. Who do you think you are? Nothing more than a fat, middle-aged has-been who can't get it up any more without those little blue pills. Don't think I haven't seen you trying to hide them.' Damien stood up, pulling the sheet around his waist and legs. 'As for leaving, I think you've lost the plot, Mr Limp Dick. I know your memory is failing, but let me remind you that this place was paid for by me and I have a letter signed by you to record the fact. So, I suggest it's you who does the packing and buggers off while I find someone who appreciates me.'

Seth glanced at the defiant expression on Damien's face, took a step forward, and slapped the man across the cheek with all the strength he could muster. Blood spurted from Damien's nose as he sobbed.

Seth's tone was ice cold. 'We'll see who is leaving and who's staying, my cheating little bum-boy. Rely on me. I'll ensure you get some suitable accommodation at the State's expense; somewhere you'll find plenty of willing partners.'

# TWENTY-THREE

## ALEXANDRA PALACE – LONDON

## 11.00 - 18 November 2065

Few delegates braved the blustery showers and north-easterly wind chill to make it into the Palace on a Saturday morning. For Jack, it was the preferred day to catch up on the never-ending stream of bureaucracy without the workday interruptions and the opportunity to avoid AR and his band of allies.

But today was special. For the first time in three years, he would miss next Monday's meeting. Jack's stand-in was Les Hawkins, a trusted colleague whom he knew would not let him down, provided the groundwork was sufficiently prepared.

Jack was just writing a note to leave with the completed dossier when his phone extension rang.

'Jack, is that you?' The male voice was strained, high-pitched.

'Who is this?'

'Who do you think it is? It's Mac. I've been trying to get hold of you for ages. I booked this call three hours ago.' He sounded out of control. 'What is it with these people?'

'Calm down. Has something happened? Harriet? The girls?'

'No. Nothing like that. Was Harriet coming around to your place this morning? She's just disappeared.'

'Not as far as I know. I'll be home within the next half hour. What has happened?'

'She's been acting out of character since she got back from seeing you. She kept denying there was anything. We usually lie in on Saturdays, and let the kids play around in the bedroom. Not today. She was up and dressed by seven. I'd just woken up. A car hooted outside, and she was off. I thought it must be you,'

'It wasn't. She didn't say where and with whom she was going?'

'Just told me to look after the kids for a few hours and everything would be alright. Whatever that means. That was five hours ago and not a word since. Do you know where she'd be?'

Jack had a good idea, but he wasn't about to say. 'Everything is bound to be alright. Perhaps she just wants to surprise you. We should give her a little longer before you start to worry, don't you think?'

There was tut-tutting on the line, Mac's temper frayed. 'What could it be about other than this wretched house business? She's convinced we are going to lose the place. There's a problem with someone in the chain.' He hesitated. 'Truth is, I don't even know whether I want to go to Exeter. It's not exactly a step up in my career.'

Jack smiled to himself – more a wry grin had he looked in the mirror. Nobody who knew him would ever accuse Mac of being ambitious or career-minded. The description 'laid back' came to mind, a synonym for 'plain lazy' as far as Rebecca was concerned. She had little time for Mac, readily irritated by his habit of looking on as Harriet took up the domestic slack. Get off your backside and do this or that, Rebecca would say in the early days. Take your head out of that book and help with the girls as the family grew. Whether it was Mac's attitude to life or her daughter's apparent acceptance of his lifestyle, which antagonised her most, Rebecca's opinion never faltered. 'I can't see what Harriet sees in him,' she confessed. 'I'm surprised he even found the energy to impregnate her', after one particularly testy set-to with him. 'The man is a piece of flotsam.'

Jack didn't see it like that. Mac was one of the disenchanted, disinterested in what the world had become compared to what it was before. He came alive, his heavy-set eyes gleaming, his conversation animated, whenever the topic was pre-eleven/eleven history, space exploration, engineering achievements, cars and the now-banned world of motor racing. Personal relationships he took for granted. They just existed; not something you needed to work at.

'I've been looking after the girls all morning,' Mac continued when there was no reaction to his last comment. 'They're in a foul mood. Why would she go off without telling me? It's inconsiderate.'

Jack needed to choose his words carefully. 'A colleague from work called in to see me whilst Harriet was at the apartment. She mentioned your housing problem, and he suggested he might be able to help. She may have followed up on his offer.'

'But shooting off without saying anything? It's so unlike her.'

'Maybe she didn't want to raise false hopes.'

Mac was unconvinced. The call ended with Jack's promise to look further into Harriet's absence when he got home.

As nonplussed as he sounded on the phone, Jack was concerned. If Harriet had gone off with AR, which was the likeliest explanation, this was no act of kindness. AR was after information, and he believed Harriet could supply it. The question was, what information and to what end? True, AR faced a complaint from Kahn which Jack was supporting with his request to Simeon. But it was just moral support. He did not witness the alleged assault, and the likelihood was the incident would be dismissed with a few soothing words from Simeon some months down the road when other forces were in play and recollections of misdeeds could be challenged as misunderstandings.

No, it was for some other reason. If AR was being true to form, he wanted to discredit Jack in the eyes of those in power. But why? Jack had no idea.

On his way out, Jack detoured via the administrative offices to pick up Alison's travel pass and subsistence vouchers. As always, the television in reception was on and broadcasting an all-areas alert from INCOL Asia to vessels in the South Atlantic. For the first time, they were offering a reward of a hundred thousand credits for any information leading to the seizure of the vessel and the apprehension of Ted Hubbard, a lone sailor believed to be heading towards South America.

Wow, they desperately want him, Jack said to himself. He must have some priceless information to be worth twenty years' salary to the average person on the street. Reference to the South Atlantic suggested Hubbard was intent on reaching Tomorrow World. If he succeeded, they would have the devil's own job trying to locate him.

# TWENTY-FOUR

## BARRA DA TIJUCA – RIO – TOMORROW WORLD

### 08.00 Local Time – 18 November 2065

It was the morning of the third day since Ted Hubbard's unexpected appearance and it was a case of so far, so good. For any new escapee arrival, the first forty-eight hours were the most critical, when he or she was most vulnerable to capture and deportation. Once integrated into the local population, the task faced by the authorities became increasingly more complicated.

No way was it lost on Lance that this was no standard induction and transformation from escapee into a new identity as a member of the TW community. Hubbard was his highest profile fugitive, with an astronomical price on his head. The Chinese would calculate he had either arrived or drowned trying and act accordingly.

His story had enthralled Lance, who was eager to know every last detail.

As he approached the eastern seaboard of South America, Hubbard calculated a flotilla of craft, big and small, would be lying off the coast, patrolling the waters along the TW shoreline, waiting for him to appear. His plan involved plotting a course seaward until he was off the coast of Santos. When dusk fell, he would make a dash for the shore using both motor and sail power, as well as employing his modified software for the Swedish Astro IV system to manipulate and jam contemporary radar signals. With any luck, he could create enough confusion and fake positioning to end up on a deserted beach by dawn. It could have all gone wrong, and it almost did.

On the last afternoon, before putting his plan into action, he allowed himself to sleep whilst strapped to the tiller. He would need all his energy for the hours to come as dusk approached.

He awoke with a start as the swell from another vessel tipped the hull and sent him careering sideways across the deck until his body jerked against the pull of the rope securing him. A fishing trawler was fast approaching from the leeward, preparing to ram the yacht. Regaining his feet and working on instinct, he tacked into the wind and headed across the path of the incoming vessel. The yacht was inches from safety when the trawler's bow clipped the stern and wrenched a tear in the fibreglass structure.

The yacht took on water. Luckily, the wind strengthened, and at full sail, he could outrun the trawler under normal circumstances, but the constant attention needed to bail out the excess water meant he could not concentrate on extending the distance between the two vessels.

Hubbard guessed from the outset there would be a hefty reward on offer for his capture. It was a calculated risk the captain of the trawler would maintain radio silence until his chance of a pot of gold was lost on the horizon. Once that became a reality, the radio waves would be buzzing and the INCOL Americas' protection detail alerted to his approximate position. His radar jamming system needed to do its job.

Under cover of darkness, he took a northerly course, parallel to the coastline and away from the chasing vessel. His calculations showed the yacht would still be several miles from land by the time daylight came and it was visible. Also, his diversionary tactics meant he had veered off course and was now much closer to Santos than intended.

As light from the sun heralded a new day, Hubbard decided to scuttle the yacht, don his wetsuit and use the rubber dinghy to make his way inshore. There was now constant radio chatter in a language he did not understand and possibly a hundred vessels out looking for him.

Coming on shore with people about was dangerous, but it was his one chance. His hope was the search would be concentrated on a deserted stretch of shoreline shown on the old Brazil map as an ecologically protected area. Nobody would expect him to come out of the sea onto a crowded beach. Luck was on his side.

As he turned the headland, he could see the sea washing onto the distant beach of Praia Grande, a handful of surfers riding the waves, but no craft patrolling the bay.

Three hundred metres from shore he punctured the dinghy, which, with the weight of the outboard motor, sank below the surface. Shouldering a knapsack filled with critical possessions, he lay on his treasured surfboard and paddled toward the shallows. Like the others now around him, he made a valiant attempt to stand as the wave surged beneath him, fell and clambered onto the sand, just another surfer vanquished by the sea, ready to return on another day.

The rest was easy. He stole a T-shirt and shorts from one of the many beach stalls and raised enough Incos for a coach ride to Rio by bartering a watch in a bar with a drunken Swedish electrical engineer with whom he struck up a casual conversation. Hubbard used the coordinates fixed from his satellite exchanges with Lance to set the approximate position of the transmission location. It was then just a question of hanging around and waiting for Lance to appear.

From the moment the two men met, Lance worked on a blueprint to ensure the new arrival could be assimilated seamlessly into the workplace. Whilst the ruling Senate in Tomorrow World was a far more benign body than its INCOL counterparts around the globe, there were clandestine groups infiltrated into the territory to deal with dissenters and activists who were considered a threat. Assassinations were rare, but kidnappings and unexplained disappearances were becoming more common as public confidence in the territory grew, natural leaders came to the fore and voices called for a return to the re-establishment of democratic institutions. Lance was in no doubt the attentions of these groups of infiltrated enforcers would now be stimulated by the offer of a reward and concentrated on locating and silencing Hubbard. There was no time to lose.

Petropolis Palace is an aparthotel complex set four blocks back from Leblon Beach, comprising three high-rise buildings overlooking the Atlantic to the front and the *Rodrigo de Freitas* Lagoon to the rear. Constructed in the 1980s, the properties had suffered the ravages of heavy tourist traffic for the first forty years and neglect and insufficient maintenance during the ensuing forty-five years.

Unable to raise the resources to refurbish the properties, the owners formed a cooperative to sell off the apartments on the first four floors of each block. The sale agreements obliged the new owners to renovate every apartment to a pre-agreed standard in exchange for a right of occupation outside of the three-month summer season plus a share of the rental income from the management company's operation of short-term lets to the home-grown tourist industry in TW.

For Lance Cody Senior and his small group of co-conspirators, it was an attractive option. He purchased a ground-floor two-bedroom condo and, using a bogus tour operator as a front, signed a five-year contract with the management company to use the unit for holiday lets. Cody now exercised total control over an apartment in a complex with a fluid and intermittent residential population where faces changed at regular intervals without attracting attention and his escapees could hide in plain sight.

Hubbard was smuggled in during the night and Lance set about changing the Australian's appearance using skills he had gained over the years.

To adopt the persona of a clean-cut, troubleshooting, Blockchain consultant visiting from the States, the first step was to remove ten weeks' worth of facial hair and convert those sun-bleached, long blond locks into a nondescript dark brown crew cut which, to Hubbard's amazement, Lance undertook with tonsorial proficiency. Contact lenses to change eye colouring and a distinguishing mole on sallow cheeks completed a mini-transformation Hubbard would enhance over the coming weeks with designer stubble and full sideburns. For the intervening period, identity photographs showed a man in his late thirties with a Latin look, sufficiently distant from the wholesome Aussie image of the man who arrived.

Establishing a new persona was a more detailed operation involving collaboration from outside TW. Lance planned the subtle changes to Hubbard's face and hair as an approximate likeness to a former colleague, Ron Coleman, once a specialist crypto investigator who was now seconded as a nurse in a secure psychiatric facility in San Diego.

From encrypted exchanges with his contact in Melbourne, Lance knew if Hubbard made it to TW, he would need a watertight and verifiable background history to escape the clandestine manhunt the Chinese were bound to mount. Hubbard possessed first hand knowledge of the iron fist wielded by the occupiers in Australia and exposing the information would be severely damaging to the image China wanted to portray of its colonial ambitions.

The US and its allies employed tactical nuclear weapons following eleven/eleven, but the aftermath left uninhabitable large tracts of the Korean Peninsula, along with vast swathes of land in the northeastern Chinese provinces of Liaoning and Jilin. Within days, the Chinese military responded, treating the infringement of its territory as a green light to employ its might in overrunning Taiwan, parts of Southeast Asia, and a three-pronged attack on Australasia. Within fourteen days, the initial conquest was complete, leaving the West no option but to look on if it wanted to avoid enlarging the conflict.

In anticipation of Hubbard's arrival, Lance convinced the administration at Campo Grande that his section required the temporary support of an experienced crypto investigator for up to a year. The administrators were little more than pen pushers in Lance's eyes, with little or no technical expertise, and agreeing to his request was a mere formality. The requisition submitted to TW vetting in New York named Ron Coleman as the preferred candidate and the period stipulated as a minimum of twelve months.

There was one weekly flight to TW from the hub in Atlanta, direct to São Paulo. Most of the passengers were visiting dignitaries from around the world, supervisory or audit teams or, as with Coleman, specialist consultants on time-limited appointments. Vetting was thorough and intrusive no matter the status of the visitor and a rejection neither required justification nor was it subject to appeal.

Approval for Coleman's secondment was agreed upon and scheduled to start as soon as Campo Grande gave the go-ahead for him to travel. He had arrived the previous day, and Lance travelled to São Paulo to meet him. That night, they stayed in a safe house in the sprawling suburbs of the city, venturing out only to a neighbourhood restaurant where they could dine undisturbed. Over a local brandy, Lance explained there would need to be a change of plan.

Instead of exchanging his identity documents and personal history chip for a forged set to begin a new life on America's West Coast with a curriculum expanding his leisure time passion as a landscape gardener, Coleman was asked to fulfil another role.

'I'm worried about our operation in the United Kingdom,' Lance told him. 'We have a good man whose status appears to be under threat. He is keen to get away. I'd like you to take his place. He has suggested a candidate, but I'm not enthusiastic. I'll tell you why.'

Coleman listened as Lance explained the circumstances and strategy. He needed little convincing. The idea of a new start in another part of the world was a dream come true. Nursing the mentally sick was a laudable task, but Coleman yearned for a life in the open air, to steep himself in the natural world.

'I have documents and a history chip prepared in the name of David Jackson. He died shortly after birth thirty-four years ago. We've hacked into the system and deleted the record. Your chip shows his progress into adulthood and his career as a horticulturist. You should have no problem embedding yourself into the INCOL environmental control workforce with the write-up I've given you.' Lance laughed. He could tell the proposal would be no hard sell.

'You can stay with a colleague in Santos for two days until you sail on a refrigerated cargo vessel across to Portsmouth. I've worked with the ship's captain before. He knows the drill for getting you on and off. You will arrive early in December. Plenty of time to work on your English accent.' Lance smiled at the expression on the other man's face.

'You planned this?' Coleman looked over a pair of thin-rimmed glasses. 'You have no intention of taking no for an answer, do you?'

'I figured you might not be averse to a change of scenery. I hear San Diego's not what it used to be.'

They parted with a hug. The resurrected David Jackson would be met on arrival by Lance's UK contact. 'He's a man of the cloth,' Lance said. 'And he is running scared. You can expect to be hurried, but don't run before you can walk. Let me know what you think of his niece. He suggested she take his place, but I need your experience. Don't take any unnecessary risks.'

The following day, Hubbard left the Petropolis Palace to travel the fifty kilometres to Campo Grande and the BC Complex. In the guise of Ron Coleman, he was introduced around the workplace to Lance's team and settled into an office next to Lance. Two days working in the apartment on his accent and Manhattan geography were not wasted. People were curious to know what was going on in the States since they had left, and Coleman did well to avoid any pitfalls as he dealt skilfully with the various enquiries in as general terms as possible.

As the new Ron Coleman was being introduced to his workmates, back in the Santa Amarta favela in Botafogo, a forger was working to substitute a photograph on Coleman's original identity document. It was a rush job. He stood back and admired the finished article. His long-time client would collect it this evening, the price, double his normal fee. The money would go toward his son's private education.

It was a spur-of-the-moment decision to pass by the lock-up in Rio once the deal with the forger had been completed. It was still daylight when Lance and Hubbard strolled through the hillside slum dwellings to where they left the motor scooter chained to the railings.

Lance had avoided a dinner invitation from the BC Human Resources director and his wife to welcome Coleman, which would undoubtedly have involved a friendly grilling of the new arrival's personal history. Better left for another day when the new Coleman had adapted to his surroundings and could confidently converse about his background. Besides, there was still something about Hubbard's escape which troubled Lance, and the chance to talk in private was opportune.

'Damn,' Lance said as he disengaged the alarm and noticed the flashing blue LED light on the black box alongside the keypad. 'There have been six unscheduled, missed satellite calls. I'm guessing the UK. Something has gone wrong.' He booted up the system and checked the log. 'Right on. It's our wayward padre. Let's see what he wants.' He sounded more upbeat than he felt.

The connection was instant. Robert's voice was full of apprehension and apology. Did Lance recall their conversation suggesting his niece, Alison, as a substitute should he be compromised? Lance did not feel his confirmation was necessary.

'When I discovered who was to be your next subject, I realised, either by an extraordinary coincidence or some complex design, my niece has an intimate relationship with a member of this person's family.' He waited for Lance to react, but there was silence. 'I have now learned she may have decided to demonstrate her ability to be of assistance to us without consulting me.'

'What does that mean?'

'I think she may try to meet with the person under some pretext?'

'Why would she do that?' Although seething inside at the man's naivety, Lance kept the tone of his voice inquisitive but calm.

173

'To gain their trust.' Robert lowered his voice as if wary of being overheard. 'Talking in this roundabout way makes it difficult to be specific.'

'I agree. Just explain why you expect her to establish contact.'

'I'm not one hundred per cent, as I haven't been able to reach her. My understanding is that she is taking time off from her normal routine to vacation in the area we associate with this individual.'

Lance exhaled slowly; his brow creased as he looked over at Hubbard, who was intrigued by the roundabout exchange. 'I'll speak with my contact in the region,' Lance said. 'If you get in touch with her, insist she desists and gets the hell out of there. She could compromise everything.'

'I'll do . . .' Lance ended the call before Robert had time to answer. He shook his head.

Hubbard broke into a grin. 'What is this Big Foot, Wet Feet business you call each other? Sounds like kids at play.'

The other man's intense stare immediately stilled the humour. 'In a way, it's just that,' Lance acknowledged. 'And it troubles me. We are a motley collection of well-intentioned, best-endeavour amateurs functioning in a world of ruthless control and oppression. We need to operate like an efficient guerilla force, not a bunch of idealists and their relatives doing their own thing like kids in some adventure novel.'

'You want to talk about it?'

Without mentioning names or locations, Lance gave a sanitised explanation of the problem.

'If there's anything I can do to help,' Hubbard said. 'Just ask.'

'Your time is best spent working your way in as quickly as possible to the Coleman profile, so much so that it feels a part of you. Let me worry about my issues.'

Hubbard clapped the other man on the shoulder. 'Don't concern yourself. I didn't survive a ten-week voyage, living every day on the edge of my nerves, fearing capture and the consequences, just to screw it up now I'm here. I dreamed about this place. I won't let either of us down.'

'While we are on the subject, I need to ask you something that's been on my mind.' Lance sat facing Hubbard. 'I get all the hype around you being the first to flee from Chinese control and, sure, judging by what you've already told me about life behind the Bamboo Curtain, I get that it's as bad, if not worse than we all imagine.' He played his tongue around the inside of his mouth. 'But come on, all this effort they're putting into catching you: television appeals, offers of hefty rewards across all INCOL territories? I just believe there is a lot more to it than one man making a break for freedom. What do you say?'

Hubbard smiled as he glanced behind at the closed front door. He turned back to stare at Lance. 'No bugs, no recording devices?'

Lance shook his head. 'Just you and me.'

'There are two things you can know.' He pulled up the cushion to support his back as he relaxed into the narrative. 'I was one of a team, one of six covert tech nerds developing similar technology to what you're working on in Tomorrow World – a sort of clandestine parallel development programme.'

'Why bother? INCOL Asia has equal rights to access whatever we develop.'

'You don't understand the Chinese psyche. They're paranoid about being cheated or excluded from any joint initiative. They only trust themselves. Everybody else is a potential threat. It's a collective paranoia, instilled in the young from primary school age.'

'And you were forced to work for them?'

'It was blatantly obvious our families would be harmed, imprisoned if we didn't.'

'Your escape will have repercussions?'

'I hope not but know not.'

'Your family?'

'My mother was my only family. My father died some years ago and the extended family is spread around the world.' He swallowed hard and coughed once. 'It's down to Mum I'm here.' He swallowed again and shook his head. 'It's not what you're thinking. Nothing to do with maternal support or encouragement; don't worry about me, I'll be fine. There was none of that, I'm sorry to say. Four months ago, she was stopped entering the butchers for her weekly meat ration. She was partially deaf and didn't hear the young Chinese community controller ask for her papers. He was embarrassed, insulted – God knows what went on inside his mind – and vented his anger by beating my mother with his nightstick. By the time they got her to an emergency centre, she was in a coma. Never recovered. She was buried in a communal grave for opponents of the regime. I was forbidden to see her or attend the burial.' He shrugged. 'I was already planning my escape. The prospect of revenge drove me on.'

'You didn't conceive the plan on your own? Don't tell me your colleagues weren't involved?'

Hubbard gave a hesitant nod, as if having just reached a decision. 'If I tell you everything, you will be in as much potential danger with the Chinese as I am. Are you certain you want to know?'

'What I do already is a capital offence. They can't kill me twice.'

'They can make it excruciatingly painful. I've seen them in action.'

'I'll take my chance.'

'Your decision.' He took the bottle of beer from Lance's extended hand. 'Cheers,' and took a gulp. 'As a specialist unit, we were given the hardware and know-how to develop systems way beyond the limited broadband and online services available to the armed forces. It also meant we could infiltrate and hack into confidential servers operated by INCOL around the world. The Chinese thought that by embedding two of their specialists into the group, they could keep us in order.' He snorted. 'The two who joined us were even more anti-establishment than we were. They were appalled at the oppressive regime and paid little more than lip service to their masters.'

Hubbard explained how the unofficial leader of the unit was one of the foremost specialists in developing and managing the worldwide commercial and maritime blockchain systems. 'Without his help, I would never have made it.'

'Won't they figure that out and come after him?'

'We were sensitive to the possibility. We fixed it so that several aspects of the chain he worked on, smart contracts, PBFT, digital certificates and suchlike, bore my name as the compiler. He can point to my access code and say it was all down to me. When their two so-called spies confirm it, they won't look any further.'

'Hopefully.'

He gave a sanguine nod. 'Anyway -' It was a topic he clearly did not want to pursue. 'Anyway,' he repeated. 'In tandem with our official tasks, we also had our private agenda.'

Through a military communications satellite using a piggy-back IP address purporting to be an army establishment in some obscure province, they were accessing 6G speeds and streaming intelligence briefs, compiled in an encrypted form which even the Chinese duo could not understand or decrypt.

'I set up the speaker in my quarters to vibrate if this parallel programme reported the appearance of any document in a language other than encrypted Mandarin.' He nodded to himself at the memory. 'Stroke of luck. Somebody uploaded a confidential report translated into English that was about to be encrypted. It stayed up in its original form for ten minutes, long enough for me to download and spirit away.'

'What was it?'

'It's a thirty-page document I've dubbed the Red Manifesto. I'm not going into details now because I haven't decided the best way to use it to maximum effect. When I do, I'll put you in the picture.' He looked at the disappointed expression on Lance's face. 'I'll just say it deals with Chinese plans as the world returns to normality and the objectives which are nothing short of inflammatory.'

'They will know it was downloaded?'

'Of course. The links in the chain won't match. An alert will have sounded. As soon as they realised some corporal on the Mongolian border was not the guilty party, attention will turn elsewhere.'

'Puts your usual suspects in danger?'

'There has to be honour amongst us thieves.' A noise outside the front door startled him into silence. Lance flicked a switch on one of the dormant monitors. The image was of a man in a drunken rage as he cursed, leaning against the door,

Lance pointed at the ceiling. 'There's a knocking shop upstairs. He must have discovered his wallet's gone missing.'

'Sorry,' Hubbard said. 'Nerves are still a little shot.' He took another mouthful of beer. 'To finish the story, I was the only one in the group aware of this report. I wiped my workstation computer but left a trace back to the download, so there was no doubt who was responsible. There was no way I could hang around. I guessed I had a two-day start before they got their act together. I slipped out of the marina at night, headed due south, and then turned east. By midnight, I was working on the GPS deviation programme. The rest, you know.'

'And this Red Manifesto. Where is it now?'

'It's in a cloud with a 256-bit cryptographic encryption protocol. The passcode algorithm is safely tucked away.'

Lance whistled. 'Man, AES 256. You certainly don't want anybody to get to it. Even with the necessary computer power, which we don't have, it could take thousands of years to crack. You must have something worth protecting?'

'I do. And when the time is right, you'll see it.'

# TWENTY-FIVE

## CHELSEA HARBOUR – LONDON

## Late Afternoon – 18 November 2065

By the time Seth raised his aching body from the living room sofa, the apartment was in total silence; no cheery greeting from Damien announcing the weekend had arrived, no evidence of the cup of tea they would take back to bed for a Saturday lie-in.

Perhaps Damien had packed his belongings and cleared out. Seth dismissed the notion. His flatmate would need a van and helpers to move the accumulated junk their eighteen months together had amassed. Forget Damien. He was yesterday's news and right now, Seth had an article to work on. It would not write itself and, boy, did he have a story to tell.

Two double espressos and a cold shower conquered a mild hangover. It was past midday, and he needed to concentrate and put his domestic concerns to one side. He flexed his fingers and reached for the work laptop.

The chunk of jewellery on Francesca Hill's wrist was the definitive link. Thanks to Arthur, he had a nitid print of that piece of one-off jewellery on the arm of the woman touching the back of Jack Tirrand's jacket as they entered his apartment. The plan was to finish the article with the innuendo firmly planted, phone Simeon's wife for a comment and, bingo, end up with two stunning quotes for his lead headline.

He was through by eight. Re-reading it several times, and making minor alterations, he was satisfied. It was a masterpiece.

The headline across the two-page inside spread read, *TIME TO FEED THE DOGS* and the teaser *Society wife threatens to cut off husband's privates.* He would need a two-column/five-centimetre block on the front page, a headshot of Jack with the question, *Is Deputy Tirrand in the doghouse?* The exclusive featured three photographs: the lonely, society wife standing isolated at the charity event alongside a blow-up of Jack leading Kahn into his apartment building, followed across the page by a blurred image of the brief hug as he ushered Simeon's wife into the collective. The narrative was all sleazy innuendo and journalistic licence, from which the reader could only draw one conclusion. And it worked. Rebecca Tirrand's explosive closing remark featured once more at the end of the piece.

Seth sat back and read it one more time. Three things were missing: a quote from Simeon's wife, a review by the paper's legal man and, most importantly, the count to ten exercise.

Many years ago, an old hack at the now defunct Sun newspaper told him to write his piece, go away and come back an hour, a day, a week later, as the publication timetable demanded, count to ten and re-read it. Changes would flow and there would be plenty. The advice always worked. There was still no reply from Simeon's number, so he saved the copy and decided on blowing a few credits on an Italian meal and a bottle of claret from the vineyards of Sussex. There would soon be plenty of credits and an apartment all to himself.

His phone pinged once more, the third time since late afternoon. The message was hours old. Rebecca Tirrand was chasing him. Foolishly, he had promised to let her have sight of the article before it went for publication. He sent back a reply; still in production; be in touch when ready. If the weekend censors were true to form, it would be midnight before she got the message.

Seth let himself back into the apartment. Damien must have returned. His coat was slung over a chair, and the bedroom door was shut. Seth's first reaction was to go barging in, but another confrontation would serve no purpose. No point. He had drunk a bottle of wine, sufficient to leave him light-headed and loosen his tongue. He needed to be stone-cold sober with a measured response when he confronted Damien in the morning. He had to be convinced to leave without causing a scene. Seth needed to choose the best way to phrase this and, if necessary, up the threat level.

Someone was shaking his arm. Seth awoke with a start, his eyes opening and quickly closing again as the sunlight blinded him. The small of his back was aching from an uncomfortable dip in the sofa cushions and the thud of a headache reminded him that the Sussex claret could be safely reclassified as plonk.

'How about we call a truce?' Damien displayed two days' growth of stubble on his chin, bloodshot eyes and he smelled of a stale deodorant Seth did not recognise.

'Truce? What does that mean?'

Damien looked confused. There were drops of congealed blood at the point of his nostrils. 'What do you think it means? Let's make up, get over it.'

Seth pulled himself up and turned around. He was still dressed in yesterday's chinos and casual shirt. 'What happened to you? Give you a bit of a beating, did he? Likes it rough, does he? You tart!'

'Doesn't always work out the way you think, does it?' Damien looked at the floor. 'I made a mistake, all right?'

Seth stood up, gyrating his neck to ease the stiffness. 'Several, I'm counting, and now it's too late.'

'What do you mean?'

'The first presentable opportunity and you're off, screwing somebody else. I doubt it's the first time, but it's the first time I've caught you at it.' He licked at the spittle that formed at the corner of his mouth. 'It's incompatible with what I want. I'm looking for a long-term, honest relationship and that's not you. I don't blame you necessarily. I know I'm not the greatest catch in the ocean, but I am loyal. You're not. I could never trust you again.' Seth studied the other man's quivering lips. It was impossible to tell if it was fear or the resentment springing from rejection. 'So, I suggest you organise your belongings, get transport and find somewhere else to live. I don't want you around me anymore.'

In an instant, contrition turned into aggression. Damien's eyes were wild, his gaze fixed on Seth's neck, his fists clenched.

Neither man spoke. Gradually, Damien's expression softened, his hands relaxed and he smiled. 'I think the old man's memory is failing him. Could be the onset of dementia. You seem to forget the credits to buy this place came exclusively from me. As a convenience, the lease may be registered in your name, but no court would uphold your ownership once the facts are established. This apartment legally belongs to me. You are the one who needs to do the packing, load the vehicle and find somewhere else to live.' He slumped backwards into an armchair and cocked his leg over an arm. 'Damien Spencer is staying put. Get the picture?'

Seth walked toward him, watching the man cower into the seat as he neared. 'Picture's crystal clear. Where you are going, you won't need an apartment.'

'What's that supposed to mean?'

'Remember the file I took back for you the other day?'

'What about it?' The words were spoken with bravado but tinged with apprehension.

'Your friend, Phil the Brief, made a copy for me. It's tucked away in a safe place. I have a mind to tell Homeland I found it in your possession and, like the good citizen I am, return it to them. I might also suggest they examine your finances to verify certain various unsubstantiated deposits.'

Damien sat bolt upright. 'You wouldn't.' His voice trembled.

'Believe me, if it wasn't the weekend and I had a deadline, I'd be along there today.' Seth chanced a smile. 'Best to avoid any nastiness, don't you think, and make alternative arrangements, like this afternoon?'

Damien held the palms of his hands against his cheeks. 'You would do that? After all we meant to each other?'

'Where do you get this B film dialogue? What we experienced was a liaison based on sex and mutual convenience. Except, your understanding of the sex bit differed from mine. There will be plenty of opportunities to broaden your sexual horizons where you'll be going unless you play ball.'

'You bastard! We'll see about this! I have some spiteful friends.'

'Get them to help you carry your stuff out.'

Damien pitched forward off the sofa and made for the bedroom. Minutes later, dressed and dragging an overcoat behind him, he careered out the door.

Seth sighed. He would take a long, leisurely shower, breakfast, and then proofread the text one last time. He had until four to file his copy at the office. The legal review and passage through the editorial and production channels would take it up to the ten o'clock print deadline. By tomorrow morning, the world would know all about Jack Tirrand and his sordid little secrets.

During the afternoon, he made several changes, significant improvements as he saw it, and dealt with three more messages from Rebecca, all replied to with various excuses, increasing in journalistic hubris as her messages became more desperate and demanding. There was no way she would get advance notice of the article and, once published, he would guarantee there would be no further contact between them. That reminded him.

The call was put through within the hour. He didn't expect a man to answer.

'Who is this?' The tone was curt, impatient.

'I'm Seth Morgan from the *Capital Review*. I booked the call to speak with Mrs Hill.'

'What about?'

'It's a personal matter. Whom am I speaking with?'

'Who are you again?'

'I told you. Seth Morgan. I'm a journalist.'

'What does a journalist want with my wife?'

'Aah, Mr Hill, is it? *The* Simeon Hill?'

'Is that supposed to be funny?'

'No offence intended. 'Tetchy' was the adjective he thought of using to describe the husband's reaction. Perhaps 'Suspicious' would be better. 'It was a personal matter I wanted to discuss with your wife. I take it Mrs Hill is not available?'

'She is not.'

'Perhaps you would like to offer a comment. Your wife, Francesca, features in an exclusive we are publishing tomorrow concerning Deputy Jack Tirrand.'

There was a lengthy pause, during which Seth could hear the man's measured breathing. When he spoke again, his voice was lighter, more inclusive. 'What about Tirrand? And what possible interest could my wife have in him?'

'I interviewed Tirrand's wife to get her reaction on the revelation that he has taken to inviting a string of women to lengthy soirees in his apartment on occasions when his wife is not present. As your wife figures in his guest list, I was hoping for a comment from her as to the motive for her visit.' He paused for a second. 'You know, business or pleasure?'

'What is this nonsense? My wife doesn't even know Tirrand, other than to shake his hand at some public function. She only met him informally and briefly at our house a few days ago.'

'Obviously, a quick worker.'

'You are mistaken, and I dislike the inference.' His temper was apparent. 'Listen carefully, Mr Morgan. If my wife's name appears in your rag, there will be a libel action on your editor's desk within hours. I have the authority to get the *Capital Review* shut down in hours and make sure you remain unemployable.'

'Sounds like a threat, Mr Hill.'

'Just some friendly advice.'

'I'll take the quote as on the record.'

'Let me tell you something off the record, Mr Morgan. I don't know what you've got on Tirrand, but if my wife is mentioned in your newsprint, you will find yourself walking on hot coals. You could get burned.'

Simeon studied the unconscious body of his wife as he replaced her mobile on the bedside table. She would be out for the next few hours. The Temazepam in her tea would see to that.

He was so sick of all the arguments, the constant rowing, the interminable fights. 'You stupid cow,' he said to her sleeping form. 'What have you gone and done?'

The direct line in the office bypassed the central call routing and censorship control system. Hill was straight through. 'Is that you, Roach?' He could hear an old lady's voice in the background querying who was telephoning on a Sunday. 'Sorry to disturb you, but I need you over at the house.' He drummed his fingers on the desk as he listened. 'It can't be helped, I understand, but I must insist. Come straight away and put one of your best men on standby for first thing tomorrow morning.' Simeon flexed his fist, the frustration apparent. 'No, I cannot explain over the phone and, yes, I *do* have a serious problem. Listen, before you come over, find the contact number for the senior editor and the owner of the *Capital Review*.'

Seth sat in the darkness of a deserted newsroom. With no heating on since Friday, the air was chill in the cavernous room. From his office, the voice of the duty editor broke the silence, advising whoever was listening and, in no uncertain terms, he was finally going home. Seth nodded and decided he would follow suit. It was past ten.

The legal opinion involved changing two sentences. Otherwise, the exclusive was good to go. The flak would fly tomorrow.

Capital's owner, a hard-headed, north countryman, who owed his fortune to a career in waste disposal withstood a lively ten-minute conversation with, as he described it, some wanker from the political class in the presence of a pet lawyer threatening brimstone and fire. There was nothing diplomatic or courteous about tipping detritus into a big hole in the ground and there was a simple, two-word stock answer for these so-called liberal elitists. He was the paper's owner, and editorial interference was something he would never countenance. Threats he treated with contempt, and he was not about to pay any heed to the mutterings of a pair of public school tarts from London.

'As my legal man says it's clean,' he said. 'We go to print.'

And they did.

# TWENTY-SIX

## STRATFORD COMMUNITY TRANSPORT MARSHALLING HUB – LONDON

### Early Morning – 19 November 2065

Alison arrived early, her intention to avoid the crowds. It was a pointless exercise. With an hour to go before its departure, the Community Express service to Paris was already packed. People were standing in the aisles, filtering into the corridors, suitcases wedged between legs or in any available floor space. Tempers were short as more and more travellers tried to move through the carriages, provoking condemnatory stares or muted complaints and an undercurrent of hostility, accentuated by the hushed mix of European languages.

Alison's heart sank. Travelling like this for the next six hours would be purgatory.

A conductor moved skilfully along the carriage, studying each travel pass as he did so. His supercilious air melted into obsequiousness as he noticed the two red lines printed on the sheet of paper Alison proffered.

'Follow me, please, Madam.' He pushed his way forward through the crowd, barking a warning whenever necessary and ensuring his charge was following unencumbered in his slipstream.

'You've done this before,' Alison said with a laugh in her voice.

He leaned forward, moving two children deftly out of his path and shooting her a questioning glance before nodding, reassured by the smile on her face. 'This time of year is the worst,' he said. 'All the seasonal labour contracts have ended, and this lot needs to get back to their own countries before the winter curfew comes into force. Most don't want to go. Too good here for them. If they stay, it's winter cleaning the streets, living off charity and then deportation.' He checked she was keeping up with him. 'They've got four months now to survive in a wood cabin in some backwater watching their savings disappear. Then, it's back in the spring to do it all over again. Ain't life grand?'

He tapped on the door of a compartment with its window blinds closed and slid it open to let her pass. 'I'll be back to take orders for your meal when we are underway.' With that, he closed the door behind her.

The single occupant was a matronly looking woman in a window seat, a collection of papers spread out on the table before her. She was a stranger to Alison, but her first impression was the air of someone in authority.

'You must be Alison,' she said. Her upper front teeth were slightly pronounced, stretching her top lip into a thin line. 'Welcome. I'm Ramona Usher. Jack has told me all about you. You're taking a break from studying for a few days, yes?'

The woman made the question sound as if she disbelieved the assertion. 'I'm taking a few days away from university. Exams in two weeks, for which I need to do some revision.'

Usher studied her over the top of a pair of wire-rimmed reading glasses, her lips pulled into a half smile. She was unnerving Alison. Those cold eyes just staring, assessing her, forming a summary judgement. How could she know there was another explanation for Alison's presence? She couldn't. Did she suspect something, or was it just Alison's guilty conscience?

Usher nodded, as if she had reached a conclusion, and returned to reading the page in front of her.

Alison stowed her overnight holdall in the rack and sat down. Out of the corner of her eye, she looked across at Usher, immersed in whatever she was studying. Given some make-up to hide the lines and crow's feet together with a tint to tone down the greying hair, Usher could be considered passably attractive. She would be a little below average height with a voluptuous figure, a little too forgiving around the hips, in Alison's opinion, but, overall, a striking woman.

'My father has not arrived yet?'

Usher shook her head. 'Probably tied up with a few last-minute issues on his mind.' Her glance rested on the folded newspaper alongside her briefcase. 'He will be here, don't worry.'

'Do you work with him?'

Usher looked bemused. 'Good Lord. No. I'm in Homeland Security. Beyond this present assignment, we have nothing to do with each other.'

'You make it sound as though you're relieved it's that way.' She knew it sounded confrontational, but the force of the denial confused her.

Usher could have taken it the wrong way, but her response was measured. 'I meant nothing more than to emphasise our paths rarely cross.'

'What brings you together on this trip?'

Alison registered the feigned startled glance she received as similar to the one her father adopted when asked a leading question. It said *You don't expect me to tell you, do you?*

'Mutual interest.'

'Fair enough. I'll mind my own business. Jack did warn me.'

'He did?'

'Not to ask leading questions and to concentrate on what I was doing.'

'In our line of work, that is good advice.' Usher reached for a file inside her briefcase and, without removing it, flicked to the corner of an inside page. She gave Alison a warm smile. 'Unconnected with what we've been talking about, I need to ask you something?'

'Ask away.'

'In my line of work, a name has cropped up which, possibly, you and your family might have come across. Tell me, when you were young, do you ever remember somebody named Gordon Bachelor? He came from Tyneside with a strong accent, hence his nickname of Geordie Bachelor. Ring any bells?'

'Sorry, no. Should it? Who is he?'

Usher shrugged. 'Nobody special. Just a guy who was around the domestic scene when your father's career got going. Jack might recall the name. It's before your time. Forget it.'

Against her inclination, Alison let it pass. What was it with these people? Her father was just the same; punctuated a conversation with the deliberate intention of discarding one topic by introducing an unrelated question without explaining the reason for the non sequitur. What the hell. Ask something mundane, she thought. 'Do you know the route we'll be taking?'

Usher nodded. 'It's a bit of a shunt, I'm afraid. When we get to Paris, we change onto the express to Strasbourg where we part company. You will get a connection to Stuttgart and we will travel on to our destination.' Alison went to interrupt. 'Don't ask,' Usher said. 'It's classified.'

The carriage door opened with a bang and a harassed-looking Jack Tirrand pushed a small suitcase and briefcase in before him. 'That was a close-run thing. Needed to go to the office first . . .' He stopped, collapsing into a seat as the train lurched away from the platform. '. . . Then the traffic was chaotic. Thought I was going to miss it.' He leaned sideways to kiss his daughter on the cheek. 'Been talking about me behind my back?' he said with a smile in his voice. 'Nothing complimentary, I expect.' He took in Usher's quizzical expression. 'Something wrong?' he asked.

'Do you mind giving us five minutes, Alison? I need to speak with your father in private.'

A look of query and incomprehension passed between father and daughter. Alison smiled and nodded, conscious of Usher's stern glance. This was a woman used to giving an order in the guise of a polite request. 'Of course. I'll go for a walk,' Alison said.

'Have you seen this morning's paper?' Usher waited for the door to slide shut before speaking.

'No. What's happened?'

'Pages eight and nine, double spread.' She handed him the *Capital Review*.

As he read, he slumped back in his seat. After a few minutes, he closed and refolded the newspaper, leaned forward and handed it back to Usher without saying a word.

'I didn't want to bring it up in front of Alison. Best you choose when and how to broach it with her.'

'Thank you,' he said, staring at the empty seat next to Usher. 'She will be devastated.'

'Alison? Don't think so. She comes over as a pragmatist.'

'No.' He shook his head as if re-calibrating his thoughts. 'Rebecca was so looking forward to the kudos flowing from this article which was supposed to recognise her work for charity. She will feel betrayed by this deliberate deception to use her to fashion some nonsense piece of scandal directed at me. I must put in a call to her when we get to Paris. She will be devastated. God knows how she'll react.'

'To the deception or the allegations . . .' She stopped herself. '. . . innuendos, I should say.'

He croaked a false laugh. 'The whole thing is just made-up rubbish. Rebecca will get that. The deception will surely hurt her, seconds before it turns to anger. This Morgan individual has made a laughingstock of her amongst her circle of acquaintances; the ones she wanted to impress. I can't imagine how many people she's told the article was to be published.'

Usher nodded in agreement. 'Someone from the *Review* is bound to ask you for a comment before they do the follow-up tomorrow. Do you intend to say something?'

'The follow-up?' He pointed a finger at the paper sticking out from her briefcase. 'There's more of this rubbish?'

'There is a teaser on the masthead. You must have missed it. Tomorrow, they intend to name the secret woman who figured on the second page of the article, doubtless with more innuendo and speculation.'

He puffed his cheeks, letting the air escape through puckered lips. 'That would be unfortunate. The person concerned came to see me on a confidential matter. It has no impact on me, but I suspect she will have to deal with certain recriminations.'

'I don't need to tell you, the problem with all this journalistic smoke and mirrors is the adage, as far as the public is concerned, there's no smoke without fire. You've just been branded as some lothario. You're instantly famous.'

'Infamous, more like. How do they get hold of these ideas?'

'A tip-off, perhaps. Someone spreading fake news who wants to see you politically wounded. Can you think of anybody?'

'That's a naïve question from someone in the same line of business. There's a queue I should think. Come on, isn't there anybody who wants your job?'

She allowed herself a knowing smile. 'Not enough to have me spread across two pages of today's paper.'

'Then you're lucky. The status of a deputy with a portfolio is both jealously guarded and jealously sought. I suppose being a civil servant with permanent employment takes the edge off your professional vulnerability.'

'In any large hierarchy, there are always people eager to clamber up the greasy pole, dislodging whoever might be in their way on the climb up. We're both as good as our next assignment, whatever this trip turns out to be all about. Have you any idea?'

'None at all. I could offer one or two suggestions, but let's leave it until we are on our own. Right now, what's uppermost on my mind is to talk to Alison about this crock of lies and how best to handle Rebecca.'

Usher chose not to comment, returning instead to comb through the files in her briefcase, back to the compelling case of Detective Inspector Gordon Bachelor. Why did the name of a Family Division liaison officer who was tortured and then murdered appear in two separate and, apparently, unrelated files? When it came to the name of Jack Tirrand, she didn't believe in coincidence.

As impatient as she felt, now was not the right time to ask questions of her travelling companion.

# TWENTY-SEVEN

## MUSWELL HILL – LONDON

### 9.00 - 19 November 2065

Emerging from the haze of semi-consciousness, Rebecca registered the intermittent buzzing of the intercom and now, the persistent knocking on the door. Her head was throbbing. 'For God's sake,' she said to herself. 'Is there a fire? I'm coming.' What time was it? Something important was happening today.

The pillow was damp. Perspiration. She remembered taking the pill, washed down with Irish vodka. Her mouth was parched. Water. Seth, the bastard, hadn't contacted her! She must have booked more than a dozen calls to his number. No answer. She wasn't able to sleep, forever tossing and turning. Then she remembered the pill.

'I'm coming. Be patient!' This time out loud. She dragged her feet onto the floor, fishing with her toes for her slippers, reaching out blindly with one hand to find her dressing gown. The banging on the door sounded even more desperate. Jack's side of the bed was empty, the sheet folded back. Last night he went to bed, leaving her pacing up and down in the lounge. He had mentioned an early start this morning and was long gone. Meticulous and sober, that would be Jack's epitaph. She continued drinking into the early hours, waiting for a damn call which never came.

'Coming!' She said it loud enough for the banging to stop. Where were her slippers? Fuck it! What did she look like? The wood block flooring in the hallway was cold to bare skin. She couldn't let anybody see her like this. 'Who is it?' She was at the door. The concierge must have known who it was to let them into the building. She peered through the spyhole.

'Jesus, you look terrible!' Rebecca let her daughter slide past her. 'I know. I don't look so great myself.' Harriet was avoiding eye contact. 'What's the problem? Did you sleep in those clothes? Are the girls alright?'

'Oh God, Mum!' She flung her arms around Rebecca's neck, gripping tight, her voice coming in staccato bursts in between tearful gasps. 'My world is falling apart. It's a disaster.'

Rebecca prised the arms away from around her neck, forcing Harriet back so that she could study her face. Her daughter was staring at the floor, her shoulders heaving as the tears ran down her bright red cheeks. 'What has happened? Pull yourself together and speak. I asked you if the girls were alright?'

Harriet's empty stare fixed on Rebecca's waist. 'They're alright. Mac took them to school. He's walked out on me. He says I've betrayed him; that it runs in the family.'

'What are you talking about, Harriet? Take a deep breath and make some sense, will you? Exactly what has happened?'

'I went out for the day yesterday; a friend . . . colleague of Dad. He said he could help me with the property chain for the house in Devon. There is a problem with the owner, a convicted criminal, who is appealing against losing the family home. We went to see him in Stafford. I didn't tell Mac I was going.'

'Why not? Who is this colleague? Are you involved with someone?'

There was a violent shake of the head. 'Shut up. Nothing like that. I didn't tell Mac because he would have told me not to bother and let things take their course. Truth is, he doesn't want to move to a new job in Exeter. He would have asked a million questions. Besides, Mr Roach told me it would be best not to tell anyone.'

'Roach? AR do you mean?' Rebecca's voice increased in pitch. 'You spent the day with AR? Are you mad? What was in it for him? Jack must have warned you. AR does nothing without some self-serving motive.'

'Nothing.' Harriet's eyes cast around the room. 'He asked me lots of questions, that's all.'

'Questions about what?'

'The family. Dad's past. Our relationships. Just general stuff.' She fiddled in her coat pocket for a tissue and rubbed her eyes. 'He seemed genuinely interested in us. That's all.'

'And did it work? Did you see this ex-criminal?'

'Arnold saw him on his own. He said it was best. He could apply pressure. I waited in the car.'

Rebecca tightened her grip on Harriet's shoulders. 'So, it's Arnold now, is it? Did you not realise this man was playing you? I expect he said everything went according to plan. There would be no problem.'

'More or less.'

'You're so gullible, Harriet. And then what?'

'It was late by the time we got back. He suggested I join him for a casual meal before I went home. I was keen to get back and explain things to Mac, but Arnold would not take no for an answer.'

'Have you lost touch with reality? You let him take you to dinner?' She could not hide the exasperation.

'We ate at his place. Just an omelette with salad.'

'What was he doing, chatting you up?'

'Don't be silly. Nothing like that. His mother was there. She is an inquisitive old lady. He was trying to get her to go to bed.'

'I bet he was.'

'She insisted on eating with us. We were halfway through the meal when a call came for him. There was an urgent matter to attend to. He arranged a collective for me.'

Rebecca signalled for her to stop talking as the realisation dawned. 'You didn't mention the pregnancy? Tell me, you didn't.'

'Not in so many words.'

'What does that mean?'

Harriet's cheeks coloured as she returned her gaze to the floor. 'I mentioned it only hypothetically. A third party with the problem. How could it be resolved?'

'And you imagine the wily old bastard didn't work out it was you? My God, whose child are you?'

Tears flowed. 'It's all such a mess. My whole family. How can you stay so calm? Mac is so angry.'

'Why? You got home, didn't you?'

'I fell asleep on the collective. I don't know why. I only drank a half glass of wine. I was the last off the collective. The house was in darkness. Felt so drunk, I could hardly stand. I was so tired. Made it to the living room and I must have collapsed in a chair. Mac woke me up this morning waving the newspaper in my face. He was shouting. I could barely focus on him. My head was . . . is thumping. The twins looked so scared. Mac never gets angry in front of them.' She slid knees first onto the carpet, her face pressed against the carpet, fists banging on the floor. 'Why? Why? Why?'

Rebecca's attention was on the folded newspaper poking from Harriet's handbag. She yanked it out. The ink on the cheap newsprint had smudged the photograph of her standing alone and looking downcast at the Film Festival. She didn't remember it being taken. A photographer must have been waiting for the opportunity to catch her at an off moment. As she unfolded the double spread, the banner headline came into view. *TIME TO FEED THE DOGS?* With a shuddered 'Oh, no,' she slumped down into a chair and read. She took in every word, each one registering a pinprick in her heart, each one seeking to destroy her, bring her down, make a fool of her.

Harriet was sitting cross-legged on the floor, studying her. 'You didn't know, did you? You haven't seen it?'

Rebecca smiled as she shook her head and stood up. 'You believe it? Mac does, I assume?'

Harriet's brow creased. 'I don't know what to believe.'

'More fool you and that good-for-nothing husband of yours. This isn't about the truth.' She crumpled the pages into a ball. 'This is a hatchet job, designed to destroy your father's career, motivated by jealousy or resentment, possibly hatred. In doing so, the aim is to bring down the entire family. As far as you are concerned, it looks as though it's already succeeding.'

'But what if Dad is having affairs with these women?'

'It's a side issue. The likelihood is it's all a pack of lies but, in any case, would any right-minded person condemn an innocent until the evidence proved otherwise? This isn't about sex. It's the start of a mission to bring down the name of Tirrand.' She walked into the bedroom to dress, eventually fetching out of the wardrobe a winter coat with a white imitation fur collar. Every muscle in her face was rigid. She wedged black, tight-fitting gloves onto her hands and pulled on a hat over uncombed hair.

'Go home, Harriet. Count yourself lucky. Imagine what could have happened if you had passed out at Roach's apartment. It was planned. Nobody in their right senses would look twice at that sick fuck. Tell Mac everything and to not pass judgement until he knows all the facts. If he doesn't come around, bring the twins back here. We'll stay with my parents for a few days.'

'What are you going to do? I don't like to leave you on your own.'

There was warmth in Rebecca's smile. 'Physician, heal thyself. The author of this piece and whoever is behind it may trash the name of Tirrand, but what they will not do is sully the Fitzwilliam dynasty. I am about to teach somebody the Fitzwilliams can be equally ruthless when it comes to trash who don't deserve to breathe the same air. Somebody will pay for this, and I intend to make sure they do.'

198

# TWENTY-EIGHT

## SAINT GEORGE'S HILL – WEYBRIDGE

## 9.00 - 19 November 2065

Roach struggled to manoeuvre his frame into the rear seat of the hybrid VW Incoletta. The effort brought beads of sweat to his forehead and damp patches on the visible areas of a blue shirt.

Simeon watched the contortion from outside the car, released his grasp on the opposite rear door handle and opted for the passenger seat next to the solemn-looking peak-capped driver.

'Sorry about this,' Simeon said with no conviction as he glanced back. 'Far too conspicuous to use the Range Rover on this mission. If there are journalists on the prowl, we certainly don't want to be recognised. Did you get the entry code to the garage?'

Roach grunted as he daubed his face with a handkerchief. 'I did it last night when we met up,' he replied testily. 'Surely, you remember? I got hold of the chief of the management company. He didn't take kindly to being disturbed at midnight. I said we would make sure he was on the list for the hospitality suite at next summer's Olympics.'

Simeon mumbled something about remembering the conversation. For some inexplicable reason, he felt the tension in his stomach. Yet, everything was under control. The journalist, Morgan, agreed to postpone naming Simeon's wife until they met in person. He sounded relaxed about it. Perhaps it was always Morgan's plan; announce he was about to unleash a scandal and then accept a substantial bribe to bury the story. Simeon was prepared to deal, but Morgan would learn not to mess with those who should not be messed with – which reminded him. 'Where are we picking up your man?' He swivelled around in his seat.

Roach grunted for a second time. 'Are you asking to check up on me?' He was decidedly irritable. 'I try to do my job to the satisfaction of those who empower me.'

Simeon said nothing.

'Battersea,' Roach said finally, with a sigh in his voice. 'The west side entrance to the sport and leisure centre.'

The driver smiled to himself and acknowledged the information. He was familiar with the sprawling building, many years ago a south-bank landmark of a disused power station with its four enormous chimneys. Laying empty and decaying until its conversion into a multi-faceted family entertainment and wellness centre, it now attracts visitors from around the Capital. It was a stone's throw from their destination across Chelsea Bridge to the northern bank of the Thames and the Chelsea Harbour residential complex.

Roach was regretting his outburst. He tapped Simeon on the shoulder and leaned forward. 'The plan is we park in the garage under the apartment building and let Sharky go up to this Morgan's apartment for a little chat about his future wellbeing.'

'Sharky?' Simeon queried.

'It's the nickname of the man joining us. I don't know his real name. He bit off someone's ear once. Hence, the nickname.'

'Not Jaws?' Simeon queried with a smile.

'I understand the nickname was already taken by another equally large and carnivorous individual. It's a question he's often asked.'

'Sorry, you were saying?'

'Once Sharky is satisfied an understanding has been reached, he will bring Morgan down to the garage where you can finalise arrangements. He will go to his editor, explain it is a case of mistaken identity and insist the story be pulled. The paper's legal team will not want to take the risk.' Roach sat back to ease the pain in his back. 'The driver and I will be on call should you need us, but a person-to-person approach will command his confidence and whatever deal you agree is between you and him.'

Simeon nodded. They drove on in silence, a stop-start crawl along the A3 as the morning rush hour developed.

Roach grinned with satisfaction. Who was he trying to convince it would go as he predicted? Morgan might well need to be softened up before he capitulated. A pity. Roach's sympathies were with the journalist. As far as he was concerned, Francesca Hill was a stuck-up slag who, whenever they met, looked down her nose at him as though he were an inconsequential minion with an unpleasant smell.

All right, he was in a bad mood. His carefully planned evening was abruptly interrupted by Hill, just when he was on the point of sending his mother to bed and getting to work on Tirrand's weak-kneed daughter. By the time she finished the glass of wine with the little additive and passed out, Mum would be tucked up in bed and he could transport the unconscious body across to the sofa bed and spend an hour of pleasurable relief before he dressed her and waited for her to come around. It was a tried and tested technique. Although one or two of his conquests had questioned what had happened, not one had ever dared accuse him.

Never mind. A second opportunity would present itself. The stupid bitch had got herself pregnant for a third time. Imagine. It was naïve of her to ask for his help. She would beg him to let her keep the little brat.

As for that charade to help remove the ex-con from his home to facilitate her move to – where was it? - that's right, Exeter. Who in their right mind wants to live in Exeter? He listened to the man's miserable story and said he would do everything possible to help him keep his home. In exchange, he might ask for a favour or two. The dossier described a hard man with a fighting streak, sentenced to three years hard labour for assaulting a doctor who refused to prescribe some addictive drug. Time among the criminal community turned him into a calculating psychopath. He could come in useful.

Roach burped. 'Better out than in,' he said. They turned off the main road toward the sports complex. 'There's Sharky,' he gestured. He pointed to a tall, thick-set man with curly black hair, sporting a duffle bag slung across his shoulders. 'Pull into the set-down parking area,' he said.

Craven, alias Sharky, was his man. Roach demanded loyalty, and Craven never let him down. The moment Roach vetted him, he knew this man would do his bidding. Here was someone who enjoyed inflicting pain, watching a victim suffer; a man who respected strength of character as much as he despised weakness in his adversaries. He put the fear of God into Kahn. The memory brought a smile to Roach's face.

Roach explained his plan. If Morgan succumbed to Hill's bribe and Craven's coercion, as was the likeliest outcome, the journalist would need another source to reinforce his exposé of Jack Tirrand.

Roach discovered early in their relationship how Craven, as a security consultant at Alexander Palace, used his position to cultivate relationships with many of the deputies who would stay over in local hotels one or two nights a week. With a little detective work, Roach learned of Craven's out-of-hours activity pimping for three so-called escorts who visited their clients in the privacy of a hotel room. It proved doubly advantageous for the big man. Not only did he enjoy the occasional pleasure from one or other of the three attractive young women, but having some valuable dirt on several holier-than-thou deputies gave him leverage when he needed to exert influence in the Assembly.

He would get together with Craven and the more voluptuous of the three women, a peroxide blonde who went by the name of Trixie, prime her with as many details of Jack Tirrand's background as possible along with a staged photo of her leaving the deputy's apartment building and then, let her loose on Morgan. For an agreed fee, Trixie would confess to her long-standing sex and bondage relationship with this lust-crazed deputy.

Whether the allegations proved baseless was irrelevant. Mud sticks and as far as Jack Tirrand's career was concerned, it was as good as over.

# TWENTY-NINE

## CHELSEA HARBOUR – LONDON

## 9.00 - 19 November 2065

Derek Willard's shift as the duty concierge at Chelsea Harbour was coming to an end. It had been a quiet night, boring, you could say, for someone on the London South Central OCD register with an overactive thyroid. Derek's obsessive, compulsive disorder was the driving need to classify everything and everybody into orderly groupings. As there were a myriad of ways to determine a group, Derek's task was never-ending and extremely time-consuming.

One of his favourite listings was to categorise the residents of the apartment block under the 'Can they afford to live here?' grouping. He arranged them under one of three headings. There were the UTOAs – 'up their own arseholes' – the rich and famous who either ignored him or treated him like dirt when they wanted something: the JAMs – 'the just about managing', who were in the main, middle-class, pleasant and polite: and, finally, the CATS – 'can't afford this shit' – a small group, mainly rental tenants rather than owners, who didn't have the credits or status to be living at such a prestigious address. This group was always late paying the service charge, suffered periodic electricity or gas outages and was regularly feted with visits from stern-looking individuals from collection agencies. Willard accorded these CATS the respect they deserved. None. His reaction to them was haughty and bordered on contempt.

The man about to enter with two companions fell into this category. He was Willard's number one CAT. The resident of apartment 319 was looking decidedly the worse for wear, unshaven, his customary mop of well-groomed blond hair like a ball of brushwood grass that had rolled across the prairie and landed atop his head, His clothes were creased and stained from continuous wear.

Mr D. Spencer lived in a small two-bedroom unit on the unfashionable north side of the building with little sun and a view of the Thames only if you strained to look sideways over the balcony railing.

Spencer also appeared in Willard's homophobic grouping as in the 'Raging' category, so classified by the way he flaunted his sexuality with a partner who was old enough to be his father. Willard had no time for him and, as for the two new arrivals Spencer left sitting in reception while he went upstairs. Well, what could he say? They were as thin as rakes, all-black leather trousers, and matching waistcoats with silver studs over tattooed chests. And what about those ridiculous black, lace-up boots with silver metal toecaps?

It would be just his luck if one of the UTOAs appeared to complain about something trivial and objected to the presence of these two threatening-looking individuals. He prayed they would leave before he was forced to confront them.

He tapped on the keyboard, activating the third-floor security camera. Spencer was at the door of his apartment. 'Hurry up', Willard said under his breath.

Seth reached to pull up his trousers. 'Stop banging on the door!' he shouted. 'The chain's on. Give me a minute. I'm on the John.'

He took the time to wash and dry his hands before strolling to the front door. 'What do you want?' He spoke from the other side of the door. 'Have you come to collect your things?'

'Let me in, please. We need to talk.'

'Done talking, Damien. Time for you to organise transport, take your belongings and . . .' He breathed deeply. '. . . And fuck off out of my life.'

'Please, please, think again. We are good together. You know that.'

'It's all "was", not "is". There is no going back for me. Get it in your head, it's final and let's both move forward.' He released the lock and let the door open to the extent the chain would allow. He looked into Damien's tired eyes. 'Don't make this difficult for both of us.'

'This is my apartment.' There was a controlled anger in Damien's voice. 'You leave if you must. I intend to stay put.' He pushed at the open door, the chain straining in the clasp.

Seth moved behind the door, shouldering it to relieve the pressure on the chain. There was a stand-off. 'We've been through all that. You should know that your girl, Janet, at Nine Elms, has put a call through to me, looking for you. Somebody from Homeland, Usher, I think the name was, is eager to speak with you. I've got a message ready to send to Homeland telling them exactly where to find the copy of a file that went missing and a suggestion they contact a certain Phil the Brief. Get my drift?'

Seth was straining against the sudden increased pressure on the door. 'You're a piece of worthless shit!' Damien shouted. 'Old and washed up. You'd see me ruined?'

'Not my intention, if you take my advice. Collect your things and agree to an assignment of your interest in the lease. Do it calmly with no fuss or tricks and your side deals with Phil will remain our little secret.'

'I won't forget this, Seth. You're having me over. Let's get it done before I change my mind. I've got two guys downstairs to help me.'

Seth moved back from the door. 'Give me ten minutes to finish dressing and then come up. But remember, no tricks, cries for help or trying to stake your claim. We have a deal, and you agree to stick to it, right? '

He waited for a reply, but there was no response from the other side of the door.

Willard studied the monitor as Spencer turned away from the door to his apartment and walked toward the elevator. His two henchmen were still sitting quietly in reception. The concierge felt the air leave his body. Thankfully, Spencer was on his way down and the three of them would soon be gone.

Willard's attention was diverted toward the double glass entrance doors to the building. What was a VW Incoletta with tinted rear windows doing driving toward the underground garage? With a perfect recall of every resident's make of car and the relevant garage space, he knew nobody owned an Incoletta with tinted windows. He would swear there was no authority from any resident authorising one of the eight visitor spaces for such a vehicle. The driver would either have to turn around and drive back out or stop at reception to seek authorisation from a resident.

Willard waited. Categorising cars, he mused, was tricky. The problem was, they were all the same. As a hangover from the days of national identity, the limited production of new, replacement vehicles, primarily commercial, was in the hands of five small-scale manufacturers in Europe: three in Germany, two in France and an assembly unit in the UK. All cars were hybrids with one of two engine sizes and parts and body shapes were homogenous.

Manufacture and distribution were strictly controlled by a branch of ISE, which issued licences to reclaim and recycle the precious lithium car batteries from retired vehicles.

Colour coding was also out of the question as all cars were painted in a one-coat, solid red ochre finish, the cheapest manufacturing process available. Painted with a large white stripe running from boot to roof to bonnet and an identity number stamped four times around the body and once on the roof, collectives were easily spotted. The only scope for individuality amongst the manufacturers was restricted to the shape of the grill and emblem, although the German designers enjoyed a two-year advantage in chassis design changes before they were available throughout the industry. Such was the Incoletta with its snub-nosed front and squared-off boot for extra space.

Optional extras, such as tinted windows and external warning lights, were restricted to public service vehicles which bore the INCOL standard on the boot lid and bonnet.

Willard was puzzled. The Incoletta did not reappear, yet without the remote control or the master code for the keypad, the garage was not accessible. As soon as the unsavoury visitors had left reception, he would investigate.

The first elevator returned to the ground floor, the hydraulics hissing as the door opened. Spencer remained inside as he called out for his colleagues to join him. Willard switched cameras on his monitor to watch the two men walk through the door as it closed.

Thank God. They must be heading for the garage and Spencer's car. Willard switched to the underground camera, level one. A hollow black image filled the screen. A malfunction? This never happened. He switched to level two – the same damn thing. The system was supposed to be top of the range. His heart was racing.

The second elevator hummed into action. It was on its way up from level two. He needed to check why the cameras were offline. Rules were rules. Only in an emergency should he leave the reception area during the graveyard shift. Two replacements were due to start at 9.15. Late again – waiting for coffee and bacon sandwiches at the café, no doubt. They would bring one for him. He wasn't hungry. Today, he was edgy. Something was wrong.

He checked the elevator control. Both registered as being on the third floor. Spencer had not gone to the garage after all. One elevator was now on the way down. It passed the ground floor level before he could get to the call button. The second elevator was still on the third floor. From higher up the building, somebody was banging on the lift shaft door. His index finger hammered against the call button. Nothing. Somebody was holding the door open.

He hurried back along the lobby corridor to reception. Damn it. The screen he needed to look at now showed the same fuzzy black image. Where was the emergency call-out number for Vigilance, the security company? Harry and Zelmo would be here at any minute. He would go up to see what the problem was.

Willard heard the strains of exertion on the stairway before the PR executive from 628 made it to reception. The elderly man stood in front of him, hands on hips, his veined, bulbous, red cheeks inflating as he struggled for breath and tried to speak at the same time.

As the concierge, Willard could only apologise for the inconvenience. He was just about to investigate the problem with the elevators when the gentleman appeared. He could not agree more. It was irregular and as soon as his colleagues arrived, the matter would be fully investigated. No, he did not have a sardonic smile on his face and was not being disrespectful. No, he did not consider he should be dismissed and was sorry the gentleman felt that way. This unfortunate occurrence was outside his control.

The tirade continued, but Willard switched off. He was watching the man's mouth move without listening. Fortunately, his supervisor was an understanding leftie who despised the residents, whom he referred to as the new bourgeoisie. As for this unpleasant UTOA standing there ranting about having to walk down six flights of stairs, if he only knew his attractive young wife received three visits in one week from the domestic appliance repair man, each lasting around three hours, he might have other things on his mind than Willard's employment status.

With a contemptuous glance at Willard, the UTOA marched toward the front door, its hydraulic damper frustrating his efforts to slam it shut. A fitting end, Willard thought, to the old man's tantrum. He stood at the full-length window to follow the man's progress toward Waterside Drive just as the Incoletta drove past on its way out. The passengers in the rear were hidden from view by the tinted windows, but he made fleeting eye-to-eye contact with the driver. As the UTOA put his thumb out to demand a lift, the Incoletta sped up, ignoring the man and the middle finger salute which followed in its wake. There's justice for you, Willard said to himself.

He caught sight of Harry and Zelmo strolling toward the entrance. Just time to return to reception and check the monitors. The garage cameras were back online, as was the unit on the third floor. He checked the internal unit on the level one car park. Spencer's space was unoccupied. He heaved a sigh of relief.

'Excuse me.' The voice came from behind him. 'I assume you work here.'

# THIRTY

## CHELSEA HARBOUR – LONDON

## 9.40 - 19 November 2065

Willard wheeled around. 'Sorry, I didn't see you. How can I help?'

The woman gave him a fixed smile. The patterned silk headscarf covered her hair and forehead and was tied under her chin. She wore large dark glasses, presumably for effect, as the sky outside was full of dark, threatening rain clouds accompanied by an unpleasant swirling wind. Her tailored beige raincoat had a turned-up collar which rubbed against her cheeks. Willard put her as late forties or early fifties: someone who put on her make-up in a hurry and was doing her best not to be recognised. It would not be the first time in his five years at Chelsea Harbour.

'I'm here to see Seth Morgan. Can you direct me to his apartment?'

He laughed. 'That's 319. It's been a hive of activity this morning. Can you let me have your name, please?'

He moved to switch on the intercom, which buzzed before he could do so. 'I am sorry,' he said to the caller. 'Can you repeat that, please?' He turned his back on the woman to tap the keyboard and bring the image from the third-floor camera onto the monitor. 'Nothing is registering on my screen,' he said. 'Could you not have contacted me first before calling the police? It's probably just a domestic difficulty which I could deal with.' He waved at Harry and Zelmo as they reached the front door. 'Say that again, please.' He listened. 'I can assure you, Signora Spinetti . . . Sorry, Signorina Spinetti, I have been right here at my station all morning. If I stepped away for a minute, it was to deal with a resident's request and I certainly did not hear the intercom if, as you say, you called me first.' The line went dead.

He turned back to speak to the woman. 'I'll call Mr Morgan. Who should I say . . ?' The sentence trailed off. The woman had gone.

'Thank God you two are here,' he said, addressing his colleagues. 'It's been a hell of a morning. Somebody's got past me before I could contact the resident.' The motion sensor on the camera returned the image on the monitor to the third-floor corridor. The woman was at the door of 319. 'I'll bring you up to speed in a minute,' he said. 'I just need the Gents. I'll be right back.'

The two new arrivals stood there bemused, reusable coffee cups and packages of bacon sandwiches in their hands. They looked at each other and shrugged.

Rebecca needed the element of surprise to gain the upper hand before Seth had time to react.

The door to Seth's apartment was ajar. Even better. She would slip in without a word and appear in front of him like an apparition from hell. She couldn't remember the speech she prepared on her way over. What a pretentious, soulless place this was. No character. Just like living in a second-rate hotel. What was she going to say? It didn't matter. She would make it up as she went along. He would get a piece of her mind. She would threaten legal proceedings if he didn't agree to an immediate retraction. Was it libel or slander? She could never remember which was which.

She eased her way along the hallway toward the lounge. The traitorous bastard would be in the kitchen area, coffee in hand, reading his fucking masterpiece for the nth time. She was going to enjoy this.

She turned the corner.

Willard was halfway through recounting the morning's happenings to Harry when the two police officers arrived. Zelmo drifted off to check the garage cameras. His English wasn't good, and he had trouble understanding Willard's west country accent. Besides, he didn't want to be around in case someone asked about his immigration status.

'There has been an emergency call reporting a disturbance in the apartment above 219.' The police officer coughed and brought his voice down an octave. 'I assume that would be 319?'

'You assume correctly,' Willard said. It was an old cliché, but so true. Police officers seemed to get younger every day. This couple hardly looked old enough to have left school, dressed up in their grey-flannel uniforms, stab-proof vests, fluorescent yellow with the letters "ISE" printed on their backs. Babes in the wood. Clichés? There was a thing. When today's confusion was over, he would relax by compiling a list of his favourite clichés and then, categorise them. The idea was inspiring.

'Third floor?' The female officer asked.

'Right again.' The woman did not appreciate his sarcastic tone. 'I'm off duty now, but Harry here will follow you up as soon as his colleague finishes downstairs, and he can leave reception.'

As he collected his overcoat, Willard watched the monitor, first as the motion sensor prompted an image of the two officers walking along the corridor and then, switching to the eighth and tenth floors as residents moved around, activating the motion sensors. 'I'm off,' he said to Harry. 'Keep me posted.'

Five minutes elapsed as Harry swallowed the last mouthful of his bacon sandwich and was on the point of going to find out what was delaying the police. Suddenly, all hell broke loose.

With sirens blaring and lights flashing, two ISE police cars screeched to a halt outside the entrance to the building. These guys were older, experienced officers with a single purpose, no-nonsense attitude. The one with the moustache shouted orders to the five men who were exiting the cars. One was ordered to man the main entrance. Nobody was to enter or leave the property. A second man was sent to seal off the garage by securing the exit to the elevator on level one. The leader and his remaining three men ignored the elevators and headed for the stairwell.

A dozen curious residents assembled in the lobby were silenced as the noise on the stairs became louder. Two officers supported a woman between them, almost lifting her off the ground as the toes of her shoes scraped against the floor. The group of onlookers parted to let them through. Harry could see the patches of blood on her raincoat and across the knuckles of her right hand. Her head was uncovered, her face, grey and pallid, her eyes lifeless.

As the police manoeuvred the woman into a car, somebody amongst the onlookers spoke up in a broad Cockney accent. 'That's the woman Morgan slagged off in this morning's paper. She obviously didn't take kindly to what he wrote.'

Harry turned to find Zelmo at his side. He poked his colleague in the ribs and gave him a knowing wink. 'Wait 'til I tell the wife,' he said.

By midday, order had returned to the building. The residents who witnessed the arrest were herded into a meeting room on the first floor to be interviewed before being allowed to leave the building. A team of uniformed police were charged with knocking on doors. Extensive areas of the building, including reception, were sealed off as potential crime scenes. Exiting and entering the building was through a rear entrance controlled by two ISE officers.

Willard was summoned back to the building. Following on from his recounting of the morning's events, a team of individuals in white protective suits, plastic overshoes and face masks were not only active on the third floor but spraying and dusting around the elevators on the ground floor and sealed off areas on the lower floor garages. The place was a hive of activity. Dozens of press teams huddled together outside the locked main entrance, waiting patiently for somebody to say something factual to quell the rumours.

Half asleep and alone in the janitors' rest room with the door ajar, Willard cursed the inactivity. He should be at home, working on a chronological listing of all that morning's events, cross-referenced and colour-coded to each resident. It was pointless for him to sit here doing nothing.

Harry was on his lunch break, leaving reception unmanned whilst a nervous Zelmo was questioned by an ISE officer. His barely audible answer was to repeat he had not seen or heard anybody. Harry told him to piss off home before he got himself and the boss into trouble.

Footsteps stopped just before the door to the restroom. Willard recognised the voice of the female ISE officer, who was the first to arrive that morning. She cursed to herself. The faint ring of the mobile suggested it was tucked inside her uniform and the one-word exclamation, perhaps a reaction to the name of the caller on the screen.

'Yes, Sir,' she stammered. 'We were the first on the scene.' She listened. 'Lying face up on the carpet in the middle of the room,' she answered. Another pause. 'I'd suggest multiple stab wounds, sir. CSI personnel are investigating as I speak.' A longer silence, but still she did not move, nor investigate if anybody was behind the partially open door. Her voice was growing in confidence. 'The woman was kneeling alongside the body, blood stains on her clothing and dripping from the kitchen knife she was holding out. Cadet Hammond ordered her to put down the weapon, but she failed to comply. He used his taser on her. We took her into custody with the assistance of officers from the rapid response team.'

A radio transmitter crackled. 'What do you want, Tina?' an irritated male voice asked.

'Assistant Commissioner Bradley is on my phone. He wants to know if we have a positive ID of the victim.'

'Right.' The frustration in his voice became measured as he tried to sound efficient rather than annoyed. 'Not confirmed, as yet, but an SCO advised me he was Seth Morgan, a journalist. I am led to believe the woman we are holding in custody was the subject of a derogatory article the journalist filed which was published this morning.' He waited while his colleague asked if the Assistant Commissioner had heard the exchange. 'With motive and caught in the act, it would seem,' he added gratuitously.

Willard heard the call end and the female officer walk away. That chronological list he intended to prepare would be essential to assist the ISE in the investigation. The woman may well have been the guilty party, but as sure as God made little apples, something else took place in that apartment before she got there.

# THIRTY-ONE

## EISENBAHNKREUZUNG – STRASSBURG – GERMANY

## 19.00 (18.00 GMT) - 19 November 2065

It was as if he were seeing the world encased in a soundless bubble, like watching the television on a giant screen with the sound off. Cut off from the familiar sounds of the commuter rush hour by the efficient treble-glazed windows of the *Schwarzwald Express,* destination Basle, Jack looked on as the crowds of people milled around the Strasbourg rail hub.

The train had been standing at the platform for ten minutes, the hubbub of passengers joining long since abated. Now, they were waiting for the connection from Frankfurt to finish coupling for the last leg of the journey south. The scheduled arrival time was just after eight.

Beneath an outwardly relaxed veneer, Jack was melancholy. Saying goodbye to Alison had been a wrench. He felt unusually protective toward her, insisting on a cuddle while he passed on some unnecessary piece of advice, as if she were that gangly youth again. In truth, he recognised she was better able to look after herself than either he or Usher. Alison claimed fluency in both German and French, a boast he willingly accepted. Every one of the conductor's bilingual announcements she translated without hesitation, including the brief historical explanation of how, after eleven/eleven and the abolition of the EU and its parliament, Strasbourg became a border city, shared by France and Germany. Both languages were officially recognised, although, over the intervening years, German became more prominent with the spelling of the city as Strassburg attributed in most official documents.

Alison even insisted on giving her father and Usher a thirty-minute course in basic conversational necessities for their visit. Listening to him, stumbling over the words, she giggled like the child he once knew and with whom he had felt so close. It was these memories tugging at his heartstrings as he watched her, backpack draped over her shoulder, walking away from him to find the connection to Stuttgart.

The contrast between the twins was striking. Harriet was always more clinging and needy, forever vulnerable as she sought the help of those around her. Alison was also vulnerable, but her transition from child to adult discarded unconditional love for a cocktail of extreme passion, tempered with bouts of self-doubt and the need to challenge the validity of every powerful emotion she experienced.

Jack's shoulders shuddered as he sighed.

'A penny – or should I say a credit for your thoughts?' Usher looked up from her paperwork and smiled. 'Still concerned about Rebecca?'

He had not managed to complete the call at the changeover in Paris. Whatever influence he tried to impose on the operator was met with a standard response, blaming the censors and promising to call back the number he gave her as soon as authorisation was granted. He waited until the last moment, almost missing the train as his frustration grew.

'I'll call from the hotel this evening.' He shook his head. 'I can still remember a time when people were never off their mobiles, texting and making calls at will. It's a paradox to be living in the future yet enduring such an archaic communication system.'

Her smile was warm and genuine. 'I get your impatience. It's understandable, but the world's obsession now is with security. The laissez-faire behaviour you mention played no small part in the catastrophe of eleven/eleven. We can't allow that to happen again, whatever the inconvenience. Besides, as I recall, people were never off their mobiles. My parents, God rest their souls, would take us kids to some swanky restaurant for dinner and then, spend all evening studying their mobiles and forcing us to look at pictures of Aunt Maude eating breakfast in Lanzarote with the enthusiasm of Moses receiving the Ten Commandments. For one, I'm grateful it's in the past.'

'I take your point. I guess you can thank this obsession with security to keep your pay cheque coming.'

'I'm not sure how to take that,' she challenged playfully. 'Put it this way; I doubt I'll ever be out of work.'

'No fear of that. Homeland plays a vital role.'

'As we're on the topic of work, can you help me with something?'

His forehead wrinkled. 'If I can.' He looked at the folder she was holding. 'With a blue ISE? I cannot imagine what.'

She removed a summary sheet from the file. 'Just over six weeks ago, a retired ISE family liaison officer was callously murdered at his home in Whitley Bay, Northumberland. The man was tortured before he died. Whoever killed him was after something, most likely information, as nothing of value was taken.'

Jack shook his head. 'I don't get it. Why is it your concern? You are Homeland, prisoner welfare and rehab, aren't you? My first reaction is it sounds like a revenge killing; somebody this ex-policeman put away, wanting to get his own back. What's your interest?'

'This victim wasn't on the task force. In the days before Homeland, when it was the Home Office in control, he would have been a consultant in the family liaison group. He boasted a psychology degree and specialised in victim support and the welfare and rehabilitation of young offenders back into the community.' She rocked forward in her seat. 'Hardly fits the revenge theory you're advancing.'

'Go on,'

Alongside his relaxed attitude, did she detect a note of wariness in his voice? 'The safe was open,' she went on. 'He must have given up the combination under duress. All it contained were old case files, ones in which he took a particular interest and felt the information would be prejudicial to the wellbeing of the subject if it became public knowledge.'

'Do you know if any were taken?'

'He had a coded record on his laptop of the files he kept. Sure enough, one was missing.'

Jack pinched his eyes closed. He knew what she was about to say.

'I guess the name Gordon Bachelor is familiar to you? Chief Inspector Gordon Bachelor?'

'My file was taken?' He did not wait for an answer. 'The resettlement paperwork covering my transfer from the children's home to my parents.'

'Your foster parents,' she specified. 'Yes. Can you think of any reason someone would murder to get it?'

Jack shook his head. 'Bachelor. Geordie Bachelor. There's a name to conjure with from my past. What a guy. From the moment I came around after the accident, he was always there when I needed someone. He was my prop during those initial months after my parents died. Looking back, I don't know where I would be now without his guidance. Whatever mood I was in, there was always Geordie's perspective on life, guiding me onto some middle ground where I could see things more clearly.

'For those first six months, until I moved in with the Pearsons, he must have spent half of his working life caring for my needs. Who would be prepared to kill such a genuine and irreplaceable human being?'

'Somebody, it seems, determined to get hold of information important to them. I was hoping you might help us?'

A scratchy announcement in German filled the compartment, followed by a jolting movement as the train shunted forward twenty metres to couple with the adjoining carriages. They now looked out on a sign displaying *Strassburg/Strasbourg Eisenbahnkreuzung*.

The diversion gave him time to recognise the signs of the onset of a panic attack. She was looking at him, studying his face, her expression seeking an answer to her request. Should he lie? She would see through any phoney explanation; possibly sour a working relationship, which was getting off to a relaxed and promising start. He would take a chance.

'I can't tell you when it will happen or why it does, but, on the odd occasion when I am forced to confront something from my youth or experience a disjointed flashback, I suffer a debilitating reaction.' He stopped and swallowed hard. 'It starts with a foul smell and a searing, acrid sensation in my nose. My throat closes. I suffer from severe palpitations and end up fighting for breath and near to collapsing. It lasts for a few minutes, which feels like a lifetime, and then recedes.'

He looked for sympathy or, at least, understanding, but sensed only incomprehension and impatience in her face. 'I felt an attack coming on just now,' he said rather weakly. 'I'm not trying to evade your questions. If you just give me a few minutes . . .' He trailed off.

The reason he confided his distress in so few people was written all over Usher's stoic expression, the pseudo-comforting, resigned look of somebody saying goodbye to a not-so-close relative for the last time. She was the product of a new regime; one that treated weakness in others as failure and related only to strength of character and purpose. It was as if individuals who wielded power were subliminally indoctrinated to look at mental suffering as defining a second-class citizen, a burden on others who should be confined to the margins of society.

She was becoming impatient. 'This physical reaction is genuine,' he said firmly, as anger overrode the symptoms of his unexplained distress. 'The only answer I can give you is a potted history of the period of my life when Geordie played a part in my development. There is no motive for murder.'

'All the same, I'd be interested to hear.'

His first recollections following the accident were of a convalescent home in southern Germany, where he remained for several weeks. Jack was treated for minor injuries in Frankfurt before being transferred, although he had no memory of the events surrounding the tragedy. A doctor at the home said he was suffering from traumatic dissociative amnesia. Eventually, he could hope for partial recall.

Geordie collected him from the home, the first English person he had spoken with since the accident. They bonded almost immediately, a relationship forged out of necessity. Jack felt a sense of abandonment when he was eventually handed over to the couple who would become his foster parents.

Jack's initial feelings of loss and despair were handled inadequately in his new environment. For all their good intentions, the Pearsons were not the best fit for their charge. Foster mother Helena was a career woman who saw her role during the few leisure hours her working day allowed, as providing the social backdrop to the family and extending moral support to her husband. As a former nurse in a psychiatric facility, Nigel Pearson was a carer with no parenting skills, who believed a controlled and regimented lifestyle was appropriate for the wellbeing of a teenage boy who craved friendship, a mentor and the emotional understanding of a kindred spirit.

It was Geordie who filled this void, always available at the end of a phone, always ready to set up a face-to-face meeting if there was a personal issue Jack could not resolve or did not feel comfortable discussing with his parents. Geordie would listen, talk through the problem and present Jack with a series of options rather than pontificate or pass summary judgement. Jack was always left to make the final decision and, more often than not, Geordie would tell him afterwards it was the choice he would have made.

On his eighteenth birthday, along with the customary card, Geordie sent a present. It was a book, well-read and dog-eared on how to overcome adversity, to deal with life's challenges single-handedly. Trust your judgement, said the note on the flyleaf in a shaky hand. Time for us both to move on. Never forgotten, it read and was signed "Geordie".

'We were never in contact again,' Jack said. 'At first, I was consumed with self-pity. I saw the comment as a sop to yet another rejection in my life; betrayed by my birth parents, who deprived me of a proper family life. Now, I was cast aside by my one genuine ally, the policeman who befriended me, only to discard me when I needed him most. Or so I thought.'

As he read the book and the months passed, Jack's view slowly changed. Geordie was never his support; that was too gracious and intimate a word. Geordie was his prop, a transition; the means to overcome the hurdles which the tragedy presented. Erecting barriers to handle disappointments, as he sought to do, was the opposite course to embracing the problem, putting it in perspective and moving on, as the handwritten note put it. The book taught him to see the gangly policeman with the stooped back and permanent frown, not as an enemy, but as his one true ally. The passage of time may have dulled the memories, but news of his death brought their relationship to the forefront of his mind.

'I remember a kind and gentle man who went beyond the call of duty to help me. Why anybody would want to kill him is beyond me.' He stopped to organise his thoughts. 'If you keep something in a safe, it either has some tangible value or you don't want anybody to see it. I can't see why my file could fall into either category. Are you certain nothing else was taken?'

Usher's attitude softened, her impatience diminished. 'I apologise. I didn't wish to appear unfeeling. Whoever it was - and we can't rule out a "she" as well as a "he" - they took an antique hunting rifle mounted on the wall but left several easy saleable items in the house. We have discounted robbery as a motive. No fingerprints; no DNA; nothing disturbed; this was a planned operation and, as far as we can judge, directed at obtaining information about you.'

'If you're asking me whether I've been contacted by a stranger interested in my past then, the answer's a definite "no".' He thought of mentioning the incident of the bullet at Sandys Hall but decided against it.

Reporting it at this late stage would provoke too many questions. Even so, he could not discount a connection. 'I can't see how details of my youthful progression could be of value to anybody.'

'Me neither,' she acknowledged.

'Sorry to press the point, but I still don't get the link to Homeland as far as the murder investigation is concerned. Okay, so, person unknown took a copy of an ancient Home Office file which Geordie kept, let's say, for old time's sake. ISE might need to ask you questions, but involve you in the investigation?'

She nodded and shuffled a single sheet of paper from her briefcase. 'It's still an ISE-led investigation, but there are additional factors which concern my department.' She passed the paper to him. 'This is a transcript of the decoded index found on Geordie's laptop identifying the files in the safe. You will note the title *J. Tirrand (Supplementary)*. The inference is another file exists which, if kept anywhere, would be stored at our Nine Elms facility.'

'And does it exist?'

Her sideways glance and a moment's thought told him a straight answer was unlikely. 'With any murder enquiry, the victim's name is flagged with all INCOL departments to establish what is known about him or her. If Geordie's name came up in any context, it would be reported to the investigating officer.'

'And it did?'

'A hard copy of a case file kept by Homeland Storage at Nine Elms went missing about a fortnight ago. It reappeared at the end of the week, but the circumstances suggest it was removed from the premises and copied before somebody made a ham-fisted attempt to return it. The section head has been under suspicion for some months, and I'll be interviewing him when we get back.'

'You're going to tell me its relevance?'

'I don't know yet. It passed across my desk on its way to ISE. All I can tell you is Gordon Bachelor was the family liaison officer in the case in question and there are large sections which have been redacted on orders of the presiding judge in a criminal case. More than that, I'm afraid you will have to wait until the file is returned. At present, it's classified.'

Jack choked back the accusation he was about to levy, deciding to wait for a more opportune moment to broach the subject. Instead, he said, 'The assumption is the murderer thinks there is a tie-up between the two?'

'And possibly tying himself up in knots doing so. I will check in with my contact at ISE later in the week. Monday's not the best day to chase after people.' She hesitated. 'And I guess you've got plenty on your plate dealing with this attempted hatchet job on you.'

'Right now, it's Rebecca I'm more concerned about.' He could just envisage her launching a verbal tirade at the journalist who tricked her. She would be feeling terrible and craving Jack's support. He must speak with her as soon as possible, take the heat and emotion out of the moment.

A cool head would be needed if he were to quash the allegations, manage the damage limitation and preserve his professional status.

# THIRTY-TWO

## ISE SERIOUS CRIMES UNIT –FULHAM – WEST LONDON

## 19.00 - 20 November 2065

She was left propped on a chair in an interview room until late in the afternoon, by which time the effects of the taser had worn off and her continuous protests and banging on the reinforced door finally attracted attention. The lock turned and a young girl dressed in civilian clothes held out a coffee in a polystyrene cup. Rebecca drank greedily as the girl retreated toward the door.

She drained the last drop of foamy milk, which settled around her lips. 'When can I get out of here?' she asked, but the door closed before she finished the question.

Two men in ISE-issue uniforms of grey bomber jackets over black shirts entered the room. The younger man – she put him in his mid-twenties – with greasy hair, a pointed chin on an angular face, held the door open. His colleague followed; a man in his forties sporting collar-length hair streaked with silver strands and with steel-blue eyes that appraised her with the look of someone accustomed to being in control.

'I am Inspector Diamond,' he said. 'My colleague is Officer Porfeiro. We are obliged to caution you.'

As the young officer began, Rebecca interrupted, turning toward the older man. 'Now, you wait a minute. You are not attempting to implicate me in Morgan's death?' She made it sound as though there could be nothing more ludicrous. 'I was trying to help him, not kill him.' She held the man's gaze.

'How would you interpret it?' the Inspector said, offhandedly. 'You are kneeling next to the body of a man who has been repeatedly stabbed. There is a substantial amount of blood on your clothing and a knife in your hand. You avoided security at the front desk to reach his apartment unannounced. Opportunity was not a problem. As for motive and premeditated intention, the victim had just written and published in today's paper a derogatory piece about you and your philandering husband. You must have been furious with him. So, tell us, why on earth shouldn't we treat you as a murder suspect?'

'Because I didn't do it.' She enunciated each word slowly. 'It should have been obvious to whichever of your people was first on the scene – the young girl, as I recall – I was trying to establish whether there were signs of life.'

'You have medical training?' Porfeiro butted in, raising his eyebrows at his colleague.

'Of course I do,' she said dismissively. 'After eleven/eleven, every able citizen had to take a four-week nursing and first aid course, not only to assist with the victims requiring longer-term care but to be prepared in case of a future attack. Tracing a pulse and CPR were basic procedures. It has come in handy more than once.'

'And I suppose holding a knife above the victim's chest is part of the survival course?'

'It was lying on his chest. I simply picked it up to remove it to apply CPR. It should be blindingly obvious.'

'What had you in mind to do when you confronted the journalist?' The Inspector took over with a hand raised toward his subordinate.

'I didn't think it through. I was offended and annoyed, more for being deceived into believing his motives were genuine and the article was to be based on my charity work. I suppose I would have screamed and shouted at him, called him a bastard and insisted he published a retraction to refute all the spurious allegations and innuendoes.' She laughed to herself. 'I certainly did not go there envisaging I would get physical with him. After all, look at me.' She bent her arm as if flexing a muscle.

Conversation stopped as the door opened and the girl who had delivered Rebecca's coffee nervously approached the Inspector to whisper in his ear. After a brief mumbled exchange, both men rose as one and, ushering the girl before them, walked out.

Alone, fearful, angry and frustrated, Rebecca banged her fist on the metal table as tears welled in her eyes.

The elder of the two ISE detectives read from the card he held between his thumb and index finger. 'Senior Deputy Arnold Roach, to what do we owe your presence? You mentioned at reception an interest in the incident at Chelsea Harbour?'

Roach withdrew his fingertips from the other man's grasp. 'Whom am I speaking with?'

'Apologies.' The Inspector introduced himself and his junior officer. 'How can you help us?'

Roach looked from one to the other as if they were begging for money and unworthy of his largesse. In his eyes, the men and women from ISE were indoctrinated to treat everyone with suspicion and would question his motives if it looked as if he was muscling in on their investigation – which is exactly what he was doing.

'I thought it appropriate to provide my assistance. You have a suspect in custody, the wife of a fellow deputy. I have her trust. By speaking with her when this conversation concludes, I can establish the facts. I am here at the express request of Senator Simeon Hill.'

Leaning forward to activate the recording machine, Diamond spoke, noting the time, place, and those present. 'Can you detail the reason for your visit to ISE today, Senior Deputy Roach?' He hesitated and smiled. 'Please?'

'To clarify an unfortunate coincidence which will surely come to your notice is the fact that we visited Chelsea Harbour this morning. We were in a VW Incoletta.'

'At what time and who is "we"?'

Roach blew air out of puckered lips. 'Around nine-forty-five. You will already know the exact time from the CCTV record. I was with Senator Hill and a driver.' He put up a hand to stop any interruption. 'We were about to park on the premises and seek the journalist's apartment. Whilst still in the car, the Senator received an urgent call, and we had to abort the visit. We stopped, remained in the car, turned around and drove out without seeing or speaking to anyone.'

'And this proposed visit was to do what?'

Roach wriggled, an uncomfortable expression on his face. The arms of the chair were pressing into his hips. He was feeling irritable, but he controlled the tone of his reply. 'There was an article in this morning's paper written by this journalist making allegations against one of my fellow deputies.'

'Jack Tirrand?'

'Correct. The Senator was given advance notice this article would appear. He was anxious to ensure there were no follow-up stories.'

'Why?'

'Deputy Tirrand is currently abroad, working on a sensitive policy issue. We do not want an important INCOL directive to be diminished or clouded by allegations relating to Tirrand's private life or his sexual conduct. You must see the difficulty we face?'

Diamond looked over a pair of steel-rimmed glasses as his subordinate nodded his agreement. 'Surely, the most effective would be to approach the paper's owner or the editor-in-chief rather than the journalist?'

'Senator Hill did indeed speak with the owner. He got the expected response, namely non-interference with editorial issues. It was the owner who suggested we approach the journalist. His editor was waiting for the follow-up story before taking any decision.'

'How did you expect to convince Morgan?'

'Hill expected he would have to offer a quid pro quo, a sweetener you would call it. He would ask for the story to be pulled in return for an assurance on a far bigger fish; advance notice of the policy issue with which Tirrand was dealing. Horse trading. Something like that, but, as I say, we never got around to it.'

Diamond appeared unimpressed. 'From the closed-circuit images, there was an eleven-minute window between the Incoletta passing reception on its entry and exit. Eleven minutes appear excessive for stopping, receiving a phone call and driving off. Don't you agree?'

Roach's cheeks coloured. 'I object to the inference.' His tone was ice cold.

'I am making none.'

'I believe you are.' His voice rose. 'All we did was wait in silence for the Senator to conduct his phone conversation, decide to leave, perform the manoeuvre and drive off. If it was eleven minutes, it took eleven minutes!'

Diamond appeared unmoved by the quivering lip and hostile expression. 'According to the record, the Senator's call lasted ninety seconds and was with his son. What occurrence was so demanding it would stop you from pursuing an important – what did you call it - policy issue?'

'It was a personal, domestic matter. If you require further information, you will have to contact the Senator.' Roach could no longer hide his frustration and irritability. 'Look, all this is irrelevant. Let me speak to the Tirrand woman. It's in our mutual interest.'

Diamond ignored the outburst. 'All in good time. In the eleven minutes you were parked, did you see anybody else enter or leave the garage area?'

'Possibly. I wasn't paying attention to traffic movement.'

'Specifically, three men in their thirties in a silver/grey compact?'

Roach shook his head. 'I'll check with my driver. He may have noticed.'

'Is there anything else you can contribute, Deputy Roach?' Diamond asked.

'Senior Deputy,' Roach corrected. He waved at the recording machine and drew his hand across his throat. Diamond gestured for Porfeiro to comply.

'This must be off the record,' Roach said.

'That has to be for me to decide.' Diamond watched as the big man grasped the arms of the chair and made to stand up. 'Withholding information is a penal offence . . . even for a senior deputy.'

Roach sat back down and folded his arms across his chest. 'I emphasise, what I can contribute is no more than gossip, hearsay and rumour.'

'Then we don't have a problem, do we?' Diamond smiled and leaned back, using the palm of his hand to smooth the material of his bomber jacket against his muscular frame. 'Gossip away.'

'Within the close community at Alexandra Palace, the word has been circulating for some weeks of a change in Tirrand's temperament, irascible, short-tempered as opposed to his normal relaxed attitude. He has taken an unhealthy interest in several younger women around the place and has confessed to difficulties in his home life. There have been tales of physical injuries, scratches, a badly bruised arm, a blue patch under his eye. I have seen none of this personally, but I assigned him a new aide with instructions for her to report back to me with anything out of the normal.' He accepted the glass of water Porfeiro offered him.

'I know he has family difficulties. His wife is a Fitzwilliam. Firebrands, the whole family. I wouldn't doubt her capacity to get violent with Tirrand if she thought he was playing away, so to speak. The old man once pinned another player's hand to the backgammon table with a steak knife. Accused the man of cheating. It's the Irish in the blood. Fiery, short tempers. Fiercely protective of their good name. Rebecca would have seen this article today as deriding the family's status. I'm sure she's capable of anything to protect their integrity. As for the daughters, one is off the rails, a loud-mouthed dissident keen to denigrate INCOL and what it stands for: the other, well, I'm guessing she's a third-pregnancy respondent who is scheming to keep the child. All in all, a dangerous bunch and one to watch.'

Diamond studied his lap as he listened and did not look up. 'Makes me wonder why you would choose somebody so volatile for your sensitive mission?'

'You are not a politician, are you, Inspector?' He made it sound like a criticism and did not wait for a comment. 'Putting his personal issues to one side, Tirrand is an experienced professional and was considered the best man for the job.' He winked at Porfeiro. 'You know what they say about keeping your friends close and your enemies closer.'

Diamond watched the politician shuffle down the corridor, his frame dwarfing the figure of the young woman sent to accompany him. 'What can we make of that?'

Porfeiro knew better than to offer an answer to a rhetorical question.

'Quite a hatchet job. If we were expected to have doubts about her beforehand, his intervention was a deliberate attempt to persuade us of her capacity to murder. Believe me, Luigi, with friends like him, you don't need enemies.'

The door opened slowly. Roach peered into the room.

Rebecca awoke at the sound of the door creaking and slowly lifted her head as she recognised the figure hovering in front of her. She gave a weak smile. 'Oh, it's you AR. A friendly face, at last.' The words belied the thoughts assembling in her head. You evil bastard, she thought. Come to gloat, have you? Well, I need to play you, for all it's worth.

'God, Rebecca, what have they done to you? I came as soon as I heard. And with Jack away on the Continent. What a terrible mess. How are you feeling? They can't believe you were involved in this awful business, can they?'

'I need a lawyer, AR. They keep ignoring my request. Can you do something about it for me, please? Contact Harbin Cuthbert. Father used to use him whenever he got into a scrape.'

'Plenty of experience, then?'

She ignored the inference. 'One of the best. Can you help me? I'll be forever in your debt.' She smiled, searching for a reaction in his eyes.

'Of course, first thing in the morning. I'll let your father know if you like?'

'Better not. My parents are getting on now, and it will come as a terrible shock. If you could have a private word with Robert, he can choose his moment and break the news to them gently. I've been told they can hold me here for up to seven days without charge or representation where national security is involved; though why the death of a gossip writer should fall into that category, I do not know.'

'What about the girls?'

'No!' From his taken-back expression, she realised her reaction was too dramatic. 'No, I don't want them to know until I know where I stand. They have busy lives and will want to offer support when, in truth, they can do nothing. Leave them out of it.'

'ISE may want to question them. Better if it comes from a friendly source first.'

'Ask Robert to do it, will you? Religious training teaches you all those soothing words. He's good at that.'

'Of course,' he bowed his head. 'Did the journalist say anything to you before he died?'

Her eyes widened. 'Good Lord, AR, what a question. Did somebody suggest you ask?'

'Not at all,' he backtracked.

'I was just curious.'

'Believe me, he was dead by the time I arrived.'

'I understand the apartment was ransacked. Were you looking for something, or was it already in that state?'

A look of realisation dawned on her face. She cast her eyes around the ceiling. 'Did they tell you to ask these questions, AR? Are they listening in?'

He waved a dismissive hand. 'I have no idea what they are doing. I can assure you, Rebecca, I am here of my own volition to help. Nobody has asked anything of me. If I let my curiosity run away with me, let me apologise.'

'Don't sound so pompous, AR. As I told the ISE men, I knocked on the door, saw it was open, walked in, announcing who I was and saw the body lying in the living room. I bent down over it at the precise moment the two uniformed officers entered. That's all I know.'

'It's all very unfortunate,' he said, shaking his head. 'Couldn't have happened at a worse time.'

Rebecca guffawed. 'On behalf of the late Seth Morgan and me, I apologise if his death and my apprehension have come at an awkward moment for you. In God's name AR, you're inconvenienced?'

He failed to acknowledge the sarcasm. 'Assuming what you say is true, and it's just a question of time before you're exonerated of any involvement in this business, I have to consider the impact on Jack, who is at the start of an important and sensitive assignment. The moment he finds out you are in custody, he will want to return. That would be a setback for our plans. The attempt to discredit him leaves the Senate in a difficult position. His credentials were impeccable but, true or false, we have been dealt a blow by the revelations.'

'Libellous lies, more like. What are you saying? You don't propose to tell him of the fix I'm in?'

'Not for a couple of days, no. There will be no publicity surrounding Morgan's death and your involve. . . presence at the scene, whilst investigations are ongoing. Even if he were here, I doubt the people at ISE would agree to his seeing you as he's likely to be followed everywhere he goes for comment until public interest wains. It would be best for everybody to leave him where he is.'

'He'll be concerned he's not able to contact me.'

Roach leaned forward to take her hand, but she withdrew it, leaving his arm outstretched across the table. He pretended to prim the cuff of his shirt and adjust his cufflinks. 'Subject to your agreement, I will suggest to these two ISE buffoons they let you put in a call to him. I suspect Jack will have read the article so, you treat it as a storm in a teacup and tell him you're going down to the family home in Devon to avoid all the press attention until it dies down. It will keep him focussed and, by the time he's back, you will be free of the chains that bind you, so to speak.'

You can't say anything without sounding like a pompous fool, she thought, as she watched the door close behind him. Even so, he was probably right. She agreed to his suggestion.

Porfeiro escorted Roach to the exit. 'Go as you planned?' he asked.

Roach's cheeks sagged in a hangdog expression. 'Tragic. Fine woman, regrettably, unable to control her temper. You know the old saying, when provoked, a woman scorned, etcetera.'

As a keen amateur dramatist, Porfeiro recognised the misquote from William Congreve's play but let it pass. Diamond's words were still ringing in his ears. 'Get that malignant old fucker off the premises before I say something I regret.'

# THIRTY-THREE

## ROTTENBURG – BAVARIA – GERMANY

## Mid-afternoon – 20 November 2065

Given the option, Alison decided she preferred her own company. It was a darn sight easier than having to deal with the baggage other people brought with them.

Leaving the train at Strasbourg yesterday had been a relief, she was sad to admit. After Paris, the atmosphere in their carriage was decidedly uncomfortable. Jack could not contact Rebecca in the time between changing trains and slipped into a sombre and pensive mood throughout the rest of the journey, saying little and answering in monosyllables. He was unduly emotional as they said their goodbyes at Strasbourg, clinging on to her, telling her to take care and kissing her with tear-filled eyes as he eventually let her go.

In stark contrast, Usher became quite a pain. She adopted a tactic of asking for translations of the conductor's announcements coupled with the odd word or phrase, skilfully interlaced with a series of probing questions into Alison's past family life. Initially, she found Usher refreshingly sympathetic, but as time passed, Alison realised she was being played, almost interrogated. It annoyed her to the point her answers became evasive, and she was about to explode.

With relief, she boarded the express to Stuttgart and a ninety-minute journey which started in hazy sunlight and ended in darkness. It was well into a chilly evening before she found and checked into the *Hostel Reisende-Osten*.

In a deserted pine-furnished dining room, with the unappetising remnants of a dinner buffet scattered over paper table covers, she ate a warming vegetable soup from an electric tureen and some slices of coarse, homemade bread laced with a pale, unsalted butter. It was no feast, but a welcome end to a tiring day.

As she fumbled in the darkness across the bedroom toward her bunk, trying to avoid waking the other three women sharing the loft space, Alison's thoughts drifted to her father and the intensity of that parting kiss on her forehead. She could not recall ever having seen him act with such affection.

Breakfast in the morning was a cacophony, raucous comments in several languages, laughing and good-natured repartee between the forty guests who occupied the various dormitories. Most were young, around Alison's age, including a women's hockey team from Hannover playing in a local competition and a group of serious-looking Czech young men in identical black shirts who were on some special skills training course. A lie about meeting up with her fiancé deterred the hiker who suggested she join him for the day.

The local train service to Rottenburg left after midday and it was three when Alison stood in the tree-lined suburban road where Dieter Eigard was recorded as a resident in the council office's citizen's register.

Compact, detached houses with regulation-sized gardens lined both sides of the road, ending in a cul-de-sac, bordered by a public park which, she discovered, also ran along the entire length of the back of the row of houses on Eigard's side of the road.

With a rehearsed storyline going around inside her head, she made her way along the pathway to the front door. Unlike most of the houses she had studied, this garden was uncared-for. Rolf's father was not the green-fingered equal to his neighbours. The door ring gave a hollow-sounding buzz. No reply. The house looked unoccupied, but she persisted with a second, longer push on the bell ring. Again, no response.

She made her way into the park and around to the back of the house. There was a creosoted, slatted wooden fence, high enough to avoid being overlooked, with a door at one end framed by the woodwork.

Alison looked around. A group of young boys were playing football nearby and, beyond them, various individuals or couples using the defined pathways to walk their dogs, occasionally stopping to use scoop-a-poop shovels and plastic bags to clear the mess. Further away still, a large children's playground was full of kids and their attentive parents.

She reached over the door to locate a large, standard bolt which creaked as she moved it. Quickly, she withdrew her hand. A boy wearing the white and black strip of the German national side was placing two coats apart on the ground in front of the fence to make space for the goal. He smiled at her and rubbed his hands together as he exhaled a cloud of hot breath into the chilled atmosphere. It was getting colder, and dusk was fast approaching.

She waited, feigning interest in the soccer match. Young kids playing kick a ball, she thought, was like a flock of birds coursing across the sky at sunset, all chasing and changing direction together as the ball was hacked across the grass. Suddenly, it span off toward a pathway where a large dog on an extended lead raced to stand over it, a low growl protecting it from the advancing players who, as if entranced, suddenly adopted statuesque positions. It was an OK Corral moment when whoever made the first move would break the spell.

As all attention was directed toward the scene, Alison reached over the fence, pulled on the bolt, slipped inside, and closed the gate behind her. She heard the game resume. The dog must have given up his prize.

The garden was fifteen metres long, laid with various bushes of hardy perennials dotted around a small, paved patio. As with the front, the original neat and cared-for configuration was now becoming overgrown and in need of attention.

There was no sign of life inside the property and no lights visible. She tried the handle on the kitchen door and the double French windows leading into the lounge. Both were locked. Beyond was a walled area, behind which she guessed was the garage. The curtains were partially open, allowing her to peer into a room furnished with old-fashioned dark wood furniture and an ageing red leather sofa.

Daylight was failing. What did she think she was doing? What could she say if the man suddenly appeared? Damn it, she was here to find out if this Eigard guy was genuine or not. Don't chicken out now.

She picked up a rock from the arrangement bordering the path. One of the small windowpanes in the kitchen door was already cracked. A tap and it would shatter into pieces. She could reach the Yale lock release. Forget it! What a stupid idea. Go around the front and wait for him to return.

She turned back to retrace her steps just as the cry of childish anguish, a sudden silence, followed by a collective groan, heralded the sight of the football as it came sailing over the fence. One bounce and it nudged against the kitchen door before coming to rest on the patio. Rock in hand, she wheeled around and thumped it against the cracked pane, shattering it into shards onto the kitchen floor. The biggest of the bushes was a metre away and large enough to hide behind.

There was a general melee on the other side of the fence; stilted conversations urging Heinrich to hurry and that it would be alright, the old man who lived there was kind and wouldn't mind. Another voice said they saw him go out, the place was empty and to hurry. They had to be home in ten minutes. Johann would bend down, and Heinrich could climb on his back.

Alison glanced up to see a sweaty face with curly brown hair and scared eyes appear over the fence. A tiny hand fumbled to release the bolt on the door. Through the leaves of the bush, she watched a boy in a football shirt of yellow and black creep gingerly into the garden toward the ball in the middle of the patio. He must have seen the broken window because she heard a whispered *Scheisse*. In an instant, the boy collected his prize and bounded back to the safety of the park, slamming the door behind him as he moved past. Unbolted, the door creaked back and forth on its hinges until the sound of the boys playing resumed and drowned the noise.

She moved into the kitchen. A selection of dirty crockery was piled in the sink alongside a stained melamine work surface with a stack of soiled packages like those she recognised from her occasional charity work on behalf of the university. Herr Eigard's meals for one were supplied by the German equivalent of HISSES, as the acronym was known in the UK: the Home INCOL Social Services Executive, supplying daily deliveries to the housebound elderly and infirm. Unlike the general untidy state of the working surfaces, the stand-alone gas hob and oven looked pristinely clean and hardly used. Don't expect to find a cookery book, she thought.

The rectangular-shaped lounge ran from the front to the back of the ground floor. She looked through net curtains toward the front. No movement: it was now dark: the hazy, orange light from the streetlamps casting a sinister glow into the room. She needed to hurry. Turning on a light, even the torch app on her mobile would alert anybody in the immediate vicinity.

Alison felt a chill run through her body. There was something uncomfortable about the room in which she was standing. First impressions from studying the detritus of newspapers, magazines and circulars scattered across the floor, a plate with remnants of fruit balanced on the arm of a tired-looking sofa, empty beer bottles lying on a rug; it all brought back memories of her early student days of living in a squat, somewhere transient and temporary with no soul. Yet, around the perimeter of the room were signs of caring, a mantlepiece above the fireplace with a set of polished brass cow bells, neatly arranged, a glass cabinet with shelves filled with trophies, engraved lidded beer steins and petite brass and porcelain figurines of skiers in various postures, all positioned with care. Set into a recess was a plain, varnished pine cupboard on top of which was centred an empty glass fruit bowl. Beyond the direct line of sight from the window, she chanced switching on the torch app. The beam of light highlighted shadowy lines in the dust right around the fruit bowl. Photo frames, she thought, but where were they now? It was a matter of seconds. There were six photographs in their frames, bundled under a pile of tablecloths and crocheted doilies in the bottom drawer. She moved the light onto the images, studying them one by one until she came to the three men, dressed in ski gear, smiling at the camera.

Someone was at the front door. She gasped and hurriedly turned off the light from the mobile. She held her breath. There was a sharp rap on the glass pane in the door. By peering around the lounge door into the hallway, she could make out the silhouette of a figure and the outline of a face pressed against the frosted glass. The shadow of another, smaller figure came into view.

There was yet another rap on the glass, this time louder.

She tucked the photograph into her identity card and travel authorisation wallet attached to the chain around her neck and made her way back through the kitchen and into the garden. Blood trickled onto the stone patio as she jarred her hand against the broken glass while locking the kitchen door from the inside. Wrapping a handkerchief around her hand, she set off through the gate into the park and back onto the road running along the front of the house.

A woman was leading the boy Alison recognised as Heinrich away from the house. She held a tight grip on the boy's collar and a troubled expression on her young but careworn face. The boy caught sight of Alison as she passed under a streetlight and said something to his mother. The woman stopped in her tracks and waited for Alison to approach.

'Heinrich said he saw you standing by the back gate of the old man's house. Are you something to do with him?' She was nervous, barely taking a breath as she talked and stumbling over the words.

'Can I help you?' Alison avoided a direct response.

'I wanted to see the gentleman before the curfew. I assume he is coming back tonight?'

Alison hesitated. She was having trouble understanding the mother's guttural German.

'I broke a window,' the boy chipped in.

The woman gave that long-suffering look Alison recognised as peculiar to mothers of errant children. 'I've told him and his friends a hundred times not to play so close to the fence. They get over-excited. I knew it would happen one day. I came to apologise and offer to pay for the damage, or, at least, his father will.' She swung round and tugged at the boy's arm. 'Wait 'til your father gets in. He'll teach you to go around breaking people's windows.'

'I didn't think I'd kicked it that hard,' Heinrich said in his defence. 'Maybe it was broken already.'

Blonde, curly hair slipped from beneath the woman's baseball cap as she turned back to address Alison. She looked so young, Alison thought, vulnerable and embarrassed.

'And maybe his father won't beat the living daylights out of him.'

The boy cowered at the prospect and, possibly, the memory of an earlier punishment.

Alison felt contrite. 'He's got a point,' she said. 'It could well have been cracked. I'm sure he didn't do it on purpose.'

'I know,' the woman said, softening. 'But this gentleman is not as understanding as old Herr Eigard. He used to come out and bring the boys water and biscuits.' She hesitated; suddenly aware she did not know who Alison was. 'That's not to say the current gentleman is unkind.'

'That was thoughtful of him. You said old . . .'

The boy's mother interrupted. 'It's all this sport. Too much running about these days. Everybody must be good at one sport or another to get ahead. Not enough brain power, thinking time. My father tells us of an age when kids could sit in front of a screen or play an electronic game for a quiet few hours, working out strategy and problem-solving. That's what they need; develop their minds, not their feet.' She drew a breath quickly. 'Somebody always has to spoil a good thing. Bad people started taking the machines to bits to make secret communications equipment, so the Senate banned everything.' She shook her head. 'Now, it's just football and TV and football on TV. No wonder they get bored.'

Alison nodded, but her mind was racing. 'You said old Herr Eigard?'

'You're not related, are you?'

Alison shook her head. 'I know a relative.'

'Then you won't mind me saying. His brother is different, a few years younger, but you would never think they were related. Not looks so much. You can see at a glance they're from the same stock. It's this one's temperament. He scares the boys. Never says a word. Just looks grumpy and bad-tempered. You must know him?' She looked puzzled.

Alison shook her head. 'It's his son I know.'

It was the woman's turn to look confused as her brow knitted. 'Knew, you mean. Bit confusing for a foreigner, German, I know, but you speak it well. The kids used to have six English lessons a week. Now, it's down to two and they make them learn Chinese.' She ruffled her hand through her son's hair. 'This one's got no flair for languages. Send him to Shanghai and he would go hungry.'

'And how is old Herr Eigard?'

'No idea. He collapsed, and they took him away late one night about six weeks ago. I had to fetch this one from the park. They play until all hours. I say to his father…'

Alison knew the conversation was about to drift away again. 'Sorry. Was he dead?'

The woman gave a snorted laugh. 'No. Think it was a stroke. That's what a paramedic said.'

'Where did they take him?'

'The hospice in Feldberg, I guess. That was the name on the side of the ambulance. It all happened suddenly and discreetly.'

'You are sure it said Feldberg?'

She nodded. 'I do because at first I thought it said Freiburg. Then, I remembered there was a report on the television. They converted an old refugee detention centre in Feldberg into a psychiatric hospital and hospice. I would have telephoned to see how he was, but you don't like to pry, do you?'

Car headlights swept into the road. Heinrich stepped close to his mother's side.

'I thought he'd be back before the curfew,' the woman said, noting her son's discomfort. 'Now, we'll see what he has to say.' She smiled at Alison. 'Are you staying here tonight?'

'No,' Alison said, conscious of the pulse beating in the side of her head.

The woman looked askance. 'Where then?'

'I booked a hostel in Stuttgart.'

'How on earth are you going to get back to Stuttgart before the curfew?' A thought occurred, and the woman reared her head back as if to look at Alison from another perspective. 'You're not one of them with special privileges, are you?'

Alison shook her head, but it was obvious the woman did not believe her.

The car pulled into a lay-by and an elderly man with thick-rimmed glasses peered out of the window, expressionless as he took in the scene before him. He slowly exited the car; his eyes fixed on the woman as she pushed the boy in front of her. The man hardly had time to stand upright before she was upon him, the words propelled from her mouth with a nervous energy.

The man looked over the woman's shoulder, his eyes locking with Alison's. He was curious, she thought, not suspicious or hostile. She could see the family resemblance. He was younger than the man in the photograph, but he had the same jutting chin and turned-up nose. What hair he had was black and outlined the bald circle on the top of his head. She guessed he would be two or three years younger than the man in the photograph. He buried his shoulders in a thick trench coat as the distraught woman pushed her son forward.

Alison held back, retreating from the glow of the streetlight so as not to appear involved in the conversation about a broken window. Her concern was about how to introduce herself, and the right words to choose.

A gloved hand gripped her arm, pulling her even further into the shadows. Her first reaction was to shout whilst trying to break the grip on her arm. A soft voice whispered in her ear, demanding she keep quiet. Before she could open her mouth, her aggressor spoke, a melodic voice that carried into the still of the night. 'Sorry to keep you waiting, my dear. You must be so angry with me. I can only apologise. Shall we go?'

The powerful hold on her arm became a squeeze as he backed her away from Eigard and the woman who was still berating her son's behaviour.

'Keep walking and say nothing if you value your life.' He spoke in English, the sound hissing in her ears.

Heinrich's mother turned her head at the sound of retreating footsteps. The foreign woman she was talking to had disappeared into the night.

'Strange,' the woman said, interrupting her anxious apology and looking at the bemused man. 'I thought she came to see you.'

# THIRTY-FOUR

## TODTNAU – BAVARIA – GERMANY

### Mid-afternoon – 21 November 2065

Jack picked up the note pushed under his hotel door. It was in Usher's handwriting. He was grateful she had respected the *Bitte Nicht Stören* - Do Not Disturb sign and his need for a few hours' downtime to work through yesterday's train of events. A car would pick them up at 3 pm. Another two hours yet. They were to meet Dr Manfred Richter and his team at the rather confusing-sounding *Das Bayerische Institut für Soziale Entwicklung* – The Bavarian Social Development Institute.

Absentmindedly, he picked up a crust of toast from his breakfast tray and held it between his thumb and index finger. He couldn't decide whether he was hungry; whether to eat it irrespective, or whether to open the window onto a bright autumn afternoon and feed it to the birds. A much better idea. The cold, dry air took away his breath, yet he relished the sensation.

He was feeling wretched, a hollow sensation in the pit of his stomach he had never experienced before. Common sense would not prevail. A combination of loneliness and confusion at the events and emotions of the previous day weighed on him.

He found saying goodbye to Alison much more challenging than he could ever have imagined. Wandering off across the platform, dragging the rucksack along with one hand, he remembered her as a child again, self-willed but vulnerable. His eyes watered at the thought of all those lost opportunities to get closer to her. Parents shouldn't have favourites, but he did.

Then there were the uncertainties. What had happened to Rebecca? Why couldn't he speak with her and put his mind at rest? What was all this business about Geordie Bachelor, God rest his soul, and a missing file surrounding Jack's fostering? The explanation Usher gave was tenable, but he doubted it was the entire story. The more likely was an attempt within the Assembly to discredit him, something in his past to be leaked to the press and added to the smear campaign to finish his career. What it could be, he had no idea.

Alighting from the train in Basle the previous evening, they were met by an overpowering woman in her thirties, square-faced with heavy features coated in foundation and with shoulder-length, peroxide-blonde hair, blackening at the roots. Once installed in the minibus, she reached for a microphone to announce herself as Katrina, Director of Public Relations, and with a theatrical sweep of the arm, presented their driver, Ruger, a dour-looking, muscle-bound individual who ignored the introduction and stared, face forward into the failing light.

As hard as her two passengers tried to follow the convoluted description of their onward journey and programme for the evening ahead, Usher was reduced to glancing at Jack with raised eyebrows and a crooked smile. Katrina's basic English was handicapped further by her need to speak before her brain was fully engaged with what she was saying. The result was a mishmash of half-complete statements, hurried corrections, and a series of non-sequiturs.

With a satisfied smile, she turned to sit alongside the driver and begin an earnest monologue in a language neither passenger understood.

The route took them north of Basle, past the abandoned frontier post that once marked the border of this Alpine enclave before the collapse of the world's monetary systems and the inevitable annexation of the Swiss territory by Germany. At least, Jack pondered, the occupation had been swift, peaceful and avoided bloodshed. They joined the old autobahn route running north along the Rhine before turning east past the picturesque town of Lorrach and into the hilly, pine-covered lower reaches of the Black Forest. Katrina pointed out they were still forty minutes from their destination, the village of Todtnau. Upon arrival, they were to check into their rooms and come straight down to dinner as the kitchen closed at 'nine on the face of the clock'.

Traffic was light, and they made good time as the road, once again, turned northward on the gradual climb along the escarpment. In halting English, Katrina described quaint-looking hamlets set in a landscape of dark-green forests alongside verdant pastures where cattle would graze, and bales of hay sit piled high in pine-clad storage barns.

The tranquillity of the surroundings did nothing to calm Jack's increasing anxiety. How much further before he could get to a telephone? His patience was at its limit.

*Willkommen in Todtnau,* the sign read. Thank God, he said to himself. At last. The feeling of relief turned into concern as they avoided the turnoff to the town and began a climb along a winding, narrow, single-lane road, rutted and ill-maintained. The headlights illuminated a high chain-link fence, topped with barbed wire which ran along the treeline as the road twisted and turned. The fence must have extended for a kilometre before they finally reached a set of double gates, manned by a security guard who acknowledged the driver's curt nod of the head and stood to attention with his rifle shouldered as they passed.

Inside the gates, a recently paved road ran parallel to the perimeter, coming to a dead end as they swung into a car park with a flag announcing '*Gasthaus Bise*'.

In the silence, Jack heard the crunch of the gravel under his feet. There was a dry chill in the air, enough to cloud his breath and provoke an involuntary shiver. The scene before him was surreal. To his front, picked out by spotlights, strategically placed to illuminate the entire area, was a chocolate-box image of an alpine chalet building in glistening pine with a pitched roof. On the upper two floors, he counted twelve small balconies straddling the carved pine frontage, all decked with suspended troughs of brightly coloured flowers. On the ground floor, on either side of the double entrance doors were a series of windows inset into the lacquered pine cladding, leading to a row of full-length sliding glass doors to allow diners in the restaurant a view of the sloping grassland beyond the car park. It looked idyllic, the place for a hideaway vacation: that was until he turned half-circle toward the perimeter fence. The spotlights shining so benignly on the hotel took on a far more sinister aspect when directed outward. The beams oscillated in wide sweeping arcs, picking out a wide drainage ditch running alongside the chain-link fence. It reminded Jack of a scene from those ancient film classics where prisoners of war looked out at the boundary of their captivity and dreamed of escape and freedom. He felt his throat constrict. As much as he could accept Katrina's explanation that the defences deterred unauthorised visitors, the converse was also true. It kept in any inmates they did not wish to let out.

They were hurried through the registration formalities, identity cards and travel warrants surrendered to reception for inspection by the authorities and led by a swarthy Middle Eastern-looking porter past the restaurant to an old-style concertina metal entrance to the elevator. Their arrival provoked little interest amongst the men at the bar.

Katrina ignored Usher's forceful suggestion she and Jack dine alone, waving the protestation away and insisting 'Please down to restaurant straight away come'.

By the time they found their way to the dining room, Katrina had already ordered their meal and sat at the table, reeling off commands to employees, all of whom, Jack realised, were of Middle Eastern appearance. Without exception, they reacted with total reverence, heads bowed and unresponsive to the obvious contempt in her voice. There were few diners around to witness Katrina's performance, just two couples finishing coffee at tables out of earshot.

Jack finally booked a call to Rebecca. Reception would contact him when the connection was made. Feeling relaxed for the first time that day, he realised how hungry he was when a plate of thick potato and vegetable soup was placed in front of him. He smiled at the waitress and remarked on how all the staff appeared to have been recruited from a pool of Middle Eastern immigrants.

He soon regretted making the comment. It was the cue for Katrina to launch into a halting and disjointed explanation, punctuated as she indelicately crammed food into her mouth and rinsed it down from a glass of wine regularly replenished by an attendant waitress. She talked of a large migratory influx of refugees from Saudi Arabia, Kuwait and the other former oil-producing states.

'They come after eleven/eleven,' she said. 'Saudi Arabia have little land not contaminated and no money when oil stop; so, people starve. Our government then silly, allow millions to come to Deutschland. They say do work German people won't do, but it don't happen like that. These peoples no want wait on tables. They want to be doctors, engineers, boss men, like they was in the desert. They want mosques, build areas just for them to live. They no want be German. They want build little Saudi Arabia in the Black Forest or in the Ruhr or the Rhineland. We couldn't have this, could we? Imagine in your country.' She teased a large chunk of pork fat into her mouth, smudging her lipstick as she did so.

'INCOL solve that problem,' she said, stopping to wipe the red-tinged globules of fat from her chin with a starched white napkin. 'All jobs now classified: A, the most important, down to F, sweep sidewalks or mend roads. Migrants only allowed to work in category E or F. Hotel and restaurants, group E. Don't like it? Go home. Bibi.'

By the time the apple strudel arrived, Katrina had exhausted her list of prejudices and Jack and Usher, weary of the company, were ready for bed.

'Any problems during night,' Katrina said, as she made to leave. 'Ruger come back after drive me. He on security duty. Speak with him. Curfew now until six. Forbidden to leave hotel unless you have one of these.' She held out the plastic identity tag around her neck. 'Gangs of bad men.' She pointed at the two waiters making up tables for breakfast. 'Their countrymen. No jobs. Go around at night, attacking people, robbing and hurting. Dangerous to go outside. These DCs nasty men.'

'DCs?' Usher queried.

'Americans give them name, Dune Coons.' She shook hands with them. 'Tomorrow morning, I send you papers to study for afternoon appointment at the Institute. Please read. Ruger will tell you when it time to go.' With that, she turned and swept out of the room.

Before they could exchange impressions, the receptionist called over to Jack to tell him his caller was on the line.

He would take it in his room. With a hurried apology and a promise to catch up with everything tomorrow, he raced for the stairs, his 'goodnight' coinciding with the hotel lights dimming to an emergency glow. Through the landing window, the external arc lights traced a pattern across the car park to highlight the boundary fence and the road beyond.

The conversation did nothing to put his mind at rest. Rebecca was distant, her answers to his questions hesitant and non-committal, as if she were under some form of external control. It was so unlike the forthright woman with a fierce tongue and spontaneous response he knew and loved.

He asked if everything was all right and she assured him it was, even though she avoided talking about the journalist, his article and her reaction. It was in the past, she said, and all she wanted was peace and quiet. In the morning, she was planning to leave for Devon and would be out of touch until he returned. She urged, almost pleaded, as it sounded to him, to get on with his assignment and not to worry about her. He could catch up with all the news when he got back at the end of the week.

Her telling him not to worry did little to address his concern. Her voice lacked her spirit, the emotion always present whenever she spoke. Perhaps it was the suggestion of his infidelity in the article. He needed to reassure her.

'You sound down, darling,' he said. 'You mustn't let a trashy newspaper article with not a shred of truth get to you. It's all innuendo with no substance. The suggestion I am or have been unfaithful to you is absurd and untrue. I can and will explain the circumstances to you as soon as I'm back.'

'It's not that, Jack. I do trust you. It's all got too much for me. Look, let's not talk anymore tonight. I need to get some rest and I'm sure you have a big day ahead.'

And so, he ended the call with so much unsaid and a sense of frustration at being apart from her. He felt cornered, unable to react as he would want. A sense of rage was building inside him, the urge to strike out at someone. He just did not know who that someone was.

He could not remember ever having felt this way before. Yet, there was a voice inside his head telling him that this vengeful, violent urge was the genuine, unrestrained Jack Tirrand, not this bland politician following the dictates of an ephemeral authority.

\* \* \*

Inspector Diamond took the receiver from her trembling hand and replaced it on the handset. He turned to see the tears rolling down her cheeks. He handed her an ironed and folded handkerchief. In between staggered sobs, she thanked him and dabbed at the tears. 'I didn't think people used hankies anymore,' she stuttered, accepting his gesture to keep it. 'Don't tell me you're old fashioned?'

'My mother always insisted on a pointed white handkerchief showing in your top pocket and another, folded in your trousers. This was the sign of a gentleman. I gave up the top pocket option after Mum's funeral, but I guess keeping one handy reminds me of her every time I need it, and that's important.' He gave a self-effacing half smile. 'You didn't let your husband know what your situation is?'

'What is my situation?' The tears stopped. She gripped the damp handkerchief in a clenched hand.

'You need to instruct a solicitor. Tell him you are under arrest but have not been charged.'

'AR said he was sorting one out for me.'

'AR?'

'Deputy Roach. It was he who insisted Jack was not to be burdened with my problems whilst on such an important mission. I asked him to contact our family lawyer.'

Diamond looked up at the ceiling and the blinking light of the camera recording the conversation. He lowered his head and nodded toward the one-way, tempered glass screen, drawing his hand across his throat as he did so. The camera light blinked once and stopped.

'Did you kill Seth Morgan?' He looked into Rebecca's eyes.

'No,' she said, returning his gaze without blinking. 'And you know I didn't.'

'Even if I believed you, and I'm not saying if I do or do not, the decision to charge you with murder rests with my superiors. Should they decide to proceed, your chance of an acquittal is unlikely.'

'Even though I am innocent?'

'Even if you are innocent,' he emphasised.

'That's preposterous.' She rounded on him, her voice measured and determined. 'Do your job. Don't look in my direction. Find the real culprit.'

'Listen and take what I have to say to heart.' There was no emotion in his voice. 'My job is to investigate all viable leads, every shred of evidence. That I will do, but I offer no guarantees and, I'm afraid, it's not the issue you face.'

'You're making no sense.'

He nodded, more to himself than to her. 'I assume you have never been involved in the criminal system?' He took the blank stare as confirmation. 'It's not like the olden days when twelve just and honest citizens sat in judgement over their fellow man, weighing up the evidence in trials that lasted weeks and months. Those days are long since gone. The credo now is summary judgement. If you are charged, the circumstantial evidence surrounding your involvement would undoubtedly see you condemned. The trial will last, possibly all morning. The judge will find you guilty and your plea for mercy would, at best, see you in a collective farm prison for the rest of your days.'

She shook her head. 'My family; my husband; they have influence,' she stuttered, shaken by his remarks.

'Your family is of the old school, now regarded as little more than an irritant by the authorities. Your husband is being discredited, possibly facing expulsion as a deputy and public humiliation. Believe me, Rebecca – you don't mind if I call you that when the recording is off? - they can do nothing for you. You must place your trust in an experienced advocate who can pre-empt the charge before the Justice Executive issues a warrant.'

'AR promised to contact someone.'

'You bring me to another topic. My advice is not to rely overly on Deputy Roach. He is a politician with several agendas, some of which might well be furthered by your husband's disappearance from the public eye and the Fitzwilliam name fatally blemished by your conviction.'

'Why would he do that? He's always been supportive of Jack and the girls.'

'Genuinely, I have no idea, and it's of no professional concern to me beyond my investigation. Off the record, if I were to tell you he was present at the property where the murder was committed just before you arrived?' He left the question hanging in the air.

Rebecca sat back in her chair. 'Why was he there?'

'I am not prepared to go into details, but I'm guessing he has little interest in contacting your lawyer until the charge is issued.'

She was lost for words. For the first time, he detected genuine fear in her eyes. 'I am only interested in the truth,' he said. 'If nobody has been in contact with you by the morning, I will speak unofficially to a first-class defence lawyer I've been cross-examined by more than once. Trust him with the truth. If anybody can put a spanner in the works, as my dad used to say, he can. I will hold off sending my charge sheet to the Justice Executive until tomorrow night. There will be time, but you need to act.'

Before she had time to reply, he spoke again. 'Now let's get back to the formal interview. Remember, we stopped for a toilet break.'

He gave a thumbs up and the camera light blinked once again.

\* \* \*

Jack flicked absentmindedly through the sheaf of papers taken from the envelope which the room service waiter delivered just before the lunch gong sounded around the complex.

The report, marked 'Strictly Confidential' and noted as having been translated from the German original, was entitled, 'CORE - Subsistence - Supply and Demand – Forecast through 2100.'

He scanned each page, highlighting the sections of interest, and paying summary attention to the reams of statistics and sensitivity analyses. It made gloomy reading. Whilst INCOL Europe population demographics looked stable with only a gentle increase in total numbers over the next three decades, the levels of supply of sustainable foodstuffs showed a sharp decline. Crop and livestock production were predicted to suffer from the continuing effects of global climate change, not only from the cumulative impact of historic carbon emissions but from the over-farming of the arable land not irradiated in the aftermath of the eleven/eleven attacks. To compound the problem, Europe's dependence on imported supplies to supplement dietary deficiencies was expected to reduce significantly as other INCOL territories struggled with similar supply problems and adopted isolationist policies.

Jack turned to the 'Conclusions'. The author suggested there was a five-year window to take several remedial measures before sections of society experienced inadequate nourishment and, eventually, starvation. The suggestions involved changing crop rotations, wide-scale re-planning of crop selection, improved husbandry techniques and a series of proposed efficiency measures demonstrating the depth and expertise which the author devoted to preparing the report.

The last paragraph was written in bold lettering. **'The author and panel responsible for submitting this document have reached the unanimous conclusion that, irrespective of implementing the changes and efficiencies detailed in the previous pages, to maintain the forecast levels** of the population until the earliest estimates of 2110/2120 when irradiated lands will start to become available for occupation, an additional 20% of basic foodstuffs over and above INCOL Europe production capacity will be required to service demand at subsistence levels. Relevant to this conclusion is that the age demographic trend is toward an older population with less productive capacity relying on a shrinking younger workforce, a trend that will eventually even out as the average age decreases.

For the next thirty/forty years, the analogy is that of the elephant balancing on a pin.'

Jack re-read the conclusion. The doom and gloom scenario did nothing to improve his mood. He tried to see a positive. However detailed, the report was a best guess and officials who put their heads above the parapets and made predictions tended to err on the pessimistic side. It was simple hierarchal self-preservation. Nobody would be upset if things turned out better than was forecast, but God help the poor soul who failed to identify an even worse scenario. He checked the author's name. Herr Doktor Dieter Eigard. The name did not register with him. He might have come across him at some convention or seminar in the past. There was no photograph.

He tossed the paperwork onto the bed. It was time to surface, shower and shave, dress ready to present himself once again to the world, a prospect that produced a dull ache in his stomach.

Raised voices outside the hotel attracted his attention. Members of the security staff were dealing with the entry of a small passenger bus stopped at the main gate. The driver was holding out paperwork, his hands raised questioningly in the air. A guard climbed in the back door. It was impossible to see what was happening inside the vehicle as the blacked-out windows impaired Jack's view. Eventually, the man re-emerged; the vehicle lurched forward, following an internal roadway and out of sight. Silence returned.

Jack looked out over the fence toward the road. A lone motorcyclist was stationary, a hundred metres from the entry gates, a man training a pair of binoculars on the receding passenger bus. He turned to study the hotel. For an uncomfortable moment, Jack got the impression the binoculars were centred on him. He pulled the curtains closed and shook his head.

There was a knock on his door. It was Usher gently reminding him they needed to leave. 'Give me ten minutes,' he said. 'I'll be down.'

# THIRTY-FIVE

## TODTNAU – BAVARIA – GERMANY

## Mid-afternoon – 21 November 2065

Whatever they injected her with was wearing off. The relaxing sensation of well-being was gone, replaced by a thumping headache, sharp pains in her chest and a feeling of dread like a stone in her stomach.

Alison collected her thoughts. It was dark inside the coach; the windows were blacked out with paint. She studied the other passengers in the gloom, a mix of the sexes, ages and skin colours, some still comatose, others barely awake. They were all poorly dressed, many filthy and uncared for, the stench unbearable, a wretched combination of that earthy scent from living in the forest, coupled with the stink of human excrement from those lying in a stupor. She gagged at the realisation.

A man in uniform shouted at someone behind him as he appeared through an open door, allowing a shaft of daylight to enter the interior of the bus. The eyes of those conscious cast around fearfully, trying to seek reassurance from each other.

The uniformed guard held a rag over his mouth and nose. Oblivious to the overpowering stench in the vehicle, the driver responded to the muffled comment by pointing toward Alison. 'She's the one with no documents. Foreign. Shouted and screamed in English.' He turned his head to show the other man. 'Look. The bitch scratched me.'

The guard loosened the rag. 'Try to explain that away to the wife,' He laughed as he moved to the back of the bus.

As his face closed on Alison's, he discarded the rag, revealing a mouth full of misshapen and rotting teeth, save for one out-of-place gold incisor. 'Who are you and how did you get here?'

Alison was about to reply but opted instead to shake her head as if she did not understand. She would wait to confide in somebody more senior who could get her out of this mess.

'She can only speak in English,' the driver said. 'And, careful, get too close and you'll get a lump taken out of you.'

The guard backed away. 'Where did you pick her up?'

'The hospice in Feldberg. The staff caught her sniffing around. She wouldn't tell them why she was there, so they contacted ISE who ordered us to pick her up. They weren't interested in some vagrant.' He rubbed the wound on his face. 'I tried to give her the onboard service. It was then she went for me. Must be a bloody dyke, I reckon.'

The guard pointed off into the distance. 'I'll let them discover who she is.' He walked back to pat the driver on the shoulder. 'Keep working on your story. Your wife likes a good fairy tale, doesn't she?'

'How would you know?'

'She told me in bed last night.'

The driver found it hard to raise a smile. 'Fuck off,' he said.

As the guard strolled back to his post, the diesel engine hammered into life and the coach pulled away.

Through the fog in her head, Alison slowly gathered her thoughts. The mention of the hospice in Feldberg brought back memories of a frightening chain of events.

She was outside the house in Rottenberg waiting to confront Herr Eigard, talking to the mother of that poor boy who was taking the blame for the window Alison had broken. Eigard had just returned when the stranger dragged her by the arm away from the scene toward a parked car, one hand clamped over her mouth.

'Quiet,' he said. 'It's for your own good. I mean you no harm.'

She tugged at the gloved hand, pulling it down to her chin. 'Who are you? What do you think you're doing?'

'Shush! Don't attract attention. Roy knows me as FreierMann. I am here to help you.' He spoke in accented English. 'Get in and let's get away from here.' He pushed her untidily into the passenger seat of a small two-door saloon and padded around the front of the car to sit behind the wheel.

As they turned the corner, he chanced a glance. Her back was pressed against the passenger door, studying him with eyes that showed no fear. 'That was a close call,' he said, exhaling slowly. 'Put your seatbelt on and stop staring at me.'

'What is this? What the Hell do you think you're doing?'

'Saving you from yourself before you ruin Roy's plan and my prospects.' He spoke with a high-pitched petulance, out of sync with the bulky appearance of the man.

'Roy? Who is Roy?' She spoke the last word at the same time as recalling the conversation with Uncle Robert when they talked of the man in Tomorrow World who changed his alias every month to the name of an old-time famous singer. She laughed when he said the current name was Roy, after Roy Orbison from a century ago. 'You're one of them?' she said with astonishment.

'You make me sound like a Martian,' he said. 'Listen, this is important. There's a curfew in force until the morning. We will keep to the minor roads. If we are stopped, I take it you have documents?' He nodded toward the rucksack on the back seat. 'I'll try to get you in at the place where I'm staying. It's a room in a private house, but the old lady's deaf and has a love affair with the brandy bottle. She'll be unconscious by now. I'll smuggle you in and, in the morning, get you out of here to safety.'

He turned off the headlights as they drove slowly through a small village, coasting wherever he could, limiting the sound of the engine noise as much as possible. 'People get reward credits for reporting the number of cars driving after curfew in this part of the world. Turn off the lights and they can't see the plate but with no streetlamps, it's hard to see where I'm going.' He strained forward in the seat to see the road ahead.

'How did you know I'd try to see Eigard?'

As they reached the limit of the village where the road ahead once again disappeared into the total darkness of the surrounding forest, he switched on the headlights. The dimmed light illuminated a stretch of patchy fog as it swirled in the breeze around them like the opening scene in a horror movie. 'Don't worry,' he said, wrongly interpreting the anxious look on her face. 'We'll be out of this soon, as we start the climb. We're in the next village, Schonberg,'

'I asked you a question.' He glanced across at her. She was still studying him.

'Roy warned me to be on the lookout for you. A contact of yours suggested you might have taken matters into your own hands to interfere with my surveillance. I've been watching Eigard for six weeks.'

'Which one?'

'What do you mean?' Alison recounted what the boy's mother had told her.

FreierMann shook his head. 'It never occurred to me I might be watching the wrong man.'

For the first time, she smiled at him, more a smile of self-satisfaction than anything else. 'It must have been the elder brother who made the original appeal for relocation. The younger one has only been in the house for six weeks. When did Roy, or whatever his name is, get the plea for help?'

'Over two months ago. I have spoken with Mila Kullenberg, who acted as a go-between. I'd say she is genuine.'

'Don't you have a photo of Eigard to compare?'

His laugh was high-pitched. 'ISE officials aren't exactly encouraged to be photogenic. I've got a print taken off an official handout that must be twenty years old. He could easily be the man I've been watching these past weeks.'

'So, what do we do now?'

'We,' he emphasised the word, 'do nothing. You will contact your father and establish where to meet up. I will see if I can get into the clinic at Feldberg.'

The climb took them out of the forest onto a stretch of road bordered by pasturelands. The sign said three kilometres to Schonberg.

The headlights were on main beam. The figure was lying, straddling the middle of the road, a motorcycle upturned on the grass verge.

'There's been an accident,' Alison cried, leaning forward, hands gripping the dashboard. 'He's come off the bike. He's not moving.'

'He will do,' FreierMann said, pressing down on the accelerator.

'What are you doing?' she gasped. 'You'll run him over.'

They were closing fast. The car was gaining speed as the road dipped.

FreierMann's knuckles turned white as he held the car on course to hit the man. His lips formed into a grimace.

'Are you mad?' Her left hand reached for the steering wheel, her fingernails digging into the veins standing out on the back of his fist. 'You'll kill him!'

'I know what I'm doing.' He released his right hand, thrusting backwards to release her grip. Resistance gone; the impetus carried the back of his hand into her nose as she bent forward. Blood spattered onto her chin.

'You're mad.' She cried in pain. They were only fifty metres from the immobile figure. Her free hand reached for the handbrake. She pulled it up with all the force she could summon.

Everything happened at once. The wheels locked as the car veered sideways.

'Oil!' FreierMann said, frantically trying to control the car as it careered out of control across the slick. The headlights illuminated a field then, the road in the direction from where they had come and, finally, a grass verge on the other side of the road.

They completed the 360-degree turn, catching a fleeting glimpse of the man as he jumped to his feet and leapt out of their path. The car carried on sideways as FreierMann struggled hopelessly to control its movement. The car reared up onto the verge, bumping into an area of uprooted vegetation, still moving at speed as the land fell away into a large drainage ditch running parallel to the road. The screeching of metal on tarmac came just before a shredded tyre spun past the driver's door and wobbled off into the distance. The braking effect of the bare wheel on the road veered the car toward the ditch as a fence pole appeared out of the pitch black and collided with the nearside headlight, casting the area into darkness.

The car came to a halt, two wheels on the ground, two in mid-air over the hollow. As FreierMann leaned across her to open the passenger door, the car rocked to the side. 'Get out.' He pushed Alison toward the void. 'Hide!'

For what seemed like seconds but could only have been a fraction of one, Alison was suspended in mid-air. The landing, in damp clumps of long vegetation, shook the air from her body. He fell in a heap alongside her, his legs thumping painfully into hers. The buttons of his shirt from collar to stomach sheared off, the sweat from his heaving chest damp against the skin of her arm.

Alison staggered to her feet, head and shoulders now above the ditch. Torchlight highlighted the road some thirty metres away. In the darkness, she could hear men's voices whooping with excitement. 'We need help!' she screamed.

An arm pulled her down. 'Don't you get it?' he said. 'It's a band of DCs out to mug us, and a lot worse. Try to stay hidden. Let me do the talking.' He pushed her further down and along into the undergrowth. It was a pointless exercise. Bracken and tangled vegetation blocked her way.

The torchlight centred on the car, which was precariously balanced, half on the verge and hovering just above the ditch. Somebody was opening one of the doors, the hinges creaking where metal was bent out of shape. The chattering of men's voices was getting closer, animated, speaking in a language Alison did not recognise. A shaft of light picked out a group of some eight men. One of them called out and shone the torchlight downwards.

FreierMann stood up. Alison could see the beam pick out his features. There was blood seeping from a wound on his forehead where he must have hit the steering wheel.

'*As-salamu alaykum*' FreierMann said.

The man with the torch laughed a derisory snort. The light played over FreierMann's bare chest before flicking across to highlight Alison's retreating figure. His voice was soft, lilting, and accented as he replied. He held the torch under his chin to highlight his face. He was full-bearded, a sign of defiance amongst the young male immigrant population who ignored the edict requiring a clean-shaven appearance.

'May the Prophet protect us, and the devil take you.' He turned back to the group of men who were now trying to manhandle the car so that all four wheels were back on the verge. 'Look what we have here,' he said, plainly intending his two captives to overhear. Apparent in the half-light was another man, a swarthy individual with the jagged white line of a healed scar across his cheek. He tossed Alison's rucksack across to the first man who felt around inside it. The torch was trained on a hostel receipt. 'English,' he said in a cultured accent. 'Alison Tirrand. Out after curfew on a country road in Germany. I look forward to hearing the explanation.' He hesitated. 'Somewhere private.' He turned to speak to the men silhouetted against the night sky. 'Like the back seat of the car.' There was an explosion of the sort of male bonding laughter Alison detested, where the not-so-subtle sexist innuendo was the obvious motive. To show his contempt, he tossed the hostel receipt and rucksack into the ditch. 'You won't be needing this where you're going,' he said.

FreierMann stood in front of her. 'I shouldn't touch her if I were you. She's important, the daughter of a very influential INCOL delegate. You'll be in big trouble. They'll pretend to pay a ransom just to get close. When they find you, they'll kill all of you and your families. Believe me, don't get involved. Let her go and I'll give you what you want.' He pulled the rest of his shirt back to reveal two augmented breasts. 'See what I mean?'

The light flickered over his chest and then, upward to his face. With his hands behind his back, FreierMann gestured for Alison to retreat further into the undergrowth, stepping back as he did to narrow the access to the area where they were trapped.

For the first time, the torchlight played on the group of men who stood behind their leader. FreierMann counted eight. They would have to approach him one at a time. The terrain was too narrow to allow a mass attack. They would rely on knives. He knew the show of guns meant nothing. There was no ammunition available anymore for these old-fashioned twentieth-century models. INCOL had seen to that. The DCs used Chinese firecrackers to imitate gunfire if they were trying to intimidate a would-be target.

'*Arschficker*,' the leader said. The torch was held alongside a short stabbing knife with an enclosed grip and serrated edge blade. 'We have an arse-fucker brothers. One for you, Armat. You've practised on the boys; now, you can have the real thing!'

There was another burst of laughter. The man called Armat moved alongside the leader. 'I'll leave him to you, Mansur. He's more your type.'

There was what sounded to Alison like a barked order, and the men moved forward to the ditch. Mansur passed the torch to one of his men and tested his footing on the ground at the start of the incline.

As he made to jump, heads turned to face the headlights of a vehicle piercing the night sky as it ran through a dip in the road and sped toward them. For an instant, the men stood transfixed, caught in the vehicle's main beam. The brakes squealed as it slowed, the shape of a large security van now visible.

'*Dunkelblau*' screamed one man. '*Raus hier.*' They ran, fanning out in all directions.

The rear doors opened and four unleashed German Shepherd dogs, teeth bared, careered into each other as they jockeyed to reach the ground first and pursue the fleeing men. Portable arc lights illuminated the scene. Behind the dogs came six helmeted men in blue uniforms, each carrying a short, single-barrelled gun with a large circular ammunition chamber.

The fattest and slowest of the Arab men received a rubber bullet in the back before he had gone ten metres. He pitched forward onto his stomach as a dog swerved to avoid him and pursue one of the other men. Alison could hear a mixture of dogs growling and whining, human screams and the regular thud as rubber bullets struck their targets.

FreierMann bundled her into the thicket. She winced as the undergrowth dug into her skin.

'He's behind you,' she cried as Mansur leapt into the drainage ditch. FreierMann turned to face him.

'Move,' he hissed. 'Say a word and I'll slice you in two.' FreierMann stood his ground as Alison felt the damp leaves and branches encircle her. She could see nothing; hearing only the thrashing sound of bushes being disturbed and a long coughing sigh.

A hand touched her on the shoulder. 'No sound,' was his whispered instruction. Beyond the thicket, the noise subsided.

'Shine the light along the ditch,' a brusque voice commanded. 'See any more down there? Shall we send the dogs?'

'Who's that lying there?' came a second voice.

'I'd take a guess at the poor fucker driving the car they ambushed.'

'Is he dead?'

'Looks like it.'

'Shall we check?'

'No. Leave it to the local community patrol. They can have the problem and the paperwork. We'll radio in we saw an abandoned car that looked as if it was in an accident. We've got enough to do processing this lot. How many did we get?'

'Six, all young and middle-aged males, all healthy looking apart from some rubber bullet wound sores and a few dog bites.'

The voices receded into the distance. 'Six. That's a good night's work. Five hundred each; that's three thousand credits for the bunch. Do that every night, we will soon be rich. Make sure they're all sedated before we lock them up. We'll take them to the farm tomorrow.'

There was the noise of dogs complaining as they were corralled back into the vehicle, men laughing and doors slamming before the big diesel engine thundered into life.

A stained hand pulled her to a stop, leaving a trail of blood on her arm. She wrenched herself free of the grip. In silence, the shadowy figure retreated toward the ditch, a thin beam from the torch highlighting the passage out of the thicket.

The moon appeared from behind a bank of dark clouds, bathing the scene in a haunted grey light. The man called Mansur was lying on his back, eyes staring blindly up into the night sky, the blood still pumping slowly out from the gash around the hilt of the knife poking out of his throat. Involuntarily, Alison gasped, her gaze transfixed on the man. 'He's still alive?' she said.

'Not for long. Help me, would you?' He held out a strip torn from his shirt. 'Pull it tight, then twist it around this stick and turn it to increase the pressure. I need to stop the flow of blood.'

'How did it . . .?' she winced as he reacted, his eyes creased with the pain.

'I put my arm up as he went to stab me. The knife struck, staying lodged in my arm, and he lost his grip. I pulled it out and didn't think. I just did. It was him or us. He lunged at me, and I swung my arm into his face. I felt the impact. I didn't stop to look. I followed you.'

'He's trying to say something.'

'Praying or cursing, it doesn't matter. We must hurry. There'll be another band of his friends and family in the vicinity. We need to get out of here.'

As they climbed out of the ditch, he sank to his knees, gasping for breath. Alison ran her arms under his armpits and clasped her hands around his back. Their eyes stared into each other. With an intake of breath, she hauled him to his feet. 'You've lost a lot of blood. We need a doctor or a hospital.'

'No!' He shook his head. 'Out of the question. Just steady me as we walk. The car is a wreck.'

'We won't get a hundred metres on foot.' She turned to look back up the road. 'The bike,' she said, 'what about the motorbike? They left it on the side of the road. Maybe it works.'

'I can't handle a motorcycle. I've no strength.'

'Chauvinist. I'm not asking you to. If it works, just sit on the back and hold on to my waist. I'm not just a pretty face, you know.'

There was no reaction. His eyelids were fluttering as if trying to stay conscious. She slapped him hard across the face. She could have sworn he mumbled something that sounded like bitch.

The bike was vintage, a 250cc model, well maintained, with two metal panniers fixed on either side of the rear wheel. The key was in the ignition. It fired into life on the second attempt. There was a strong smell of petrol.

His arms lay lifelessly on her thighs; his head couched against the back of her shoulders. 'Hold on,' she said. 'I need directions, so start talking and don't stop.'

# THIRTY-SIX

## SCHONBERG – BAVARIA – GERMANY

## 01.00 (24.00 GMT) - 21 November 2065

FreierMann was right about his landlady. Fifteen minutes later, they were tiptoeing past her suite of rooms up the stairs to his studio accommodation in the first-floor annexe. The sound of intense snoring was typical of the alcohol-induced sleep Alison knew so well from university parties.

The tourniquet had stopped the bleeding, and Alison found a first aid kit with enough components to clean and bandage the wound. He lay back on the bed, eyes closed. She did all she could. He needed hospital attention, at least a doctor, but his refusal was immediate and expressed with all the force he could muster. 'No! Either way would lead us into the hands of ISE. We can't take that chance. Just let me rest. I am past thinking.' He closed his eyes.

Alison studied the unconscious man. Beyond his exaggerated mannerisms and gesticulations, his body now relaxed, she tried to imagine the personal crisis this human being confronted every day of his life. The square-cut, rough features of his face and build were of a man, yet he longed to complete the transformation into a woman. In the bathroom cabinet, there must be a dozen or more long out-of-date containers of various shapes and sizes with hormone capsules, testosterone and oestrogen enhancements, massage creams for breast enlargement, all of which must have been purchased on the black market and, God knows, at what cost. There were some signs of physical change, the fuller breasts that the late Mansur observed, little bodily hair and a softening of some of his facial tissue, the rounding and slackening of some muscular features.

He snored, at first gently, then short, sharp grunts as if providing sound effects to the pictures going on inside his head. Alison pulled the sheet up to cover his torso.

There were rumours of places where illegal, clandestine treatment was available. Places in Eastern Europe were mentioned where procedures outlawed by INCOL could be found at a certain risk and cost that only the desperate would contemplate. Cosmetic plastic surgery, gender reassignment, and organ transplants were facets of medicine no longer tolerated, branded as the misuse of valuable resources to defy the ways dictated by nature.

Alison settled back on the sofa, covering herself with an overcoat she found in the wardrobe. For all the excitement and the horrors she had witnessed over the last few hours, the thought that filled her head as she drifted into sleep was the vision of FreierMann as a woman. Whatever the physiology driving the biological man into womanhood, this tall, well-built individual with strong, aggressive features and the strength to go with it would fit awkwardly into a female form, even if it were possible to complete the transformation.

She sensed someone close by, the rattle of laboured breathing, the gash of white upon red where the knife had torn flesh apart. Her eyes were wide open but refused to focus, the sensation of beads of sweat nestling above her top lip.

'Are you alright?' he asked. 'Sorry to wake you like this.' She blinked and shook her head to clear the fog. FreierMann stood at the end of the sofa, clad in a shiny blue Lycra tracksuit, looking like someone out for a cross-country run. Behind him, watery sunlight pierced the gap in the curtains, illuminating a strip of worn parquet flooring across the room. Memories of last night came flooding back.

'What are you doing up?' she admonished. 'You should be in bed. You have lost a lot of blood and even after I bandaged your arm, there was still seepage from the wound.'

He put a finger over his lips and smiled. His voice was little more than a whisper. 'I should say thanks for driving me back and patching up this.' He held up his bandaged forearm. 'I feel light-headed, hungry and this aches like hell, but I'll survive. We must be discreet. If the old lady hears I have company, there will be trouble. She goes out mid-morning for fresh supplies.' He held an imaginary bottle up to his mouth. 'We'll wait. I'll report the car stolen in Rottenburg. You need to ask your father to sort things out. All your belongings were in the rucksack and are God knows where now.' He stopped to gather breath. 'As soon as the coast is clear, I'll go back to see if anything is still there.'

'Not all,' Alison said, tugging at the chain around her neck and showing him the identity wallet with the travel vouchers and photograph tucked inside.

She reached for his hand and pulled him nearer to say something, smiled to herself, and let the thought go. 'The wound needs medical attention,' she said. 'Properly cleaned with antiseptic, x-rayed to establish if there is any internal muscular or ligament damage and a few stitches to avoid an unsightly scar.'

The exchange of an embarrassed smile and fleeting eye contact signalled a mutual appreciation of her last remark.

'It's the reason I'm involved with Tomorrow World and Roy. I am no adventurer and risk taker in real life. I think of myself as a landscape gardener. My joy is flower and plant arrangements for public festivals and sporting events. All this cloak and dagger stuff.' He sniffed. 'I do it for the promise of surgery.'

'Gender reassignment? How? It's all illegal, even cosmetic plastic surgery.'

'There is always someone, a specialist somewhere prepared to provide a service if the money is right. Roy says he has contact and influence. He put me in touch with a doctor in Bulgaria who will help us. We have to get to Varna next spring. The rest is down to Roy.'

'Us? We?'

'I have a friend who also craves the procedure. He helps me out doing Roy's work.' He walked toward the kitchenette. 'I'll make coffee and toast.' His step faltered as a siren echoed on the road outside.

'Don't worry,' she said. 'I hid the motorcycle under a tarpaulin.'

'You are stronger than you look.'

'Believe me, it was quite a struggle. The panniers on the back are full of fireworks, or whatever you called them.'

'Firecrackers. They sound just like gunfire. The DCs sound off a dozen or so as they wave their guns around. It's enough for most unsuspecting victims to surrender without a fight.'

The sound of the siren receded into the distance.

Alison pulled on the clothes she had discarded on the floor before settling down. 'Who were those people with the van and the dogs? Was it an

ISE patrol?' She put the palms of her hands together. 'Whoever they were, I am grateful they showed up when they did.'

'They were not ISE. What I've heard is only anecdotal. People in this part of the world talk of a medical facility dependent on volunteers to take part in what they call social engineering advancements. When candidates cease to come forward of their own free will, the powers-that-be are forced to hire private security firms to round up illegals with no citizen rights. The Saudi gangs who move around at night and anyone else without documentation are ideal targets for these unauthorised round-up heavies who are identified by their blue uniforms. You heard the guys talking. Five hundred credits a head is a big incentive not to be over-selective.' He handed her a cup of black coffee and a slice of buttered toast. 'Excuse fingers,' he said. 'Need to wash up the plates. Housework's not my strong suit.' Butter was oozing down his chin. 'You must contact your father and meet up with him.'

'I'll put in a call. My mobile was in the rucksack. I will have to use yours. It is bound to take forever; here to London and patched back to wherever he is in Germany.' She watched as he slumped into a chair, his breathing heavy. 'It's down to me to go to the hospice in Feldberg. We need to get to the truth, and that won't happen until I speak to the real Herr Eigard. You need to rest . . .' She puffed a cushion for his head to rest on. 'Do you realise? I don't even know your real name.'

He managed a smile. 'I will answer to the name Hans. There is no way you can visit the hospice alone. Too dangerous. The chances are you will be caught. You cannot use your real identity. Think of your father. Best solution is to wait until you speak to him and ask for his help. I need to rest a little longer. When I awake, we will work on a plan.'

Her eyes followed him as he discarded his cup on a side table and shuffled back toward the bedroom, stopping as he got to the door. 'There's Kullenberg, remember. She can identify the Eigard whose cause she championed.'

'They are all moving parts, don't you see? You don't know who, if anybody, is genuinely seeking asylum. What if this woman, Kullenberg, turns out to be part of some plot to infiltrate Roy's operation in Tomorrow World?

By advancing the fact you know there are two Eigard brothers, you could simply put yourself in line for immediate arrest.'

'And, if she's genuine, as I believe? I'll know the truth.' 'You won't. She could be misled and used as an innocent in the deception. I'm the only one who can help you resolve the dilemma.'

'How come?'

'I know the man who calls himself Rolf Eigard. If I can find out who he is and where he fits into the Eigard family puzzle, we will have a clearer idea of who is who and who we can believe. Old man Eigard is the only way we can do this. We have no option but to take a chance.' She could tell from the look, a mixture of exhaustion and resignation, she was winning him over.

'Let me sleep on it. These places all have visiting hours, so, even if we do as you propose, it will be the afternoon period, which I guess will finish at five, leaving time for visitors to get indoors before the curfew. We don't want to be caught out again.'

After a few hours of hectic housework which Alison accepted was out of character but which took her mind off the events of the previous evening, she sat and dozed off. It was the door to the apartment slamming shut with the force of the draught from the window she left open which woke her up.

He held up his hand in apology. 'Sorry. Just checked visiting hours at Feldberg and that our landlady is enjoying her afternoon siesta after a liquid lunch. Visiting is three to five and with over an hour's travelling time, we should think about making a move.'

'Did you report the car missing? You look ten times better than you did this morning.'

FreierMann gave a big smile. 'Thanks to you, I feel it. Don't suppose you fancy coming in regularly to do the cleaning?' He ducked to avoid the cushion she lobbed at him. 'And I reported the car as stolen, putting down the delay in reporting the theft to the pressure of work. I said I needed to get a lift with a friend to a business meeting out-of-town today. They hinted the vehicle had been located and requested I attend at ISE in Rottenburg first thing in the morning to explain the circumstances. That should be fun. I intend to almost faint when they bring up the matter of a dead body.'

'Any success with the call to my father, though God knows what I'll say to him.'

'Best guess is sometime tomorrow, probably the afternoon.'

With Hans up front and Alison riding pillion, they headed south on the A81, leaving Oberdorf and skirting the eastern edge of the Black Forest. She was grateful she could snuggle into his broad back and avoid the worst of a chill, swirling wind.

On any other day, she would have found the scenery of majestic woodlands, tracts of rich grazing land and viaducts crossing valley landscapes, both impressive and beautiful. But, today, she was apprehensive, the bravado of yesterday gone, replaced by a sense of foreboding. Against Han's better judgement, she was once more rushing headlong into the unknown, unprepared and ignorant of whatever danger there might be. She was about to approach a stranger in a strange place with no one to guide or give her counsel. She felt very much alone.

Hans pointed a gloved hand over to the right at a lake spreading into the distance and a thumbs-up, which she took to show they were nearing their destination. According to the sign, there were still seventeen kilometres to Feldberg, but the route they now followed avoided the main road, skirting through Titisee-Neustadt and along the winding lakeside road.

It was just after three when Hans tucked the motorcycle behind a local bus as it swung left through an electronically controlled gate and the driver changed down a gear with a grating sound to slow as he crossed a rusted cattle grid. A weatherworn copper plate read *Schloss Feldberg-Adler – Hospital – Pflegeheim*

The driveway climbed up from the lakeside with manicured lawns on either sound, ending at a central parking and turning circle built around a waterless fountain topped with the winged figure of Icarus looking up toward the sun. Although covered in bird droppings and chipped and pitted by the erosion of countless changing seasons, the ornate structure portrayed a sense of majesty.

The building in front of them was of much the same character. The long, four-storey castle was of baroque design, with undulating grey slate roofs. The central section, dominated by a pair of sturdy wooden entrance doors, stood proud of the east and west wings. Moss and lichen covered sections of the beige stonework hidden in the shadows away from the sun. The mortice between the joints had long since become brittle and crumbled away. Behind wooden-framed windows lacking a coat of paint, Alison made out the silhouette of people staring at the bus as it came to a stop. Fourteen people alighted and made their way toward the entrance.

'Join the group,' Hans said. 'It'll make it easier for you to get in if you're treated as one of the crowd. I'll be waiting for you at the side of the building.'

'That's fifty metres away. Why not stay here in the car park with the bike?'

'I don't want to answer questions. Now, go. Any sign of trouble, get out of there.'

The visitors in the queue were providing names to a receptionist and receiving identity badges to pin on their clothes.

'Who you visiting?' The woman wore a grey peaked cap hiding her face as she studied a computer screen.

'Dieter Eigard.'

The woman tapped on the keyboard, read the detail on the screen and, slowly, looked up to meet Alison's gaze. 'You are?'

'Alison Eigard, niece.'

'Not German, are you?'

'No. Belgium.'

The woman typed again. 'Why has it taken so long for you to get here?'

'Sorry?'

'He's had no visitors since he arrived. We were concerned there were no relatives. Document, please.'

Alison tried a demure smile. 'I was afraid you'd ask. I left my identity card and travel pass in the hotel. I did so want to see him and make sure he got this.' She pulled from her coat pocket the photograph removed from the identity wallet on the chain around her neck. 'It's of his son, my cousin. I know he treasures it.'

The woman puffed her cheeks in exasperation. 'What is it today? People don't have documents or the right documents. What do they expect me to do? Do you know your identity card number?'

Alison watched as the woman typed in the false number, and the screen changed. The matrix printer clattered into life. 'These old machines are still the best,' she said, the smile on her lips not reflected in her eyes. 'Much like the staff in this place.' She took the slip of paper from the printer and folded it into a plastic holder. 'Keep this visible and don't go wandering away from Mannheim Ward, 3rd floor. That's where you'll find the inmate.'

Alison avoided the queue for the elevator and took one of the sweeping staircases which curved upward from both sides of the main atrium. Staff and visitors inter-mingled, some stopping en route to talk, forcing her to change direction as she climbed. The anonymity of simply feeling one of the crowd, the indifference to her presence as people hurried past with the odd dismissive glance at her visitor's badge; it calmed the sensation of butterflies in her stomach.

Leaving the original ornate décor of the atrium behind, the transformation along the corridors of the third floor could not have been starker. Once spacious rooms were now stud-partitioned with plasterboard to make individual wards and social areas. The character of the original building, still present at ceiling height with colourful stucco designs, had been transformed at ground level into regular-sized, functional units, some open to view inside, others closed with signs restricting entry to staff only.

Mannheim Ward comprised six beds, all but one, unoccupied and neatly made-up, each with a regulation cupboard and chest-of-drawers alongside.

The cleaner looked up as Alison hovered alongside the row of beds. The woman pointed to the door at the other end of the room where there was a sitting room with a collection of well-worn sofa chairs arranged around a large bay window overlooking the parking zone.

Four of the chairs were taken by men in various states of dress, two in pyjamas, one in a frayed and baggy tracksuit and an elderly black man with a white beard and wispy hair wearing, what Alison could only describe as a sartorial, tropical-design dressing gown.

Nobody stirred at her presence or reacted to the false cough. All four appeared mesmerised by whatever was happening outside the window, which was nothing, as far as she could see. She waved a hand in front of the blank faces. Whatever sedative was in the small, plastic dosage cups clenched in the hands of two of the men, it must be potent, she thought.

'Are you looking for someone?' The voice came from a hunched figure sitting at the back of the room, next to a bookcase. A dirt-encrusted volume lay open on the lap of an old man in a creased white shirt, stained with sweat marks around the open collar and with a button missing over the neat, rounded paunch of his stomach. The waistband of his trousers failed to meet in the middle and were held together by a length of thin pink tape tied in a neat bow.

'Ascites,' he said, his gaze following the passage of her eyes. 'It happens after a lifetime of drinking alcohol to excess. The liver deteriorates to a point where it seeks vengeance by inflating your gut like a balloon.' His lined face contorted into a grimace as he levered himself off the sofa to pass wind with a piercing whine. 'Sorry. Force majeure. They can't give me the same thing they dose that lot with.' He waved at the four men. 'It makes me throw up immediately. They give me a pill instead. It's not as potent as the liquid. I don't end up a zombie like them, but it makes me fart.'

His comment tested Alison's German vocabulary, but she guessed what she didn't understand. Studying him, she thought she saw a passing similarity to the man in the photograph, but this careworn individual with sallow cheeks, a less prominent chin and glazed eyes set back into sockets of brown-shadowed skin, left her in doubt. 'I'm looking for Herr Eigard. Could you point him out to me?'

The man raised one eye, squinting to focus on her and saying nothing. 'You are too late,' he said, finally. 'They came for him yesterday. Lost his mind, it seems. You would be?'

'I'm a friend of his son. You wouldn't know where he is now? They said downstairs he was in this ward.'

'His son, you say? He talked a lot when he first arrived, never stopped. Nobody was listening. Only me. And even I gave up when they medicated him. Just drivel in the end. Poor chap. If they told you he's still here, I suspect they must have taken him to the hospital wing and will bring him back when he's been treated for whatever it is. Who knows when that will be?'

'Where will I find the hospital wing? I have something for him.'

'Different visiting hours, I'm afraid. Over for today. You'll have to come back tomorrow and check in again.' He registered the disappointed look on her face. 'If there's anything I can help with, pass on a message. Even if you manage to see him, I don't expect you'll get any sense out of him. He'll be in a worse state than this lot.' He studied the look of indecision on her face. 'His son, you say?' he repeated, looking around as if checking if anyone was in earshot. 'As I say, he talked a lot when he first arrived. Some of it, quite alarming, about important secrets that were troubling him. He mentioned his son a great deal. They must have been close.'

'I have a photograph which suggests they were.'

'May I see?'

She held it out for him to take with two skeletal hands that trembled as he moved it to within five centimetres of his squinting eye. 'Must have been taken some time ago,' he said. 'You can just about see it's him. This place ages us all.'

'How long have you been here, Herr . .? Sorry, I don't know what to call you.'

He looked away from the photograph and smiled. 'The people here know me as Rilke. And your name is?'

'Alison. I've been Rolf's girlfriend for a few months.'

'His son?'

'Yes.'

'Point out which one of the two boys he is. I'm curious, having heard so much about him.'

She indicated Rolf.

'Handsome young man,' he said. 'Nothing like his father. Must take after his mother or some other family member. Who is the other fellow with the big smile on his face?'

'I don't know. A friend of Rolf's, I suppose. They must ski together.' She checked her watch, drumming her fingers on the glass anxiously, her eyes looking up at the ceiling. 'You said he talked of secrets. What did he mean?'

'Who knows? He picked up a book with a plastic protective covering, thumbing through the last pages as if it applied to his answer. 'He never specified anything. Just as well. Information in the wrong hands can be dangerous, both for the recipient as for the giver. I can only give you a flavour of what he offered. Come closer.' He pulled her toward him, his hands closing over her shoulders as their cheeks touched. His mouth was against her ear. 'What is your surname?' he whispered.

'Tirrand. Alison Tirrand.'

'Get out now, while you can. They know you're here. Listen. The man you know is not my son. Rolf is dead. Franz is my nephew. Take this and show it to only those you trust.' He thrust sheets of what felt like folded toilet paper together with the photograph into her hand. 'Octogen must not happen. We must learn from the past, not repeat it.'

There was shouting in the corridor.

'Go. There are cameras with sound activators everywhere. Take the stairs. Don't use the elevator. Now, go!' As the door crashed open behind them, he pushed her away from his side. 'Why are you asking me these questions?' he said with a stutter. 'Don't you know who I am?'

To her left was one of the security guards she saw in reception, holding what looked like a spray can. Close behind was a second man in blue overalls, waving a nightstick in the air.

Alison reacted quickly as the adrenalin kicked in. She wheeled around and dodged, as the man with the club flayed it in her direction and headed for the nearest door. More anxious voices were raised in the corridor. There was an emergency exit sign light with an arrow pointing left. A nurse moved to block her path. With her free hand, Alison lunged wildly, causing the woman to lose balance and crash into the wall. 'Sorry,' she said to herself. The sound of Eigard's neurotic voice screaming, 'Tell her to go away,' faded as the damper slowly closed the door to the fire exit behind her. She took the stairs two at a time. Surely, two overweight security guards would never keep up.

One more flight and she was at ground level. She could hear people behind her, but they were at least two floors higher. The push bar on the exit door gave way with a groan. She was back in the courtyard and running toward the car park. She prayed Hans was mounted and ready to go.

Conscious that she was not in immediate danger, she glanced at the paper clasped in her hands. There must be a dozen sheets, filled with writing, frequent tears where the tip of the biro ripped the tissue, dirt lines along the creases where the papers had been folded and hidden from prying eyes.

She turned into the parking zone. The motorcycle was where Hans had left it, but he was nowhere in sight. Shit! As she ran toward it, out of the corner of her eye, she saw a flash of black and grey dart between two parked vehicles. From the opposite side, there was the sight of a mane of black hair and the sound of scampering in the gravel. Alison froze.

The Alsatian stopped three metres from her and crouched on its haunches, its head turned, tongue hanging out to cool its body. It looked around, waiting for instructions. Alison backed away toward the motorcycle, her hand on the panniers, as a second dog appeared behind her and adopted a similar posture to the first.

'If you try to run, they will take pieces out of you.' The voice came from behind her.

She looked up. It was the van from the previous evening and the same men she remembered from their blue uniforms. The tall man with the lanky ginger-coloured hair was strolling toward her. He was thirty metres away. She looked around. Still no Hans. For all she knew, they had already captured him.

The two dogs watched her every move. The jet-black Alsatian behind her was slowly edging nearer, head straining forward in expectation. She could see the sinews and pulse in its neck, its every instinct to attack.

'Do not make any sudden movements.' He was three cars away and hidden from view behind a large people carrier. Taking the opportunity, she slid the papers along with the identity wallet and chain into the side pocket of the pannier, stuffing it between two sets of firecrackers.

The first dog looked at her and cocked its head as if to say, 'I'm going to tell on you,' but glanced away and bared its teeth to attend to some foreign body on its paw.

The man came closer and stood next to her. His first command was to the dogs, upon which they stood and ambled away: his second was to order Alison to walk in front of him. Her protestations grew louder and more desperate the nearer she got to the van. She was English: her father was an important man: she was in Germany on holiday while he was working: her documents were stolen by a group of muggers: she had done nothing wrong: didn't you hear? She has done nothing wrong.

Alison was still demanding her release when someone jabbed a hypodermic needle into her arm. She collapsed onto the bench seat of the van, unaware of the order given to the youngest of the uniformed men to body search her. Neither did she hear the stream of bandied comments and suggestions from his amused colleagues, which accentuated the flush on his cheeks.

'We should get a thousand for this one,' the leader said, casually feeling Alison's breast. 'Let's get them transferred to the coach and off to the Institute.'

# THIRTY-SEVEN

## TODTNAU – BAVARIA – GERMANY

## Mid-afternoon – 21 November 2065

'If I didn't know better, I'd say you have been avoiding me?' Usher cocked her head with a smile. They were standing in reception, waiting for either Ruger or Katrina, or both to appear.

'And do you?'

'Do I what?'

Jack mimicked the movement of her head. 'Know better?'

'The jury's out.'

'Actually, apart from my overriding concern for Rebecca's state of mind and niggling concerns about family issues, I've been giving some thought to your interest in Geordie, the missing file and the link to Nine Elms.'

'Any revelations?'

'Nothing leaps out at me, but I feel I should know something I cannot get a handle on as yet.' He sucked his teeth. 'The atmosphere in this place isn't exactly conducive to immersive thought. It's giving me the creeps. I can't decide whether we're guests or prisoners. After reading that report they gave us, I have a sense of foreboding about what we are about to learn today.'

Usher placed a hand on his shoulder. 'I must admit being around Kommandant Katrina and Stormtrooper Ruger is not the most relaxing of atmospheres, but I'm intrigued by this cloak of secrecy around our presence here.' She hesitated whilst seeming to judge the moment. 'Going back to you and Geordie, do you mind if I ask a question?'

'Depends.'

'Don't worry, it's nothing intrusive. I was curious. You said your biological parents were both killed with you in the car?'

'Yes.' He stopped. 'Or rather, I am told so. I have no memory of the accident.'

'You would have been what . . . a teenager?'

'Early teens, yes. It happened here in Germany. Frankfurt area, I think.'

'And from here you went back to the UK and into foster care?'

'Yes.'

'Did your parents have no relatives who could have stepped in?'

His answer was almost a reflex, but it stalled in his throat. He coughed. 'I asked Geordie once. According to him, my biological parents were Malaysian Tamils.'

'I always thought Tamils were from India or Sri Lanka?'

'They make up a large minority segment of the Malaysian population. I discovered my mother was the illegitimate child of a Tamil house servant and a Dutch forester. My father's family disapproved of their relationship and disowned them when they ran away to get married. Geordie didn't have any names or addresses, and after a bit of half-hearted research, I gave up looking. As Geordie said, if they disowned my parents, even if I traced them, they would disown me. So, I never bothered. By that time, I was with the Pearsons and experiencing a typical English upbringing.'

He turned as he caught the scent of Katrina's overpowering perfume.

'Have you followed your instructions?' she barked, feeding strands of windblown, brittle blonde hair from her face.

'Say again,' Usher said, wheeling around, her face a mask of anger. 'Watch your tone.'

The reprimand triggered an instant reaction. Katrina's expression softened, her look wary, no longer aggressive. 'Bad English, I speak. Not come out the way I meant. Not intentional.'

Jack doubted it but was impatient to move forward. 'An interesting and alarming prognosis. We are keen to understand our role.'

'Of course,' Katrina said. 'Ruger wait outside.'

The only way Jack could describe the electric vehicle in which sat an uncomfortable-looking Ruger was a stretch golf buggy, the sort he remembered from ancient American films that moved guests around a motel-style complex. There seemed insufficient space between the steering wheel and the big man's chest to guide the vehicle, but he somehow managed – by breathing in and holding his breath - Jack guessed from his seat in the back.

They circled away from the hotel past a series of barrack-style, black creosoted wooden huts with shutters covering small windows, an electricity substation and generator housing. The tarmac track they were on followed the contours of the main road, turning sharply to the north and completing almost a semi-circle around a thick bank of tall pine trees. Almost immediately, the track opened out into what was once a parade ground, immaculately asphalted and bordered on two sides by two cream-painted, rectangular buildings, simple in design with symmetrically distanced, identical timber-framed windows, small and equally spaced over the three floors. Both buildings were covered by sharply pitched roofs in dark grey slate with equidistantly placed chimneys in red brick. Usher pulled a face at Jack. The entire area had a bleak feel to it, as if it were a monument to another era.

'Once a military barracks.' Katrina broke the silence in a tour guide's voice. 'This . . .marching place.' She pointed to the fence which bordered the third side of the square. 'Half now car park for staff and some visitors. Electronic gate. Need to show pass. Original entry over there.' She pointed to the double gates, forming part of the fencing between the car park and what remained of the parade ground. 'Now, just emergency exit. Layout changed when hotel built.' She drew a tight ellipse with her finger in the air. 'We come long way round. Hotel very close, walking through the pine trees. A hundred metres from where we are to back door. Crazy, eh?'

'Why all the barbed wire around the place?' Usher asked.

'Place become Bavarian Institute for Social Development when army left past forty years. There are many drugs on site. Crazy DCs try to get in and steal anything to get high – to forget how now without oil they poor.'

'Do they attack the place regularly?' Usher could not hide her astonishment. 'This is bizarre.'

'Not so much now. We have good security.' She patted Ruger on the back. 'Men like him. He break DCs like that.' She held clenched fists together horizontally and then turned them down so that her knuckles touched.

Ruger grunted as he stopped the buggy outside the double-door entrance to the main building.

'You take elevator to second floor. Someone meet you.'

'You're not coming?' Jack queried.

'Not allowed inside. Only on special days, with permit.'

'Why not?'

'Secret work. Very important. Ruger and me, just public relations.' Ruger raised his eyebrows. 'Public relations also important.' she said.

The electronic lock on the doors buzzed open, leading to a narrow corridor with white painted walls and stone floor. The elevator was of the antiquated variety which neither Jack nor Usher had come across in twenty years: a concertina metal door which required locking into position before the motor engaged.

Cranking the door open, they found themselves alone with a choice of three identically sized corridors leading off from the small atrium. Everywhere was painted white, except the floors, which were covered with a plain grey linoleum. There was nobody in sight or any sound of activity.

Usher cleared her throat nervously and raised her eyebrows. 'There are woman-eating tigers at the end of two of these corridors and Utopia at the end of the third. Which do I take?'

'If I hear a scream, I'll know not to follow you.'

'Thanks a bunch. Well, which one?'

As if in answer to the question, a strip of blue LED lighting pinned to the skirting board came alight, leading off along one corridor and stopping in front of a closed door.

'I guess this is the way to Utopia,' he said.

'Come,' said a voice in a heavy guttural accent, in response to Jack's rap on the door.

They entered what once must have been a classroom to accommodate around forty students, complete with blackboard and a large mahogany veneered table from where the teacher or invigilator would have sat. In place of the students' desks was a circular table sized to accommodate around a dozen people and, to the side, a video projector and screen.

Three people, seated in evenly spaced oak carver chairs, occupied the top quadrant of the table. A middle-aged man in a white laboratory coat and a woman of a similar age in civilian clothing rose to greet them. A second man, also elderly, wearing an ISE military uniform, remained in his chair. Two matching oak dining chairs, placed together at the bottom quadrant, were intended for their guests.

'Welcome to our Institute,' the man in the white coat said. 'Thank you for coming and please sit.'

Still standing, he waited for them to settle into their chairs. 'My name is Professor Max Bayer, head of this establishment. The colleague to my left is *gnädige Frau* Mila Kullenberg.' She nodded and gave Usher a warm smile. 'Our special guest' - he gave a deferential bow of the head and extended his palm as if releasing a bird into the air - 'is General Christian Ludwig von Kempeler from ISE headquarters in Berlin.'

There was no acknowledgement from the General, who stared steadfastly at a point in the distance and with the air of somebody who found the occasion tedious.

For the first time, Jack realised there were two more people in the room, seated against the rear wall. Bayer followed his eyes. 'Aah, yes. The gentlemen behind me are on the General's staff. I believe you may know them. They were in London recently: Herr Willi Schmidt and Herr Tomas Muller.'

Jack guessed they would follow the General's lead and ignore any form of acknowledgement. He was not to be disappointed.

With everybody seated, Bayer relaxed, his attention directed to parting the starched-white coat to reveal a double-breasted sea-blue blazer with a white silk handkerchief erupting from the breast pocket. 'I understand you two have been specially chosen to oversee the UK aspect of what we will discuss today. Congratulations.' He clapped his two hands together, displaying polished manicured nails. 'You have been bestowed with a great honour.'

He turned to face Usher. 'For my benefit and that of my colleagues, can you give us a brief description of who you are and what is your function in London?' He gestured for Usher to begin and, as she was about to speak, indicated she should stand.

'Back at school,' Jack said under his breath.

It was an opportunity for Jack to assess the trio who sat before him. Bayer was a man conscious of his appearance; mid-sixties with an oval face, receding hair line and a cultivated grey/brown cross between stubble and a moustache, the width of his top lip. Directly below the centre of his bottom lip was a similar furry appendage, no longer than an inch which, if intended to enhance his appearance, could equally be seen as an omission when shaving.

Usher was answering a question from the woman about the treatment of political dissidents as Jack watched on. He calculated Kullenberg was around about his age, an attractive woman who looked out-of-place wearing a wide brown headband which covered half of her forehead and scalp and hid most of her short-cropped blonde hair. The pale foundation and faint touch of makeup, along with the plain white blouse and two-piece dark blue suit, were all designed to give the impression of a serious, imposing woman succeeding in a man's world. In Jack's assessment, the laughter lines around her mouth and twinkling blue eyes could not disguise her true personality.

It was Jack's turn to verbalise a brief CV. He ended with a question, intended more to impose their presence on the meeting than appear subservient. 'We have been given zero detail as to the nature of this assignment, other than sight of a report dealing with supply and demand issues in the forthcoming years. It's about time we were told exactly why you require our services. I trust you are about to give us this information?' His gaze moved across from one to the other.

The General grunted and rattled off a sentence in German, which caused an embarrassed exchange of glances.

Bayer was quick to take the initiative. 'Of course, everything will be explained, although I need to emphasise the involvement of this Institute is strictly limited to the first phase of the project.'

'Which is?' Jack asked.

'Let me give you a little background.' Bayer played with the handkerchief in his breast pocket. 'This establishment, under one name or another, has been involved with the development and experimentation of various classes of a group of drugs known as hallucinogens for over a century. I have been engaged in this work for over thirty years.'

'We're here to talk about a drug problem in the UK?' Jack asked, his voice rising an octave. 'I don't believe it.'

Bayer shook his head. 'I need you to control your temper, Mr Tirrand, and let me complete my explanation. We understand you have issues which may influence your behaviour but challenging me before I could explain does you no credit.'

The chair creaked as Jack sat back in it. 'Please, go on,' he said.

'Let us be clear,' Bayer said, acknowledging the comment with a curt nod. 'Hallucinogens and, by that term, I am including psychedelics, entactogens, empathogens and dissociatives; these all have one similarity, namely the ability to bring about temporary, but profound alterations of consciousness. This can involve significant changes in somatic, perceptual, cognitive and affective responses.'

'Affective?' Usher queried.

'A change in moods, emotions, attitudes – let's say the way you feel.' He smiled. 'Beyond the notoriety which these drugs have, many have been around for centuries, used mainly in a religious context. Some occur naturally: mushrooms, cacti, the bark of trees, various tropical plants. Latterly, synthetics have augmented our field of study.

'Our work has largely involved the medical and psychological benefits which can be achieved with these drugs. Efforts were needed in the years immediately following eleven/eleven. The population suffered greatly, and we played our part – continue to play our part – in many areas, such as chronic pain, PTSD, cluster headaches, alcoholism, mood disorders and, of course, psychological distress.'

'Does your work involve cocaine and heroin?' Usher was warming to the man.

'Rarely. These are opiates as opposed to hallucinogens and we do not seek to resolve one problem by substituting addiction as another.'

The clap of a leather boot on the floor turned heads to face the General. He spat out a sentence to which Bayer reacted in kind, much to Jack's surprise. He appeared unwilling to let his authority be undermined. The General's next remark was in a softer, conciliatory tone.

Bayer bowed his head. 'It is true, I do tend to get carried away sometimes with my field of work. General von Kempelar suggests you are acquainted with a basic knowledge of these drugs, and I need not provide so much background detail.'

'I doubt he put it so diplomatically,' Jack said loud enough for Usher to hear.

'Just over a year ago, the author of the report you were given yesterday, Herr Doktor Dieter Eigard, approached me to assist in a project he was developing at ISE Stuttgart. What he needed was a compound or various compounds which could be taken in tablet or intravenous form by persons with no related drug history to enable that individual to experience a unique psychedelic event.'

'Come again,' Jack said, his mouth left open in amazement. 'You want to give people happy pills so they won't feel hungry?'

'Nothing so crude, Mr Tirrand. Let's imagine somebody's life dream is to visit the Taj Mahal or meet a deceased relative or attend some historical or religious event. Let's also imagine that by combining psychological autosuggestion to stimulate the individual's imagination with a simple pill, this life dream could be fulfilled. That is the task we were asked to undertake.'

Usher leaned forward in her chair, her eyes locking on Bayer's. 'Are we not to have the pleasure of Doctor Eigard's input at this meeting, seeing that he is the driving force behind the project?'

Bayer clapped his hands together. 'Regrettably, some weeks ago, Herr Doktor Eigard was taken seriously ill and is now in a peaceful environment where he can spend the rest of his days. Unfortunately, he is no longer able to contribute to the assignment.' He turned to place an arm on his colleague's shoulder. 'In his place, we have with us *gnädige* – the charming - *Frau Mila Kullenberg*—'

'Mila, please,' the woman said. 'Otherwise, you make me sound so old.' She rounded with a smile, which nobody reciprocated.

'Sobeit, if you insist. Mila is helping this Institution's Stuttgart office and is a long-time friend of Herr Doktor Eigard,' Bayer went on. 'She assisted with his analysis of the influencing factors—'

'I was more like a sounding board. Dear Dieter would read passages to me, and I would play devil's advocate, challenging his assertions. I understood his thinking. I hope, if you have questions concerning his report, I may be able to help . . .' She looked past Bayer towards the General. '. . . in some small way.'

'Thank you,' Bayer said, the tendons in his neck taut as he reacted to the interruption. 'Perhaps I can deal with your questions after my explanation is complete.'

Jack ignored the plea. 'I assume we are here because you have fulfilled Eigard's request?'

'If you would *please* just let me explain.' Bayer pleaded. 'In simple terms, what was required was a base component to ensure a set of stable emotional responses in all subjects. Once this was achieved, we could then adjust the mix with either natural or synthetic components to help produce a psychotic experience, be it mystic, insightful, transcendental or whatever.

'For years, we have been working to modify a chemical hallucinogen, known in abbreviated form as MDMA, the original and crudest stage of which is known as ecstasy. We have come a long way since those early days . . .' He stopped as the General rose, using a walking stick to steady himself as he made to stand.

'Go on, if you must,' the General said. He straightened his back and walked over to sit alongside Schmidt and Muller.

Having been given the green light, Bayer explained how they came to develop a base substance which would impair negative emotions and stimulate a general state of empathy, out of which would flow generosity of spirit, emotional communion and self-compassion. With this sense of well-being and openness to hyper-suggestion, each candidate would engage in a brief consultation with a psychotherapist to describe their ultimate desire and receive instructions on how to prepare their thoughts as the drug in one of its four forms was taken orally or administered by injection.

'In honour of the project which Eigard entitled Octogen, I have named the drug Octomax and the variants as 1,2,3 and 4.'

'It works on everybody?' Usher asked. 'Surely, there must be a failure rate?'

'To date, we have tested it on eighteen thousand volunteers . . .' He hesitated again as the General returned to his seat. 'The success rate is a little over eighty per cent, but we expect it to peak at well over ninety. You will appreciate conditions were different in the early days of trials and the failure level was higher.'

'You had fatalities?' Jack asked.

The General leaned forward. 'There are few fields in life where personal sacrifice is not required. This project is no exception.'

For the first time, Jack studied the features behind the uniform. The man would be in his late sixties, medium build with a long angular face set off by a square jaw and a deep crease in the skin under his bottom lip. A pencil-thin moustache and deep-set, dark brown eyes gave him the menacing air which Jack had reacted to when he first spoke. His hair was hidden under a peaked cap, but judging by the long sideburns, was tinted black. His only concession to the good life, which Jack guessed he enjoyed, was the slight paunch around his midriff.

'That translates into how many deaths?' Jack asked.

'We are not here to moralise or present accounts to you. Men die building bridges. Nobody says to stop building bridges because a worker dies. People understand and accept the risks they take. There would be no military otherwise.' The General shook his head. 'Can you finish? We have commitments.' The question was directed at Bayer.

'The next phase to conclude our pre-release requirements will be a full trial of five hundred persons selected at random, principally from the over-eighty population in and around London.' Bayer did not wait for a reaction. 'This trial will be organised and overseen under my guidance by Mr Tirrand and Madame Usher. To prepare you for the inevitable press interest and questions, we require you to experience the impact of Octomax first-hand. Tonight—'

'Hold up a minute. Don't we get a say in this?' Jack rose to his feet, his cheeks flushed. 'First, why the over-eighties and why London? Don't you have any over-eighties in Frankfurt or Hannover you can use as guinea pigs?'

Bayer held up his arm. 'The logic behind the trial will be explained in due course,' he said. 'Tonight, you will meet an externally contracted psychotherapist who will spend around thirty minutes with you. Please get to know them and provide whatever background information they require. It is expected they will work with you when the trial gets underway. Before they leave, you will be primed on how to approach your own experience of Octomax, starting at nine tomorrow morning. Public relations will pick you up and bring you to the test centre.'

'Just supposing one or both of us are not interested in participating in your mind-boggling experiment, at least until we understand the logic behind it.' Jack felt his cheeks redden and the blood throb in his head. 'You surely are not serious about expecting a ten-minute trip to the Hanging Gardens of Babylon and a chat with Moses is going to assuage the pangs of hunger for the next six months.' He glanced over at Mila Kullenberg. 'You can't even be certain Eigard's forecast of basic foodstuff shortfalls will reflect the reality. Things change. People adapt.'

'They do,' Kullenberg said, a softness in her voice. 'I'm sure you didn't have time to read every detail, but there are sensitivity tests to reflect variations in supply availability. Even the most optimistic outlook results in a significant staple food shortfall.'

'Whatever the merits of this experiment,' Usher said. 'I don't understand why I am here. My role is with Homeland and, principally, the prison service. Nothing I have heard so far would suggest a need for my presence. And frankly, I have a long to-do list.'

Bayer gave another of his half smiles and a shake of the head as if admonishing himself for some unspoken misdeed. 'You will forgive me. We refer to the sample group as the over eighties because they make up the bulk of the total. In fact, around fifteen per cent will be hardened criminals whom we expect to show some resistance to the suggestive process and five per cent from the ethnic minorities group, chosen to reflect variant cultural and religious approaches to drug use.' He appeared to offer his hands in supplication. 'Hence, your involvement in the project and, besides, you bring a world of knowledge about social intercourse.' He placed some emphasis on the last word and nodded.

'Enough,' the General said. 'Tomorrow, after you have your experience, I will explain the mechanics of the operation. We deal with questions, and you spend a day going through the details. *Donnerstag* . . . Thursday, we have a final meeting—.'

The phone on the table next to Schmidt gave a shrill ring. He answered and whispered in the General's ear.

'As I was saying, we have a final meeting, and you pack and start your journey back.' He turned to Jack. 'You have a telephone call, redirected from England. You need to get back to the hotel to take it.'

Bayer stood up, urging Jack to follow suit. 'You only have five minutes before they cut off the call. Best to hurry back through the trees. You will come to the back of the hotel. Go in through the service door and use the phone at reception.'

Jack made it in three minutes.

Out of breath, he grabbed the phone to hear the operator from the UK call centre. 'The call was booked yesterday by Alison Tirrand in Schonberg to Jack Tirrand. Is that Mr Tirrand?'

'Yes.'
'Do you accept the call?'
'Of course, I do.'

# THIRTY-EIGHT

## TODTNAU – BAVARIA – GERMANY

### Late afternoon – 21 November 2065

'Alison? Are you there?'

There was a moment's silence on the line.

'Hello.' It was a man's voice, softly spoken. 'Mr Tirrand?'

'Who is this? Where is Alison?'

'She's not here at the moment. She asked me to complete the call she booked to you. My name is Hans. I am Alison's friend.'

'What's going on? If Alison wanted to speak with me, she would have waited until the call came through.' Jack's thoughts were muddled. 'Has something happened to her? Who are you?' He was bordering on panic.

'Please listen to me, Mr Tirrand. My name is Hans and I met her at the hostel in Stuttgart. She is not presently with me. Before you ask, I don't know where. She didn't tell me. All she asked me to do was pass on a message if the call occurred before she returned.'

'What message?'

'The message is this.' It was obvious he was about to recite something already written. 'When I got off the train at Strasbourg.' He hesitated. 'You understand, Mr Tirrand, this is Alison speaking, not me.'

'Of course, I do.' Jack sounded exasperated. 'Go on.'

'. . . the train at Strasbourg, I must have taken one of your notebooks with me by mistake. I'm sorry. I only realised when I arrived in Stuttgart. Fortunately, Hans will be travelling in the Basle area, and I have asked him to return the notebook. If you can meet him, I guarantee you will need the contents to help with your meetings.'

'What notebook? I'm not missing—'

There was a bout of coughing on the end of the phone, stopping Jack from finishing the denial. 'It's the one with the cuttings of your speeches at the London Assembly meetings. I took the liberty of reading the one on the denial of human rights to persons held without trial. Very interesting. I'm sure you must need the notebook.'

'You're making a big . . .' His voice tailed off. Censorship. Whoever this guy was and whatever his relationship with Alison was, he was trying to say something he dared not put into words for fear of alerting the authorities. 'I was about to say you are making a big sacrifice to go out of your way for me. The problem is my location is a secret. The only way out of this is for me to arrange for somebody to meet up with you and—'

'Sorry to interrupt, but I'm guessing you're at the Institute in Todtnau?'

'How could you possibly know that? I've told nobody, not even my wife.'

'How do you say, a calculated guess? When I checked with the telephone service this morning, the operator asked me to confirm I was waiting for the patch to Todtnau. Apart from some textile factories, Todtnau is an agricultural and tourist location. The only destination a politician from London concerned with social services could head for is the Institute.'

'You must know the area?'

'I can be there at seven.' The voice was more forceful now, commanding and confident. 'Tell security at the gate you are expecting a delivery and to let me through. I won't take up much of your time. It's a favour we owe to Alison.'

Jack handed the phone back to the receptionist. If today had left him feeling decidedly uneasy, this call had set alarm bells sounding. The underlying beat of the conversation with Hans said Alison was in some kind of trouble. He checked his watch. Five-thirty. He was impatient to know what was going on.

'Everything alright with the offspring?' Usher was installed on a stool at the corner of the bar, idly picking the remnants from a plate of what was supposed to pass for potato crisps.

'You on the gin?' Jack acknowledged the tumbler in front of her.

'After the session today, I needed something potent. What do you think all this psychedelic babble is about?'

Jack attracted the barman's attention and pointed at Usher's glass. 'I think I'll join you.' He waited until two men passed by and were out of earshot. 'I'm more intrigued by what we don't know yet, rather than what we heard today. I get Bayer's role and I understand why they drafted in

Kullenberg, but we don't have a clue what part our esteemed general plays in all this. If the intention is to enforce even tighter food rationing on the elderly by offering a onetime jolly, it will not ward off starvation. It makes no sense.'

They talked on as they sipped their drinks until Usher drained the remnants from her glass. 'What time are we expecting these shrinks?' she asked. 'I need a good long, hot shower and to get into something comfortable.'

'I'm guessing between seven and half-past. If we turn up for dinner after eight, Katrina will have one of her blue fits and we'll be sent to bed with bread and water.'

'I'd better go now,' Usher said. 'I'll see you at the witching hour in the restaurant.'

'Will do.' Jack played with his tumbler as he let his mind wander over the events of the day. With all the developments, he was in danger of forgetting the predicament facing Rebecca. Did she get down to Devon? He needed to talk to her again. How was Harriet? Was she being led by the nose by that bastard, Roach? Above all, where and how was Alison? The whole family was now in one crisis or another. He gritted his teeth in frustration.

Thirty minutes to go. The receptionist raised her eyebrows as he explained he was expecting somebody to turn up with a delivery for him. He needed to thank them personally. Please advise security.

Jack was in his room, showered and changed when the internal phone tweeted on his bedside table.

'Your visitor has arrived, Mr Tirrand.'

# THIRTY-NINE

## FREIBURG – BAVARIA – GERMANY

### 19.00 - 21 November 2065

'I cannot say I am impressed with your protegee, Mr Senator.' Sitting back in a frayed, chenille fabric armchair which had long since seen better days, General Kempeler switched the call to speaker mode. He beckoned for the young subaltern waiting by the door to come closer. 'He strikes me as being headstrong and adversarial, nowhere near as pliable as the woman. She appears to be getting on well with my head scientist.'

The subaltern stopped alongside the armchair and saluted. 'Give me a minute, would you, Simeon? I'm going to put you on hold while I deal with somebody.' The phone clicked as the junior officer bent to talk into the General's one good ear. He listened carefully, nodded and waved the man away as he switched the phone to active. 'You see, that's exactly what I mean. Tirrand is a loose cannon. He's arranged for delivery of a package to the Institute which means a breach of security. Total confidentiality. Did you not impress that on him?'

'Of course, Christian. If you want to get someone to bring him to the phone, I'll lay down the law.'

'I'm not calling you from the Institute. Fearful place. I'm at the Officer's Club in Freiburg. Leave it with me. I'll get the package intercepted and the delivery man interrogated. You can deal with Tirrand when he's back in England. Frankly, I can't see him heading up this operation.'

'You leave Tirrand to me. You know the story about his wife?'

'Held on suspicion of murdering a journalist, I heard. Deserves a commendation, not the death sentence. They're sniffing around all the time, looking for a story. Shoot the lot of them.'

'She's innocent,' Hill said. 'But there's enough circumstantial evidence to convict her. We will keep the pressure on. There's also a problem for him with his daughter. She's expecting her third; desperate to keep it, according to my source. That's another lever to pull.'

'I thought his daughter was here in Germany, sightseeing or,' - he pulled a face and put on a sarcastic voice - 'soaking up the local culture.'

'They're twins, Christian. The pregnant daughter will try for family transfer rights, but we'll say her sister is unstable and incapable of raising a kid. We'll insist on third-party adoption.'

'You've got it all worked out, Simeon. I hope, for your sake, Tirrand tows the line.'

Hill's tone was firm. 'He will. Remember, he's the public face of this project. When the news breaks, he will be the most hated man in Britain. He'll be gone within a month, by which time, Octogen will be well and truly underway.'

'And the woman?'

'She will be low key and will stay on after Tirrand has been dispatched. We need continuity.' The General could hear the shuffle of papers at the other end of the line. 'According to my timetable, my two are having the experience of a lifetime tomorrow. Is that correct?'

'They are seeing the psychotherapists tonight.'

'I'll be fascinated to hear what events they choose to experience.'

The General laughed. 'As far as the woman's concerned, I think Bayer is planning her ultimate adventure way beyond a pill and the prying eyes of half the research team.'

The call ended; the room was in silence as the General waited for a call to be put through to the security gate at the Institute. His thoughts turned to Simeon Hill. Here was a superstar; a sportsman whose name was known and revered throughout the world. Worse of all, he was respected and trusted. His aura was akin to – what was his name? The soccer player sixty years ago who ruled the sporting world? Ronaldo, that was it. He could not recall whether Ronaldo was the man's first or last name.

Hill's charisma stood in the way of Berlin's ambitions. There was no other personality in the UK capable of galvanising public opinion the way he could. With Hill out of the way, there would be a void that Germany could fill. Perhaps a car accident and today's equivalent of a state funeral would pave the way to more dynamic relations.

The phone rang.

# FORTY

## TODTNAU – BAVARIA – GERMANY

## 19.00 - 21 November 2065

Jack stood as the stranger entered the bar and acknowledged the man's raised hand. A father's intuition told him this was not the style of man his daughter would seek as a friend. Possibly late thirties or turned forty, the man was a careful dresser who saw his figure in the mirror as it once was and chose his clothes to match.

Behind the biker's leather jacket, his flowing, white linen shirt was buttoned tight around his midriff and oversized bust, leaving gaps where folds of exposed white flesh poked through. His slimline, lime-green chinos bore the boast of the man who fools himself his waist measurement has not changed in twenty years. There was a hostile arrogance in the way he looked around.

Jack avoided touching the man's sweaty palm or returning the hesitant smile. 'Has Alison turned up?' he asked.

Hans shook his head. 'I don't have much time. They took me for someone else. Asked if I was the head doctor and laughed amongst themselves. I just ignored the question and they let me through. The other person you are expecting will arrive and I would prefer to have left.' He stopped for breath. 'Any chance of a glass of water?' His forehead was damp with sweat.

Jack called over a waitress. 'Just water?' he queried.

Hans nodded and pushed a black cover notebook onto the table. 'Can you check it's all there please?' Hans said.

'All in good time. First, let me get something straight—'
'Please check everything is in order.' There was determination in his voice, but also a sense of pleading, willing the other person to do what was asked. Jack glowered. 'Very well, but . . .' His voice tailed off as he opened the notebook. There were three A4-sized loose pages in the front, handwritten in ink, every word printed in small block capitals. The context left Jack in no doubt about what the message meant.

After reading and re-reading the three pages, Jack closed the notebook and smiled. 'Thank you,' he said. 'It all appears in order.' He looked through the open door of the bar toward reception. Usher was greeting a woman, the psychotherapist sent to interview her. It could not be long before his guy would show up.

The closing two sentences of the man's message prompted him into action. 'I'll just use the toilet and I'll see you out to the main gate. I can't thank you enough for bringing me this. Tell Alison I forgive her.' He made his way to the washroom at the corner of the bar, glancing toward reception as he did. He watched Ruger join Usher and the psychotherapist in conversation.

Hans was standing as he returned. 'I must be going. There is so much to do.'

The man is jittery, Jack thought. Looking at Ruger and imagining the punishment he could inflict would make anybody jittery. 'Of course, I'll see you out.'

Once in the open, Jack measured the distance to the main gate. Thirty seconds with no audio surveillance. 'Are you sure there are no cameras on us?' he asked.

'One on our backs, intended for visitors entering the hotel: two pointing at the gate, monitoring arrivals. You can talk.'

'I don't see why I can't go straight to the head man here, Bayer, and say my daughter was wrongfully taken and get her released.'

'You would be dicing with our lives. I'm guessing while you are here, tests on so-called volunteers are suspended. By tomorrow, they will have all the information from her. You and I will be implicated with her in espionage or plotting against the coalition, tried and executed. You want to take that chance.' He bent down to pretend to tie a lace of his brown boots. 'I have a plan, but it's down to you.'

'Go on.'

'The personnel shift, security, lab and nursing staff change at four in the afternoon and again at midnight. There is a fifteen-minute overlap for the handover. People are off their guard, meeting and chatting in the locker rooms.'

'How do you know all this?'

'Except for a few hours' sleep. I've been watching the place since she was brought in yesterday. In part, it's guesswork.' He rose to his feet. 'Listen, we have no time. Just before midnight tomorrow, I will set off a series of explosions in the woods on the other side of the road. It will sound like gunfire. This is your cue. By then, you will have stolen an employee name tag with the magnetic strip and set a fire in the main building. Look for a maintenance room where there is combustible material. It must be a large enough fire to trigger the sprinklers and activate the fire alarm. This will signal evacuation to the assembly area next to the employee car park.'

'How do you imagine I can do all this?'

'You'll work it out. Your daughter's life is at stake.'

'Then what happens?' Jack looked up. They had twenty metres in which to talk.

'You evacuate with the pass. I will wait in the car park dressed in a nurse's uniform. Exit with the pass through the electronically controlled gate and give me the pass. Tell me where she is, and I'll go back in and get Alison. I'll get her away on my bike and make sure she is at Strasbourg to meet your train on Friday.'

Hans waited for the guard to open the gate. Jack stepped out and grasped Hans's hand. 'Give my love to Alison,' he said in a loud enough voice to have the audio recorded. 'Thanks for bringing my notebook. Drive safely.'

Jack turned to witness a bespectacled young man driving an old two-door compact with faded paintwork and a perforated exhaust. He guessed this was his scheduled appointment. There was bound to be some confusion as identities were checked and Jack would be well advised to be back in the hotel and out of the picture when they realised Jack's previous visitor was not who they assumed it was.

Usher was describing her meeting with psychotherapist Silvia to a distracted Jack, who was trying hard to appear interested in what she was saying when Willi Schmidt appeared alongside them.

Usher immediately stopped talking, but Jack smiled at the newcomer, turned back to Usher and said, 'Do finish what you were saying. I am sure Mr Schmidt can wait. Besides, he has no interpreter with him.'

'I don't need an interpreter,' Schmidt said. 'I need to speak with you, Mr Tirrand.'

'Look, the dinner gong is about to sound. They do like us to be punctual.' He looked past the man's angry gaze to see the young man and a guard in attendance.

'I need to speak now.'

Jack was fighting a rage inside him. He was in no mood to concede. 'And I said, after dinner, when I shall be pleased to talk to this gentleman, whom I assume is the psychotherapist.'

Schmidt's face was centimetres from Jack, the alcohol on his stale breath discernible. A hand gripped Jack's forearm and squeezed. 'Now and not later'.

The pain was intense, but Jack's face was impassive, his gaze of contempt fixed on Schmidt, the adrenalin combatting the urge to wince or cry out. With all his might, he wrenched his arm free. 'The use of force when words fail is a sign of character weakness, Mr Schmidt. This incident will be reported to my superiors.' It even sounded pretentious to Jack, but the German was incensed by the comment.

'You think we are concerned with your tinpot ineffectual assembly? I am not interested in what you intend to do. I want some answers.'

'"Tinpot", is it? My word, your English has improved since you played games in London, pretending not to understand a word that was being said. What was all that about?'

'Strategic, Mr Tirrand. It was appropriate.'

'What? To look better when somebody rightfully complained about Berlin ignoring the language dictates already established?'

'Can I make a suggestion?' Usher moved to separate the two men. She spoke in a slow, measured voice, as if appealing to a child. 'If you two would like to go off for a quiet word somewhere, I will entertain your young man in the restaurant. Choose your meal, Jack. I'll order it and when you are back, I'll retire to another table and leave you two to run through the psychotherapy programme. I could do with a little me time after the excitement of today.'

Her intervention diffused the incendiary mood. Jack nodded and indicated for Schmidt to lead the way.

Sleep would not come, however hard he tried to concentrate on the positives. What positives? There were none. For the umpteenth time, Jack turned in his bed, his eyes focussing on the luminous dial of the alarm clock. Almost three.

Passages from the three pages of Han's handwritten text he shredded and flushed away in the toilet passed like a slideshow through his head.

'*Take what I have written on trust. Do not question me. This place is bugged. There are spy cameras everywhere with audio pickup. They will be in your bedroom, even your bathroom. You are under constant surveillance. Let them only see you treat me as a friend of Alison's who is doing her a favour by delivering a notebook she picked up by mistake on the train.*'

'*Alison is in grave danger. She is a prisoner in this place, captured after curfew by the team who round up victims to be used as subjects for their drug trials. She was trying to help a friend in England with an investigation concerning a German citizen. If she is forced to confess, she will be tried for treason and executed. Do not think you can help her by approaching the people in charge. You will be implicated along with me, and we will meet the same fate.*'

'*I have an idea. When we leave the hotel, and you walk me to the main gate, we can speak freely.*'

'*Your daughter's survival depends on us working together.*'

Alison, my darling Alison, what have you done? Why on earth did I let you come with me? Why did I agree to do this? These people are insane.

Ten minutes sitting, arms crossed, across a table from Schmidt did nothing to improve the growing hostility between the two men. Jack was adamant. There had been no breach of security on his part. He challenged the man named Hans as to how he could know Jack's location. Listen to the recorded conversation. The breach was down to the telephone operator. No, he did not know who Hans was, other than his name and the claim he was Alison's friend.

The notebook? There was nothing special about it. Why should Schmidt want to see it? None of his business. Go take a hike.

All right. All right. Threats were pointless. If it meant they could end this meeting, Schmidt could see the notebook. There. Nothing more than transcripts of his various speeches in the Chapter of the London Assembly which Schmidt held in such contempt. Satisfied?

Credit where it was due. Hans had done a good job of downloading and printing out all that verbiage from the INCOL website. He even went to the trouble of underlining passages of text, inserting exclamation and question marks. It could not have looked more authentic, and Schmidt's cursory examination took only a few seconds.

'What's all the underlining?' Schmidt asked. 'Some sort of code?'

'You've been watching too many twentieth-century spy films.'

For the first time, Schmidt's jaw slackened into something resembling a smile. 'Be ready at nine tomorrow. Someone will pick you up.' Schmidt stood up to leave, reaching for Jack's shoulder before he had time to move. 'Have you decided what event to simulate during your hallucination?'

'Yes,' Jack said. 'Resurrecting my biological parents seems like a sufficiently demanding challenge.'

Schmidt nodded. 'We will follow up on this unprogrammed visit today. When our investigations are complete, the General will deal with the consequences.'

'What consequences?'

Schmidt just shrugged.

# FORTY-ONE

## TODTNAU – BAVARIA – GERMANY

## 09.30 - 22 November 2065

Professor Max Bayer sat behind a small desk in an anteroom on the ground floor of the main building, a warm smile on his face as he motioned for Jack to join him. 'I have just had the pleasure of escorting your colleague into the test area. My staff will watch over her and monitor vital signs.' He nodded as if congratulations were in order. 'Indeed, she is the most obliging and charming individual, a very compelling lady.'

Jack's expression was neutral. He said nothing. After just two hours' disturbed sleep, the last thing he wanted was to comment on Usher's virtues.

'Quite so,' Bayer said, acknowledging the mood music had changed with Jack's arrival. 'You will follow as soon as she comes around and moves to the recovery room.' He coughed. 'Tell me, how did you get on with Dr Weber last evening? Did you follow his instructions?'

'If you mean did I take the relaxant pill after breakfast and will I concentrate my thoughts on my chosen experience? The answer is "yes".'

'Good. Dr Weber is a recent addition to our consultancy group and is keen to please.'

'He certainly is.' Jack reflected on the meal with an over-eager Lukas Weber – 'Let's not be formal. Please call me Dr Lukas.' 'Okay. Only if you call me Deputy Jack.' - He even controlled his brittle temper when dealing with a barrage of questions on every conceivable aspect of old age in England, lifestyle choices, social cohesion and dealing with the prospect of death.

'Can we move on?' Bayer said. He flicked open a beige folder.

'No General Kempeler this morning?' Jack asked.

'He has been held up on some investigation or the other. As I was about to say, you have chosen to revert to your childhood and try to recapture images of life before your parents died. It is a difficult choice.'

'Why is that?'

'There is a severe trauma in the train of events which has caused you to lose your memory of life prior to the accident. You may find it difficult, if not impossible, to bypass the trauma.'

'Would you rather I changed to fantasising about having sex with Marilyn Monroe?'

'Who?' He looked confused. 'No. I am just explaining why we have modified your hallucinogen. We felt a higher trace of a psilocybin component might help you confront your past.'

Jack shrugged. 'You know what you are doing, I hope.'

'As I told you, we enjoy an eighty-plus-per cent success rate. We would hate it for you to be one of the twenty per cent.'

He was interrupted by a laboratory assistant in blue overalls, who gestured to him from the doorway.

Bayer stood up. 'Madame Usher is now in the recovery room. It's your turn, Mr Tirrand. Please follow Silvia. Enjoy the experience.'

The laboratory assistant led the way into a corridor, which opened out into a rectangular room where several more blue-clad workers were sitting in front of monitors. A wall, topped with black tinted glass, ran the length of one side of the room.

Nobody spoke. Silvia handed him a glass of water and a beige-coloured pill the size of a blazer button. 'Take, please,' she said. 'No chew, just swallow.' He did as he was told.

Somebody came from behind and covered his head in what felt like the webbing from the inside of a crash helmet. Silvia smiled at the suspicious look on his face. 'Monitor brain waves,' she said. 'Tells us when you are ready.' She walked away to talk with a colleague.

Jack looked around. He could vaguely see images on the other side of the glass wall. If it wasn't tinted, it must be a one-way mirror, allowing them visual access to whatever was taking place on the other side.

He was about to find out. 'Ready.'

Silvia checked the wiring attached to his body. 'Go through door, please. Sit anywhere you like and fasten safety belt.'

The door was locked behind him. To his utter amazement, he was in the carriage of a moving train, recreated to the tiniest detail in the style of travel a hundred-plus years ago. Scenery rushed past the windows with an occasional trail of smoke from an engine: the sound of wheels speeding over sleepers, the sensation of movement as the carriage appeared to bank and straighten. It was an amazing reconstruction.

He was feeling a little lightheaded. He walked to the end of the carriage. Even the wooden-framed publicity poster advertising a brand of pastilles to cure catarrh looked authentic.

'Sit down, please.' Silvia's voice came over the intercom.

'Bet you'd be good in bed.' Did he think that or actually say it out loud? He staggered into a window seat.

'Now do up your seat belt.' He heard a man's laugh.

He wasn't on the train anymore. *There was a little brown face looking up at him, tears in its eyes, pleading for him to come home.* The searing sensation of burnt flesh in his nose was there again. He was falling into the blackness.

Jack sensed a hand was prising an eyelid open and the light from a torch blinding him. He went to move his hand to shield the light, but he was paralysed. He tried with the other hand. The same thing. 'What the hell!' Now he was conscious, drowsy, with a head like cotton wool but awake.

He was in bed, his hands bound with plastic ties to the guard rails. Bayer stood alongside him, a male nurse in attendance.

'You experienced a bad trip, Mr Tirrand, a very bad trip.'

'Why am I being restrained?'

'You were trying to harm yourself.' He touched Jack's neck. 'Feel anything?'

'It's sore.'

'No doubt. You tried to strangle yourself with the seatbelt. Kneeling, with your head on the seat, you wrapped it around your neck. Do you remember whatever it was prompting you to want to take your own life?'

Jack shook his head.

'Do you recall anything at all?'

The image of the little brown face flashed across his eyes, but he continued to shake his head.

'Where am I?'

'You are in the hospital wing. We're going to keep you under observation for twenty-four hours.'

'Good.'

'Good?'

'I don't know why I said that. I just did. I need to rest.' His eyes opened wide. 'Cut me free, please. I prefer to sleep on my side.'

'We gave you a shot of diazepam. When that didn't work, we tried lorazepam. You are bound to feel drowsy for a few hours.' Bayer made a scissor cutting gesture to the nurse. Jack's hands fell limply by his side. He was already asleep.

He awoke with a start, aware of every part of his body, his senses heightened. Somebody coughed in a hallway. He knew it was a hallway because of the faint echo of a noise in a confined space. He studied the uniform folds in the plastic curtain. How neat and tidy. His sense of smell was heightened. There was a scent of pine on the breeze which caressed the contours of his face, light and intermittent.

Beyond all these intense reactions, he felt euphoric; exhilarated at the prospect . . . The prospect of what? He didn't know. He must concentrate. He had something important to do.

His eyes closed.

'You are awake, Mr Tirrand? I need to examine you.' Silvia stood alongside the bed; a heavy red topcoat was open to reveal a tailored black trouser suit. She laughed at his expression. 'I am not a senior lab technician twenty-four hours a day. My shift finish.'

Jack looked toward the window at the far end of the ward. Daylight was failing. The sudden realisation of what he was yet entrusted to do was like a punch in the stomach. 'What time is it?'

'I leave at four. It must be three and forty-five.' She handed him a pill and a plastic cup of water. 'Take this. It will keep you relaxed; help you remember.'

He feigned taking the pill, letting it slip from his hand into a fold in the sheet. 'I have a suspicion I may have said something to offend you?'

She laughed again. It was an attractive laugh, but he wasn't about to comment. 'No,' she said. 'You were a perfect gentleman.'

'I don't think I've ever been that.'

'Answer me.' Her mood changed to serious. 'Do you use drugs in England?'

'I answered the question on my disclaimer form. No. Never.'

'Have you ever had medical treatment involving the use of hallucinogens or memory enhancers or suppressants?'

'No.' He felt irritated at the question. 'Again, it's on the form I signed.'

'I ask because your reaction very unusual. Nobody saying you not telling the truth. Perhaps you just forget or don't remember.'

'If anything comes to mind, I will tell you.'

She nodded enthusiastically. 'It is possible you will experience HPPD over the next hours.'

'What's that?'

She struggled with the pronunciation. 'Hallucinogen persisting perceptual disorder. It's difficult to say.'

'A tongue twister, yes, but I'm still none the wiser.'

'Wiser about what?' The curtain was pulled back, and Bayer stood at Silvia's side. He was also dressed in an overcoat, briefcase in hand. 'I'm on my way home. Called in to see how you are doing.'

Silvia spoke in German to him.

He nodded. 'You want to know about HPPD? In one word, it is flashbacks, specifically after experiencing a bad trip. You are likely to get visual hallucinations or distortions of reality or perception over the coming weeks, possibly months.' He shrugged. 'We are hoping during the next eighteen hours you have some recall. It may be disturbing, alarming or, possibly, horrific, but one of us will be on call to accompany you through the trauma. You can be certain,' He tapped his watch. 'I must be off. It's the rehearsal for the children's carol concert tonight. A dutiful uncle must always be on hand.' Silvia gave a polite cough. 'Sorry, yes, I forgot to say. Silvia will come to fetch you in the morning. Presuming your vital signs are normal, you will be discharged, and we will meet with the General and his staff upstairs for a final briefing. The following day, you will leave us.'

He turned smartly and parted the curtain before spinning back around. His voice was hesitant. 'I thought as . . . instead of being left to dine alone tonight, I took the liberty of inviting Madame Usher to join me at the carol concert rehearsal and something to eat afterwards in Todtnau . . . I consider it a courtesy to advise you.'

'Have a pleasant time. Did Ramona get through the test all right?'

'Amazingly well. She said it was the most wonderful experience of her life.'

'Pleased to hear it. I look forward to learning all about it.'

Except for the three other occupants of beds who looked more dead than alive, Jack was left undisturbed. He got to his feet too quickly, staggering, almost falling to his knees, grasping at the curtain and pulling on the metal rings so that the sound rang around the ward. Nobody reacted. His head was spinning. He put his hands back down on the bed to steady himself. Get a grip, man.

Fate had offered him one chance to save his daughter. He had imagined a scenario the previous night as he tossed and turned of putting on a show once the effect of the drug had worn off. He would throw himself around the room, make vomiting noises, talk nonsense and whatever else came to mind to end up exactly where he was now. His pessimistic conclusion of the likely outcome of pretending to have a bad trip was the probability of a return to his hotel bedroom, a sedative, and a nurse sent to monitor him. He would be in a worse position and incapable of fulfilling his part of Han's crazy plan. Now, circumstances had worked in his favour. Don't mess it up, he told himself.

Eight minutes to four. If Hans was right, the daytime staff were presently handing over to the evening shift. There would be few people about. Time enough to get his bearings.

His ward was at the corner of the building on the second floor. Moving along the corridor, he passed two further wards, one male, one female, both of which, from a cursory glance through the small window in the door, were fully occupied. He took an extra thirty seconds to check the female section. No Alison.

The passageway to the lobby he recognised from his previous visit led to the elevator doors and the route to the meeting room. To one side of the elevator was a wall with a recessed door. He tried it. Locked. It must be where the cleaning and maintenance equipment was kept. The layout would be repeated on the floor below. He headed for the stairs.

Lights came on throughout the building as he made his way cautiously down the staircase. The noise made him stop in his tracks. Peering around the wall, he could see the open door of the identical room to the one he had tried on the floor above. A woman was humming a tune and shuffling around inside. A cleaning trolley partially barred his view into the room. The humming grew louder as the woman reappeared, arms loaded with a selection of cloths and bottles, which she loaded into a plastic bucket. She locked the door, throwing a set of keys onto a small swivel tray built into the trolley and wheeled it into the corridor.

Jack reached the lobby and followed the path the woman had taken. His first reaction was to wait until she was separated from the trolley and then to take the keys, but it was too soon. She would notice they were missing and alert security.

The rooms on this floor were of an identical size, where a dozen soldiers would once have been billeted. Now, there were bunk beds crammed together, a central, square mess table and a row of lockers along one wall. He counted twenty individuals per room, men on one side of the corridor, women on the other. The door he tried was locked.

Alison was in one of these rooms. He sensed it. Which one? He strained to look through the wire-mesh glass window. There was something about that small pane of glass, but the memory was of it being higher up and set into metal. The image flashed through his mind and left his throat tight and dry.

*'Wo gehen sie hin?'* A man dressed in a green cloth jacket and matching trousers emerged from the room behind him. He carried a similar coloured overcoat over his arm and was obviously about to leave the building. His brow creased as he studied Jack's hospital gown.

Jack's voice was hoarse. *'Hospital. Toiletten* – he remembered the word from the sign in the hotel – *Kaput.'* He pointed at the male and female symbols on the doors at the end of the corridor.

The man muttered something under his breath. *'Seien sie schnell,'* he said as he turned and walked away.

*'Absolut.'* Jack smiled to himself.

The door was to a large toilet and washroom, old but well-maintained. At one end, past a bank of stalls and lockers, was a communal shower. There was nobody around.

Somewhere close by there was the sound of voices talking and laughing, but the corridor from where he came was deserted, the lighting dimmer. He turned toward the noise.

A door opened, lighting up a small passageway and a sign with the words *Eintritt nur für Personal* hanging from the ceiling on a chain. A woman in kitchen whites ambled along the passageway. He retreated behind the door, waiting until she passed and rounded through double swing doors, which he assumed led to the kitchen and what was once the soldiers' mess.

Jack made his way back, this time stopping long enough at each of the rooms to eliminate them from his search.

She was in the third room he came to, slumped on a hardback chair next to a bunk, staring aimlessly at the wall on the other side of the room. His fist slammed on the glass. 'Alison, look at me,' he said under his breath. 'Please look at me.'

Either she could not hear, or was under the influence of one of Bayer's concoctions. 'Damn you to hell,' he said out loud as he went to turn away.

The old woman's face appeared inches away from the other side of the glass. The grin was horrific. What remained of her teeth were brown and stained, like the colour of her gums. She looked at him with tired eyes set deep in sockets encrusted with blackened furrows extending across her forehead.

Cracked lips kissed the glass, her tongue coursing around like a goldfish in a bowl as the saliva ran down the glass. Jack caught a brief sight of two younger women standing behind her, laughing as they pointed toward the floor. For a second, the old woman disappeared from his sight, only to reappear standing on something which placed her chest at the level of the pane of glass. With gnarled fingers, she unbuttoned a worn pyjama top and thrust the nipple of a breast that resembled a creased and deflated balloon hard against the glass. As Jack looked away, he felt, not heard, the sound of the crowd as they jeered and called after him.

Jack retraced his steps to the ward. A man was standing by his bed. He looked on impassively as Jack slipped back between the sheets.

'Well, Mr Muller,' Jack said, fluffing up his pillow. 'To what do I owe the pleasure of your company? I suspect you're not here to take my temperature.'

'Where have you been?'

'Just like Mr Schmidt, straight to the point. No idle chatter. Where is Mr Schmidt, by the way? Having a well-deserved break, I expect.' A smile flickered across his face. 'Well, not that it's any of your business, but I woke up, felt fine and needed a shit.' He hesitated. 'Still following my English?'

'Perfectly,' Muller said. 'Fluency in English is a pre-requisite for joining ISE. I spent eighteen months teaching Wing Chun and other martial arts in Battersea. Plenty of my students shit themselves. Now, please, explain why you were on another floor.'

'I wondered down the corridor looking for a toilet, came to a flight of stairs and ended up on the floor below. There I found what I was looking for. I came back and here we are.'

'Security alerted us because the camera caught you looking through the windows of the female dormitories.'

Damn, he thought. He forgot about the security cameras. Of course, they must have caught him. He would need to avoid them during his next sortie. 'Curiosity,' he said. 'Dormitories, you say you call them. More like collective prison cells to me.' He yawned. 'Just curiosity.'

'Are you a sexual voyeur, Mr Tirrand, a peeping Tom, as you call it? Silly language, all these ridiculous little sayings. Perhaps, even worse, a predator, molester, maybe even a rapist. The newspapers certainly impute to you a heightened sexual appetite.'

Jack yawned again, aware that the relaxing effect of the drugs was still in his system. 'Dear Mr Muller, beyond extolling your command of English, the accusation, if that is what you impute to me, has no foundation and is untrue.' He smiled. 'I need to rest.' He moved as if to go to sleep but turned back. 'By the way, I think if you intend to use the word "shit" as a verb, "to shit", I suggest the past participle would be "shat", Hence, "My students shat themselves." Just saying.' He turned over and settled his head into the pillow.

The smell of food hit his nostrils before his eyes opened. He was conscious of feeling hungry. God, what time was it? He fumbled for his watch, trying to focus with sleep-filled eyes. Just after six. He sank back in relief.

A dark-skinned man with a fixed smile was standing alongside his bed. He pointed at the food trolley. *'Willst du Saftgulasch oder Hühnchen?'*

'A choice,' he said. 'Things are looking up.' He sat up to study the two trays. 'I'll take the meaty-looking soup.' He pointed at the goulash. 'The chicken looks as though it did the rounds at lunch.'

The man's fixed smile remained as he put the tray on Jack's bed. He looked at the overfilled plate and gave Jack the thumbs-up. 'Your grandmother's recipe?' Jack said with a laugh. The man nodded and moved along the ward.

Two of the three patients were awake and sitting up in bed. Both their faces were covered in bloody scratches and deep welts, their hands bound in bandages, as were their eyes. The dark-skinned man lost his fixed smile as he sat on the first man's bed and spooned goulash into his mouth, hardly giving him time to swallow.

Even in haste, feeding the men was a lengthy process. The third man had to be roused from his troubled slumber and protested by upending the plate and cursing in a language Jack did not recognise. Few words were spoken, none exchanged between the patients; the silence sometimes fractured by a curse, a phrase in some far-off language or a drawn-out moan, telling more of resignation than of pain.

At nine, the main lighting went off, leaving a small, localised glow from the light fixtures above the emergency exit doors.

Jack took a deep breath. He was ready to make his move.

# FORTY-TWO

## ISE SERIOUS CRIME UNIT – FULHAM – WEST LONDON

## 19.00 - 22 November 2065

Rebecca forced her fingers through a clump of matted hair. At eight that morning, she washed as best she could in the basic facilities allowed to detainees. She even forced herself to use the chemical loo in the cell without gagging, but now, as she contemplated her second night in custody, she felt both dirty and alone.

There was a knock at the door, then a key turning and the squeak of unoiled hinges as the guard appeared in the doorway. He motioned for her to follow him.

The man was pacing back and forth in a reception room complete with casual chairs and a large, square coffee table. The door closed with a dull thud as he walked toward her, his hand outstretched. 'Mrs Tirrand. What a pleasure.'

She raised her eyebrows. This man was impeccably dressed, a tailored herring-bone suit over a slender frame and with film star features. 'You would be?' she asked.

'Sorry.' He flipped a fringe of grey/black hair from his forehead. 'I'm Henry Randall. Detective Diamond suggested you might need legal representation. My field is criminal law.'

Rebecca looked him up and down. She put him in his mid-fifties. If his legal talents matched the little boy lost look, betrayed by those come to bed eyes, he could certainly represent her. Jesus! How could she be thinking so stupidly? Her freedom, her life, were in the balance. Get to grips. This is serious. 'I was expecting the family lawyer,' she said. 'But he hasn't made an appearance and I'm getting desperate.'

'Just as well, if I may be blunt. Somebody from the old school, well-versed in will-writing, countryside conveyancing law and contracts to buy and sell livestock, would be of little use to you.'

'I appreciate the distinction. Can you get this sorted out? I didn't kill anybody.'

He smiled knowingly. 'All my clients are innocent, Ms Tirrand—'

'Please. Rebecca. I *do* have an identity beyond my husband's surname.'

Randall appeared startled by the vehemence of her interjection. 'Apologies,' he said. 'Some of my clients may well be innocent, but it is irrelevant to me. My job is to provide the best defence possible, irrespective of my opinion, if I have one, as to their guilt or innocence.'

'I understand, but you must appreciate I couldn't allow you to defend me unless I believed you were convinced of my innocence.'

He held his hands up in mock submission. 'Then, let's start from that premise and, of course, my firm belief you will settle my account when the time comes.'

She opened her eyes wide. 'You can depend on that.'

'Good.' He pulled his chair nearer to the coffee table and took a lined A4 pad from his briefcase. 'Let's get started.' From his inside pocket, he drew a tortoise shell fountain pen.

'Good grief,' she said. 'That's something I expected my family lawyer would sport, not you.'

He beamed at her. 'Well spotted. I wasn't around when these were in fashion, but some judges I deal with are old enough to remember and associate a writing style with gravitas and class. Remember, Rebecca, your future hangs on the single decision of one person, the judge. The outcome is based on not only the evidence, proven or circumstantial, but also on an element of theatre. The judge is human with prejudices, likes and dislikes and human nature means they play a part in his assessment. When and if the time comes, I'm going to worry about your dress, your appearance, demeanour, facial expressions; all things with zero relevance to the facts, but still important.' He waited for her nod of acknowledgement. 'Now, let's start. I have the basic outline of Inspector Diamond's submission. I need you to tell me everything in precise detail from your very first contact with,' – he checked the notepad - 'journalist, Seth Morgan. Take your time. We have all night if need be.'

'Don't you have a home to go to?'

'Rattling around in an empty house has no particular attraction for me.'

Rebecca smiled, deciding to bank the next obvious question until they knew each other better and could talk man to woman rather than lawyer to client. Her lot was on the up.

# FORTY-THREE

## TODTNAU – BAVARIA – GERMANY

## 22.00 (21.00 GMT) - 22 November 2065

The last hour had been very productive.

As the main lights were switched off, a security guard appeared at Jack's bedside, checked his name on a list and took a tablet from a pill box, mimicking for Jack to swallow it with a cup of water. He pretended to swallow the relaxant and gave the man a thumbs-up signal.

Play acting followed as Jack pointed at the unmanned nurses' station by the door. *Morgen,* the guard said, reacting to Jack's look of concern by going toward the cord hanging above his bed, making to pull it and then, with a finger pointing at his chest, begin running on the spot.

'Okay. I get the picture,' Jack said and gave another thumbs-up. 'The nurse comes on duty in the morning. In the meantime, you'll come to save me if I'm dying. Some comfort, that is.' The man returned the thumbs-up salute.

The laundry chute was set in a recess halfway along the internal dividing wall against which Jack's bed was placed. He would never have seen if the man serving the food had not halted alongside it to recycle the cloth saturated in goulash from the upturned plate of the disgruntled patient. Unaware Jack was watching him, the man took a small cloth bag from his pocket, filled it with six pieces of chicken, pulled together the string ties, and sent it down the chute. Doubtless, he was feeding a family and would collect the bag from the stack of dirty linen when his shift was over. There was no security at the exit gate other than a surveillance camera. He and likely others would be well-versed in the art of petty pilfering.

The chute was wide enough to take a folded single mattress. The height was a problem. Jack could lay sideways across the riveted metal plates, his head and shoulders pressing on one side, his knees bent, feet tight against the other. By applying sufficient pressure, he could control his descent without careering down three floor levels to the basement and ending up both damaged and detained. However, as he eased himself into the space, he realised headroom would be his problem. His back was flat against the base of the chute, his knees and chin almost touching the top. There would be more room in his coffin, he thought wryly to himself. If the chute narrowed, he would be wedged in like a cork in a wine bottle, unable to move up or down.

'Here goes,' he said in a whisper. He arranged the bedclothes to give the impression of a body asleep and took one last look around the ward. Whatever the outcome, there was no alternative. He could not repeat his stroll around the building dressed in a hospital gown. A camera was bound to record his movements and associate him with whatever disturbance was to follow. He needed anonymity, a disguise.

The drop to the first floor was almost vertical. Beyond was a turn in the chute, necessary to bypass the entrance hall on the ground floor. How and where the chute went after the turn, he had no idea.

'Don't look down,' he told himself. 'Even if you could.'

He pushed his head and knees up as hard as he could. His body slid, shoulders chafing against the rivetted metal. He was speeding up. Feet out, head and shoulders back, he shuddered to a stop. He felt he must be at the turn but, looking back, he had travelled just three metres.

Once again, he forced his body to contract, sliding slowly, at first, his shoulders and the back of his head now sticky with blood from the friction burns.

He felt the acceleration, but something was going wrong. The weight of his head and torso, being greater than his legs and feet, meant he was falling faster, his body turning from the horizontal to an angle of sixty degrees. Unless he could correct the movement, he would end up turning a full ninety degrees from the horizontal and diving headfirst toward the basement, his arms pinned against his side like the man shot from a cannon at the circus.

Using every ounce of strength, he tried to drag his feet and legs forward, but however hard he tried, he was again picking up speed. Any second now, he was about to lose control and cascade headlong into the unknown.

His shoulder hit the bend in the chute with a painful thud just as his legs pirouetted upwards, wedging his knees between two protruding cast iron stanchions. His forward impetus finally stopped as his torso turned, leaving his body prostrate, trapped with his head looking down into the black void.

He closed his eyes. A feeling of nausea swept over him. *The little boy's voice was asking him if he could hear the moaning coming from below. He said no, but he knew it wasn't the truth. Of course, he could hear the fear and hurt in that wailing sound, but there was nothing he could do about it. Too late. It was too late. It was an accident. He never meant for it to happen. No remorse, the man said. He had shown no remorse. Stand up.*

He tried to stand up before the image faded, and he realised where he was. His head rang against the metal roof of the chute. He looked down again. The bend had saved him from serious injury, possibly death. Battered and bruised, he undoubtedly was, but he was confident no bones were broken.

There was nothing for it. He must keep going. For Alison's sake. He pictured her sitting in that chair and shook his head. Regrouping his faculties, he inched around the corner.

The first-floor access flap to the chute was just in front of him. He edged past as noiselessly as possible, discounting the thought of exiting and making his way on foot down the remaining two floors. It was tempting, but having got this far, illogical.

To his relief, the height of the chute increased after the access flap and the drop was no longer vertical, but at a modest incline of twenty or thirty degrees. He could now use his hands to apply as a brake if his rate of descent sped up or his body moved out of position.

Ten metres further down and he stopped for breath. The flap, now above him, opened and a mass of bed linen and blankets landed on him. The stench from fouled sheets made him gag as he used his hands to filter the items past him to fall with only a swish on their way down the chute.

The bunk bed mattress tumbled onto his back without warning and almost dislodged him. The flock inside and the outer fabric cover were sodden with fresh blood and urine. Try as he might, he could not compress the mattress sufficiently to bypass his body.

It was a risk, but a risk worth taking. Ignoring the fetid smell, he pulled the mattress toward him and wrapped it partially around his body.

He stopped. The flap opened again, and a man's voice echoed down the chute. He must be checking to see if the mattress had fallen or was wedged against the sides of the chute. If he shone a torch, Jack was doomed. Kicking out, his arms pulling the mattress tight to his head and body, he launched himself into the void.

What had taken almost an hour so far was completed in seconds. The sensation of fear mixed with exhilaration was something Jack would never forget. The mattress broke his fall, splitting and shedding its insides over the concrete floor and the bed linen that had gone before.

The cavernous basement was poorly lit. Jack sat up and checked his body. Nothing broken, but his gown was torn and stained with his sweat and blood. His shoulders and neck felt like a hot poker was being drawn across his back. His knees were skinned, the soles of his feet raw.

There was nobody in view, although he could hear two people talking in the distance.

He struggled to his feet, his eyes focussing in the dim light. The basement extended along the length of the building. Several carts full of dirty linen were parked in front of a bank of ten industrial washing machines cemented into raised concrete bases. Two were working and of the rest, three or four, looked as though they had been cannibalised for parts.

Further on was the drying and ironing section, a vast and confusing arrangement of cords running from pillar to pillar over an area as big as half a soccer pitch. Sheets, blankets, uniforms and gowns were draped over every conceivable inch of cord, turning the entire area into a glorified maze. Stands with vertical steam irons, professional ironing tables and hand presses stood grouped together. Folded linen was stacked on large square tables.

Running parallel to Jack as he traversed the basement was the external wall, half brick, half window, through which light filtered in from above. All that Jack could see on the other side was a service passage and a stone wall, no doubt constructed to stop the earth from encroaching on the building. Midway along, through the glow of a tired fluorescent light, he saw a door ajar and a flight of steps leading up to the former parade ground. This was where the noise was coming from. The glow from cigarettes reflected on the window pane as two men chatted and smoked.

The extent of the laundry was defined by a timber-studded wall running right across the building with a double-door in the middle, sealed with a chain and padlock. To the side of the door, there was a makeshift partitioned office. A solitary bulb illuminated two desks, a small table and two large filing cabinets. Alongside the office was a large, covered incinerator, hot to the touch, embers glowing bright against the dark surroundings. Jack crisscrossed through lines of washing, unable to find what he was looking for.

The two men were still outside. Jack crept into the office. Only one of the two filing cabinets was locked. He found a bunch of keys on a desk, tried three before the fourth turned in the lock. The large bottom drawer was packed with reinforced polythene, single use sterile kits. He took out a packet marked *mittelgross*, discarded his torn gown and pulled the medium-sized blue suit over what was left of his vest and briefs. The elasticated scrub cap was too small to cover his forehead, and the shoe covers were not made to go over bare feet, but they would have to do. He thought about wearing the mask, but away from the laboratory, it would look ridiculous. He clipped the elastic ties around his arm.

Satisfied it was as good as it would get, Jack opened the incinerator and dropped his torn gown and the plastic packaging into the embers.

The two men were returning, their lumbering progress slow, the conversation laboured. Jack hurried to the drying area, hiding between two rows of sheets. In the event, the sound of the men's footsteps receded toward the washing machines. One uttered what sounded like a curse. Jack guessed the man had just seen the new delivery from the chute.

Ten-thirty. With neither a location to start a fire nor an employee pass for Hans, time was running out.

There were two ways of exiting the laundry: one, via the stairs out to the parade ground, the other, a service elevator in the corner opposite the washing machines. He could use neither without drawing attention to himself, which, at this stage, he was not prepared to do. Perhaps there was another way. He went back to the office and the bunch of keys. He found one to fit the padlock securing the double doors built into the partition wall. He returned the keys to the desk and opened the door into the other half of the basement, pulling it shut behind him.

Save for a sheen of tepid lamplight filtering in close to the external wall, the area was in darkness. There was no way he could move forward without a torch. His mobile was God knows where, doubtless in the hands of a technician trying to locate the source of Han's call. He would need a light to guide him across what looked like a storage warehouse. He returned through the double doors.

Somebody was in the office. Jack waited in the shadows. Eventually, the man rose, pocketed a keyring and left, swinging a small toolbox in one hand.

Along with a selection of candles, some new, some part used, there were three torches in the top drawer of the open filing cabinet. Power cuts must be a regular problem. He realised the wiring circuit down here was not linked to the generator. Laundry was not a priority when emergency power was needed. He chose the torch with the strongest beam.

The warehouse contained a disorderly confusion of surplus detritus, simply dumped on the floor and left to decay or collapse, untended. In one corner, there were piles of single mattresses like the one discharged into the chute. He calculated hundreds, leftover from the days when a battalion of soldiers was garrisoned here. To one side was a heap of rusting bayonets, next to a collection of wooden poles, fencing and netting, used for assault course training, and a row of battered, metal lockers, many with doors bent open revealing the remnants of clothing and personal items. There was no storage plan or organisation. Surplus items were simply brought here and cast aside.

Not so in the far corner alongside the external wall. There, next to an open cargo lift operating between the basement and ground-floor levels was a hand-operated, battery fork-lift, and an organised grouping of six pallets, stacked with boxes of cleaning materials, sanitising gel along with medical and first aid supplies.

Jack felt the tremor of exhilaration run through his body. He had found the means and place to become a novice arsonist. The next task was to find and steal a magnetic personnel ID card.

The internal exits from the basement were in the far corner, an elevator, summoned and operated by a key or a push-bar door opening onto a flight of stairs. He was careful to leave the door ajar, using a blanket as a wedge to stop it closing and locking from the outside.

It was past eleven. He needed to hurry. How long did he need to set a fire before Hans let off his diversionary firecrackers in the forest? He had no idea. Twenty minutes, he guessed, for it to take hold and trigger the alarm.

Did the basement have smoke sensors and a sprinkler system? Whatever, it was too late to look for somewhere else.

The building was in almost total darkness, the common areas partially illuminated by the emergency lighting system. He passed no one on his way to the first floor until the sound of talking brought him to a sudden stop. He slipped into the passageway to the kitchens and chanced a quick glance into the corridor. Muller stood alongside the door to the dormitory in which Alison was being held. He was on the telephone, his gaze either at the floor as he listened or peering through the window into the room when he spoke.

Jack told himself the call could be about anything or anyone, but in his heart of hearts, he sensed it was about Alison. Could they have discovered who she was? Time was critical.

Muller finished the call and walked back to the main staircase. Casting a glance into the darkened room and failing to catch sight of his daughter, Jack urged himself to move on.

The entrance to the personnel rest rooms was in darkness. In twenty-five minutes, the shift changeover would occur, and he imagined a bustle of activity in place of the eerie silence as he opened the door to the male toilets. It was larger than he had calculated. A changing room full of wooden benches and lockers with toilets to one side leading into a shower room in which he could hear running water and a cracked tenor voice singing at full volume. He looked around. One set of dungarees and an apron hung on a clothes hook, but there was no identity badge.

His luck was also out in the female washroom. A cursory look around an empty room told him just how careful everybody was about securing their belongings inside lockers.

Disheartened, he made his way back to the basement. Just maybe, in the confusion about to ensue, he could dislodge one from somebody's uniform. He acknowledged it was a slim possibility.

Ten minutes to set a fire. Taking one of the less corroded bayonets from the heap, Jack began by slicing open mattresses, exposing the contents of cotton waste, wool and lint. He made a circular pile of ten shredded mattresses placed on top of a further ten, for which he only had time to slit the studded fabric cover along its length.

Dousing the pyre of with hand sanitiser, he used a two-metre length of sisal rope to fashion a make-do fuse. He emptied the contents of a case of litre bottles over the remaining mattresses, just in case. There should be enough alcohol to get a healthy blaze underway. Now, all he had to do was light the fuse, make sure it was burning, and get out. That was the exact moment he realised without matches or a lighter, there was no way of igniting the damn fuse. Panic. Think, man! Think!

Jack had reached the double doors when he heard the first retort. My God, it sounded just like gunfire. It was quickly succeeded by a barrage of noise. Floodlights must have been switched on around the parade ground, as the intensity of light reaching the basement increased tenfold.

There was commotion, shouts from inside and out, the sound of feet trampling on the gravel. A siren wailed.

What was he doing? He was not going to find a box of matches just lying conveniently on the ground. Panic consumed him. *A boy's face flashed in front of his eyes. Not the one he remembered from before. This time it was a younger boy, pale-faced and frail. The boy opened his mouth, shouting at him, yet his lips moved in total silence.* The vision passed.

The office. There must be a solution somewhere. Remember the two men smoking outside?

He shook his head to clear it as he opened the connecting door.

The man was walking toward the office, a stack of neatly ironed sheets in his arms. He stopped as Jack appeared through the door. Both men stood still, unsure of what to do.

This was not one of the two men Jack had seen earlier, but a shorter and slimmer youth who must have just come on shift. As his gaze took in Jack's blue laboratory gear, the man's mouth fell open, his eyes wide with fear. He dropped the sheets onto the floor, holding his hands up, palms outward, as if trying to stop Jack from coming nearer. *'Nicht Ich. Nicht heute!'* he pleaded.

There was another barrage as more firecrackers burst into life.

The man turned and ran, banging into the finishing tables and careering headlong into lines of laundry. He kept shouting out, repeating the mantra that it wasn't his turn today as he disappeared into the morass of laundry.

The intensity of the noise was increasing. Jack ran to the office, going back to the desk. Matches, a lighter. He ransacked the drawers, tossing paperwork onto the floor. What was that? Amongst the checklists was something he recognised. Feeling the rigid plastic between his fingers, he pulled out an identity card with the magnetic strip across the back. The portrait photo was of an elderly man, partially covered by a white label with the word '*tot*' written on it. It was of a dead maintenance worker and must have been missed before his uniform was sent for cleaning and recycling. Perhaps it still worked. He pocketed it.

No matches. No lighter. He must find someone who smoked. Not wearing this, he realised. They must be terrified of being co-opted as guinea pigs for laboratory testing. The last thing they saw before their bodies were pumped full of drugs was a group of people in blue suits. No wonder the man ran.

He found a hospital gown on one of the drying lines and stripped off the blue plastic sterile suit. The incinerator. How stupid could he be? Back in the office, he took a candle from the drawer in which he found the torch, waited until his blue suit started to melt in the embers, wrapped a towel around his arm and hand and lowered the wick of the candle into a flickering flame. He waited. The towel smoked and his hand sensed the intense heat as the candle came to life, flickering in the draught.

Protecting the flame with a cupped hand, he returned to the warehouse. In an instant, the entire length of sisal erupted, feeding flame into the shredded mattresses almost immediately and producing an explosion of light and smoke which reached the ceiling in seconds.

God, Jack thought, as he turned for the adjoining door, I'll burn down the entire building.

His last glance caught a line of barely visible blue flame coursing toward the remaining mattresses and feeding across the floor to where the accelerant must have spilled in his haste.

Jack's way out was via the door onto the steps up to the parade ground. Alongside the door frame, he saw a manual fire alarm activation box with a white pull-down handle. The response was immediate. The moment he activated the unit, sirens and bells rang around the building and the annex. As if in sympathy, another salvo of firecrackers sounded in the distance.

Jack held back, hiding behind two empty linen containers until three men, the original two plus the younger man he had unwittingly terrorised, ran to the exit and disappeared up the steps. He could now hear anxious voices. Peering just above ground level, he saw a line of people shunted by a guard toward the assembly point. A group of what looked like supposed test volunteers were leaving the building through the main door, shepherded by two women holding torches, the beams now lost in the floodlights which drenched the area and the woodland beyond. To Jack's chagrin, there was no way he could help these poor souls, shivering in their night clothes, heads bowed before the two female guards, who poked and prodded their charges as if herding cattle.

As soon as a group of five kitchen staff passed, talking and laughing as if nothing out of the ordinary was happening, Jack advanced to ground level. The icy wind ran through his flimsy gown. He shivered, his teeth chattering, his arms flaying around his body. He ran toward the largest group of people, veering at the last moment to the gateway next to the employees' car park.

Nobody. Hans was supposed to be there waiting.

'Have you got what I need?' came a voice from the shadows of a parked INCOL Frei saloon car.

'I don't know,' Jack said, reaching into his pocket. 'It's from a dead person. It may not work.'

Hans came into view, wearing the exact uniform worn by the nurses in the Institute. 'Give it here and stay aside. Don't talk within camera range.' The tension in his voice was palpable. Jack poked the card through the wire netting.

Hans swiped the magnetic strip through the reader to the sound of a double beep and a red light.

'Shit,' Jack said under his breath.

Hans retreated and handed the card back to Jack. 'Try it on your side.'

Jack looked around. The crowd in the assembly area had swollen, but nobody was looking in his direction as far as he could see. He ran the card through the reader. There was a continuous beep, a green light, and the door swung open. Hans pulled it closed, locking it into position.

'What the fuck are you doing?' Jack whispered angrily when out of earshot of the camera. 'You could have walked through.'

'People who are registered as "in" have to exit before they can return. It's logical. If I'm right, I'll be able to get back out again when I return with your daughter. Now, spare me any more talk and give me the card.'

Hans ran it through a second time, and the light went green as the door swung open. He stood next to Jack. 'Where do I go?'

'First floor; western corridor; straight on; third door on the left, possibly locked.'

'I'll worry about that when I get there.' With that he was gone, disappearing in between the growing crowd exiting from the building.

Jack suddenly realised he was freezing. The adrenalin rush was fading and his body was shaking uncontrollably.

Someone handed him a blanket, then took it back, unfolded it and wrapped it around his shoulders. He was trying to say *danke* when the explosion came.

The crowd fell silent as the basement windows exploded and the flames and smoke billowed upward from below as if the earth had caught fire. The sound of fire engines roared as they closed in on the scene.

The burning sensation in Jack's nose was so intense it made him double up, his eyes pressed tight shut.

'Are you all right?' He recognised the voice.

*They had put him in a van. No windows. That's not right. There was one, but high up. Two policemen were in there with him, stern faces, saying nothing. People were banging on the outside of the van, calling him names. Murderer. Devil child. The window shattered as something hit it. Liquid and fire poured into the interior. "Burn in hell," someone shouted. The policemen stamped on the flames, extinguishing them. Someone alongside him was crying. It was the little boy's face, covered in tears and snot, his eyes pleading. "Don't worry, Jamil," he said. "I'll look after you."*

'I asked if you were all right?' Muller stood next to him, a look of genuine concern on his face.

Jack nodded. 'What's going on?' he asked.

'Looks like a fire broke out over there.' He pointed toward the firemen, extending hoses at close quarters to the building. 'I expect it looks worse than it is. They'll have it under control soon.'

'I heard what sounded like gunfire.'

Muller's brow creased. 'You did?'

'I think that was what woke me up.'

Jack's eyes were on the main doors, where people were still leaving the building. In amongst them he saw Hans wearing a mask and pushing a wheelchair, his charge wrapped head to foot in blankets. A surge of relief swept over him, then panic. Muller was following his eyeline. Jack turned to block his view. 'When do you think we can get back inside?'

Muller looked past him, ignoring the question. 'If that is who I think it is . .' He stopped in mid-sentence. 'I've got to see someone.' He hurried to where Hans was manoeuvring past a group of people. In his haste, Muller almost stumbled into the wheelchair, sidestepping at the last moment and grabbing the metal arms to halt its progress as he moved past. Hans stood his ground, his free hand reaching inside his tunic.

Muller regained his footing, rubbing his shin as he stared into Hans's face. 'No panic,' he said in German. 'Take your time. Everything is under control.' He moved past Hans to a guard escorting an old lady and spoke, pointing at the building as he did so.

There must have been a hundred people crowded around the assembly point, all eyes but one focussed on the blaze and the firemen fighting it. Jack watched as Hans pushed the wheelchair through the access gate and across the uneven surface to disappear into the night. A minute later, he heard an engine splutter into life, accelerate and gradually fade into the night.

Jack let out a long sigh of relief, his breath condensing into the chill night air.

# FORTY-FOUR

## TODTNAU – BAVARIA – GERMANY

## 16.00 (15.00 GMT) - 23 November 2065

'Our apologies for the delay in calling this meeting.' Bayer looked uncomfortable as he sat wedged into a double seat next to General Kempeler in the room fitted out as a replica train carriage from the previous century. Opposite him, across a table covered in a starched white linen cloth, sat Usher and Jack. Facing them on the other side of the aisle were Schmidt and Muller.

'There was a breach of security here last night and a person, or persons unknown, gained entry to the premises, murdered a guard and set a fire of some intensity in the basement.'

Usher gasped at the news. Jack bit his lip as he studied the floor. Hans must have needed to use violence to free Alison. That someone died in the attempt was tragic.

'To what end?' Usher asked.

Bayer gave her a warm smile. 'We are unsure. When raids have occurred in the past, it has been to secure drugs.'

'Not so this time?' Jack asked.

'We are still checking, but so far—'

Schmidt leaned over. 'I'd like to ask you a question about last night, Mr Tirrand.'

'What about?'

'You were one of the first to reach safety outside the building. How come?'

'As I told your oppo, the gunfire woke me up, a fire alarm started, and I made my way downstairs out of the building.'

'Gunfire?' Usher said in amazement. Jack looked at her. It was apparent she had not spent last night in the hotel.

'It's a ploy used by the DCs to create a diversion. They use firecrackers. We sent out a security detail to chase them off, but they had fled.' He smiled again at Usher. 'Nobody in the hotel was unduly inconvenienced.'

'As I was saying,' Schmidt glared at Bayer before holding Jack's gaze. 'Did you see anybody on your way out of the building, specifically a person in a blue plastic suit, similar to those worn in the adjoining room?'

'Nobody of that description. I'd just woken up and was in a hurry to get out of harm's way. I wasn't interested in who was who.'

'As you say, you just woke up and were in a hurry. Tell me, does a man getting out of bed not leave the bedclothes in disarray, the mattress cover exposed? Your bedding was pulled up, even suggesting somebody could have been in the bed.'

'Am I suspected of something?' Jack decided attack was his best approach.

'No. Not at all. Just a strange thing to do.'

'Well, if you must know, your man gave me a sleeping pill, and I fell into a heavy sleep. When the gunfire or whatever it was woke me up, I felt my damp crotch and the sensation I might have had an accident whilst asleep. I didn't stop to look, just pulled the blankets up to cover my embarrassment. Happy?'

Bayer tut-tutted. 'Can we please proceed with what we are here to do and leave other matters for later?'

Ignoring Bayer's plea, the General placed two images in front of Jack. 'Recognise either of these two men?' he asked.

The grainy stills were from the camera in the corridor leading to the dormitory where Alison was held. One showed Jack, head bowed, clad in his blue sterile suit and elasticated cap; the other, Hans, also with head bowed and a towel covering his head and half his face. It was tied under his chin.

'I didn't see anybody looking like that in here last night.'

'We think the taller man bears a resemblance to the man who visited you two days ago.' The General made the statement sound like a question.

Jack studied the photo again. 'Heights about right, but as to the rest, I couldn't say. I don't know the man who delivered the notebook other than what he told me and that was next to nothing.' He hesitated. 'Or is the implication of your bizarre comment to suggest I was somehow involved in last night? If so, I must have done it in my dreams.'

The General, stone-faced, made no move to reply.

An uncomfortable silence was broken by Usher. 'You've still not said, Max . . . Professor Bayer, what you think they were after?'

Bayer coughed, adjusting the elastic of a red bow tie under the collar of a white shirt. 'We don't know for sure. We are fairly certain it was DC initiated, their objective being to free a group of fellow criminals rounded up the previous evening and sent to us for evaluation. They are housed in a separate area. When their mission failed, they kidnapped a female volunteer and made off with her.'

'How awful,' Usher said. 'Who was the poor woman?'

'That's what we don't know and, regrettably, that's down to you two,' Bayer joked, in a failed attempt to lighten the atmosphere.

'Down to us?' Usher retaliated.

'We suspended induction procedures during the days dedicated to your hallucinatory experience so that all of my front-line staff could help evaluate the results. The woman in question was due to provide us with her name and relevant background today. A profile with photograph would go on to our data base.'

Jack clenched his fists under the table. He tried to sound impassive. 'Didn't she simply volunteer that information when she arrived of her own free will?'

'Why do you want to know?' Schmidt leaned across the aisle once again.

'Curiosity. Don't you like people asking questions?'

'Please,' Bayer said. 'She came to us under abnormal circumstances and did not utter a word all the time she was here. Eventually, we would have extracted the information.'

'Drug her, you mean?'

'Enough.' The General retorted. 'It's irrelevant. We will send images today of the woman and the two men who infiltrated this place with such ease . . .' He hesitated to give Bayer an appraising glance. '. . . to Berlin, where they still have some facial recognition software. The process is slow, but in three weeks, if they are anywhere on file within INCOL, we will know their identity.' He waved his hand toward Schmidt and Muller. 'We still have a lot of work to do investigating the events of last night and taking the appropriate disciplinary action.' He let the last three words hang in the air. 'Now, to conclude our business with you two. Have you finished talking, Bayer?'

The professor looked stunned, then affronted by the vehemence of the question. 'All I wanted to comment on was our failure to achieve a satisfactory result with Mr Tirrand. We will re-examine the video of his experience, and we ask him to report to us any HPPD occurrences – that's to say, flashbacks – should they occur during the coming months.'

Jack nodded his agreement.

'Over to you, General,' Bayer said. 'Our involvement in this project has been explained.'

The General ran his tongue across nicotine-stained teeth and looked from Usher to Jack and back again. 'This has been an unsatisfactory week and I have serious reservations about your suitability for the assignment. However, you have been selected and will see this through, even if we have to monitor your performance.'

'Thanks for the vote of confidence.' It was Usher's turn to sound affronted. Jack said nothing.

Easing himself out of his seat, the General rose and stood in the aisle. He took Schmidt's hand to steady himself, his eyes still moving between the two visitors. 'Of course, you realise you are not returning to London just to give a few old people a trip into their dreams. You are not that stupid. Here's how it will work.'

He spoke in short, clipped sentences. The conclusions reached in Eigard's paper on supply and demand were accepted unanimously by the Senate, including every UK senator. He stressed the last point. His role had been to assemble a team with one remit – to come up with a solution. This, he was pleased to say, they had done.

The answer, he stressed, was based on the concept of reward and sacrifice. People who spent their lives contributing to society were to be rewarded with an experience of a lifetime when, for a short while, they could live out their wildest fantasy. This initial trial phase of the project, named Octogen, will be micro-managed in London by Mr Tirrand, supported by Madame Usher.

Using specially written software, a random selection of five hundred persons, in the main, those with dates of birth up to 1985, would be chosen to take part.

The day prior to the experience, everyone selected will be accompanied to a reception centre where they will speak to a psychotherapist to establish the medication they are to receive the following day. They will be given a relaxant, which they are asked to take before going to bed.

'It's a mild hallucinogenic designed to stimulate the thought process of the individual person's fantasy.'

Jack could feel the tendons in his neck tighten, and his pulse rate increase. Usher glanced round to receive a reassuring smile from Bayer.

'Four carriages, identical internally to this room, are currently in transit to London, Charing Cross, a station which I believe was once one of the busiest commuter terminals in the Capital.' He nodded to Jack. 'One day, may it be so again. They will arrive early next week.'

'You will assign seats to each . . . passenger, shall we call them?.. and they take their prescribed medication. As the train moves off, the passengers drift into their fantasy.'

General Kempeler explained how the train would leave the station, travelling for a kilometre across the Thames to Waterloo where an area had been adapted for their requirements.

'Let's pretend we are on board,' he said and retook a seat opposite Schmidt.

The lights dimmed, and the noise was of a steam engine racing over points. A countryside landscape raced across the windows to give the impression the train was moving.

'Realistic, is it not?' he said. 'Now imagine the ten minutes during which the hallucinogenic drug has performed its miracle comes to an end. Our travellers will remain asleep because a side ingredient in their medication was a five milligram, delayed action dosage of Lunesta, a potent sleeping supplement.'

He rose and walked to the end of the would-be carriage, unscrewing a small glass lampshade from the protruding metal tube. 'From this tube and three others like it, placed strategically, will be pumped a mixture, predominantly of nitrogen, but mixed with $CO_2$. For the uninitiated, it purges the confined space of oxygen, displacing it with an inert gas. The individual's organs and bodily functions shut down through lack of oxygen and death follows, painlessly and with dignity within a few minutes.'

Jack went to stand up, but Schmidt leaned across and pushed him back into his seat.

'Let me finish,' Kempeler grunted. 'Waiting in convoy at the marshalling yard are the local undertakers nominated by the traveller. Bodies are tastefully sealed in a funereal manner and transported to the relevant address for burial or cremation. All expense is borne by INCOL. The train returns to Charing Cross and the process is repeated three times over an eight-hour period.'

Jack was on his feet before Schmidt could react. 'You are out of your fucking minds!' His voice quavered. 'The idea is to murder enough people, so there's sufficient sauerkraut to go around. The idea is both pathetic and crazy and I'll have no part of it.' Saliva was bubbling around his lips. 'What's more, your crazy idea needs to be exposed. You are intending to exterminate people?'

Schmidt was alongside him. 'Sit down, Mr Tirrand, and listen.'

Kempeler shook his head. 'Nobody is murdering anybody, nor are we exterminating. These are callous terms based on hatred. We are involved in a programme of social euthanasia, thanking the elderly for their contribution, and protecting the young and vulnerable so that they have a life to fulfil. I expected you, of all people, with your background in care for the elderly to recognise the dichotomy.'

Shaking his head and saying, 'No. No. No,' Jack turned on Kempeler, his finger poking at the General's chest. 'Why England? Why London? Can't you run your updated gas chamber in Frankfurt or Dusseldorf? How many do you expect to kill before Eigard's questionable predictions can be fulfilled? Suppose he's wrong? There's no nuance in his conclusions.' His mind was racing. 'Just because one man says you're going to run out of food doesn't give you the right to execute a section of the population just because they're old.'

Kempeler brushed a hand across his chest as if to wipe away Jack's protests. 'I will answer your questions, Mr Tirrand if you calm down and start thinking rationally.' He motioned for Jack to sit back in his seat. 'The Senate agreed on London for the trial based on various criteria, amongst them, the bias toward homeownership when compared to other European cities where rental is prevalent. A large amount of property will be released in which relatively few have been living, yet which could house so many more.' He put his hand up. 'Ask your questions when I have finished, please, and do not interrupt.' He nodded at Schmidt.

'Once any problems have been resolved resulting from the trial, Octogen will be expanded all over Europe: Paris, Brussels – the German cities you mentioned. We estimate around five million fatalities will suffice in this first phase. As to the veracity of Eigard's proposals, he did not work in isolation. A team composed of individuals from many countries worked with him and a panel of experts spent a month testing his calculations and conclusions. We have no doubt the poorest and most vulnerable will starve unless action is taken. Would you want your grandchildren to suffer whilst their grandparents took the food from their mouths, so to speak?'

Jack continued to shake his head. 'You make your flawed ideology sound rational. As far as I recall, your forefathers also rationalised a similar ideology last century, which cost millions of innocent lives. You are just repeating the same horrific mistakes.'

Kempeler's thin lips quivered. 'How dare you? There is no comparison. The Nazi ideology was founded on fear, hatred and mass hysteria. We seek a compassionate and humane way of ensuring there is a young and vibrant population when the world recovers from the cloud under which we survive. You and your colleague are tasked with ensuring this objective is properly explained and understood.'

'I cannot be a part of this madness.' Jack wheeled around to glare at Usher. 'Haven't you got anything to say about this lunacy?' He studied her expression. 'You knew already, didn't you?' The wry smile was directed at Bayer. 'Your boyfriend told you, didn't he? What was it, pillow talk? A shared cigarette while you talk about exterminating five million and then roll over and do it again?'

Tears filled her eyes. 'You bastard,' she said. 'Don't cheapen me like that. Yes, I was told and, if you must know, my initial reaction was much the same as yours. Unlike you, I've spent several hours thinking it through. As distasteful as I find it, the argument is powerful and rational. Whether you should bother to give people a jolly before they die is no more than a sop to history, a desire to inject humanity and sensitivity into what is perceived as a callous act.'

'My God, they've brainwashed you already. That didn't take long. You're the reincarnation of Eva Braun, are you?'

'Don't be so fucking insulting, Jack. You're being ridiculous.' Her cheeks coloured, but she controlled her temper. 'I'll forget you said that. You're in shock and disturbed by what you've just heard. Lie down and give yourself a few hours of quiet reflection. Let's see if we can have a civilised dinner together. Max will join us. It's our last night.' There was a tinge of regret in her voice.

Jack took her advice. Lying on the bed, staring at the ceiling, a thousand thoughts careering endlessly through his mind, there was no way he could find the release into sleep his body needed.

He skipped dinner, preferring to leave the two lovebirds to escape the dreadful reality Usher and he faced when they returned to the UK. Whatever Bayer's conscience dictated, the compromise he hid behind was a role limited to the creation and production of hallucinogens. Once outside his laboratory door, the responsibility lay with others and, like so many conspirators in the past, he aligned with those three wise monkeys.

Disinterestedly, Jack lifted the top slice of bread off a sandwich to examine the contents. He was beyond trusting anybody in this place. It looked like ham and cheese. Perhaps it would even taste like ham and cheese, though he suspected the outcome would seem more like cardboard. He was replacing the top slice when there was a sharp rap on the door.

'Go away.'

Another sharp rap.

'Whatever it is, I don't want it.'

'I need to speak with you before you leave, Mr Tirrand. I assure you it is of the utmost importance.' Jack recognised Schmidt's husky voice, as if he needed to cough, but could not.

'I've got nothing to say you would want to hear.'

'But I've got something to say you *need* to hear.'

Reluctantly, Jack opened the door. Both Schmidt and Muller were standing there.

'Come to beat me into submission, have you?' He let the two men pass him and closed the door.

Muller motioned for Jack to sit. 'If we felt it would do the trick, we might be tempted. We are guessing in this case, it wouldn't.'

'You're right,' Jack said.

'We do not believe in unnecessary force,' Schmidt said. 'Not when words will serve.'

'I'll tell that to Samantha Kahn, shall I?'

'Who?' Schmidt queried.

'The Pakistani woman in London you let Roach intimidate.'

'A dinosaur with limited persuasive powers other than force. His talent is obsequiousness.'

Jack sat on the bed. 'Before you two ...what did I hear someone describe you as? Facilitators? Before you two facilitators tell me why you are here, satisfy my curiosity. How do you all come to speak English so well? It's beyond fluent.'

'Thank you for the compliment,' Muller said, and turning to his colleague, 'Maybe we won't hit him so hard as he's being so nice to us.'

Schmidt gave a maybe, maybe not shake of the head.

Muller continued. 'General Kempeler will only recruit to his private staff those who speak English well enough to detect the intention behind the words – what was the word used in the meeting? Nuances - the nuances of accent and tone which speak louder than words. The General learnt his English at Sandhurst during a five-year stint to gain officer status way before eleven/eleven. Both I and my colleague have spent several years on overseas exchange postings in English-speaking countries. The General considers it vital to understand the intention behind the words.'

'Satisfied?' Schmidt asked, a look telling Muller to be quiet. 'The General gained the impression you are not willing to proceed with the Octogen trial?'

'I'm past not willing. I'll do everything in my power to curtail it.'

'You realise you won't succeed? Too much has been invested, both in resources and personal reputations to shut it down.'

'I can only try.'

'And fail,' Schmidt said with a wry smile. 'Also, I suspect you will be arrested and accused of treason for planning to work against the coalition. You know the penalty for treason, I'm sure?'

Jack raised both his hands in apparent submission. 'I can't betray my conscience.'

'Try,' Schmidt said. 'It's not that hard. Let me present you with two scenarios and see how your conscience reacts. Your wife is about to be charged with the murder of a journalist. There is substantial circumstantial evidence to link her to the crime and, as you know, guilty verdicts can be reached by the judge where there are reasonable grounds to believe the defendant committed the crime. I just talked about personal reputations being at stake. Those at stake in the UK will guarantee your wife is found guilty and – he checked his watch – three weeks to the day, she will be executed by a single bullet to the back of her shaved head.'

'You wouldn't.' Jack sensed the bile in his throat and the burning in his nostrils. 'She would never harm a soul.' Closing his eyes to cope with a pain he knew so well, he saw in his hand an empty calliper, a rat perched on the end, looking at him. 'I would,' he mumbled. 'I did.'

'Say again.' Schmidt said.

'Nothing. Just thinking out loud.' The image passed.

'There's one more thing. Your daughter is expecting her third child. With both parents gone under such notorious circumstances, the people's court would be bound to take the view, not only should the newborn be taken from her for adoption, but both she and her husband be sterilised, and the twins placed into care for educational reassignment and subsequent fostering. Your other daughter is likely to be arrested for dissident behaviour and given a lengthy prison sentence.'

Jack allowed himself to tip sideways, his head and shoulders coming to rest on the bed. 'You'd do it as well, wouldn't you?'

'As I said, reputations are at stake. People have too much to lose.'

Jack fell quiet, eyes closed, and head bowed.

Schmidt sat down on the bed next to him. 'Let me paint your conscience another picture. You fulfil your obligations to Octogen and see the

London phase through to completion. From then on, somebody else takes over.'

'And what?'

'No charges are preferred against Rebecca. In ten days, when the trial is due to begin, she is released without charge and pronounced of no interest to the investigation, subject to her status as a witness. Concurrently, the newspaper which accused you of sexual impropriety prints a full retraction and offers to make X number of credits available to the charity of your choosing. Your pregnant daughter has her third child, which is nominally adopted by her sister and moves to her new home in wherever it is. I forget.'

'And Alison?'

'That's her twin, is it?'

'Yes.'

'Of no interest to the authorities. How does that sound? I'm guessing your conscience will find it irresistible.'

Jack sat up and stared at Schmidt. 'Talking about nuances, I'm guessing the look behind that impassive face is saying, don't shoot the messenger.'

Schmidt managed a tired smile. 'As the old saying goes, if I told you, I'd have to kill you.'

# FORTY-FIVE

## EISENBAHNKREUZUNG – STRASSBURG – GERMANY

## 13.30 (12.30 GMT) - 24 November 2065

The *Schwarzwald Express* barely slowed to a halt at the platform before Jack was at the window waiting for the doors to open. The station was alive with people, some pushing past him to get off, others milling around on the platform waiting to board the train. He strained above the crowd to see. There was no sign of Alison.

Ten minutes came the announcement in German, then in French. The train would decouple, and the front eight coaches head north to Frankfurt, the rear eight, west to Paris. As much as he longed to be off German soil, he would disembark if she did not show. He was not leaving without her.

The doors closed and locked as the carriages separated with a jolt. Usher was standing just behind him. They had exchanged few words all morning. Jack ignored her attempt to make conversation, and she fell quiet, prepared to wait until after his daughter boarded.

As the Frankfurt Express pulled away, Jack stood on the platform, his heart pounding, hands clammy with sweat. The crowd dwindled to a few well-wishers waving off friends or relatives.

'Hello, Dad.'

He swung around and did a double take. Had it not been for the smile, he swore he would not have recognised her. She seemed even more slender than a few days ago; her face an unhealthy grey pallor, her normally vibrant eyes, lifeless. The most striking feature was her hair, now of crewcut length and dyed a hooker's shade of peroxide blonde.

'My rucksack was stolen,' she said in a monotone.

Out of the corner of his eye, Jack saw Usher standing waiting just inside the door. He hugged Alison, kissing her, tears streaming from his eyes. He struggled to compose himself and whisper to her. 'Say nothing in her presence. Do you understand? She is a traitor. Tell her the last two days you were ill and are glad to be going home. Mention nothing that has happened. Got it?' He felt her nod.

She was looking over his shoulder, her hand raised. 'Just saying goodbye to my saviour,' she said. 'Don't look round.'

Usher was curious, full of questions. To Jack's amazement, his daughter reacted well, answering positively, yet emphasising how the food poisoning laid her low and she was still dealing with the consequences. As for the haircut, it was an aberration, a lost bet over a card game in the hostel with some friends. She could do nothing now except wait for it to grow out.

'Excuse me,' Alison said, as Usher was about to speak. 'I need to use the loo and find somewhere to crash out for an hour. I'm still feeling weak.'

'She looks terrible,' Usher said when the two were alone.

He nodded.

'We need to talk,' she said. 'You can't go on acting like a petulant schoolboy. We have to work together. Max told me you have accepted your assignment.'

'Oh, Max did, did he? And what other little titbits of information did Max give you?'

'Don't talk to me as if I have a foot in both camps. Okay, not that's it anything to do with you, I spent a very enjoyable evening with Max. Maybe something will come of it, maybe not. It doesn't alter my thinking on Octogen, nor will it alter the fact they are suspicious as to our – principally, your – willingness to see the trial through. They will have people watching us every step of the way.'

Jack gave a wry smile. 'I never doubted it. We – principally, me – will become the public face of this crazy project and we – principally, me – will become the most hated twosome in Britain. Our faces may disappear from public view after the trial, but I will be remembered as the public executioner of five hundred innocent souls and the man who opened the gateway to selective mass extermination throughout Europe. That's exactly what they want. After what happened in the last century, no self-respecting German or UK senator or influencer can be linked to this particular killing field. You see that, don't you?'

Her eyes flickered as her tongue moistened cracked lips. 'Maybe it's time for a change. Perhaps I'll organise a transfer abroad, start a new life.'

His stuttered laugh was full of scepticism. 'Then I'll avoid giving you my reading of Professor Max Bayer and the chances of a happy forever after scenario.'

'Even if you did, I'd say it was too biased to be of any value.'

'Perhaps,' he said.

# FORTY-SIX

## SANDYS HALL – DEVON – ENGLAND

## 21.00 - 27 November 2065

Jack shivered involuntarily. It wasn't just the humidity in the near freezing temperature making his skin feel chilled, but the reason behind the array of maps of South America and shipping charts pinned to the wall in the undercroft of the chapel. He bunched his shoulders inside his overcoat and looked across the table at the two of them, their expressions a mixture of uncertainty and contrition.

'Would the real Robert Fitzwilliam stand up, please?' Jack said. 'Not quite the hapless preacher he would have us believe he is, but a scheming conspirator working against the Establishment. And in his shadow, as Robin was to Batman, my daughter Alison.'

'Robin? Batman?' Alison queried.

'A reference to a fictional superhero long before your time. He gets the analogy, don't you, Robert?'

'Look, old man—'

'Let's drop the "old man" persona, shall we?'

'Old habits and all that. The comparison is spot on if you accept we are working for the good of humanity. The people we help are being unfairly persecuted and are now in a place where they can use their skills for the benefit of mankind.' He leaned across the table. 'Surely, you can see that?'

Jack stamped up and down on the stone floor, his face expressionless. 'Alison's given me the background of what you've been up to and this character, Roy, or whatever his real name is. After what happened in Germany, she had no option but to tell me.'

Robert looked around at Alison and clasped his hands together as if about to pray. 'I want you to accept I had no idea what she planned and, had I known, I would have done everything in my power to stop her. She took an unacceptable risk by putting her life and that of our German collaborator on the line.' He put his arm around her shoulder. 'Having said that, the information she came up with was priceless and avoided us sending saboteurs over the water.'

'To sabotage what, exactly?'

'We will have a better idea when I talk with Roy, but I assume, to destroy the *AF* network at source.'

'*AF?*'

'We call the network after *Adeste Fidelis*, you know the Christmas carol, "O Come All Ye Faithful".'

'And you plan to join Roy as soon as possible?'

'I am convinced my cover is about to be blown. That bullet fired when you were last here was meant for me. I'm certain. But it's not just me now. Alison needs to come with me. She was held at the Institute. They have her photograph and will eventually identify her. That puts both of you at risk.'

'I don't remember my photograph being taken or being asked questions beyond my captors demanding a name,' Alison said. 'I know I said Sandra.'

Jack shook his head. 'You can't guarantee it. You were drugged to the eyeballs when I saw you and there were cameras around the place. I suspect you're on record somewhere.'

Alison nodded. 'I've only just about recovered. I can understand how people become addicted. Hans slapped me twice when I started shouting for something to ease the longing. He was afraid his landlady would hear.' She laughed. 'I hope he's okay. He's a genuine friend.'

'And your boyfriend?' Jack queried. 'How does he figure in all this?'

'My ex, you mean.' Alison folded her arms. 'He has gone missing from campus. No longer in his digs, and his so-called mother has no idea. He's disappeared off the face of the earth. Probably gone back to Germany now his real identity is known to us.'

'Let me get this straight,' Robert said. 'The man you saw in the home who wrote the report is the Eigard who, for the want of a better term, sought asylum and was referred to us? His son, Rolf, died in a skiing accident some years ago?'

'According to the talkative neighbour, yes,' Alison confirmed. 'The man I went to meet is Eigard's younger brother, and he has a son of Rolf's age, named Franz. I assume both father and son are ISE officials.'

Jack nodded. 'Franz certainly bears out my impression of a man with military training who knew exactly what he was doing during and after the shooting incident. He was no novice to the sound of gunfire.'

Robert shivered. 'Fancy a shot of something yourself?' Robert took a hip flask from his inside pocket. When the others declined, he took a large swig. 'So, they bundle old Eigard off to a home and the brother takes his place, whilst Franz takes Rolf's identity with the records doctored to show he's still alive. I expect the plan was for the impostor to turn up and demand his son be sent to TW with him. It still doesn't explain how Rolf ended up with Alison and so close to my operation down here. The authorities must be on to me.'

'Maybe not,' Jack said. 'My guess is Hill and his cronies set me up as the patsy for a project I'm scheduled to give a press conference about tomorrow.' He shook his head. 'Sorry, I'm not going into details. I'm betting the Germans put Rolf in play to get closer to me through Alison and form their own assessment of my suitability. Had he been investigating your operation, I doubt he would have left when he did. He would have concentrated on uncovering what you were up to.'

'Sounds reasonable,' Alison said.

Robert looked disappointed. 'If it's not me, you must be in danger after what happened in Germany?'

'Once they work it out, I imagine so. Until my current assignment is over, they need me and I'm safe. You will understand why tomorrow.' He shrugged. 'I guess trying to get all family members to a safe place is out of the question, so I'll have to stay and deal with the consequences once you've both gone.'

'If it means putting you in danger, I won't go, Dad. I got you into this mess.'

'I am distressed to say you have no option. Your meddling has thwarted an ISE operation, which constitutes treason and you know the penalty for that. If it means talking to you on some makeshift satellite system rather than not talk to you at all . . .' He left the sentence unfinished.

'What about Mum? How does she figure in this? And Harriet? Has my screw-up prejudiced the entire family?'

'Calm down.' Jack reached for her hand. 'I'll not give you platitudes. Life can never be the same for any of us: not so much for what you did, but for the situation I'm involved in. It will all come clear to you both tomorrow. As for Rebecca . . .' His voice tailed off. He would have to choose his words carefully.

Yesterday's reunion with his wife in one of the interview rooms at ISE in Fulham left him feeling the one under threat. Rebecca had a right to feel euphoric. She was told by her new lawyer there would be no charges brought against her. The praise for her attorney was boundless. Without him, she could only imagine what might have befallen her. The man was her saviour. Yes, it was inconvenient having to remain under lock and key for the next few days until the judge could formalise her release and, no, it didn't seem strange to have to do so. Henry told her it was quite normal procedure.

Jack had to suffer a barrage of Henry said this or Henry said that before she must have seen the hurt look in her husband's eyes and finally asked him how his trip had gone. But she paid no attention to the answer, interrupting to talk about her plans. Things needed to change in her life. What exactly? She would look for new horizons, meet different people, enjoy the company of friends in places new to her. This experience had taught her life was too short to make personal compromises.

There was no 'we' in any of her rapid fire monologue. The two things that stuck in his mind were the cursory peck on the cheek she gave him as they stood up to say goodbye and the fact she never once mentioned or asked how Alison was.

Jack gave both Alison and Robert a big smile. 'She's relieved the ordeal will be finally over by the end of the week and is looking forward to getting home. We all share that sentiment.'

Before Robert could reply, the sound of the satellite connection reverberated around the cavernous space. He pulled the microphone closer and went through the identification routine. Alison smiled at Lance's soft American drawl.

'I advised you my niece and her father would be present during this call.'

'You did.' Lance's voice sounded grave. 'You are putting a great deal at risk. You realise that?'

'I have every confidence in their integrity.'

'You have no option but to trust them given the headstrong girl's unauthorised actions which may still have serious, unintended consequences.'

Alison squeezed in front of her uncle. 'I am no headstrong girl, as you patronisingly call me—'

'Then don't act like one,' Lance said.

She waved her fist at the microphone. 'I was about to say, my involvement has saved you a great deal of time and effort, let alone embarrassment and possibly disaster.' She hesitated. 'I'm sorry if the unintended consequences concern our mutual friend.'

'I have lost the benefit of his services, I am sad to say. He is currently a fugitive.'

'But he *is* okay?' Alison said, desperation in her voice.

'As of last night, he was.'

'I'd die if anything happened to him.'

'I'd happily kill you if anything happened to him.' There was a hint of irony in Lance's voice. 'He is somebody who has learned the hard way how to look after himself.' His voice was stifled into a mumble as he covered the microphone to speak to somebody. 'Put Wet Feet back on, please.'

'What news?' Robert asked.

'As there is now no need to advance with your last assignment, arrangements have been made to transfer you as early as next week. I will give you coded details later.'

'The arrangements include my niece?'

'As agreed. I look forward to meeting her.'

Jack prompted Robert with a dig in the back, which he acknowledged with a nod. 'What was the outcome of the papers recovered from the real – for want of a better word – Eigard, which she hid in the motorcycle pannier?'

'Yes. Intriguing. Our German friend translated them. There was a great deal of information. Boiled down, Eigard believed the report must be put on hold or, at least, the conclusions amended. Rumours were circulating of a breakthrough in the development of a highly effective fertiliser for GMC yields—'

'GMC?' Robert queried.

'Genetically modified crops. Eigard said he possessed a document suggesting yields per acre of certain basic crops could be more than doubled.

The problem has always been the lack of the basic components of fertilisers, phosphorous and potassium. Eigard contended that if the synthetic enhancement suggested could achieve the projected yields, both fertiliser availability and food supplies would nullify his preliminary report conclusions.'

'Good news?' Robert suggested.

'You would think so, but Eigard's revised report was dismissed out of hand in Berlin. He was told his original document would be released and the Octogen project, whatever that is, would continue. Eigard argued vociferously, but his pleas were ignored. It forced him to seek through Mila Kullenberg an escape route to a safe place where he believed his objections could be voiced. In the end, one of Kullenberg's messages to her parents was intercepted. She was coerced into confessing and collaborating with the authorities as a mouthpiece for Eigard, who was shipped into a home for the terminally ill. This is where your niece found him. I'm guessing a plot was hatched to get Eigard's brother and nephew shipped to TW to destroy our network.'

Jack moved close to the microphone. 'Suppose the rumours are false? Eigard's objections would be groundless.'

There was a moment's hesitation on the other end of the connection before Lance spoke. 'Coincidentally, I have independent confirmation the rumour is correct.'

Jack motioned for Robert to get up and took his seat. 'In which case,' he said. 'I need a private conversation with you. I'm going to ask my daughter and Robert to leave the room whilst we speak. I'll call them back when we've finished.'

Bemused, Robert put his arm around Alison's shoulder and escorted her to the door. 'Never mind,' he said. 'I've got another little something to keep us warm in the vestry.'

After checking no one was listening, Jack huddled close to the microphone, his voice a whisper. 'Robert tells me you are an expert in communications and computers?'

'That's a little like asking a champion surfboarder if he can swim.'

'Modesty, not your problem?'

'If you've got it, flout it.'

'I hope you are right. What I am about to tell you may need all your skills.'

# FORTY-SEVEN

## FREIBURG – BAVARIA – GERMANY

## 13.00 (12.00 GMT) - 1 December 2065

The Adler suite in the officers' club was reserved for General Kempeler and five guests. Lunch would now be served at fourteen-hundred hours in view of the delayed arrival of the two visitors from England. The heavy mist around the local airfield was finally lifting, but expected to return by night fall. There would be little time for socialising. Thank God, Kempeler thought. He could only tolerate smarmy English politicians for so long before his temper frayed.

He stood, heels clicking, as the guests arrived. 'Welcome, Senator Hill and Deputy Roach. A great pity your flight was delayed. I believe you have met my colleagues from ISE, Willi Schmidt and Tomas Muller. That just leaves me to introduce Professor Max Bayer, head of the Institute, which carries out all this amazing research.'

There were handshakes and pleasantries all round as they took their seats. Schmidt ordered the waiting staff to serve the Rossbach Chardonnay and doily covered plates of local hors d'oeuvres. *'Prost', 'Zum Wohl'* and 'Cheers' filled the air as glasses clinked and the group exchanged smiles.

'Right,' Kempeler said. 'Let's get down to business. We have an agenda. Tell us, Senator, what is the reaction in Britain to Tirrand's press conference? We are two days on, now. How has the public taken it?'

Hill combed the fingers of one hand through his hair and loosened his tie with the other. 'Thank you, General, for the invitation. I think the short answer to your question is "Surprising".'

Hill eased effortlessly into his public speaking mode, explaining how well Tirrand crafted his introduction, summarising Eigard's report and emphasising the need to protect the young and vulnerable from the real possibility of starvation and the likelihood of disease turning into pandemics which could threaten the health and wellbeing of every citizen.

A responsible authority could not allow its people to drift into this nightmare. Action must be taken now, and he called upon the population to shoulder its responsibility, protect its young, the future of our civilization and, for some, take a step into the unknown.

He then turned to the sacrifice he was asking the elderly to make. Those over eighty and those with terminal illnesses had lived the best of their lives, be it short or long, and now moved into what a preacher once described as God's waiting room. Some would be required to join in a programme entitled Octogen, endure a quick and painless passing, and a funeral with all costs borne by the authorities. But such a sacrifice would not be borne without its compensations. For those selected at random by computer, their last experience on this earth would be their most rewarding, living out the fantasy of their dreams or choosing to experience a precious moment from their past.

'Usher was then moved into the spotlight to recount her experience under the influence, which she did with unbridled enthusiasm.' Hill laughed as he turned to Bayer. 'She talked about the fantasy of shagging someone she had recently met. Not her words. I can only assume she was referring to you.' He gave a dry chuckle.

'Not a particularly high-grade fantasy and, shall I say, likely to be of limited appeal to the over-eighties.' Kempeler looked derisively at Bayer. 'Nevertheless, her dream came true, did it not, Professor?'

Bayer ignored the jibe. 'Do proceed, Mr Hill. I'm intrigued.'

Hill acknowledged the request with a flat smile, going on to explain how Tirrand eulogised those martyrs who would not be forgotten before turning to the practicalities of the operation. He highlighted the option for those who wished to volunteer for places in the trial; those who, of their own free will, see no future for themselves in this life and choose to dignify their passing, accompanied, if so desired, by their spouses.

Kempeler turned to Schmidt. 'Where are we up to on that?'

'We will only know about spouse requests when the invitations are issued tomorrow. As far as volunteers go, life must seem bleak in the UK. We could have filled every space with applicants and more keep coming.'

Hill reacted. 'I would point out you have people with terminal illnesses or in hospices who accept their lives are over and recognise the financial benefits for their families of a no-cost funeral and wake. Coupled with the last sweetener of double credits awarded to the beneficiaries for the appropriation of the properties owned by the deceased, it's a big incentive to put your name forward.'

'We'll select around a hundred,' Schmidt said. 'The rest can wait until we go live with the project.'

'Why not accept them all?' It was the first time Roach had spoken. 'You won't incite adverse public reaction if you are proposing voluntary euthanasia.'

There was a false expression of amazement on the General's face as he looked first at Roach and then at Hill. 'Deputy Roach, your question surprises me. I thought you understood. Your security services have identified over a thousand individuals, many of the old guard whose attitudes and opinions are motivated by memories of a different world, who are considered a threat or an undesirable influence, likely to support terrorist acts against the authorities. We will filter these individuals into the programme over the forthcoming weeks. For the trial, we have selected those individuals currently under selective surveillance.'

Roach looked at Hill for confirmation. 'Of course,' he said. 'I understand. I was confused by the reference to a random computer selection.'

The General gave a studied laugh. 'Don't be naïve, Deputy Roach. We have already identified all the trial candidates. There are more than a hundred names from this blacklist included.'

Roach's cheeks burned red as he sat back in his seat.

'Tirrand is behaving himself, I take it?'

'Yes, General,' Hill said. 'He knows his wife is to be released at the weekend and Roach here has sorted out his daughter's housing and third child dilemma. Tirrand will toe the line.'

'On no account is he to see the list of candidates for this weekend. There will be an adverse reaction from him if he does. See to that Schmidt.'

Schmidt acknowledged the order with a nod.

'Good. I'll come back to him and the woman later. Let's talk over lunch. I've been reading the report on the incident last week at the Institute.' He raised a glass as if to propose a toast. 'Heads will roll. I am certain of that.'

# FORTY-EIGHT

## MUSWELL HILL – LONDON – ENGLAND

## 14.00 - 1 December 2065

He woke with a start, irritable, unsettled. Whoever but the elderly dozed off halfway through the day? The trouble was he couldn't sleep at night for the dreams – sometimes dreams, sometimes nightmares. Vivid images of another time before eleven/eleven, *two young boys playing and laughing in the sun; a mother, Asian in appearance, verbally chastising them for being late, dirtying their clothes, not paying attention. She said she loved them and only rebuked them for their own good. They had to learn fast because they were different from other children. There were people who didn't understand their customs, their appearance, and who resented them living close by.*

*But Dad was like these people,* the elder of the two boys protested. *Doesn't that make us the same as they are? Your Dad isn't like them because he chose me as his wife. He is betraying his birthright – you don't understand? - his people. They despise and hate him for it. How could they? He was such a kind and peace-loving man who never argued and could always see their side of the story. Even so, he always did as she said. I like a quiet life, he would tell them.*

*On one occasion, after ten beatings with a slipper that left him fighting to still the tears and his father with an equally pained expression, he asked through the sobs why his father had married her. Because I loved her and knew she was the one for me. I still do and always will, his Dad said. Where were these people now?*

*Then there were the dark images: the pitch blackness and the whimpering of the voice from below: the crying of that little face as tears mixed with snot ran into his mouth: the shouting of the crowd as they bayed for blood: the man with the curly white hair who said he showed no remorse. What was remorse and how did you show it?*

Jack emerged from the daydream to the ringing tone of the phone. He was waiting for a call to speak to Robert, but, to his surprise, the voice was Rebecca's.

There were no introductory intimacies. 'I watched your press conference on Monday.' Her voice was flat, devoid of emotion. 'How could the Jack Tirrand I knew be involved in such a monstrous plot to bring about the death of innocent people? It's horrendous. I can't believe it. I can only assume you have abandoned whatever conscience you once possessed.'

'Rebecca, please watch what you say. It's unwise to speak your mind over the phone.'

'Don't concern yourself. You can say what you want. The Inspector has allowed me to use his official phone. For obvious reasons, it is not monitored. I don't understand how you could let yourself be used by them. I have been spat at in the washroom. One of the other women on remand tried to attack me. The name of Tirrand is reviled.'

'You must understand, I have no choice. The circumstances gave me no option.' He struggled to find the right words.

'What circumstances?' Two words, but somehow spoken with both incredulity and contempt. 'What did they promise you? Henry told me the paper is to print a retraction for that stupid article they published. Is that the pound of flesh you demanded for the lives of my parents?'

'I have no control over this operation, nor any idea who has been selected. They will not let me see the list. I will do everything in my power to ensure our family members are not included.'

'My family members,' she corrected. 'The Fitzwilliams. Jack Tirrand no longer has a place in my family or anywhere amongst my circle of friends. You have turned yourself into a pariah, an executioner who justifies his actions with mealy-mouthed excuses. Thank God for Henry Randall. He rescued me from death's door and I worship the ground he walks on. It's a world away from following in your bloody footsteps.'

Jack looked up to see Alison standing just inside the door. No warning to advise she was on her way up. The concierge must have also blackballed him. 'The only defence I can offer and ask you to believe is that, for the sake of us all, I have no way out, as much as it troubles my conscience.'

'What conscience?' Her voice rose in pitch but changed to a hollow, sombre tone. 'Listen. I don't want you to visit or try to contact me. On Saturday, when I'm released, I'm setting off for Devon to stay with and protect my parents along with Robert. I have asked Henry to start divorce proceedings and to change my name immediately by deed poll to Fitzwilliam. The girls will make their own decisions, but I doubt they will want to have anything to do with the name Tirrand in the future. This is goodbye, as far as I am concerned.' The line went dead.

Jack held out his arms. 'Have you come to disown me as well?'

Alison cocked her head and gave him a questioning stare. 'That was Mum on the phone?'

He nodded.

'Giving you the "Dear John"?'

'Am I supposed to know what that is?'

'The brush off. You're the big baddy who is supposed to have some control over these morons?'

'More or less.'

'She phoned me earlier. I tried to argue your corner, but she's been embarrassed by association and feels she needs to protect herself from the fallout. It came as quite a shock to all of us.'

'Where does love and cherish come in all this? I thought we loved each other.'

Alison moved forward and put her arms around him, resting her head on his shoulder. 'You old romantic. I love Mum too, but I'm not blind to the fact she is only interested in number One. She figures having brought us twins into the world, nurtured and cared for us until adulthood, she now deserves some "me" time. Not unreasonable as "me, me" comes naturally to the Fitzwilliam side of the family.' Feeling his shoulders trembling, she nestled even tighter into him. 'Can I tell you a secret or two?' She sensed his nod. 'Mum was a Fitzwilliam until it was better to be a Tirrand and going places. Now, it's the kiss of death being a Tirrand, so it's back to being a Fitzwilliam. But I think she sees the move as transient.'

'What do you mean?' he said, gently pushing away to study her face with his tear-flushed eyes.

'My reading is she has the hots for this lawyer who's on her case. By trading in the old, dependable model for a later, shinier version, she believes she will cast off all the problems associated with the past and find a brighter, livelier future with a new beau.'

'I don't appreciate the analogy,' he said. 'You make your mother sound callous.'

'After what happened to her, she sees life as finite and doesn't want to waste a moment compromising. You might see that as not caring about others. She would say it's living life to the full.'

'With no deep emotional attachments?'

'You can answer your own question. You know her better than I do.'

Jack stroked the stubble of blonde hair and let her head come back onto his shoulder. 'And what about you? You seem nonplussed about losing your boyfriend, uprooting your life, losing all your friends, and not seeing your family again.'

Her shoulders sagged. 'It's just bravado. I'm shit-scared about what's happening to me. I wake up and feel I'm living some sort of horrific fantasy which quickly becomes my reality.'

'Robert has a great deal to answer for in all this. Thinking just about himself, he tries to steamroller you into the hot seat. His attitude was deplorable.'

'I get it you've got a thing against the Fitzwilliams, but he's only partially to blame. He didn't ask me to do anything. Stupidly, I thought I was taking a pleasant excursion to Germany for a casual chat with an old man on the pretext of being his son's girlfriend. I'd find out all about him, come back and show Robert and friend, Roy, just how useful I could be. Naïve. I didn't contemplate what could go so wrong and how others would be implicated and risk their lives. I know I must go with Robert, but I fear what the future holds. I'm so sorry I fucked up.'

Jack could feel the damp patch on his shoulder. Trying to make her feel better about herself would only bring on more tears. 'I'm not going to give you platitudes and say it was alright, because we both know it wasn't. What we must accept is the past cannot be changed and you must move forward with the same sense of commitment and energy you've always shown. Only the next time, your decisions will be tempered by the knowledge of what went before and who you are.'

She pulled away from him and went to sit, motioning for him to join her. She smiled through cracked lips and puffy eyes, her cheeks glowing red. 'That's the trouble,' she said. 'Right now, I'm not sure of anything. I had a boyfriend whom I thought felt something for me, only to discover the only reason he was with me was to get near to my father and report back to his masters.' She shook her head. 'I took stupid actions which have created serious repercussions for you and my friend, Hans. On top of all that, I turned away my sister's plea for help when it was the least I could do for her.'

'Have you spoken to Harriet? I've tried to reach her, but she hasn't called me back.'

'I wouldn't read anything into it. She's ecstatic, rushing around, getting prepared to move to Devon. Your colleague, Roach, has taken her under his wing and sorted out the problem. He also gave her the green light for an inter-family adoption, which I agreed to.'

'But you won't be here?'

'Right. I told her to organise the paperwork this week and get Roach to sign it as her sponsor. I gave her a story about having to be absent from London and her needing to strike while the iron's hot. I said you'd told me Roach could run hot and cold and she should catch him while he was in a good mood.'

'Pretty much the truth, I'd say. How did she take my press conference?'

'She is so wrapped up in her own little world, it was hardly mentioned. She said the idea was potty and would never work because the people would never let it happen.' Alison reached for her father's hand. 'Do you know what her reaction was when I said the name of Tirrand would be tarnished by your involvement?'

He shook his head.

'She didn't care. As far as the rest of the world is concerned, her surname is MacDonald, and she would never have to admit her parentage.' Alison's brow creased. 'You don't seem put out by her attitude?'

'I'll tell you something in confidence—'

The telephone ringing and the tap on the front door came almost simultaneously. 'Keep whoever it is at the door waiting until I've finished this call,' he said, as he moved across the lounge toward the kitchen.

'Jack, what can I do for you?' Robert's voice boomed across the line as if he were in the next room. 'I'm just finishing lunch with my parents. I won't say who is calling. I take it you're not phoning to talk about your spine-chilling revelations?'

'No. I need a favour. You remember I was talking to that friend of yours about a print job? I wondered, if you're in contact, tell him I need his personal input to strike the right balance. Let him know he can have my input early tomorrow. Could you do that for me, please, Robert?'

'Will he know what you mean?'

'Yes. I need to preserve my public profile.'

'You certainly need to do that,' Robert said as he ended the call.

'It's Christopher,' Alison called from the door, the surprise in her voice apparent.

'Christopher?' Jack's voice grew nearer. 'Do I know a Christopher?'

'Chris Hill,' Alison said, embarrassment now having overtaken the surprise. 'Simeon Hill's son.'

'Of course. Tell him to come in and take a seat. I'll put on the kettle.'

Christopher was sitting perched on the arm of the sofa when Jack returned with three steaming mugs of tea on a tray. Alison was making the small talk, with the young man hanging on her every word.

'What can I do for you?' Jack asked.

'I didn't realise,' he stammered. 'That Alison would be here. Like your new hairstyle.'

'You must be joking.' She beamed a smile. 'I can't wait for it to grow out.'

'It suits you, though.'

'Do you mind if we get to the point, Chris? I must leave soon.'

'Sorry. Sorry. I wanted to ask you whether you have any say over who can go into the trial this weekend?'

'Why do you ask?'

Chris looked from one to the other. 'If you do, I wanted to put my grandmother's name forward.'

'Do what?' Jack looked at the young man in amazement. 'Putting people's names forward just because you want to be rid of them is not an option.'

Christopher bristled, his sagging shoulders now upright. 'Good Lord. No! How could you think that?'

'When I last saw you, the sentiment I picked up was your frustration with her.'

'You've got it all wrong. I was angry with that cow my father is married to. She's the one who would be glad to see the back of my grandmother. And of me too.' He hesitated. 'No, I love and adore nanna. She's the only reason I hang around at home. Sure, I get frustrated sometimes with being put on to look after her. That's also down to my father as well as the bitch. It's not at all what you imagine at home. You could cut the atmosphere with a knife.'

'What are you trying to say?' Alison asked.

'Nanna saw your broadcast, Mr Tirrand, and asked . . . begged me to speak with Dad about putting her name on the volunteer's list. He refused point blank. She's in a terrible state, both mentally and physically, and just wants out of it. He got angry when I pressed him, more so when Francesca joined in for her selfish motives. He said the list was designed to include those who didn't deserve to draw breath and we would be well rid of. He would not let anybody connected with him be included.'

'He said that?' Jack pressed.

'Scouts honour. So, I thought if it's not a random selection, as you said on the broadcast, and you're choosing people to be put to death, my grandmother deserves to have her wishes considered.'

Jack stood up. 'Thanks for coming, Chris and sorry to chase you out, but I need to be somewhere. Ask your grandmother to call me when she's on her own and we'll have a chat. I promise you that, at least.'

'Thank you.'

'I need to go to the Assembly library and consult the Citizen's Register.' He looked at Alison. 'Coming with me?'

'There's a dozen press guys waiting downstairs,' Chris said. 'And a handful of protestors.'

'I've got a pool car. We'll use the garage exit.'

'Just one more thing,' Chris said, holding the handshake with Alison for too long. 'The rumour at Uni is you've broken up with Rolf.'

Alison nodded. 'Why?'

'Only, on my way into this apartment, I saw him in the coffee shop downstairs. He recognised me and got up and left. If looks could kill, I'm a dead man.'

# FORTY-NINE

## FREIBURG – BAVARIA – GERMANY

## 15.00 (14.00 GMT) - 1 December 2065

The General broke off his conversation to study the embossed menu card. 'Tell the chef I enjoyed the *Rouladen,* even if the red wine sauce was a little too heavy to bring out the taste of the beef.' He looked the waitress up and down. 'I'll take the roast pear with goat's cheese for dessert. Bring a bottle of Marsala and fresh glasses.' He looked across the table at Simeon Hill. 'Not to your liking, Senator?'

Hill motioned for the girl to take away his half-eaten main course. 'Everything was fine,' he lied. 'I feel as though I left my stomach on the plane.'

The General smiled passively. 'You were going to finish your report on the public reaction to the press conference. It appears putting extra manpower on the streets proved unnecessary.'

'I said surprising, and I mean in every sense. I think the initial reaction was shock, perhaps disbelief. There was little immediate reaction, no crowds thronging the streets, protesting. It took a while for the reality to sink in before we saw the usual suspects appear; a sprinkling of human rights activists, age concern and the right to life contingent, but nothing on any grand scale. We believe protest will intensify as we approach Sunday and there are live images of the candidates on their final journey. Some disruption is inevitable.'

'Make sure there's plenty of TV coverage of Tirrand and the woman.'

'Roach has that aspect in hand.' Hill nodded toward his colleague. 'We've been helped by a couple of factors. The supermarket shelves have looked bare in places and what is available is taking up more and more credits as prices rise. There are also editorials in the two main news sheets not exactly backing Octogen but providing an understanding of the logic behind the project. For the elderly who have enjoyed a full and active life, plus up to fifteen years of a meaningful retirement, the future paints a picture of illness, reduced mobility, and cognitive degeneration. Sacrificing these hardships to ensure the younger generations thrive and prosper is a worthwhile trade-off.

That's the thrust of these articles. I believe a significant proportion of the population is, at best, supportive of, or, at worst, neutral to the argument.'

'Nevertheless, you will have a large deployment of armed security on standby over the weekend?'

'Of course. I emphasise the positives, but there are negative forces making their objections known. Professors from a group of prestigious universities have questioned Eigard's conclusions and presented cogent scientific back up to support their findings. The Peace Foundation, which helped establish INCOL as a global phenomenon has come out and said aging cleansing is no different in its ideology than the ethnic cleansing practiced by the Germans one hundred and twenty years ago because it discriminates against a particular section of society.'

'We must proceed, expecting the worst.' The General wiped away the port wine droplets on his chin with a fresh serviette.

Bayer, who had said little throughout the lunch, attracted the General's attention by rising from his seat and pointing at the watch on his wrist.

'I am well aware of the time, Professor, and our guest's departure schedule,' the General said. 'Since you press, let us turn to the troubles at the Institute last week.'

He gave Simeon a run down on the events before and during the fire, leading into the investigation which he instigated.

'At first, we thought the individual in the blue laboratory uniform could be Tirrand and the man who came in and took away the woman, the individual who visited Tirrand at the hotel the previous evening. From the images, Berlin gave us a twenty per cent probability on both, which is about as good as saying they are both male.'

'You ruled out Tirrand?'

'From starting the fire, yes. There are no images of him leaving the hospital ward and making his way downstairs prior to the alarm sounding. In fact, the intruder is seen approaching from the basement and moving up to the first floor. With the melee that followed, smoke everywhere, sprinklers in action and camera malfunction, it's not possible to say at what point Tirrand left the ward and made his way downstairs, but he next appears standing outside in his hospital gown where he stayed until the fire was brought under control.'

'So, he's in the clear?'

There was a throat clearing cough from Schmidt. 'Not to our satisfaction,' he said. 'Tirrand claimed his visitor guessed his location from a misstatement by the telephone operator. I've listened to the tape and no such disclosure was made. The only viable explanation is, having arrived here, Tirrand managed to tell somebody.'

'Or he was followed,' Roach suggested.

'Feasible, but unlikely. Our driver is trained to know if he is being tailed.'

'What about the man who visited Tirrand?' Kempeler asked, 'Can we identify him even if we can't place him as the phoney nurse who took the woman?'

'The image of him arriving at the front gate gives a near forty percent view of his face, even though he tried to shield it. They are working on it in Berlin, but it's a lengthy process.'

'Tell them it's urgent,' Kempeler demanded.

'Everybody tells them that,' Schmidt said, careful to sound diplomatic. 'I used your name to apply pressure, but they are a law unto themselves.'

'What about the woman? Any developments?'

Muller straightened in his chair. 'At first, we guessed she had been taken by the DCs as a hostage to bargain with for the release of their guys we rounded up the day before. That's not the case.' Muller paused for effect. 'Whoever this woman is, she was taken from the hospice. She claimed to be Eigard's niece from Belgium. He sounded the alarm when she tried to speak with him. She also fits the description of the woman who was in Rottenburg trying to talk with Martin Eigard, the younger brother. He was dealing with someone else as she approached and only glimpsed her briefly before she disappeared.'

Simeon Hill stifled a yawn and stretched his legs under the table. 'Is this relevant to our meeting? I'm sure it's important, but can we get to the crux of why I'm here?'

'Please be patient, Senator,' Kempeler said. 'The background information is important. Just a little longer. Go on, Muller. Keep it brief.'

Muller reacted to the instruction by talking in staccato sentences, explaining why they failed to identify the woman whilst under their control and to establish for whom or what organisation she was working.

'To put the ball in your court, Senator,' Muller said. 'We considered the coincidence of this woman appearing at the same time as Tirrand's daughter was holidaying in Stuttgart. However, the description of the woman suggests she was older than Tirrand's daughter with fluent German as spoken by somebody from a neighbouring country. I was also told by our operative in the UK who has been in place as the daughter's boyfriend for some months—'

'To do what exactly?' Simeon asked. 'And why wasn't I informed?'

Kempeler held up his hand to stop Muller from replying. 'When Tirrand's name came up several months ago as a potential candidate to front the Octogen trial, we sent our man to find out as much as possible, get close to Tirrand and his family and give us his assessment. We did so by enrolling him at the same university as the man's daughter, where he formed a relationship with her. He is convinced she could not be the woman we are after, describing her as a left-wing activist who is a force within the university campus but as demonstrative as a puff of wind on the outside with no links to any dissident organisations. We didn't want to trouble you with all this detail.'

'That's patronising and masks the truth,' Hill said. 'Notwithstanding, what do you want us to do?'

'Nothing until Tirrand has completed his task. I suggest next Monday you interrogate his daughter and find out exactly what she was up to during the time she was here. Be firm with her. If our man is wrong and she was involved, we need to know who she is working for.'

'What about Tirrand? How does he figure in your plans?'

Bayer stood up, with one hand brushing biscuit crumbs from the lapel of his jacket whilst he held a slice of cheese between two fingers of the other hand. 'May I say something at this juncture?'

'Is it relevant?' Kempeler asked.

'Very.'

Kempeler nodded.

Bayer sat back down, discarding the cheese onto a plate. His attention was centred on Simeon Hill. 'I have given some thought to Tirrand's response to the trial drug we gave him. It caused him significant distress before he returned to full consciousness with no immediate recall. It can happen if the subject has a history of serious drug abuse which I discounted in this instance or, more specifically, if the person has received a course of drug-based treatment in the past to adjust the function of the hippocampus and the amygdala in the temporal lobe.'

'Can you repeat that in plain English?' Hill said.

Bayer studied a piece of cheese before picking it up and placing it into his mouth. 'In the days before eleven/eleven and occasionally since, our research was centred on aiding the recall or suppressing the episodic memory in the temporal lobe.' He pointed to the side of his head, just above the ear.

'Brainwashing?' Hill asked.

'Or stimulation, if recall was required.'

'Are you suggesting Tirrand had this treatment? I don't believe it.'

'I didn't, but in conversation about the incident with Ramona . . . Ramona Usher, she told me about a file which mysteriously disappeared and reappeared. It dealt with Tirrand's history as a juvenile. Most of the information leading up to his fifteenth birthday was redacted, but his parents dying in a car crash in Germany alerted me. It's a classic reset during the brainwashing process, which can last a week or more, to establish a starting point for the episodic memory. A fatal car crash is final and the one who survives, in inverted commas, has both a point of reference and an acceptance of the trauma as a reason for the memory loss of events before the accident.'

'It could equally be true there was a car accident.'

'I am a conscientious record keeper, Mr Hill. Seven days after the supposed date of the car crash, we performed a memory wipe using a scopolamine derivative and lysergic acid . . . LSD compound on a fifteen-year-old British juvenile, four years into a fifteen-year sentence for the culpable homicide of a younger boy who was handicapped.'

'You are saying this juvenile was Tirrand?'

Bayer nodded. 'You will remember the turmoil following INCOL's fragile beginnings. The prison population was reduced and sentences for young or non-violent offenders were commuted all over the globe.'

Roach caught his breath. 'If you are saying Tirrand was the lad you describe, God help him if it ever comes out. I remember the trial. I was a junior in the Home Office, as Homeland was called in those days. Public outrage was incensed. A brown man was accused of the murder of a white kid with a withered leg who lay in a well dying for days. They would have strung him up if they could have got their hands on him. The papers never named him. Legal reasons. When the judge read out the sentence, the victim's elder brother tried to make it to the dock and attack the boy. People in court cheered the attempt and attacked the van he . . . wait a minute. It was the van *they* were in. His younger brother was in the dock too on that day. Poor little sod didn't have a clue what was going on.'

Bayer nodded. 'I can believe it. The boy came here with his police guard, who stayed close to him the entire time. I was the only lab assistant then who spoke decent English, and I used to take the policeman out for the occasional meal when the boy was sleeping. He was conversational, but I found it difficult to understand his strange accent. What I learned was horrific. Following eleven/eleven and while he was still in juvenile detention, the boy's mother was repatriated to her native land, somewhere in Indonesia. His father was hounded remorselessly by the press and ended up falling or being pushed under a metro train. The younger brother suffered physical abuse and, at the age of eleven, hung himself in his cell. The elder boy had several tragedies to overcome and forget. It took many sessions.

'The hallucinogen we recently administered to Tirrand acts as – for want of a better word – an antidote to stimulate the hippocampus. He is bound to have flashbacks, HPPD, as we call it. Eventually, either with partial or total recall, these events will return to haunt him.'

'Do you have a photo of the boy?' Hill asked.

Bayer drew a faded black and white Polaroid print from a file.

'That's Tirrand,' Hill said. 'What was his real name?'

'Turn it over.'

'Aashif Firman,' Hill said, repeating the name to himself.

Kempeler tapped a spoon against his empty dessert plate. 'Fascinating, I am sure, but his real identity has no bearing on the future. Once the Octogen trial is over, we have no further use for Tirrand. Correct?'

Nobody disagreed or assented. Blank faces stared back at him.

'I will take that as an endorsement. I find Tirrand an unwilling and troublesome individual. Whatever part he played in last week's happenings at the Institute, he is best out of the picture. Our man has him under surveillance. He will be instructed to terminate him next week, at a suitable opportunity. If he can't make it look like an accident, we will need to lay the blame on an extremist protester bent on revenge. I will leave it to Schmidt to organise it. He has experience in these matters.'

He stood to shake hands as his visitors filed out of the room. 'Let's make Octogen a great success and rid ourselves of some of the worst elements in society.'

Schmidt stood aside to let them pass but blocked Bayer's attempt to follow them.

'We have some unfinished business to attend to, Professor,' Kempeler said. 'Do take . . .' He finished the sentence in German.

Hill and Roach exchanged a questioning look as the door closed behind them.

# FIFTY

## SANDYS HALL – DEVON – ENGLAND

### 06.30 - 2 December 2065

Jack's shoes crunched into the frosted crust of the grass, the headlights of the pool car absorbed into the blanket of mist and barely reaching through the darkness to identify the door into the chapel.

'This is eerie,' Alison said. 'It's a scene set for the murderer to appear and commit his savage crime.'

'Shut up, will you? You're giving me the spooks. Come on. Robert will be in the undercroft.'

The fact the heater was on full blast made little difference to the chill, damp feel of the place. The stone walls were as cold to the touch as the inside of a freezer.

An old matrix printer was churning through a ream of continuous, perforated paper, the noise echoing around the chamber like machine gun fire.

'Just finishing,' Robert said. 'There was no time for me to decrypt all the information. Look at it. It would take a week. Roy sent it unprotected. It will show up if there is ever a data download from the satellite. It puts us at risk.'

Jack flicked through the printed pages, stopping now and again when a particular name or address caught his eye. 'Any coffee?' he asked. 'We've been driving most of the night. I'll need an hour or two to go through these.'

'Anything I can do?' Alison asked.

'Keep the coffee coming and sit down with Robert and his encryption book and start coding these pages.' He pulled three sheets of folded paper from his inside pocket.

She started to read. 'But these are—'

'Exactly,' he said. 'Now get on with it.'

Robert sat down next to Alison. 'Roy spoke with me earlier. We leave on Monday.' His Adam's apple oscillated in his throat as he saw her expression. 'There is a bulk carrier leaving from Plymouth with recycled plastic pellets. It will collect more en route in Florida and the northern Brazilian port of Recife. The next scheduled stop is Buenos Aires, where border controls are strict, so he is altering the route filed to include a brief stop in Montevideo. From there, we will transfer to a tramp steamer north to the port of Paranaguá, which is within TW territorial boundaries.'

She fought to gather her composure. 'Will the crew know we are on board?'

'The captain and first mate will. They will be well paid, and Roy says the captain needs a special favour. Exactly what that is, I don't know. Our movements will be restricted, but it's only two weeks.'

Jack looked up from the sheet, his gaze fixed on his daughter.

'Did you want something?' she asked.

He coughed and cleared his throat. 'No,' he mumbled, turning back to the printouts. 'Can you two get on with the encryption, please?'

Five coffees and two hours later, they finished.

'It's the middle of the night in TW,' Robert said. 'I never call at this hour.'

'He'll be expecting and waiting anxiously for this data.'

The call was acknowledged before the second ring. Robert went through the identity verification protocol. 'Somebody here to speak with you,' he said.

'Put them on.' Lance's voice crackled through the speaker, a sense of urgency detectable above the interference.

'Thank you for the list,' Jack said. 'It's what I thought. Do you still have control of the data?'

'I'm fortunate to have someone here with me who is an expert in blockchain technology. I could never have done it on my own. He's been at it solid for the last eight hours.'

Jack recognised the plaudits were not for his ears but for those of the person working alongside Lance.

'I'm grateful,' Jack said. 'It's an area I know nothing about.'

'Blockchain is like a ledger registering transactions or information available to the users with no trusted third-party intervention, like a bank, for example. It does this by defining protocols, so the computers know how to process and verify transactions.'

'You are already losing me,' Jack said.

'Okay. This is what my colleague does. To complete the verification and register a block in the chain, individuals known as "miners" use sophisticated computers to test and verify the information. If a hacker can gain control of over half the mining process, they can create a second version of the blockchain, known as a fork, and register an original set of data which appears authentic. That's what we are attempting.'

'Sounds like a means to syphon off some extra credits into your account with nobody noticing.'

Lance tut-tutted. 'We have a golden rule never to go near currency chains. They are complex and well-protected. Gaining a 51% mining control can be a lengthy, costly and energy-intensive process involving trillions of checks. Our colleague has developed a mirror programme which speeds up the mining procedure exponentially until the technical limits of the checking computer are reached. It gives results in minutes rather than hours and days.'

'Can we do what needs to be done? We have encrypted the information, and we are ready to send it.'

'Stream it to us. It's too late to worry about the data trail at this stage. It's down to luck they don't come across it and locate the source. Your associate has been told to dismantle and hide everything before he leaves.' Lance hesitated. 'Have you considered your position?'

'Asleep and awake, twenty-four/seven. I don't have any options. I'm safe until Sunday. After that, I guess I become expendable.'

'On Saturday, we will release the text of Eigard's retraction of his original conclusions to the press, along with a sworn affidavit from a guy called Ted Hubbard. You may have heard of him.'

'The Australian who fled from Chinese-controlled Australia?'

'You've got it. It will make the Sunday newssheets. The disclosures will blow the Octogen project wide open.'

'What about censorship? It will never pass.'

There was a laugh, echoed by a second person. 'Give us credit. The download will arrive censor approved. We know what we are doing.'

Jack fell silent.

'Are you still there?' Lance queried.

'Yes.'

'You know what all this means for you?'

'That's what I was contemplating.'

'They will know you were behind this. You'll be arrested and interrogated. You will talk. Guaranteed. They have ways and means. You will implicate everybody involved, us, your daughter, our colleague there. When you've told them everything, they will kill you and look to arrest your family members. You will have told your captors where they are, and they will never complete their journey. You have no choice.'

'Come with them?'

'Either that or a far more unpalatable but less painful conclusion.'

'I understand.'

'We could use your talents, I am sure. We know all about you.'

'No, you don't. Every day, I learn a little more about my past and who I really am. There are plenty of blanks still, but memories are returning.'

'I look forward to discussing the subject with you.' Lance broke off to speak to somebody else. 'Listen,' he said. 'I've just been told the invitations, in inverted commas, to Sunday's death ride have been issued and will be delivered later today to the candidates, as they are called. According to the chatter, you are expected to be making the announcement at a press conference this afternoon. They can't locate you. Your phone must be out of range of a signal. I suggest you get moving.'

'Just one more thing,' Jack said.

In a small copse beyond the chapel, a gloved hand focussed a pair of binoculars on Jack and Alison as they made their way to the car. The red light glowed on a hand-held recorder as a voice noted the time and place. Adjusting the belt of a black raincoat, the observer stood and replaced the recorder in a side pocket, the plastic casing resting against the butt of an old Walther 99 revolver.

From a hollow in the ground which once served as a fairway bunker on a golf course, a slender, muscular man in his late fifties focussed the sight of an M16 automatic assault rifle on the man dressed in a black raincoat as he appeared from a small group of trees. He lined up the crosshairs as the subject walked to a compact car and opened the door. Refocussing the sight, he zoomed in as the man removed a peaked cap and took the driver's seat. Nestling the M16 into his shoulder, the man lying in the hollow pulled an imaginary trigger and mouthed a phut as he pictured the bullet obliterating the side of the young man's head.

He dismantled his rifle as he watched the compact drive away. It was the second time he had visited this location. On the previous occasion, he fired a real bullet just as a young girl screamed.

# FIFTY-ONE

## CHARING CROSS STATION – LONDON – ENGLAND

### 16.00 - 2 December 2065

'Thank God, you're back.' There were beads of sweat above Ramona Usher's top lip. 'I was beginning to think you were leaving me to handle this press conference. Frankly, the crowd gathering outside unnerved me. Since the summons—'

'Don't you mean the invitations?' Jack said with a sarcastic smile.

'Call them what you like. The reality seems to have sunk in and we are experiencing a level of public dissent I haven't witnessed since the enforced repatriation legislation many years ago.'

Jack looked through the window of their makeshift office in a disused pub on the upper level of Charing Cross station, down to the dimly lit main concourse. It was deserted except for the workers completing the final touches to the marquee, intended as a reception centre for the first intake on Saturday, just two days from now. The enclosed passageway led into the adjoining hotel where the five-hundred poor souls would spend their last night on earth.

The few trains scheduled to run into Charing Cross were cancelled until the following Monday. The dozen guests the hotel would have catered for were moved to alternative lodgings and extra part-time staff recruited to deal with one night of high occupancy.

'What are Kempeler's two enforcers up to?' Jack asked, looking around at the three operatives grouped into one corner, studying computer monitors.

'Muller went down to the hotel foyer to organise the press conference. Schmidt said he had to take part in a video call with all ISE stations involved. It must be to do with the arrangements for picking up and bringing the chosen ones here.'

'Where's the train?'

'Platform six. Heavy security. Nobody is allowed near it in case of sabotage. Schmidt says he is determined the event, as he calls it, will go off without a single hitch.'

'Tell that to the crowd outside.' The background noise of chanting and the occasional shouted demand filtered through the concourse, the intensity steadily increasing. Jack looked Usher up and down and raised his eyebrows. 'You've got your coat on. You planning to go somewhere and leave me to face the anger of the press corps?'

'I've got a ready-made excuse; that's if I can get past the protestors. ISE has arrested the manager at Nine Elms, whom I suspect of illegally renting out files. They have charged him with the murder of his flatmate, the journalist, Morgan. Lets your wife off the hook,' she said, with a nod of the head. 'The Inspector will give me fifteen minutes with him before they start their interrogation.'

'I was told Rebecca would not be facing any charges.' He watched her tighten the belt of her coat. 'I'd say, if I didn't know you better, that you were trying to avoid being seen with me in public. In fact, the way it's panning out, half the people do not want to be seen dead with me and the other half want to see me dead.'

It merited a smile from Usher. 'An exaggeration, I hope.' She walked toward him and touched his hand. 'The way I see it, Jack, is they wanted a respected Brit to front their killing game, and you were their choice. My role was to select a bunch of nasty characters serving life sentences to join the death ride and play the obligatory female support role. I've played my part, and I don't see the logic in the two of us shouldering the burden when it can be borne by one. Selfish maybe, but not without logic. I'm hoping I've found a future I didn't have before and didn't think I'd ever have.'

'With Bayer?'

'It's early days, but the signs are positive.'

Jack watched as Muller strode across the concourse in their direction. 'I hope it works out for you. You'd better—'

'I was waiting for the "but".'

'Alright, but I don't trust any of them. Now, get your butt out of here before Muller comes up those stairs. Use the side exit. When I came in, there were no protestors about.'

'Good luck with the press,' she said, picking up her handbag and walking to the service door.

Usher's scent still hung in the air as Muller pushed the door open. 'Where the hell have you been?'

'In case you didn't notice, my wife is still locked up. Her parents needed support and guidance. I went down to see them.'

'Twice?'

'Not intentionally. The second time was specifically at my wife's request following the initial announcement. They were alarmed.'

'I understand you have a brother-in-law living with them. Couldn't he do it?'

'I don't know why I'm explaining my movements to you, but, if you must know, the man is a bumbling idiot, a cleric who sticks to praying and confessionals. If you had let my wife go, it's something she could have done. Satisfied?'

'Things are moving fast now. You need to be around.'

'We've got a press conference. Yes?'

'Where's Usher?'

'With ISE in Fulham. She was summoned. I'll handle the press.'

'*Himmel Hergott nochmal.* What is it with you two?'

Jack closed the bedroom door and checked the minibar. Schmidt told him it was too dangerous for him to leave the hotel. The number of protestors had swollen to several thousand, and ISE officers were too busy dealing with crowd control to provide a personal bodyguard service. Jack's daughter had been contacted and would bring him toiletries and a change of clothes. He would remain on site until the trial was underway. On Monday, he was to give a final public statement and answer questions.

Expecting to find the minibar empty, Jack opened the door. It was full: spirits, beers, soft drinks, savoury snacks and a printed card which read, *'This complimentary minibar has been stocked for your enjoyment, courtesy of Deputy Jack Tirrand.'*

Jack Tirrand and Octogen were becoming synonymous. His name would always be the one associated with the next holocaust.

Closing his eyes did not relieve the shooting pain in his nose and throat, the acid which seared the soft tissue and left him gasping for breath.

The card swam before his eyes '. . . *courtesy of Aashif Firman, unrepentant murderer of little Stanley Ford.*'

'*. . . showed no remorse. How do you show remorse? It was just a tragic accident. Of course, he was sorry.*'

For how long the telephone rang, he did not register. The mineral water was chilled. It dulled the taste of panic, the urge to run, to free himself from all these nightmares.

'Hello.'

'You bastard! My parents! How could you? You're nothing but a cold bloodied murderer.'

He was about to say, 'I am,' but the words froze on his tongue. 'Rebecca?'

'Of course, it's me. How could you include my mother and father in this act of mass murder?'

'I didn't know,' was all he could say.

'What do you mean you didn't know?' Her voice reflected both anger and despair. The words stuttered as she sobbed. 'Your name is the one on the fucking invitation the courier delivered! How you've got the nerve to deny it, I can't imagine.'

The fog in Jack's head dissipated. He had no idea on what line she was calling, whether the conversation was being monitored. He suspected it was. There was no way he could say he was trying to do something about it.

'I don't have the names of the people selected. I did not know your parents were on it. You must understand these things are all beyond my control. The people responsible for Octogen are the ones who decide on the names. I will only get the details in the morning.'

'Well, you had better become responsible and get my parents off your extermination list or I swear I will kill you with my bare hands. You know something, Jack Tirrand? You're a worthless piece of shit. How I could have let you talk me into marrying you, I don't know. Now, stand up and be counted and save my parents from this lunacy.'

The line went dead.

He was on his second vodka miniature when someone knocked on the door.

'Hi, Dad,' Alison said, pressing a piece of paper into his hand as he let her in.

He read the note. She suspected the room was bugged, possibly with concealed cameras. 'I reached the same conclusion,' he whispered in her ear as they hugged.

'I brought you a change of clothes and a book to read. It's short stories,' she said. 'There's one about football you will like.'

'Thank.' He nodded his understanding. He hated football.

'The porter will bring the case up. It was going through security. Did mum call you?'

'Yes. She's beside herself with worry. I said I'd do everything in my power to get your grandparents removed from the list.'

'Do you think you can do it?'

'I don't know how they got on there. It's supposed to be restricted to London and the suburbs. Apparently, there is another agenda in play. I'll have the list in the morning. I'll speak with Schmidt. They owe me that much for fronting this business.'

They talked on for another twenty minutes: the protestors, family issues and the latest news. Nothing contentious and nothing to suggest they suspected the room was bugged.

As Alison went to leave, she blew him a kiss from the door. 'Try to get some sleep tonight,' she said. 'I always find I start reading something and I've fallen asleep before I've finished the first page.'

'I'll take your advice,' he said.

The thin strip of paper was tucked into the binding on the second page of the story about World Cup heroes. It was a way out for him. Six pm, Sunday afternoon. He would do everything in his power to be there.

# FIFTY-TWO

## SANDYS HALL – DEVON - ENGLAND

### 07.00 - 3 December 2065

The rain was fine, chilled droplets spiking his skin and running down his cheeks as if he were crying. It was almost invigorating, he thought, as he made his way using the cover of the trees to reach the pathway leading to the chapel.

The man Alison knew as Rolf, real name Franz Eigard, decided the deviation from his orders to maintain surveillance on Jack Tirrand was warranted and could be justified if he was ever held to task.

He watched the previous evening as Alison struggled with a suitcase through a throng of protestors to the entrance to the hotel above Charing Cross station. The ISE security cordon let her through with what must be clothes and personal items for her father. Twenty minutes later, she emerged with that stern look on her face, one of those assertive expressions she adopted when under stress and disappeared into the crowd.

Franz regretted their relationship was about to end so abruptly. He so much wanted to approach her, explain how he felt and why he had to follow orders. He imagined a way back into her life, but when the surveillance changed to a kill order and the target was her father, that possibility was no longer.

Confident Tirrand would now remain ensconced in the hotel until after Sunday, Franz followed a hunch. On both occasions he had tailed Tirrand all the way from London to Sandys Hall, neither Alison nor her father visited the main house, as he would have expected. Instead, they went straight to the chapel to meet up with that pompous idiot of a clergyman who called everyone 'old man'. And do what exactly? He was about to find out.

The latch creaked as he pushed open the heavy wooden door. The early morning light percolated through the stained-glass windows, casting eerie shadows over the pews.

The interior was smaller than he envisaged, room for just thirty worshippers with a raised chancel at the front, dominated by a figure of the crucifixion. On either side of the pulpit and altar, thick velvet curtains in what looked like a deep purple colour were drawn across to keep from view whatever lay behind.

Franz lifted his head and strained to listen. There was the mumbling sound of two men talking. It was impossible to hear what was being said unless he moved nearer to the drawn curtain. As he did so, his knee caught on a pew, causing it to scrape on the stone floor and dislodge a pile of hymn books which cascaded onto the floor. The talking stopped.

Cursing under his breath, he moved nearer to the curtain. He stopped. The silence was overpowering. His rasped breathing sounded so loud.

In a single movement, the curtain on the other side of the chancel was drawn back. 'Can I help? . . My goodness, it's Rolf, isn't it? What are you doing here, old man? At this time of the morning?'

Franz straightened his back, taking a moment to regain his composure. 'I could ask the same of you,' he said.

Robert moved forward and extended his hand. 'If you did, that would be impertinent, would it not? This is my place of work and worship. In the heyday of this estate, two dozen workers would file in here every day at six for morning mass before commencing their allotted tasks. Now we are down to just one soul who shuns my pastoral attentions and wishes only to talk of his duties. Perhaps you will be good enough to tell me why you are here?'

'I was hoping to find Alison?'

'What made you think she was here?'

The conversation was not panning out the way Franz imagined it would. His cover was being challenged, and he had to assert himself. 'I was in the area and thought I'd check to see if she was around.'

Robert chuckled in genuine amusement. 'You'll have to do better than that, Rolf, old man. This is Devon, next stop Cornwall and the Atlantic Ocean. Nobody is just in this area by accident. Beit work or holiday, people come to Devon for a reason, especially a university student based in Manchester, if that is who you are.'

Franz felt the comforting touch of his hand on the butt of the Walther 99. 'You've got me all wrong,' he protested. 'Alison and I have sort of broken up, and I'm desperate to locate her. I've tried her place in London and the regular haunts, but no luck.'

Robert turned to lock the door behind him. 'Let's go up to the house. My parents have a trying day before them and I need to be with them to offer support.'

'Haven't you just locked your worker in the cellar or whatever it is?'

'The undercroft is a storage area, originally for corpses, but now, for all the bits and pieces accumulated over the years. There's another exit into the grounds. I can assure you there are no bodies, dead or alive, downstairs. Now, let's go. I'm desperate for a coffee and a livener. How about you?'

# FIFTY-THREE

## CHARING CROSS HOTEL – LONDON – ENGLAND

## 14.00 - 3 December 2065

The view from his room took in the main entrance into the concourse and the front section of the large marquee erected as a reception centre. Had it been down to him, Jack would have stayed in the room and tried his best to avoid looking down on the line of confused and distressed souls waiting patiently to begin the registration process. But it wasn't down to him. Schmidt insisted he and Usher make a regular appearance to greet the arrivals "in a serious and dignified manner" as the German put it.

From around midday, a trickle of people emerged from their 'courtesy' ISE car into the station. Within the space of two hours, a trickle turned into a stream. Although the noise of the protestors erupted every time a car appeared, most of those arriving stayed silent, staring straight ahead to avoid his or Usher's presence. Most were old, some in wheelchairs, pushed by their spouses or ISE facilitators.

Only one woman accosted him, at first begging him to alter the course of his heinous crime and repent his sins. When he explained it was not within his gift to do so, she condemned him to hell, demanding to know how such a caring man could change into a beast and how he could live with his conscience. He looked at the surrounding faces. Nobody spoke, but he could tell they all felt the same way.

Back in his room, Jack found himself drawn to the window, his depression increasing as the reality and momentum of what would happen tomorrow filled his thoughts. He pictured the line of people inside the marquee, their names checked, room cards issued and the time of their appointment with the psychotherapist noted. An escort would lead them to their room and accompany them whenever they visited some other area of the hotel. Within these walls, they were prisoners, the hotel no more than their condemned cell.

It had been so different earlier that morning. His heart beating fast, palms sweaty, he tore open the manila envelope. There were twenty-five continuous printed sheets, each with twenty names and addresses. Roy and his colleague had done it. How, he could not imagine, but there it was in black and white in front of him. For the next hour, he felt nothing but exhilaration.

Now, like the pleading voice from the bottom of the well, he felt nothing but despair.

As the car pulled up outside the house on the private estate at Saint George's Hill in Weybridge, one of the two ISE officers looked at the other with raised eyebrows. The other shrugged. 'It's the address on the list,' he said.

The door was opened by a young man dressed in a baggy track suit and no shoes. He looked quizzically at the young couple. 'What do you want?' he asked.

'We are here to collect Mrs Bianca Hill and take her to Charing Cross. Is she ready?'

'No shit!' Christopher said. 'He swung it for her. Good on you. I'll go and tell her.'

'She should have received an invitation,' the female officer said.

'Special case,' Christopher said. 'She won't be long.' he left them standing at the front door and ran upstairs.

From inside the house, a female voice shouted, 'What's going on, Chris?'

'Nothing,' he called back.

The male officer stamped his feet up and down on the ground to combat the cold. 'He could have invited us in,' he said.

A woman appeared at the door, also clad in a track suit, although hers was fitted to a shapely body. 'What's going on?' she asked.

'I have just advised the gentleman we are here to collect Mrs Bianca Hill and take her to Charing Cross.'

'What for?'

'She is joining the Octogen trial.' The explanation was part of a prepared list of responses all ISE officers received to deal with a hostile or negative reaction.

'Are you mad?' Francesca Hill said. 'You've got the wrong person.' She grabbed the requisition from the female officer's hand. 'There must be some mistake,' she said, after reading the detail. 'Bianca Hill is Simeon Hill's mother, *the Simeon Hill,* you know? I'm his wife. It can't possibly be for his mother.'

'You must let us do as we are instructed, Mrs Hill. I take it Mr Hill is not here?'

'He's working, as far as I know.'

'There is a procedure you can follow, Mrs Hill. I'll give you the contact detail for the liaison officer at Charing Cross. He will deal with your queries from eighteen-hundred hours onward.'

At that moment, Chris and his grandmother appeared at the door. He carried a small suitcase for her. 'What's all the fuss about?' she said.

'There's been a terrible mix-up,' Francesca said. 'These men intend to take you to Charing Cross in the mistaken belief you are a candidate.' She shook her head and reached out to put her hands on Bianca's shoulders. The old lady backed away.

'No mistake,' Bianca said. 'I asked to be put on the list.'

'You what?' Francesca's voice rose an octave.

'Do you imagine I can stand another day of you all arguing and shouting at each other over me? You have made it plain, Francesca, that I am a burden to you. I choose to be a burden no longer.' She turned and pinched Chris's cheek with thumb and index finger. 'My boy here is helping me to find some dignity in my last hours. Please do the same.'

'Simeon will never allow it.' Francesca swallowed. 'It will be the death of him.'

Bianca smiled. 'I sincerely doubt that.' She took the suitcase from her grandson's hand and gently placed a kiss on his forehead. 'I hope you get everything you deserve, Francesca. Now, officers. If we are ready.'

Another pair of ISE officers waited on the doorstep of a large semi-detached house on a tree-lined road on the outskirts of Hertford. 'I'm just coming,' a voice said from inside the front door. 'Who is it?'

'We're ISE officers, madam. We've come to collect Mrs Deborah Roach to take her to Charing Cross.'

The door opened to reveal an elderly lady with heavy-set features and a scarf over her head covering a series of rollers around which her hair was curled. She held a wooden walking stick in one hand.

'Why am I going to Charing Cross?' she asked.

'Did you not get an invitation?' the officer asked.

She gave a knowing smile. 'Must be something my son organised,' she said. 'He's such a caring boy. Wanted to surprise me, I expect.'

The two officers looked at each other.

'He's influential in politics, you know. Almost runs the London Assembly single-handed. I felt something special was going to happen today. Lucky I permed my hair. Can you wait while I take out the rollers?'

'Best you hang on until you're at the hotel,' the female officer said. 'You will need to pack a change of clothes.'

'I'll be staying the night? How wonderful! I'll leave a note to let Arthur pack for me. He knows where everything is. Does all the washing, ironing and cooking for me, you know. Sometimes he brings home a lady friend to help him, but these young girls . . .' She hesitated. 'They've got no stamina these days. He makes them dinner, gives them wine – treats them like royalty, in fact – then they fall asleep on him before you can count to ten. He has to carry them up to the spare room and put them to bed. When I get up in the morning, there's no trace of them. Ungrateful little madams.'

She hobbled forward, head bent, intent on imparting a confidence. 'Do you know, one of the trollops he brought home even messed up the bed with her, period? Saturated in blood, the bedding. All over his clothes as well. He burned all the sheets and the mattress along with everything he was wearing. You'd think with all the products these days to protect a woman's nature . . .' She left the rest of the sentence hanging in the air and just shook her head as if it were beyond her comprehension.

The officer had run out of patience. 'Never mind all that. Lock up and let's be on our way. Eternity can't wait.'

Between the hours of midday and four, ISE officials knocked on another twenty front doors of some of the most politically influential families: senators, senior deputies, judges and high-ranking civil servants. In every case, the result was the same. Some came confused, some hostile, some refusing to cooperate; but by late afternoon, twenty elderly relatives of the politically motivated Who's Who of London and the Home counties joined the long line of people in the concourse waiting to be processed.

It was just after six in the afternoon, as Jack watched the confusion begin to develop when he was called to the phone.

'This is Samantha Khan, Mr Tirrand. You recall helping me following the last Assembly meeting?'

'Yes, I do. What can I do for you?'

'Let me say I understand all this Octogen business is not of your making, and you are obliged to cooperate.'

'I appreciate your support, Samantha. I wish the rest of the population could see it your way.'

'That was not my purpose in calling. I just wanted you to know that.' She didn't wait for a reaction. 'Yesterday, I and my family received those so-called invitations, saying we would be picked up and taken to Charing Cross. We have been patiently waiting all day, but nobody has come.'

'Before you say anything else, let me check.' He rustled some papers as if searching for names. 'No, you are not on this list. It must have been a rather distressing clerical error. I'm most sorry for the upset caused to your family.'

'I see,' she said slowly, as if trying to fathom what lay behind his apology. 'So, we do nothing?'

'Today? No. I'm not suggesting there could not be a repeat invitation at some later date.'

'Thank you,' she said. 'We will do as you say and take the necessary steps.'

'I'd see how things pan out tomorrow, if I were you.' He ended the call before she had time to speak.

It was just after seven when Jack stood in the makeshift office and watched the disturbance on the concourse. Simeon Hill and Roach arrived together, pushing their way through an angry crowd of protestors, and flashing their identity cards at the guard at the head of the ISE security cordon. Hill berated a woman responsible for reception duties before his gaze fixed on the mezzanine floor office. He mounted the steps two at a time.

Three hours had passed, and Usher was still not back from her fifteen-minute interrogation window. Wise woman, Jack thought, as he stood alone in the room. Keep her head down and she might survive the blowback when the shit hits the fan.

'What the fuck is going on, Jack?' For a fit man, the stress left Hill out of breath. Body bowed, hands on his knees, he looked up at Jack, his eyes charged with fury. 'Somebody put my mother on the list, along with Roach's mother, and a handful of colleagues who have already contacted me, concerned about their relatives.'

More than a handful, Jack thought. 'No,' he said. 'How could that have happened?'

'Chris thought you could explain.'

'Me? No. I have nothing to do with the list. It's compiled in Berlin. I understood, with your inputs.'

'You are telling me you know nothing about it?'

'Come on, Simeon. You know damn well I'm just a fucking stooge for this trial, the fall guy who gets the full force of the public's invective. It was planned this way, and you were strategically involved in the selection process. It's too late to pretend it's all down to "the others". Well, in this case, it's exactly that.'

'What do you mean? Chris gave me the impression you included his grandmother at her request.'

Jack thumped his fist on the table. 'Wise up, Simeon! Do you think Berlin would give me access to the list? They wouldn't even show it to me until this morning and, to be honest, I didn't study it.' He felt his heart beating in his chest. 'If you must know, I haven't got the balls to look at the names of all those poor souls you've condemned to death.'

'You're saying the name of my mother was included in Berlin?'

'Where else?'

'Have you seen Schmidt and that beefcake of a sidekick of his?' His eyes darted around the room.

'Best guess is they are off site, dining somewhere nearby, away from the confusion. Usher is supposed to be the liaison officer tonight, but she has not returned, so I guess it's down to me.'

Jack found he was talking to himself. The door banged shut as the figure of Hill disappeared.

# FIFTY-FOUR

## FREIBURG – BAVARIA – GERMANY

## 09.00 (08.00GMT) - 4 December 2065

Kempeler paced across the meeting room, his face pallid and drawn through lack of sleep, his customary precise and measured reactions usurped by a series of impatient demands to the technicians working on the video link. He didn't want to hear that the technology for installing online gatherings at non-registered locations had been outlawed after eleven/eleven. Perhaps the reasons were valid. Yes, the terrorists used video conferencing to coordinate their attacks on the oil installations and refineries, but times changed and today was different.

'Don't waste time telling me things I don't want to hear,' he said. 'Just make the damn thing work. We need to see what is going on.' He turned to the couple sitting at the table, their faces expressionless. 'We'll soon have it resolved. Be patient.'

A grainy image of the darkened interior of what had once been a bar flickered on the screen and then turned into a grey/black sandstorm. A distorted voice was asking whether the problem was something to do with the weather.

Suddenly, Schmidt's face appeared on the monitor, his hair dishevelled, and the customary white shirt and tie swapped for a casual roll neck jumper. 'Are we through?' he asked someone.

Kempeler lowered his head, his mouth almost touching the microphone. He mouthed an expletive that made Schmidt sit at attention. They had a link. Kempeler introduced the two people sitting alongside him as compliance officers from the Senate in Berlin.

'What's the status over there?' he asked. 'I've got Hill and another dozen local bigwigs sounding off at me and accusing us of a conspiracy to undermine political stability in the UK? How did their relatives end up on the list?'

'That's a question for Berlin, not for me,' Schmidt said. 'The atmosphere here is febrile. The crowd of protestors outside is in the tens of thousands. The Strand is a solid mass of humanity and Trafalgar Square has been overrun. Security is stretched to the limit. They don't know how long they can restrain the mob. There's been over a hundred arrests and eight officers are receiving treatment for a range of injuries.'

'Forget that,' Kempeler said. 'Can't you just remove the twenty relatives, apologise and get on with it?'

Schmidt shook his head. 'We are way past a simple solution. Over thirty applications for writs of *habeas corpus* have been lodged with the PCJ. The magistrate ordered the Octogen trial be suspended until the applications can be heard at eleven local time, twelve, where you are.'

The force of Kempeler's fist on the table tipped a glass of water to wash over the table. He ignored the protest from the visitor. 'Since when have we taken any notice of directives from the People's Court of Justice? We simply overrule any order and carry on with our timetable.' As an afterthought, he said, 'You're not holding anyone in custody. You've got five-hundred people living it up in style at INCOL's expense.'

'That's debatable,' Schmidt said. 'The problem is that the people who should argue on INCOL's behalf are the ones who are pressing for the writs. The PCJ is likely to suspend the trial for seven days and defer the applications until both sides can present their arguments.'

Kempeler looked around at his visitors. 'I'll ask Berlin to countermand the directive. You prepare for the first trainload, and I'll get the order sent to the PCJ.'

'I don't recommend such a course of action. For one, if you override the PCJ, you will put Berlin in direct conflict with London. Do you want that? Second, the magistrate ordered a troop of Homeland reservists guard the train with orders to restrict access. If I order officers from the concourse to break this cordon, we could have open hostilities, possibly fatalities, inside the station. And by doing that, we weaken the force at the front.'

Somebody alongside Schmidt said something, forcing him to break off the conversation and turn to listen.

'I will have to call you back in a few minutes, General. The death row convicts extracted for the trial were all locked into rooms on the fifth floor and the floor sealed. They've broken out into the hallway and shattered windows to call down to people in the crowd of protestors. There's smoke pouring out of windows. I need to deal with it.'

'Can't Tirrand or the woman – I forget her name – Can't they handle it?'

'Usher has gone AWOL. Nobody has seen her since yesterday. Tirrand's handling a meeting of the candidates in the old ballroom; trying to calm them down. You cannot imagine the atmosphere in this place. It's ready to explode. Sorry, but I must go.'

Before Kempeler could protest, the screen showed an unoccupied chair and the backdrop of an illuminated sign showing the doors to the toilets. 'Schmidt!' he stormed.

Muller slipped into the vacant chair and adjusted the camera and microphone. 'Permission to speak, General,' he said.

'Where's Schmidt? I am not finished.'

'He's gone to handle the revolt. There's a real danger they could break out of the fifth floor and start harassing the other candidates.'

Kempeler's voice lost its heightened sense of urgency and frustration. He spoke in a quiet, resigned tone. 'Go ahead with what you wanted to say, Muller.'

'There is a new element you should know about, General.'

'Go on, if you must.'

'The later editions of the UK morning daily news sheets and, I understand, the first editions of the evening press, include or will include an open letter from Dr Dieter Eigard, dealing with the impact of an agronomical breakthrough which has caused him to change the conclusions reached in his original report on future foodstuff supply and demand.'

'Do what? Who released it and who, in God's name, authorised it?'

Muller hesitated, wary of the reaction his answer was likely to illicit. 'It was released by Dr Eigard through an INCOL server in Munich and is shown as having complied with all the censorship protocols and release authorisation.'

'Impossible. The old bugger is drugged up to the eyeballs in a closed facility. He couldn't even release a fart! Who appended their password to the authorisation?'

There was silence as Muller looked away from the camera mounted on the monitor.

'Did you hear me, Muller? I asked who authorised the release.'

'You did, General. It's your encrypted password.'

# FIFTY-FIVE

## WEST LONDON – ENGLAND

### 16.30 - 4 December 2065

'Whose apartment is this?' Robert asked.

Alison hooked the rucksack over her shoulder and patted his shoulder to show she was ready to leave. 'It's a girlfriend who used to be at Uni with me. I'm ready.'

He pointed at the rucksack. 'Is that all you're taking?'

'Dad said I dare not go back to Manchester. They could be after me. And what's the point? They're only possessions. I've got a couple of changes of clothes, a toilet bag and a book to read. I expect when I get to where we're going, I'll accumulate some more possessions.'

'That's a philosophical outlook to adopt. It rather undermines my need for a heavy suitcase.'

'Each to their own. Did you read the news sheet?'

'I take my hat off to Roy and his mate for what they've achieved. Substituting names and addresses was one thing, but getting Eigard's letter into the papers with his retraction and detailing all that fertiliser and GM crop business - well, that was sheer genius.'

'Do you know how they do it?' Alison asked.

'Not a clue. It's all this blockchain technology. That's about the limit of my understanding.'

'The Chinese are going to be incensed by the revelations. It's their science. How do you think they will react?'

With a shake of the head, Robert ushered her to the door, checking his watch as he did so. 'If they've got any sense, they will take the credit, make some grandiose speech about helping humanity and offer to supply the recipe and process at government level on a global basis. They've lost control of the information. They might as well get all the kudos possible out of the situation.' He gestured for her to speed up. 'Come on. We need to keep moving.'

Alison stopped in her tracks. 'What's the rush, Uncle? We have ninety minutes before we pick up Dad. That look on your face? Something's wrong you're not telling me about.'

Robert moved back inside the apartment and closed the front door. He took a deep breath, exhaling slowly through his nose. 'I didn't want to tell you until we were safely away from here, but I can see I'm not going to get away with that.'

'You're making me nervous.'

'I'd packed up most of the communications gear in the undercroft ready to bury it and was having a final briefing with Roy when your boyfriend showed up.'

'Rolf?' She reacted to the nod. 'What was he doing there?'

'He said he was looking for you; gave an excuse why he was in the area. My guess is he followed Jack the last time he came and returned to find out what was going on. Remember, it must have looked suspicious. Jack came straight to the chapel, did not go to the main house, stayed for an hour and then returned to London.'

'What happened?'

'I could tell your man was suspicious, intent on finding out what was in the undercroft. An hour alone was what I needed to finish dismantling everything and secreting it in one of the burial spaces in the churchyard I'd already excavated. He wasn't going to give me that.'

'You didn't . . .?'

'Lord, forgive the girl! Spare the thought. I invited him back to the main house for coffee and slipped in a couple of those Clopixols we give to Verity when she gets anxious and needs to rest. He must have been tired. Within a minute, he was fast asleep in an armchair and still not stirring when I returned.'

'You just left him? Where is he now?'

'No idea. My parents were sitting huddled together in their overcoats, waiting to be collected and taken to London. I told Dad they wouldn't be coming, that he was off the list, but he didn't believe me. I asked him to apologise to Rolf when he woke up; that I needed to leave on diocese business and would see him next time he was *in the area*. Nice touch, don't you think?'

'Don't look so smug. He's an ISE agent who infiltrated into my knickers with the single ambition of getting close to my father and the UK political scene. He had no interest in me.'

'It didn't seem that way when he came to Verity's birthday bash.'

'No, it didn't, did it? Maybe he's just a damn good actor.'

# FIFTY-SIX

## FREIBURG – BAVARIA – GERMANY

## 18.00 (17.00 GMT) - 4 December 2065

The brandy glass shattered as it hit the brickwork fireplace, the remnants of the alcohol exciting the embers of the coals into one last explosion of flame.

General Kempeler sat alone, lounging in an armchair, his long legs bent at the knees, the toes of his boots the only part of his feet in contact with the carpet. He stared as the flames flickered one final time and died.

The adjutant appeared at his side. Schmidt was on the line. Somebody needed to make a statement to the press. His position was untenable.

'Do you have a directive for me, General?'

'Berlin has spoken, and in no uncertain terms.'

The British contingent to the Senate presented a formal charge accusing the German High Command of attempting to undermine the UK's political stability. INCOL's supreme tribunal would hear the complaint the following week. As an interim measure, the PCJ has ordered an indefinite stay of execution of the Octogen project pending the outcome of a series of applications for writs of *habeas corpus*.

China has recalled its team of observers in Berlin for further instructions whilst an investigation is carried out into the release of a text to the newspapers containing information obtained by treachery and deception and prejudicial to INCOL Asia. An employee in the Indonesian Agricultural Development Commission had been arrested on suspicion of passing classified information to a fellow researcher in Munich. An agronomist, Martin Eigard, currently resident in Rottenburg, has been arrested and taken to Berlin, where he will answer charges of committing acts prejudicial to the Coalition of Nations. Proven guilty, the automatic sentence was summary execution without the right of appeal.

'With what you tell me and the reaction from Berlin, we have little choice. The Octogen trial is suspended indefinitely, pending the outcome of an investigation into these recent revelations. Get Tirrand to make the announcement and then—'

'May I ask a question, General?'

Kempeler did not react to the interruption. 'As long as it's not to ask how I'm feeling.'

Schmidt sounded unsure whether this was humorous or serious. 'No, of course not,' he said blandly. 'Have you any idea how your name came to be on the censorship authorisation? Berlin has asked me to comment.'

'No idea.'

'It is your signature?'

'It appears to be. Papers cross my desk and some I sign without studying the content, but I cannot envisage I would ever let such a document pass uninspected and certainly not authorise it.'

'Berlin says the Blockchain sequence cannot be hacked, and an initial inspection has not thrown up any anomalies.'

Kempeler stood up, brushed the crumbs from his shirt, straightened his braces and reached for his jacket. 'I have a strong suspicion Tirrand is behind all this: the names on the list with no corresponding invitations . . .' The sentence tailed off. 'I'm just thinking. Don't we have a copy of the list from which the original invitations were printed?'

'I checked. No. Instructions were given that no lists were to be printed until yesterday morning. The database was used to print the invitations and addresses. If you replicated them now, you would get a data set in line with the printed lists we now have.'

'Somebody's done this,' Kempeler concluded. 'And I'm certain Tirrand knows something. Rescind the kill order and apprehend him as soon as he has made the announcement. Take him straight to Berlin. In the meantime, get someone to check his movements since he returned to the UK. I want to know exactly what he's been doing down to the last detail and with whom. Understand?'

# FIFTY-SEVEN

## CHARING CROSS HOTEL – LONDON – ENGLAND

### 17.45 - 4 December 2065

Jack wiped his forehead with a handkerchief. His announcement was met with both euphoria and relief. Cheers erupted from the crowds in the surrounding streets, banners waved in triumph. Gradually, they dispersed. The so-called candidates filed slowly out of the hotel, a confused look on many faces as they were reunited with their relatives, their ordeal over.

Looking down on a concourse emptying rapidly, the large reception marquee now almost deserted, Jack glanced at the clock. He was due to be on the Embankment at six. He would get his things together and try to leave as inconspicuously as possible.

'Where do you think you're going?' Schmidt was standing at the doorway, Muller close behind.

'My job's done. You don't need me anymore.'

Schmidt smiled and shook his head. 'You are under arrest, Mr Tirrand, on suspicion of treason against the Coalition. We are to take you to Berlin, leaving this evening.'

'Don't be ridiculous,' Jack protested. 'I've done everything you asked of me. Treason? All I've done is cooperate.' He went to pass Schmidt, who pushed him backwards, forcing him down into a chair.

'It would be useful if you could help your cause and tell me now how you came by and got into print, a copy of a document purported to be written by Dr Eigard with General Kempeler's authorisation?'

Jack shook his head. 'I have no idea what you are talking about. The article in the news sheet was as much a surprise to me as to you.'

The back of Schmidt's hand flashed across Jack's face, the signet ring tearing his cheek as the blood welled and then trickled down his chin. 'Wrong answer,' Schmidt said. 'Think a little harder.' He went to lift his hand a second time. 'You might as well stop pretending. We've got Eigard's brother in custody. He won't protect you.'

'Who? Never met him or heard of him.'

The hand struck him across the other cheek, but the skin remained intact.

'Willi Schmidt? Tomas Muller?' The voice came from an ISE ground force officer dressed in full riot gear, standing just inside the doorway, flanked by three similarly dressed officers.

'Don't worry,' Schmidt said. 'We've got him. He's under our control.'

The ISE officer approached, ignoring Jack. 'You are Willi Schmidt? I have a warrant for your arrest and that of Tomas Muller on the grounds of sedition and acts prejudicial to the governance of INCOL.' He read both men their rights.

'This is crazy,' Schmidt protested as the lead officer grabbed his arm and pushed him toward the door. 'You can tell Hill we will be out within the hour. Trying to use us as pawns in his sordid attempt to pressurise Berlin will never work. We'll be back for you, Tirrand.'

'Are you alright, Sir?' the officer asked Jack.

'Better now you're here,' he said, accepting the handkerchief to wipe the blood from his face.

The officer bent down to whisper. 'Confidentially, Sir, I don't know how you did it, but you've stopped a bloody riot. Getting that lot to back down; you're a bloody miracle worker. Well done. The men said you didn't seem like the sort of guy who would go along with executing people.'

Six o'clock. Jack had told Alison they must not hang around. If he wasn't at the agreed meeting point at six, they were to leave.

He struggled through the crowds toward the Embankment. The car was there. Fifty metres. The engine started. A puff of white smoke drifted from the exhaust. The driver was manoeuvring to leave its space between two illegally parked cars. The traffic coordinator was four vehicles away, patiently registering the details and fixing a penalty notice on the windscreen before moving along the row.

Jack ran, increasing his stride, his hand thumping on the boot as the car pulled away.

The brake lights glowed in the dark. The passenger seat was empty. Headlights from an oncoming car picked him out as he darted from the road toward the pavement. Someone opened the passenger door. He scrambled in and fell into the seat as the car accelerated.

'Good of you to come,' a voice said from the rear.

Jack wheeled around to find himself looking into the barrel of a Walther 99 handgun.

# FIFTY-EIGHT

## BARRA DA TIJUCA – RIO DE JANEIRO – TOMORROW WORLD

### 18.00 (21.00 GMT) – 4 December 2065

It was Lance's favourite time of the day; the in-between hour when he could sit at his favourite beach bar and watch the sun worshippers as they ambled languidly from the sand to mingle with the early revellers dressed in colourful attire, drifting, laughing and chatting along the mosaic cobbled walkways.

All the tables were taken, the beers and caipirinhas flowing, the conversations animated, as Ron Coleman, alias Ted Hubbard, slid into the seat opposite Lance and ordered mineral water.

'You get some sleep?' Lance asked.

'Like a baby,' Coleman said. 'Any developments?'

'What do you think? You created absolute confusion. The trial was put on indefinite hold, and I'm guessing with the revelations about the way to an enhanced GM crop yield, the Octogen project is dead in the water.'

'Did your padre and his group get away?'

'I'm out of contact now until they make the ship. The skipper will ping me to confirm.' Lance played with the empty beer glass, running his finger around the rim. 'The real Ron Coleman, now David Jackson, contacted the padre yesterday. He knows where the equipment is buried and will collect it for transfer to a new location. It should be back online within the next couple of days.' He held out his hand. 'By the way, congratulations!'

'What for?'

'Two counts. Your transfer papers came through. Pack your things ready for a move to Campinas in Sao Paulo and the Centre for AI Development Research. You are deemed over-qualified for Campo Grande, and you get to work with the nerds and the robots.'

'Sounds like fun.'

'It also puts some distance between the two of us, which is no bad thing as far as you are concerned.'

Coleman smiled. 'I'm always available if you need me. And the second count?'

'Our eternal gratitude for your efforts over the past few days. I couldn't have done it without you. The blockchain hack was incredible, the touch of replicating Kempeler's signature on the censorship requisition, a touch of real genius.'

'Stop. You'll have me blushing.'

'Under that tan? You wouldn't see it.' Lance pushed his glass to one side and leaned forward. 'This Red Manifesto; is the fertiliser formula the secret you were waiting to spring on the world?'

'A small part. It's more complex, a strategy designed to achieve world dominance in certain critical areas to coincide with the return of some semblance of normality. The Chinese intend to assume the role of the major player. I intend to do my best to frustrate them.'

'You've done pretty well so far.'

'One step at a time. I'll put you in the picture as and when.'

'You do that. Don't take any risks. They will not stop looking for you.'

Three tables away, a woman in a blue-striped T-shirt looked over her magazine at the two men. On orders from Washington, she had been tailing Cody for the last two days. The man with him she did not recognise. She would do some digging.

# FIFTY-NINE

## THURROCK – ESSEX – ENGLAND

## 21.00 - 4 December 2065

The three captives looked at each other as the lock turned, the door opened, and out of the darkness, a single bulb cast a dim glow over the cellar in which they were being held. The man they now knew as Franz slowly descended the wooden steps from the hallway, carrying a tray with three steaming mugs. Without saying a word, he placed the tray on the floor, took a knife from the sheaf on his waist and sliced the length of telephone wire which bound Alison's wrists behind her back. She rubbed at the skin furiously as the blood flow circulated.

'She can feed you,' he said to Jack, who was seated on a mattress, hands bound, his back propped against the brick wall.

'What about going to the toilet?' Robert asked. 'I've been wanting to relieve myself for some time.'

A preoccupation with his bladder and a dicky prostate had been Robert's constant complaint since the moment Jack appeared at the front passenger door of the car on the Embankment. Ten minutes earlier, the rear door had opened, and Rolf moved into the car alongside Alison, pressing the barrel of his gun against the back of Robert's seat.

Her initial surprise and fear masked by anger and indignation, Alison let her feelings loose in a tirade of rebuke. The slap across his face caused him to turn the pistol on her.

'Put that silly thing away,' she chided. 'Who do you think you're trying to threaten, you pathetic individual?'

One hand couched the red welt across his cheek, the other returned the gun to centre on Robert's back. 'I accept I used you to get to your father,' he said. 'But if it's any consolation, I do have feelings for you.'

'Bullshit words,' she retorted. 'You're just a despicable undercover ISE agent sent to spy on us, Rolf, or whatever your real name is.'

'I think you know who I am. I'm guessing you are the mystery woman who turned up to speak with my father in Rottenburg. Yes, I am Franz Eigard.

My father, Martin, is Dieter's younger brother. Dieter's son, Rolf, died in a skiing accident some years ago.'

'Why the subterfuge?'

'You didn't stay around to speak to my father, did you? Had you done so, the unenviable position in which we find ourselves might have been avoided.'

Alison looked puzzled. 'You're not making any sense.'

At that moment, Jack's face appeared at the front passenger window, took in the scene, and reacted as the gun in Rolf's hand pointed at Alison. Jack raised his hands before reaching for the handle and clambering untidily into the seat. He ignored Rolf and addressed his brother-in-law. 'Drive, please, Robert,' he said. 'I am being followed.'

The car pulled into a gap in the traffic.

'Get to the A13, heading eastward,' Rolf said.

Jack swung around in his seat to face Alison. 'Are you all right?' he asked.

She glared at the man sitting next to her. 'Rolf, real name Franz, was about to explain why he has hijacked the car and is pointing a gun at us.'

'I was going to ask,' Robert said. 'How Franz knew where to find us. Last time I saw him, he was sleeping like a baby.'

'Thanks to you, *old man*.' Franz snorted through his nose. 'All ISE fleet cars are protected via a tracker linked to the INCOL satellite. I detached mine and fixed it on the underside of this car while it was parked at the chapel.' He reached around the headrest, poking the barrel of the gun into Robert's temple, causing Robert and the car to veer to the left.

Jack reached for the steering wheel to correct the movement.

'You will be interested to learn, Priest, that after waking from my enforced sleep, I revisited the chapel and its interesting basement, now bereft of the equipment necessary to operate as a communications centre. I suspect the newly turned earth in a cemetery that has not seen a burial in a hundred years will provide some answers. I'll check it out on my return.'

You'll be too late, Robert thought. My replacement should be there right now, retrieving the equipment for installation in a new location. But he said nothing, staring straight ahead as he manoeuvred the car into the outside lane to overtake a lorry.

Alison poked a finger into the gunman's side. 'You were blaming me for what? Messing up your plans?'

'For making assumptions, drawing the wrong conclusions.'

'Explain yourself.'

The lights from the office blocks in Canary Wharf illuminated the night sky as Franz pointed at a sign for the A13 and Tilbury docks.

It all started, Franz explained, when Uncle Dieter distributed drafts of his report on the Octogen project to Berlin with a copy to his brother. As an agronomist, brother Martin's intended role was to endorse the radical measures proposed by Dieter and his group. But Martin did the exact opposite. His clandestine contact in Indonesia had detailed knowledge of a revolutionary fertiliser developed by the Chinese for significantly enhancing GM crop production. Presented with this fresh evidence, Dieter redrafted his report to include this information and conditioned his conclusions.

The powers in Berlin were hostile to the changes, demanding to know the source of this speculative and, most likely, false news. They insisted the original conclusions be restated. Dieter capitulated but, in doing so, recognised he had put his brother at risk. The idea of relocating him to a haven prompted Dieter's approach to his friend and ally, Mila Kullenberg, whom he knew had relatives with links to Tomorrow World. To protect his brother, Dieter made out it was he who wished to escape, intending to explain the deception when he established contact with his facilitator.

By design or coincidence, Rolf was seconded as an ISE field operative to undertake covert surveillance in England of three individuals recommended by Senate member, Hill, as potential candidates to front the trial of Octogen toward the end of the year.

'I quickly settled on Jack Tirrand as the best-qualified candidate and experienced the intense pleasure of starting a relationship with his daughter to get close to Tirrand. It evolved into something more meaningful as we got to know each other.' He chanced a smile at Alison, which was not returned.

The car radio crackled into life, programmed as standard to turn on or interrupt whenever a public service message needed to be broadcast. A cultured male voice spoke ' . . . a warrant for the arrest and detention of Deputy Jack Tirrand, wanted for acts prejudicial to the Coalition. Tirrand is believed to be desperate and dangerous and should not be approached.

Information leading to his arrest will be rewarded with ten thousand Free to Spend Credits.'

Robert whistled. 'They certainly want to get hold of you. I'm even tempted,' he said, trying to lighten the atmosphere.

'They don't know of your involvement?' Jack asked.

Franz shook his head. 'My orders are to get you to Berlin. If you are arrested here, the authorities will insist on you remaining in London. In the space of a day, you've gone from zero to hero. Public opinion is on your side. Crowds will soon be in the streets chanting your name as the man who thwarted the system and caused Octogen to be cancelled. The authorities will bow to public pressure and trump up some legal loophole for you.'

'Then, let the authorities here arrest him. What's stopping you, Franz?' Alison pleaded. 'If you care for me, as you say, it's a way out of this mess.' Franz reacted to the excitement in her voice by lowering his eyes to fix on the floor.

'I can't. I didn't finish telling you.' His voice adopted a sombre tone.

Desperate to know the source of Dieter's knowledge of the fertiliser, ISE interrogators questioned everybody close to him. Under pressure, Mila Kullenberg confessed. Martin was arrested and the plan to flee to Tomorrow World came to light.

'Under normal circumstances,' Franz said. 'My father would have just disappeared, but the ISE command had different ideas. Dieter, who has terminal bowel cancer, was moved to an end-of-life facility. Martin was to assume his persona together with me in the guise of his resurrected son, Rolf. He would plead with the facilitators to allow me to travel with him and we would both end up in TW where I would set to work dismantling the resistance movement.' He looked at Alison. 'As it is, your snooping around thwarted that plan and left my father trapped and staring a death sentence in the face.'

'That's ridiculous,' Jack said, shaking his head. 'You blame Alison for failing to talk to your father and listening to gossip from a neighbour? Put the blame where it belongs.'

Franz shrugged. 'I do as I am ordered, or my father is transferred to Berlin. My instructions are to bring you back alive. That is what I intend to do.'

'What about us?' Alison asked, placing her hand on Robert's shoulder. 'Where do we figure in your plan?'

Franz glanced away, looking at the road junction ahead. 'Take a right,' he said. 'Follow the sign to Tilbury dock and turn off toward Chadwell St. Mary.' He turned back to face Alison. 'I don't know. I expect once your father and I are safely on a cargo vessel back to Hamburg, you'll be released.'

Alison recognised the faltering smile and the lack of conviction in his eyes. 'You'll follow your orders, won't you?' she asked.

His expression told her all she needed to know.

# SIXTY

## MUSWELL HILL – LONDON

## 18.00 - 4 December 2065

Rebecca pushed her way through the crowd of people thronging the street outside the apartment building, the mood good-humoured as the name of Jack Tirrand was chanted in unison.

'Give us some room, please,' she demanded, forcing Harriet to move in front of her. 'Space! Let her through. She's pregnant.'

The welcome calm of the apartment was unreal, the noise from below, nothing more than a rumble reverberating against the lounge window.

'Do you know what is going on?' Harriet asked. 'The radio calls Dad a wanted man, dangerous. Do not approach. There's an enormous reward on offer, yet everywhere you go, people are calling his name as if he were the Messiah. Nothing makes sense. Do you know where he is?'

Rebecca shed her topcoat onto the sofa, making her way to the drinks cabinet and pouring a neat vodka. She held out the glass. 'After a week in a cell, I need this. Want one?'

Harriet shook her head. 'Are you going to answer me?'

Rebecca closed her eyes as the alcohol penetrated her senses. 'I don't know and what's more, I don't care. All I *do* know is Jack put my parents on the death list and pretended he knew nothing about it. Mind you . . .' She took another gulp. 'He's never liked them, always annoying Dad and disrespectful when it came to dealing with Mother.' She hesitated. 'If you must know, I'm divorcing him.'

'Why? The crowd is saying he sabotaged the Octogen thing. Nobody died.'

'He only came to his senses after I reasoned with him and did what I asked. That's all well and good, but I couldn't live with a man who was capable of betraying my family name. We are finished. Full stop.' She looked around at the clock. 'I need to be somewhere at eight. Where's that grey trouser suit I bought the other week? I want to look as if I were a high-powered executive in a legal firm. A long, hot bath is my priority. How are the twins, by the way?' She strode from the room. 'Keep talking,' she shouted. 'I'm just going to turn on the bath.'

'Fine,' Harriet said to an empty room in as loud a voice as she could muster. 'Looking forward to our move to the West Country and the prospect of a new baby brother. That's the reason I wanted to talk with you.'

'And Mac?' asked the disembodied voice.

'Morose and jealous of my relationship with Arnold.' Her voice tailed off to normal volume as Rebecca returned.

'What do you think?' Rebecca held up the trouser suit. 'Suitable for a quiet dinner with my lawyer, don't you think?'

'I thought you were free, no charges?'

'There are a few loose ends to tie up. I need an excellent lawyer onside in case this death list business rears its ugly head again. He's a widower; lost his wife in a drowning accident. Tragic. Still, one door closes, another opens.'

'You wouldn't know of Arnold's whereabouts, would you?' Harriet said. 'He's been so helpful in organising the property relocation. I need to ask him what I should do with the adoption request Alison signed. I put through call requests, but none are accepted.'

'What's the rush? You're not expecting for another six months, are you?'

'Ask Alison. She told me she's got the travelling bug and expects to spend a year out of the country. She was insistent. I should get Roach to countersign it whilst he was in a friendly mood. He could change in an instant. Best to strike while the iron and all that.'

'Your sister is a law unto herself. Do you know where she is?'

'Last time I spoke to her, she gave me the adoption paperwork and said she was planning to meet up with Dad. This was before all the confusion.'

Rebecca sighed theatrically. 'One day she's calling your father a dinosaur; the next, she's holding his hand. I must get going. Can't be late.'

Harriet grabbed her arm. 'Any idea where I can contact Roach?'

'I heard the police inspector on the phone. Roach's mother somehow ended up on the death list and suffered a stroke or something. She was carted off to hospital and I expect AR went with her. He'll surface soon enough. You watch your step with him. There are no free lunches as far as he is concerned.'

# SIXTY-ONE

## THURROCK – ESSEX – ENGLAND

### 07.00 - 5 December 2065

Robert awoke to the muffled sound of raised voices speaking in a language he did not understand. Fear gripped him as he cast his eyes around the bare, distempered walls and rough stone floor. There were no windows. The only way he could tell day from night was through a ventilation grill close to the ceiling. Shreds of light illuminated the side of a wall of the outbuilding attached to the main house. His two fellow prisoners lay asleep on camp bed mattresses.

Exhaustion had finally overtaken them in the early hours, and they drifted in and out of troubled sleep.

His hands bound in front of him with plastic ties, Robert staggered toward the bucket to relieve himself. As he made his way back, he stopped, pressing his ear to the slatted wooden door. The woman's voice dominated the conversation. Whatever it was they were discussing, and it was most likely about their three hostages, Franz was losing the argument. If only he understood what they were saying. His glance fell on Alison. He would wake her. She would understand why the woman sounded so angry. He gritted his teeth. Perhaps it was best not to know. She had looked angry and hostile from the moment they had first seen her.

The car had turned onto the dirt track as it passed the village, turned left and then swung onto a gravel-surfaced roadway leading to a small, abandoned industrial estate. The gravel deteriorated into the rutted dirt track, furrowed by the rain as they passed a sign which said 'Star of the Alps – Guest House', with the design of a small white flower alongside the name. Underneath hung a second, smaller sign announcing, 'No Vacancies'.

The guest house amounted to a two-storey, brick-built detached farmhouse style property with an annex created from what must have once been the stables. The building stood alone, at the head of a clearing bordered by scrubland for as far as the eye could see. In the distance, they could hear the steady bass thump of a machine, pounding with monotonous regularity every few seconds.

As Franz ushered them from the car toward the front door, the woman stood, clad in a blue plastic apron, hands on hips, barring their way. At the last moment, she stood aside and studied them as they passed. Jack put her at mid to late forties, a tall, statuesque figure, although tending to thick around the waist and hips. Her hands were unusually large for a woman of one metre-seventy, scored with ingrained dirt accumulated over the years. Her nails were bitten to the quick.

She was of mixed race, African and white European, her face dotted with patches of depigmented skin, bright white against the natural light brown. Her cheeks were pitted, her black hair thinning, signs of a protein deficiency in childhood, and her emotionless expression compounded by the result of a cleft pallet operation inexpertly completed.

There was a brief exchange in German between Franz and the woman. The familiarity in the way they reacted to each other was not lost on Jack.

'I'll take the room with the jacuzzi,' Robert said to his companions with a forced smile.

'Mine's the one next to the fire escape,' Jack retorted, keen to defuse the tension he knew they felt.

'Along there,' the woman said in accented English, pushing Robert through the kitchen toward the outhouse.

Alison tugged at Franz's arm. 'You know you don't have to do this,' she said. 'I know your heart isn't in this. It's a big mistake. Let us go.'

Franz pulled away, avoiding her pleading eyes, conscious the woman was studying him.

The door closed behind them as they staggered, wrists bound, across the chill, stone floor.

'She was surprised to see the three of us,' Alison said, breaking the silence, her eyes now accustomed to the growing darkness. 'That's what she said to him when we arrived. She was told to expect just one man. They would need new orders.'

'Do they realise you speak German?' Jack said.

'I always spoke to Rolf . . . Franz, in English. I could have mentioned it.'

Jack poked with his feet at a cigarette butt on the floor. 'We're not the first to have been imprisoned here. What do you think this place is, a safe house for people smuggled in and out of the Country?'

'Looks like it,' Robert said. 'We've got to get away somehow.'

They were talking in whispers when the light came on; the key turned and Franz entered, closing the door behind him. 'You heard somebody knocking at the front door, I'm sure.'

They hadn't, but nobody reacted.

'I urge you, for your sake and that of the person at the door, to keep silent. I don't want to gag you, but I will if you make a sound.'

'You said that as if you regretted having to threaten us,' Robert said.

'Just be quiet.'

The faint hum of conversation could just be heard, receding as the sound of two people climbed the stairs, followed minutes later by another momentary burst of conversation, the squeak of the front door closing and a return to silence.

'All clear.' The woman's voice came from just outside the cellar.

*'Was geht ab?'* Franz asked as he opened the door.

For the first time since they arrived, the woman laughed, a phlegmy cackle that turned into a cough.

'What did she say?' Jack asked Alison when Franz had gone.

'As far as I could make out with her references to *vogel*, somebody came to the door asking about booking accommodation next spring for a group of birdwatchers planning a visit to the marshes. Whoever it was, asked to see one of the rooms.'

'Makes sense,' Jack said. 'The banks of the Thames from here and running out to sea are covered with marshlands and protected areas for hundreds of species. Doesn't sound like our saviour, does it?'

'Let's make a plan,' Robert said. 'After all, there's three of us and only two of them.'

A bedraggled Alison responded to the light grip on her exposed foot and climbed sleepily from the mattress to join Robert at the door. 'Sorry to wake you,' he said. 'But there are raised voices. Can you translate it?'

Alison listened intently. 'The woman is saying, "I've just told you, we have our orders, and we will carry them out. You should not have brought them here in the first place. Live with the consequences".' She hesitated. 'He's protesting, claiming they all have information and should be transported to Berlin. "How many times do I have to say it?", she is repeating. "We will follow the instructions I have been given.".' She hesitated. 'His voice has lost its anger. I think he said, "I won't do it. You will have to.".'

'You know what that means?' Jack was now awake and frantically running his wrists down the exposed brickwork, trying to free himself from the binding. Blood and brick dust covered his hands as he gritted his teeth and repeated the action.

'I'm afraid so,' Robert said, glancing at Alison, whose lip quivered as she tried to smile.

'We must take them by surprise,' Jack said. 'If we can free our hands, wait until they are both together and then jump them. I'll go for whoever is holding the gun. You two, try to stall the other one.'

With a final grimace of pain, Jack pulled the wire apart and vigorously rubbed his chafed wrists. He looked up at the small grill on the external wall and beckoned Robert. 'I'll climb on your shoulders to reach that. The glass has long since gone, but I'm hoping there's a shard or two still in the frame.'

Five minutes later, the thin triangle of glass cut through the ties on the other two, the plastic remnants arranged around their wrists as a light came on and a key turned in the lock. They backed away, hands clasped together.

Franz was first through the door. 'Good morning. Time to go.' A matter-of-fact statement that conveyed nothing, yet Jack could see the burden in the man's eyes. You may feel the distress of the moment, he said to himself, yet you are resigned to an uncomfortable reality. You have convinced yourself you are doing it to save your father, though I doubt he will survive to embrace your achievement.

Behind Franz was the woman, the revolver couched in the folds of her apron. She stood, legs apart in the doorway, her gaze travelling from one side of the room to the other, her expression resolute.

'Where are we going?' Robert asked, advancing two steps closer to Franz. 'What's happening to us?'

Jack moved around, now side on to the woman.

'There's a bulk carrier in Tilbury waiting to take you to Hamburg,' Franz said.

'Enough,' the woman said.

'I agree,' Jack said and launched himself at the woman, grabbing her arm as he pinched her wrist and forced the gun out of her hand. It landed with a clang on the stone floor. The impetus of his thrust knocked the woman backwards against the cellar door, but she remained upright, her legs flexing at the knees as she turned sideways to defend herself. Jack jumped at her, his hands meeting her shoulders with a shudder as they both fell to the floor, a flurry of arms and legs straining to gain an advantage.

Robert swung his right arm back and aimed at Franz's chin, which was in his line of sight one second and gone the next. His arm met no resistance as he straightened from the punch, only to receive an uppercut into the solar plexus which took the breath from his body. He doubled up and tried to focus on his assailant.

Franz turned to face a new challenge, but his reflexes were not quick enough to avoid this frenzied attack. Alison swung the bucket containing their waste at his head. Franz moved sideways to avoid direct contact with his face, but took the blow on his temple, the urine pouring over his head; the faeces sticking to his hair as particles dropped into his eyes and down his chin. Dazed by the blow, he sunk to his knees.

'Run,' Jack called from the doorway, beating back the woman's arms as she tried to gouge lumps from his face. He straddled her, although he could do little more than restrain her arms. She was stronger than he could ever have imagined. Unless he got away from her, there was every likelihood she would gain the advantage.

Alison came to his rescue. With one hand supporting Robert around the waist, she pulled the cellar door as hard as she could, driving it against the woman's head. The woman groaned and her arms went limp. Jack pushed her to one side, leaving enough space for the three to exit single file.

There was no sound from behind them as they limped through the front door and looked for the car in the yard.

'No keys,' Robert said.

'Forget it,' Jack said. 'Head for the main road.' They picked up pace as they jogged across the yard toward the exit.

The two-tone whistle sounded from somewhere behind them. Two jet black Cane Corsos careered from the stable, teeth bared as they stood their ground, barring the way forward. Jack made a move to sidle past, causing one of the huge dogs to ready for the attack.

'I wouldn't try it if I were you.' Franz shouted as he appeared from the house. 'They will happily tear you to pieces if given the command. They are trained to immobilise. It's a painful experience, so I'm told.'

The woman stepped from behind the front door, a towel compressed against her head with one hand, the handgun in the other.

'Turn around slowly and retrace your steps,' Franz said, rubbing the remnants of the urine dousing from his eyes.

# SIXTY-TWO

## THURROCK – ESSEX – ENGLAND

## 09.30 - 5 December 2065

Alison pulled at the plastic restraints fastened around her wrists. The pain as they dug into her flesh didn't seem to matter anymore. What now awaited her was so unimaginable and final, the panic gave way to a strange sense of anger and impatience. Not anger with the woman holding the handgun and prodding at them to walk faster across the marshland toward the shrub-lined ditch. Not even anger with Franz as he avoided her stare and pushed her father toward Robert's car. Dad turned and looked so lovingly at her as Franz ordered him to climb into the boot. Watching the car pull away, she felt as if she would cry, but that was a satisfaction their captors would not witness. No, the anger was directed at herself as the architect of their final misery and impatience for the guilt weighing her body down to end.

Hands bound behind their backs, they said their goodbyes. An hour had passed as they waited for Franz to reappear, showered and in changed clothes. The woman had a three-inch square of gauze taped to her head and the start of a nasty-looking black eye. Neither spoke as they herded their captives out of the house.

Robert was two steps in front, mumbling what she assumed was a prayer, his feet making a noise like a plunger clearing a blockage as they sunk into the marshland. Progress was slow. The morning frost had melted and what had earlier been crisp under foot was now a bog.

'Stop here,' the woman ordered as they reached the ditch. Two white sacks were stacked against a bush. 'Quicklime,' she said, acknowledging Robert's glance at them. 'It will turn your bodies into a slurry. The rain and the animals will do the rest.' She laughed to herself at the prospect. 'Kneel.' She used the barrel of the gun to force him to his knees.

Alison charged forward as fast as the marsh would allow, her feet rising and falling as if she were in a slow-motion movie sequence. The woman stepped back just as Alison leapt off her feet and cascaded head-first into the mud.

'God rest our souls,' Robert said, turning his face to look at the woman.

'Enough of this,' she said and raised the gun.

Alison fought for breath; her face caked in mud as she heard the gunshot break the silence of the still winter's day and reverberate around the field. Rolling onto her back, she looked up at the woman, teeth gritted. She blinked to clear her eyes. Get on with it, she thought.

The woman turned, her face a mask frozen in time. The gun pointed at Alison's chest, then continued round in an arc as her body rotated. Alison looked up in horror. The left side of the woman's head was not there anymore, just a mass of pink flesh and white bone. The woman's knees collapsed under her, and her body pitched into the ditch.

Alison turned to see Robert, still kneeling, his eyes closed tight, his lips moving frantically.

'Are you all right?' Alison asked.

Robert opened his eyes. 'What happened?'

'I don't know. We are still alive.'

'God is great.'

Alison crawled to her feet, eyes transfixed on the body of the woman as it lay unmoving in the ditch.

'Who in heaven's name is that?' Robert said.

'Where?'

From a hide a hundred metres away, a figure emerged and strolled toward them, a rifle couched in his arms, flat across his chest, barrel pointed upward. Dressed in military camouflage issue with trousers tucked into calf-length, lace-up leather boots, he appeared to make it across the marshland with ease, choosing his path with care as he approached them.

Alison wiped the mud and weeds from her face, her gaze fixed on what she could only conceive as a new danger.

Robert felt no such restraint. 'We have to thank you for saving our lives,' he said, as if addressing the Rotary Club dinner. The man was twenty metres away. He did not reply. He shouldered the rifle and walked forward, bending to retrieve the Walther 99 handgun the woman had been holding. He jumped into the ditch, where he pulled the woman's body onto her back and fired a bullet into the mass of flesh and bone on the left side of her face. He wiped the butt of the gun before wrapping the fingers of her left hand around it and placing it on her stomach.

He used his rifle as support to climb from the ditch and smiled at the bedraggled figure in front of him. 'Nobody will believe it's a suicide; just made to look like one. The gun is a Walther 99, the model issued to ISE operatives. Whoever investigates this will think it's an official execution and not spend too much time looking for a culprit.' He spoke with a twang, accentuating a heavy Midlands's accent.

Alison guessed the man was around sixty years old, but with a slender, muscular body and an agility suggesting he spent time in the gym. His black African features cracked into a smile, enhancing a flattened nose that looked as though it had been broken on more than one occasion.

Robert marched forward, holding out his hand. 'You have the better of us,' he said. 'I'm Robert Fitzwilliam. You would be . . .?'

'I know who you are, man. And your crazy little espionage operation.' He ignored the outstretched hand and turned to Alison, who was now standing and wiping off the surface mud. 'You must be Firman's daughter . . .' He shook his head. 'Sorry. I mean Jack Tirrand's girl.'

'Who are you? Why have you saved us?'

'All in good time. Let's go find the man I'm after.'

'Rolf? I mean, Franz?'

He shook his head. 'Your Dad.'

They walked almost halfway to the village along the dirt track before they saw the car, parked at an angle on a grass verge.

'I'm surprised it got this far,' the stranger said. 'I sabotaged the fuel filter last night. I didn't want anyone making a surprise getaway. My car's parked up ahead.'

Alison pulled at his sleeve. 'Be careful. Franz must be around somewhere. He's a trained soldier.'

The man shook his head. 'I imagine he's gone to the village for help or to get hold of another vehicle.'

He raised his rifle, scouting around the car and into the adjacent fields before relaxing his grip. 'As I thought,' he said. He leaned inside the car and popped the boot release.

Jack lay in a foetal position, his eyes pinched tight as the light penetrated the darkness. His voice sounded thick and incoherent as he tried to speak.

Alison rushed forward and couched his head in her hands. 'You're alive.' He struggled to talk. 'You smell lovely.'

She laughed as she turned to look at the stranger. 'That's my mud pack,' she said. '*L'eau de* Tilbury.'

She helped her father out of the boot whilst the stranger and Robert looked on. Jack's feet were unsteady, his body weaving from side to side like a drunk as he tried to focus on a face he did not recognise.

'This man saved us,' Alison said. 'She was about to shoot us, but he killed her.'

Jack's brow creased. 'Who are you?' he asked.

'I've spent forty years imagining this moment,' the man said.

Jack froze. He stared at the man; his senses galvanised by the comment. 'If you're who I think you are, I now know why you have been searching for me.'

The man nodded as he cocked the rifle. 'To kill you,' he said.

# SIXTY-THREE

## SOUTHERN ENGLAND

## 11.00 - 5 December 2065

The black INCOL Jetta saloon joined a line of vehicles crawling through the single lane restriction, as a team of traffic control officers selected cars to pull over for document inspection. A fresh-faced inspector, barely out of his teens, came to the driver's window and asked Robert for the identity cards of the three occupants. The man in the back seat wound down his window to point out he was late getting back to barracks in Salisbury and these friends were kindly giving him a lift. If the officer could complete whatever checks he needed to do as quickly as possible, he would be extremely grateful. The young man straightened at the sight of the winged dagger badge on the man's cap, identifying him as an ISE Special Services operative, and handed back the identity cards unchecked.

'Don't suppose you've seen this man?' He flashed a photo of Jack at them.

'Only all over the television and this morning's news sheets. He appears to have upset a few important people, though I suspect many are secretly relieved.'

The inspector leaned forward, his head almost inside the open rear window. 'Between you and me,' he said conspiratorially. 'I don't know how he did it, but he's given them in Berlin a real bloodied nose. Wherever he is, I hope he makes it.'

'Between you and me,' the man copied the secretive tone. 'He's in the boot.'

The inspector laughed out loud, saluted and stood aside to let the car pass.

They gathered speed and joined the western link highway. Traffic was light. They drove in silence.

'It pays to hang on to my military paraphernalia,' the man said eventually. 'Gets you into a variety of places beyond the reach of most people.'

Alison studied him. 'You took a chance with that stupid remark. He could have easily checked the boot?'

'You understand little about human relationships. We had established a trust based on rank. An officer making a humorous aside to a rank-and-file esteems the latter. He would do nothing to compromise this new status.'

Robert chanced a backward glance. 'Do you agree with what he said about Jack? If so, . . .' He left the sentence unspoken.

'Pull over to this rest area,' the man said, ignoring the question. 'Park tail-on to those bushes.'

Alison helped her father out of the boot, brushing the dust off his creased suit.

The man fished in his holdall and brought out a pair of dirty trainers, a worn tracksuit bottom, a sweatshirt and a peaked cap. 'Change behind the bushes, and stow your clothes in this bag.'

Jack sat in the back, alongside the stranger, as they pulled out into the traffic.

'Where to?' Robert asked.

'I told you to drive, and you chose this route. You must have a destination in mind. So, keep going.'

Robert shrugged. 'How did you know we were in danger?'

'I've a special interest in Mr Tirrand. I followed you to the guest house on the marshes. I needed to establish whether you were in league with the young man or his captives. I used an excuse to visit the place. You weren't around, so I guessed he had you locked up somewhere. Lucky I checked out marsh birds on the SocioLine browser beforehand. The woman was suspicious. Asked me what breed of birds we were looking out for. I'm sure my explanation sounded kosher. I looked for a suitable place to wait for you to come out. The rest you know.'

Robert nodded and glanced a smile at a stern-faced Alison. 'Who are you?' she said. 'And what do you want with us?'

'I think I can answer that question,' Jack said, turning to face the man. 'You are somehow related to the boy who fell down the well. How, I don't know. He was white and you . . .'

'Are black,' the man finished. 'And Stanley did not fall down the well. You held him over the well and let him fall. You then told nobody and left him injured and petrified to die a lonely, painful death.'

'What is all this?' There was alarm in Alison's voice. 'What are you talking about?'

Jack nodded. 'I want you to believe what I am about to tell you I knew nothing about – rather, no recollection of – until a week ago, when the effect of a drug I was administered in Germany brought back memories of my past. I've put almost everything together now and can tell you my real name is not Jack Tirrand. It's Aasif Firman and I'm the son of an Indonesian mother and a white English father. Together with my younger brother, Jamil, who is totally blameless, I take responsibility for the death forty years ago of a young, crippled boy named Stanley. Right so far?'

The man nodded.

Before his incredulous audience could react, Jack recounted the events of those fateful two weeks, the confrontation with the gang of bikers and his quest for revenge the following Saturday, eventually leading to the tragic accident and the arrest of the two brothers.

'You can believe me or not, but I never intended to harm the boy. We just wanted to scare him in return for the treatment meted out to us the previous week. Suddenly, all we were securing was an open calliper. Stanley slipped from our grasp. I remember him threatening us with a beating from his older brother. Would that be you?' Jack looked across at the man, who gave a wry smile.

'My name is Terry Hopkins. You are right. Stanley was my adopted brother. He was left on our mother's doorstep, three months old, already cursed with the infection which caused his leg to wither. My mother is Constance Hopkins. You may have heard of her.' He waited for an acknowledgement. 'No? Why should you? She's well known in Derbyshire, even now, into her eighties. Spent her life as an activist; seeking justice for the underclasses; a constant thorn in the flesh of the authorities with her petitions and street protests.' He smiled to himself at the recollection.

Alison studied her father, an expression of incomprehension on her face. 'Where did the name of Jack Tirrand come from if you are someone else?'

'Please listen to him, my darling. He's seen papers and files which explain everything. I'm still relying on a memory sketchy in parts. Please go on.'

Hopkins nodded. 'We lived in a large ground-floor council flat in a tower block called Middle England. At the time Stanley came into our lives, Mum ran an unofficial creche, mainly for single-parent blacks who worked and didn't have enough money to pay for a licensed nursery. My Dad pissed off when he knew she was pregnant and I grew up with the warped idea I was the man of the house, so to speak, and if I couldn't use my tongue as a weapon, I'd learn to use my fists. I became a keep-fit fanatic and a real hard nut as far as the other residents in the block were concerned.'

'How old were you when Stanley died?' Jack asked.

'I was six years older. I'd have been fifteen or sixteen.'

'You know what happened after the trial?'

'Mum followed every detail. All I wanted to do was to somehow get access and kill you and your brother. You got ten years in a young offenders' facility. He got five. Mum said you would have got less if you had showed remorse.'

'That word has plagued me in recent days. I've tried to analyse my state of mind at the time.' Jack squeezed his eyes tight shut as he tried to concentrate. 'I have a mental image of my mother impressing on us the need to remain expressionless, never show our emotions when people tried to intimidate us because of our colour or the fact we were the product of a mixed marriage. I can only think I carried this mantra into the courtroom. In my heart, I was so sorry and angry with myself for not telling the police as soon as it happened.'

'But you didn't,' Hopkins said, a flash of anger in his eyes. 'You left Stanley to rot, hoping he would never be found. I can still feel the raw emotion I felt then well inside me now.'

'I understand.'

'Do you? I doubt it.'

Jack shrugged.

'I tried all sorts of shit to get put inside where you were, even down to putting the two bikers who attacked you into hospital, but all I got were suspended sentences and probation officers. I gained such a hard man reputation, the only thing Mum could do was get me recruited into the army. It was the best move she ever made.'

Alison tapped Robert's arm. 'I thought it was Southampton we were supposed to be heading? If so, you've missed the exit to join the A3.'

'Change of plans. The man guessed our exit with Jack would be high profile. Montevideo was added to the ports of call to lead the chasing pack away from our actual destination. We have an alternative vessel sailing later today from a different port. With Mr Hopkins' forbearance, that's the direction in which we are headed.'

Hopkins nodded. 'I've got no beef with you two. Get to where you've got to go to.' A stifled laugh turned into a bout of chesty coughing, which he struggled to control. 'Though I have to say, vicar,' he said hoarsely. 'You came close to getting yourself shot when the girl popped up out of the undergrowth down at your place in Devon and compromised my aim.'

'That was you?' Robert asked, incredulously.

'I was intending to put Aashif, aka Jack, out of my misery, but his granddaughter saved the day. She got herself wet in the process, poor kid.'

'You stopped to save her,' Jack said. 'She could have drowned.'

'Can't be all like you, can we?' Hopkins retorted.

'That's unfair,' Alison raged, turning to glare at the man. 'What I understood from these revelations, Dad was eleven, from an ethnic minority, picked on by a bunch of hooligans, which, by the way, included your brother, and beaten and humiliated. He looked to even the score, reassert his status in his brother's eyes and became the perpetrator of a tragic accident.'

Jack reached for her hand. 'His anger stems from the fact I did nothing to save his brother. I should have called the emergency services, alerted somebody. I was convinced the boy was dead and wanted to save my skin and protect Jamil. He has every right to condemn me.'

'Where is Jamil now?' Alison asked. 'I never knew I had an uncle on my father's side.'

'Let Mr Hopkins continue with his recollections. It will help me remember.'

'Look, let's get one thing straight. Nobody except the magistrate and the bank manager call me Mr Hopkins. I've spent most of my life, either as Terry or Staff Sergeant. Take your pick.'

'You said you joined the army,' Jack prompted.

Hopkins relaxed into the narrative. For the immediate years following Aashif's trial and conviction, army life gave him little opportunity or desire to dwell on his need for revenge. He excelled as a soldier and was soon short-listed for a place in an SAS training programme and a transfer to Hereford. It coincided with the events of eleven/eleven and, in the aftermath, he saw active service on the ground in Korea, clandestine attacks on terrorist targets and drone production facilities in Iran, Turkey and Syria. He had lost count of the number of targeted assassination missions ordered and completed. It would run into hundreds.

The evolution of INCOL involved the integration of the SAS into a new European ISE elite combat division and fighting force with less restrictive rules of engagement. He took part in atrocities which he wished he could forget but was not able.

Back then, an operation to round up a renegade band of social media executives was just concluding, and he was looking forward to a two-week furlow to visit his mother – the first time in eighteen months. She was beside herself, angry and raving like he'd never seen her before. Her growing suspicions of INCOL's intentions led to her joining a protest group as a vociferous and critical spokesperson, which soon saw her as one of their main attack dogs, so to speak. The enactment dealing with prisoner release touched a nerve and infuriated her. All young offenders were to be freed.

'She was weeping as she complained of how the perpetrators of Stanley's horrific death paid with five years in a comfy open prison. Where was the justice? We didn't know the plan was for you and your brother to be given new identities and certainly nothing about the brainwashing you were to undergo.'

Jack bowed his head. 'Jamil never got to go, did he?'

A shake of the head. 'Jamil was regularly abused during his five years inside. I guess someone was worried he would complain to his carer on the outside and make problems for the abusers. The day before he was due to be released, he was attacked by an inmate. They made it look like he hanged himself.'

Jack's eyes filled with tears. He blinked rapidly.

'It did for your old man,' Hopkins said in his matter-of-fact voice.

'My Dad? He died?'

'With you gone out of his life, your brother dead, and your mother shipped off under the repatriation legislation back to wherever it was she came from, I guess he thought life wasn't worth living anymore. According to the file the bent solicitor got for me from his Homeland connection, your dad took some pills and walked in front of a tube train.'

The bald facts, spoken so callously with no emotion, stung Jack, but he held himself in check. He looked out of the window at the countryside to hide the hurt.

Nobody spoke as the scenery changed from urban to rural and back again as they eventually reached the outskirts of Bristol. Isolated memories filtered into Jack's mind as he thought of the tragedy brought on his family. No way would his killer witness the despair he felt. He took a deep breath. 'Was this file you got hold of the lead to Geordie Bachelor?'

Hopkins shook his head. 'His image shows up twice in the press coverage of your trial. He was your family liaison officer, the responsible adult present during your interrogation, and there to escort you and your brother as minors. Mum got his name from her police officer contact.'

'Why did you kill him? He must have been well into his eighties; a quiet, even-tempered man as I remember.'

'You're joking. Once the miserable sod realised who I was and the motive for my visit, he was intent on stopping me. There was no way he would have opened the safe with your file without some encouragement.'

'You tortured him?'

'The old bastard must have wanted to protect your identity. He tried to finish me. I got a stab wound from a kitchen knife in my arm.' He drew up the sleeve of his camouflage jacket to reveal a jagged scar across his forearm. 'Bled like buggery. I was forced to stay around ages to clear up once I'd topped him.'

'All for a few sheets of paper. You must be a callous man.'

Hopkins nodded. 'I spent my entire working life as a soldier; thirty-five years of active service as a killing machine; the latter years overseeing the training of new generations of special forces. There's nothing I've not seen or done to one human being by another. I have no qualms.'

Alison grimaced at him. 'As far as I can see, you've wasted the best part of this life you talk of, seeking vengeance from somebody with no memory of the crime he committed. Seems to me a life wasted.'

'I promised Mum a long time ago I would not let Stanley's death go unpunished. It is a promise I always intended to keep.'

'And does she still feel that way all these years later? Would she condone you killing my father in cold blood today?'

'We never talk about it. Her choice. She has a weak heart.' His face brightened. 'Though you wouldn't think so from all the protesting she still does; mainly letters and emails these days, sometimes indoors with a few friends of the group. She's been a firebrand all her life.'

'We're here.' Robert steered the car off the main road into the beginning of a dock complex. The sign read Avonmouth. He parked on a side road opposite the main gates and pointed to a single door further along the road. 'It's the employees' entrance.' He took slips of paper from his inside pocket. 'We have visitors' passes. Just wave the barcode at the reader and go through the security check.'

'Where are you going?' Hopkins asked.

Robert looked at Jack for guidance and received a shrug in return. 'It wouldn't take five minutes for someone to work it out,' Jack said. 'He says he's not interested in you two and has no intention of telling the authorities.' He looked at Hopkins for confirmation.

'What would be my motivation?' Hopkins's question was rhetorical. 'I get it you've been working to undermine INCOL's authority. Mum would be proud of you. And if she is, I am.'

'We're on a small cargo vessel, taking slate and china clay to Angola. The plan is to hide away in Luanda for a week and wait for a transfer across the Atlantic to Tomorrow World.'

'China clay?' Hopkins said. 'What do they need china clay for in darkest Africa?'

'I asked the same question,' Robert said. 'Of all the oil-producing countries, Angola suffered the least and is still supplying the rest of Africa. The clay is used to make ceramic parts for the extracting and refining operations.'

Hopkins nodded pensively. 'One thing. You get in with the passes, but no one comes back through security. How do you square that one?'

'I'm told there are illegals trapped inside the dock who are waiting to get out. Two lucky souls will be on the streets of Bristol before nightfall. Someone in security has a scam going selling these passes to the highest bidder. They're like gold dust.'

Jack was sitting alongside Hopkins, his thoughts lost in a past he was only starting to remember in vivid detail. 'You two better get going,' he said. 'Time to disappear.'

Alison spun around in her seat, her eyes locked on their captor. 'I'm not going anywhere without my father. Do you understand? What's in the past has gone and the mistakes we've all made gone with us. Maybe we've learned from them. Maybe, somewhere inside my father, the subconscious recognition of having done something wrong has made him the kind, generous, caring person he is today. You're not taking that away from me.'

Robert retracted the hand about to open the driver's door, his eyes moving from Alison to Jack and fixing on Hopkins. 'From my experience,' he said. 'The prospect of revenge is a far more vital emotion than the sensation of revenge realised. You will feel a great deal more fulfilled if you show mercy and allow the rage inside you to dissipate into the generosity of your actions.'

Hopkins burst out laughing. 'Spoken like a true vicar, preaching from the pulpit. And tell me more, Reverend, will God welcome me into his Kingdom? I think not. I have spilled too much blood on his prayer book to read the words. My soul is already condemned.'

'My God is all-embracing and all-forgiving.'

'Let's stop this,' Jack said. 'I need you two to concentrate on saving your hides. Stop trying to influence the outcome of a crime committed way before you two became a part of my life. If you respect and love me, as you say you do, then please just go and make something positive of your futures. What would be the point of putting yourselves in harm's way? It will change nothing.'

Tears were rolling down Alison's cheeks. 'I am not leaving—'

'You're right, of course,' Robert said, his voice booming. 'We must let you do what your conscience dictates.' He held out his hand to shake

Jack's, then opened the driver's door and walked around the front to the passenger side. 'Come on, Alison.' He pulled her door open. 'Do as your father requests.'

Her hand gripped the top of her seat. She gulped back the tears that fed into the corners of her mouth. Her eyes held Hopkin's passive stare. 'If you lay a finger on my father, I promise I'll find you wherever you are, and I'll kill you. Never forget that.'

Hopkins smiled. 'Now you know what the desire for vengeance feels like. It's all possessing. Never a day will pass when you don't feel the hurt and anger well up inside you.'

'You bastard!' She spat in his face.

Robert yanked at Alison's free hand and pulled her from the vehicle. As he dragged her along the road, her head turned, cheeks red and translucent from the tears. Robert grabbed her by both arms, shook her and said something, which, by his expression, could only have been a demand for her to pull herself together and concentrate on their next move.

Jack's nostrils flared, his eyes watering, teeth grinding together as he fought to contain his emotions. He felt the piece of paper Robert palmed him as they shook hands, smiled and folded it into his inside pocket. His daughter and her uncle reached the doorway. She turned, blew a kiss, and was gone.

'You going to do it here?' Jack asked. For once, he felt a sense of calm and a strange sense of self-confidence. He was not afraid.

'You drive,' Hopkins said. 'Turn around and go back the way we came. First left, I thought I saw an abandoned warehouse. Let's do it there, shall we?'

# EPILOGUE

Jack sat forward, both forearms resting on the steering wheel of the stationary car, his eyes looking straight ahead at the derelict building. Judging by the state of the brickwork, the dirt encrusted on what remained of the windows, and the vegetation springing up through the deserted concrete forecourt; the industrial unit had lain abandoned for about the same time as he had been alive. Like him, it had come to the end of its existence. The sign at the entrance, which said the area was monitored by a security firm and trespassers would be prosecuted, also announced the imminent arrival of a dockside expansion development to build temporary housing for dock workers and their families.

The two men sat in silence. What would it be? A bullet in the back of the head. A knife slashed across his throat. He was not about to plead for his life. It would make no difference. His killer had spent a lifetime waiting for this moment. He would not give him the satisfaction of grovelling.

Hopkins broke the silence. 'You've had quite a week, Jack,' he said. 'The transformation from the most hated man in Britain who many would have happily seen dead to a renegade saviour who had bloodied INCOL's nose; and all in the space of forty-eight hours. Even the official line has changed. The radio originally talked of apprehending a dangerous man, possibly armed. Now, it's all about protecting you from potential harm.'

'A little late for that.'

Hopkins laughed. 'I need to know something. Was it you who sabotaged this death train business?'

'With help from others, yes.'

'Why? Change of heart?'

Jack turned to look at the man. 'Why do you want to know?'

'Call it curiosity.'

'I was never on board with their project, but I had no choice. They threatened to implicate my wife in a murder she did not commit and destroy the life of Alison's twin sister. I couldn't let that happen.'

Hopkins nodded. 'You know ISE has arrested the journalist's flatmate for the murder? He's the Homeland official who got your file to me via a middleman. He's for the high jump, but he didn't do it.'

'How do you know?'

'While you were in Germany, I passed the time by tailing your wife. I thought I might need her to get to you. She turned up at the apartment in Chelsea Harbour and went inside. I was about to when I almost got run down by this car speeding away. Through the windscreen, I got a good look at the man in the passenger seat. He was wiping blood from his face with a handkerchief in one hand and turning to speak to whoever was in the back. If I hadn't jumped, you wouldn't have me to worry about today.'

'Hardly conclusive,' Jack said.

'Circumstantial, but good enough for me. I am not about to tell anybody.'

'An innocent man will be executed.'

'Seen plenty of them. What's one more?'

Jack said nothing for a few seconds. 'When I looked at that file, most of the text had been redacted. There was little in it.'

'It must have been doctored before you saw it, pages removed. There was enough for me to confirm your real identity and the family history following Stanley's death.' He hesitated, then discounted what he was about to say. 'Do you know who decided on the name Tirrand for you?'

Jack shook his head.

'It was that laughing policeman you were so attached to. He was proud of his research. It originates from France and means master of his destiny. Quite apt in the circumstances, don't you think?'

Jack creased his brow. 'Are you dragging this out on purpose?'

Hopkins ignored the question. 'You were saying you did not agree with the project, but were blackmailed into cooperating?' He did not wait for confirmation. 'What made you sabotage it?'

'No move was made until I was certain Rebecca and my daughter, Harriet, were in the clear. Apart from the obvious abhorrence of a plan designed to kill people, I sensed there were other factors more sinister in play. They kept the victim data from me, but I got to look at an advance copy and my doubts were confirmed. Amongst all the over-eighties and a handful of prisoners with whole life tariffs, there were a number of individuals ISE would class as terrorists, disruptive and vociferous individuals who see

INCOL as the enemy and are not afraid to broadcast their point-of-view. That number of undesirables included my parents-in-law.'

'And you did what?'

'I consulted the Citizens' Register and came up with thirty-two names of individuals over or around eighty who were related to Senate members, senior deputies, or anyone influential in the public eye. We substituted these names for a similar number of named dissidents and produced a new data chain to replace the original.'

'And it worked?'

Jack shook his head. 'It almost didn't. The so-called "invitations" were already issued based on the original data. Had ISE operatives been provided with a list based on this record to organise the collection of the five-hundred souls, our work would have been in vain.'

'But they were not?'

'No. Berlin was so paranoid about releasing the names that it was left until the last moment. What ISE got was a revised list based on the data link in the chain which we compiled.'

'Couldn't they compare the two and discover the manipulation?'

'Why are you so interested in the process?'

Hopkins took the snub-nosed automatic pistol he retrieved from his pocket and pressed the barrel against Jack's temple. 'Don't challenge my motives. Just answer the question.'

Jack raised his hands to shoulder level, palms facing the windscreen. 'The Blockchain programme does not work that way. Once the revised data was inserted and verified, it replaced the original, which would never have existed within the system, had it not been used as the data source to print out the invitations. The only critical parameter to obey was to provide the same number of substitute names and addresses as were removed from the original listing.'

'And you met these criteria? How?'

'You're joking, aren't you? What possible interest can it be to you?'

Hopkins poked the barrel harder. 'Don't second guess me? Just follow my lead. You said you had thirty-two new names and addresses to insert?'

'Correct.' Jack leaned his head forward to relieve the pressure.

'How many names did you have from the original list you wanted to remove?'

'From memory, thirty, including my parents-in-law and a friend from the Assembly and her parents.'

'So, how did you choose the two names from the original list to balance things up?'

'I flicked through the pages looking for anything that struck a chord with me?'

'What like an address?'

'Possibly. I was in a hurry. I needed to get the revised list of names to the tech guys.'

'Does Middle-England Towers, Broadbent, ring a bell?'

Jack nodded. 'Of course it does. We lived three streets away. The Towers were where most of the kids in school came from. Now you mention it, I think I do remember seeing it on the list, though I would not have had such a clear recollection as I do now of its significance.'

Hopkins withdrew the pistol, flicked on the safety and let the weapon fall into his lap.

They both turned at the sound of an engine racing to a stop behind them. The van screeched to a halt several metres away, blocking their exit. The sign on the side read 'Protsafe Security Services – Protect and Safeguard.' The uniformed guard with the company insignia on his breast pocket ambled across to the car. He was a tall, well-built young man, the look on his pitted face one of confidence that the cosh fixed to the holder on his belt and the two-way radio swinging on a plastic strap from his neck would be adequate to see off these two interlopers.

Hopkins wound down the rear passenger side window. 'Sorry,' he shouted. 'Are we in the wrong place?'

The man said nothing, just kept on walking until he reached the car and bent down to survey the interior.

'Not here, lads,' he said. 'Can't you read?' He pointed to the sign on the gate. 'This is private property, and we prosecute trespassers.' He glanced at Jack and then back at Hopkins. 'There's a quiet place for you two to get it on about a mile down the main road. It's a wooded area. I send quite a few couples down there.' He took a longer look at Jack.

'Sorry,' Hopkins said. 'We'll be on our way in a minute. My turn to drive.'

He opened the rear door, forcing the guard to step back. As he did so, the man moved forward to stand in front of the car, his eyes riveted on Jack in the driver's seat. He took a step back, his hand reaching for the transmit button on his two-way radio. 'Hang on,' he said. 'He's the guy everybody's looking for. There's a reward for bringing . . .' He never finished the sentence. The sound of the gunshot echoed around the deserted buildings. The man's body pitched forward onto the bonnet, blood smearing the paintwork as he slid to the ground.

'Get out of the car!' Hopkins shouted as he pulled a pair of acrylic gloves from his pocket, forcing his fingers into the blue plastic.

Jack reacted to the order as if a zombie, his mind both unable and unwilling to process what had just happened. His hand pressed against the door, supporting his body as he struggled to remain standing.

'Take this,' Hopkins said, holding the barrel of the gun toward Jack, who remained motionless. 'What's wrong with you? I told you to take this. I need to get him back in his van and park it out of sight.'

Jack took the gun and held it to his side. 'Is he dead?' He knew it was a ridiculous question. There was a black hole in the socket where the man's eye should have been. Blood seeped slowly from the wound.

'What do you think? He was about to tell the world he had just found Jack Tirrand.' His hands under the man's armpits, Hopkins levered the man up into the passenger seat of the van, the head and body slumped forward. 'Wait here while I dump this around the back of the building.'

In the two minutes it took for Hopkins to return on foot, Jack had recovered some of his composure. 'Why did you do that?' he asked. 'Why not let him take me in? My fate would ultimately be no different than if that bullet had been meant for me.'

Hopkins reached for the gun Jack was still holding at his side. 'I'll tell you why,' he said. 'My Mum was supposed to be on that death train, but nobody came to collect her. Had they done so, neither of us would have survived. Mum has got a dicky heart. She would never have lasted the journey and all the confusion, let alone make it through, only to end up dead in some railway siding. I would never have let them take her. By mid-afternoon, I knew something had happened, and they weren't coming for her. The GPS tracker on the padre's car showed he was on the move – I guessed to meet up with you. I headed back to London. The rest you know.'

Jack said nothing.

'You don't get it, do you? Something inside your head recognised Mum's address, and you took her off the list. We are both alive because of you. She would not want me to persist in seeking revenge for Stanley.'

'And you?'

Hopkins laughed. 'I don't feel quite that benevolent. I'm going to give you a fighting chance. I guess the slip of paper the priest palmed you was your visitor's pass to get on that ship. I suggest you use it. I also suggest you develop a serious head cold and use this to cover your face as you pass the security check.' He handed Jack a freshly laundered handkerchief.

'Is that it? Can I go?'

'Just one more thing. In a day or two, the security guard's body will be discovered. The bullet they retrieve from his skull will match the gun they find in the glove box of the priest's car, which I will leave in a car park in the centre of Bristol. If you're lucky, it will take a week for the car and gun to turn up, by which time you will be well on the high seas. Just as well, because the murder weapon now has your fingerprints on it; an open and shut case in a world of circumstantial evidence. Today's folk hero will be tomorrow's whipping boy.'

Jack took a step toward Hopkins, who reacted as if about to be attacked. 'Listen to me, Terry.' He waited until their eyes met. 'You treat all this,' Jack pointed at the bloodstain on the ground, 'like some macabre game. Maybe it makes it easier to process. I don't know. But I will tell you this with absolute certainty. Your mother is safe for now, but this is not the end. They will try again to achieve what they set out to do.'

Hopkins took a pace back, surprised by the ferocity of the comment. 'How can you say that? You have no idea.'

'It's straightforward. Over the next four to five decades, beyond our lifetimes, the world will emerge from energy starvation, with economies starting to grow and expand once more. Oil will flow again. Nobody can be naïve enough to think it will all go back to the way it was before eleven/eleven. Powerful forces have already started to manoeuvre into position to rise from these ashes with power and control. Can you imagine China ceding its conquests in Southeast Asia and Australasia and retrenching to its historic borders? Do you imagine the former USA will willingly share all the progress made in Tomorrow World with the rest of the globe? Will Germany not strive to be the master of a new Europe with borders stretching east into Asia and south into the Africas?'

'I don't see what that has got to do with my Mum and a death train.'

'You don't? I do. If you are trying to leap into an unassailable lead, nothing is worse than a terrier snapping and tearing at your ankles, trying to halt your progress. Protestors breed dissidents who breed terrorists prepared to use violence. Violence escalates. If you can rid yourself of the problem at the source and suppress dissent once and for all, your path is clear. That's what Octogen is all about. Your mother's voice in isolation will do nothing. Put it alongside a hundred thousand others and it has immense strength.'

Hopkins walked to the car. 'I should get going if I were you. Let's hope the world you're keen on saving is worth the effort.' The engine spluttered into life as he drove toward the exit without looking back.

Jack kicked at a stone, felt for the paper in his pocket and exhaled slowly. If everything went to plan, he would be resurrected again, only this time he would remember everything.

Extract from the Musk Foundation Definitive Dictionary (UK Edition) – June 2110

# OCTOGEN

**noun**

🔊 UK /ˌɒk.təʊ.dʒəˈn - US /ˌɑːk.toʊ.dʒəˈn

A programme developed by *INCOL* Berlin in 2060 of enforced *euthanasia* for the over-eighties and other *selected individuals*. Designed to conserve and strategically allocate resources during the *dark century*, the project was halted and subsequently abandoned following the disclosure of previously suppressed information by *London Assembly* Deputy, *Jack Tirrand*.

References: ^*Cook, Geoff - OCTOGEN*

# PREVIOUS RELEASES FROM GEOFF

April 1945 - As the war in Europe draws to a close and the days of the Third Reich are numbered, a train filled with a cargo of Nazi gold sets off from Berlin, destined for a secret location in Bavaria. On board, a young Polish Jew is about to witness a chain of events leading to the greatest robbery and criminal conspiracy of all time.

October 2018 - After eighty years, a Lisbon bank is set to close its safe-deposit facility. The secrets locked away for decades are about to be revealed. Influential people in powerful positions have reasons to be concerned.

After twelve years of marriage, Caroline and Dominio are set to divorce, citing irreconcilable differences. Really? With six-year-old twin girls and an eye-watering mortgage to take into consideration, can the reason for the split be that pat?
Their fathers, Len, a retired police detective, and Charlie, a former motor trader, are sceptical, but there can be no united response. For years, their pent-up hatred for each other has been contained under a veneer of civility. Now, it turns into open warfare as they seek to gain the upper hand. The trouble is, digging up dirt on each other's past can be dangerous especially when family and friends become involved.

'Believe me, there is nothing bold or courageous in taking the decision to sacrifice everyone and everything you have lived and worked for since you were a young man in exchange for the uncertainty of a new life thousands of miles away, with a woman you have convinced yourself you love, but, in truth, you hardly know.
Don't kid yourself. All it takes is a heady mix of bravado, false conviction, cowardice and a total lack of conscience.
I should know. I did it. Sixteen years have passed and an opportunity comes out of the blue to make amends, to rekindle the bonds of family I once too easily discarded. Or so I hoped.
But I was naïve.
I thought that words could heal. They can't. All they achieved was to distort the pain of rejection that feeds the prospect of revenge. Nor could I foresee the treacherous path that lay ahead as I stumbled into the bitter secrets of all our pasts and the trail of lies, deception and murder that would lay bare secrets for so long hidden.
But I do now.
The deaf may not hear the swish of the assailant's blade but they still feel the pain of the cut.
My name? It's Gilbert Hart, but call me Gil. Some people know me as Hartless.'

Milton Keynes UK
Ingram Content Group UK Ltd.
UKHW022155010824
446420UK00010B/126